Coming into Focus

EAGAN DANIELS

CHAMPAGNE BOOK GROUP

Published by Champagne Book Group
2373 NE Evergreen Avenue, Albany OR 97321 U.S.A.

~ ~ ~

First Edition 2022

pISBN: 978-1-957228-64-8

Cover Art by Robyn Hart

www.champagnebooks.com

Version_1

For Jesse. I would pick exactly this life and exactly you, every, every, every time. I love you.

Dear Reader,

Thank you for reading! I hope you enjoy getting to know Willa and her boys as much as I enjoyed writing them.

This book started out as a fun daydream about what it would be like to be the personal assistant for a flamboyant musician, but along the way, it became something closer my heart—a reflection on what it means to strike a balance in a world that tells women how they must exist. I wanted Willa to build her own version of having it all. She is a caregiver because she finds joy and connection in it. But she's also an artist, and a lover, a sister, a daughter, and a friend. She learns to listen to her own heart and what she wants, rather than to be swept up in an idea of what other people think she "should" be.

It's what I hope for myself, and for you—to be the truest version of ourselves.

And if that comes with a found-family of pretty rock stars, so be it.

Chapter One

My favorite thing about working in a coffee shop was the free coffee. Obviously. My second favorite thing was that once I learned how to make the drinks, my brain was free to do other things, like make mental portraits of customers. The guy who'd just ordered an extra hot, half-caf, nonfat milk, sugar-free almond syrup extra large, for example.

I made his coffee with a fraction of my mindshare while I used the rest of my mental energy to imagine how I'd photograph him. I landed on black and white, in profile. His eyelashes alone would warrant the side view, but his nose would also be fantastic outlined against a stark background. Noses don't get enough attention in portrait photography. I've always thought so.

I kept the ideas to myself. Nobody wants an artistic treatise from their barista. It was true I had an insightful, sparkling, unique portfolio… but it was made entirely of imaginary photographs. It wasn't satisfying, and it wasn't enough, but it I told myself I was keeping my creative muscles limber—so it was better than nothing.

More importantly, I had a brother to take care of. Maybe this wasn't a dream job, but it was a job that kept me close to home and helped me stay on top of our bills.

My phone vibrated in my pocket—the alarm announcing it was time to leave my second job of the day and head to the third.

My jobs were scheduled in order of preference, least to most. First job: computer lab at the community college. Boring. My only responsibility was to make sure the kids surfing porn didn't hog the computers.

Second job: coffee shop.

The third job was the best one—working in the photo lab at my Uncle Ken's music magazine, *Offstage*. It was the closest I was going to get to doing my own photography any time soon.

I pulled out my phone to silence the alarm but instead found an urgent text from Hope Harper: *Willa! I have the world's most flamboyant rock star crashed on my couch. We're HOURS behind schedule, I can't reach any of our photographers, and I can't let him leave town without pictures. Help meeeeeee.*

I slid off the stool and called Hope, holding my phone to my ear with one hand and wiping the counters with the other. She started talking as soon as she answered. "I'm off schedule, and all our photographers are booked. Your uncle-slash-my-editor is breathing down my neck. I need a break today, kid. If I don't get pictures, I'll have to use his press kit material, and it's boring."

I hesitated. I didn't want to disappoint her, but there was a ton of work I needed to get to in the photo lab, and—

"If you nail this, it could be the feature story, Willa," she said in a sing-song voice. "Those pay well."

I was sold. Paying bills before they were past due would be a joy I was unaccustomed to. Maybe I could even pay extra on Toby's medical bills to chip away at those faster.

I couldn't deny it would be a good "career" move, such as my career was. Uncle Ken said I could leave the lab and begin work with the magazine as a junior staff photographer. If I was going to take a job with the magazine, though, I wanted it to be because I earned it. I wanted to be sure Uncle Ken would have hired me off the street if I walked into his office. Not because I was his niece, not because he pitied Toby and me. It was stupid to be proud when I couldn't afford it, but I *was* proud. I'd work in the coffee shop and the lab before I'd take a handout—even if that handout was my dream job.

This was an opportunity I couldn't afford to pass up.

I gave the counters a last swipe before I tossed the washrag in the sink behind me. "I'll be there in fifteen minutes," I told Hope. How lucky for both of us my camera was with me—because it always was. It was locked, lonely and impotent, in the trunk of my car. It was finally going to see some action.

I'd call Toby on the way to Hope's to tell him I'd be late, and I'd make up the darkroom time later. I poured three coffees to go, shoved them in a carrier, and shouldered my way out the door.

I was halfway to Hope's before I realized I hadn't even asked her who it was.

Chapter Two

The sun was setting by the time I let myself into Hope's house to find her darting around with an open purse hanging off her arm and a scarf trailing out of it, chanting, "Keys, keys, keys."

She patted her pockets and checked under the stacks of unopened mail on the glossy black mantle above her fireplace, sighing with relief when she noticed me.

"Oh, thank God, Willa. We are…" She glanced at her watch, and then side-eyed the man on her couch. "Very behind schedule."

"I can't help being interesting, love," said the man of the hour. "You should have allowed more time to get to know me."

His English accent wasn't a surprise. Even the brief glance I'd given him was enough to know he wasn't from here. The soil in Nashville doesn't grow men who look like him. He was reclining on his elbows on Hope's zebra-print couch, watching her with a half-smile. A mass of curly hair, dark eyes, ridiculous eyelashes… He was familiar, but I couldn't quite place him.

This assignment would be a piece of cake. I didn't want to jinx myself, but short of cataclysmic equipment failure, there was no way to blow it. He was probably the most photogenic person I'd ever seen.

Hope ignored him and focused on me. "This is what we're going to do. Oh!" She interrupted herself. "Did you bring me coffee? You're the best." She took a cup from the carrier and drained it. "Ah, God. I needed that." She gave her head a shake. "Take the pictures, do whatever editing you need to do, then send them to me ASAP. I need them to be great to help me pitch it for the feature story. I'm sure you can do it." She gave him an appreciative glance. "The raw material is definitely there."

The couch man gestured at his body with one hand.

I ignored him for now and concentrated on her. "What do you mean, send them to you? Where will you be?"

"I have to run to the office. I have two articles due by morning, including a stupid review of stupid Benny Walker's stupid band's stupid new album. Something more elaborate than 'tired Dad-rock from a so-called legend who has worn out his welcome.'"

Oh, hell no. Some things were sacred. Or should be. Things like Benny Walker. I glared at Hope.

"I forgot you're a fan," she said, with an exaggerated eye roll. "Believe me, that guy doesn't need you to defend him. Here's the thing, Willa. I've reviewed a million albums by his band. I don't have anything else to say at this point."

She hopped on one foot, trying to get her other one into a high-heeled leather boot. Her hair was a long, wavy mess, currently red. No matter what color it was or what she did with it, it was perpetually perfect. She was tall and leggy, and I felt like an awkward kid next to her.

What she'd said was starting to sink in. "Wait. You're going to leave me here with—"

She focused her attention on the man. "It was great to meet you. Be good for Willa. Behave yourself. Oh, keys!" She dumped them out of a fancy vase on the coffee table.

"Don't worry about a thing," he said. "I'm good to my photographers."

I wanted to make the distinction that I wasn't *his* photographer, I was *a* photographer, but I held my tongue. "Hope, who is he?"

She choked on a laugh. "You don't know?"

I frowned. "His name isn't coming to me."

"You're so funny, Willa! You need to work less, enjoy yourself more." She patted me on the cheek.

"What are you girls talking about?" he called from the couch.

"Women," I corrected automatically.

He swung his feet to the floor. "You're talking about women? I want to talk about women," he said. "Let me in on that."

Hope laughed, but I ignored him. I prompted her again. "Hope?"

"He's Jimmy Standish."

"Ohhhh. Right, right, right. From the band…" She wasn't going to help me out. No problem. I knew it. Sort of. "Starts with a 'c,' right? Corkscrew? Cocksure?"

She laughed again. "Cocksure would probably have been a better name, but it's Corporate. They're *exploding*, Willa. How do you not know?"

I snapped my fingers. "No, right, of course. It was on the tip of my tongue." It hadn't been.

I needed more. Right now, all I had to work with was that he was a pretty pop singer. Photographs showing an attractive man being attractive would not be the breakthrough I needed.

Hope wasn't going to help, though. She was shrugging into a jacket on her way to the door. "Jimmy Standish, meet Willa Reynolds. Be nice to her because she's saving our asses." To me, she said, "Love to Toby. Remember to send these to me when they're ready."

She took another coffee from the carrier, did a "cheers" lift to me, and she was gone.

Leaving me with Jimmy Standish.

I squared my shoulders and stood taller, projecting the air of someone who'd done this a million times—or at least more times than never. "Right. Let's get started. Will anyone else be joining us?"

He frowned, then his face cleared. "Oh, you mean the lads?"

"Mmhm. Exactly. The lads."

"From the band...?" He prompted with a wicked smile.

"Corporate! I knew as soon as I walked in, obviously. I was just, uh, flustered. Because I'm such a huge fan, Mr. Standish."

His full-on smile lit up the room. My fingers itched to get to my camera, and he wasn't even trying. "Ooh, you are the most adorable girl!" He swung his feet to the ground. "Never call me Mr. Standish again. It's Jimmy. You are a terrible liar, but I appreciate the effort to protect my ego."

"I'm older than eighteen," I pointed out. "You must have meant to say 'woman.'"

He approached me, beaming and holding my hand for a long moment as he loomed over me. It should have been intimidating, but it wasn't.

"The other two aren't here yet. I'm here doing a press tour before the real tour. It's our manager's idea, not mine. Hawk's an asshole, but since he's an asshole with great business sense, we usually listen to him anyway. I want us to sell out this entire tour, and we're close, Willa. You can help me get there."

Even close-up, he was beautiful. His skin was perfect. Like he was lit from the inside.

I was studying him, but he didn't care since he was studying me at the same time. "Adorable," he said again.

"Professional," I said, countering him. "I'm not here to be cute; I'm here to do a job."

"All right," he agreed. "Professional. In a little, endearing way. We're going to be a great pair, Willa."

Maybe, if I could decide what to do with him. I didn't know a lot about his career or his persona. There was nothing to do but ask. He didn't seem like the kind of guy who'd be reluctant to talk about himself. "Tell me about your music."

"Would you rather listen to it?" he suggested, finally dropping my hands. He crossed the room and sank gracefully into a chair. "I'm sure you'll like us because we are very good." He gestured to my phone. "Search for 'Corporate.' Or 'best band in Britain at least since The Beatles but possibly including the Beatles.' Or maybe 'English rock stars who could be models because they're so attractive.' That would bring me up. And probably the other two, to be honest. They get overlooked sometimes because of the glare coming off me, but they're both lovely." He shifted in the chair he was in and frowned down at it. "This is a wretched chair. I thought it would be comfortable because it looks cool, but it's awful."

"Don't tell Hope." I carried my camera bag to her dining room table and arranged my lenses. "Elvis Costello sent it to her. It's her prized possession."

"Prized for what? Not for sitting in, surely."

"Prized for giving her a chance to say, 'Elvis Costello himself sent me this chair,' I guess. Check out the photo behind you of the two of them in sitting in it together."

He craned around in the chair then turned back to me with wide eyes. "Um, you don't seem to know a lot about music, darling. That's Hope with *Madonna*."

"Other shoulder."

He turned the other way and came face-to-face with an even bigger framed photograph of Hope and Elvis, both in fedoras. She was sitting on the arm of the chair; his glasses were perched on her nose, and she was resting her chin on his head. A high-heeled shoe dangled off the toes of one of her crossed legs. They were cuddled up like they'd been besties their whole lives. The real story was they'd met about fifteen minutes before the image was taken.

Jimmy wasn't impressed. He'd also sat in Elvis Costello's lap for all I knew. "He probably sent her this chair so he wouldn't ever make the mistake of accidentally sitting it in again himself." He brought the conversation back to research suggestions for me. "Did you Google me yet?"

"I don't want to learn about you from someone else," I said. "That will be their point of view, not mine. How about…what if we walked through a day in your life? We'll pretend you're going through a normal day, starting with first thing in the morning."

It couldn't fail. Hope could use it as a photo essay if she wanted, or she could cherry-pick any images she liked. Since he'd be driving the action, it would be authentic.

He nodded. "I like where you're going with this."

"We can call it 'A Day in the Life of an Emerging Legend.'"

He countered with 'A Day in the Life of a Legend as He Becomes More Legendary Even.' I agreed it could be our working title.

He headed down the hallway toward Hope's bedroom.

"What are you doing?" I called.

"A day starts in bed, darling! Let's check out Hope's...oh, perfect. It's lovely. Look at this."

I followed him. Hope's bed was covered by a huge fluffy white comforter with pristine, white pillows. Jimmy yanked his shirt over his head, kicked off his shoes, and nestled into the blankets.

He slipped one heavily tattooed arm out of the covers to display it on the snowy white bedding. "How's this?"

It was perfect.

"Um, yes. Let me get a couple shots to check the light."

For the next several minutes, the only sound was my camera clicking. I reviewed the images on my camera display and frowned. They were beautiful, but...predictable.

"What's the matter?" he asked.

"Nothing. It's just you're...so aware of getting your picture taken."

"Of course I'm aware you're taking my picture," he said. "I'm in the bed of a woman I just met—well, that's hardly a first. Being *photographed* in the bed of a—no, not a first, either, come to think of it. My point is it's hard to ignore the camera at a photo shoot."

I arranged his hair on the pillow to make sure I was doing justice to his haphazard curls.

His brown eyes studied me. "How long have you been doing this? You can't be old enough to have much experience."

I couldn't tell him this was my first official assignment. "I always wanted to be a photographer," I told him instead.

"Not an answer."

I stood on Hope's bed, straddling him, and pointing my camera down. "I'm not actually a staff photographer for the magazine yet. I'm helping Hope because she was in a bind. If you would stop talking, we'd get done a lot faster."

He posed for the camera, and I took a couple pictures. They were beautiful but stilted. "Hope said the magazine editor is your uncle," he said. "Don't you work for him?"

Answering personal questions from a stranger wasn't something

I was comfortable with. I rearranged the blankets to show more of his arm.

When I straightened, his attention went right back to the camera. Unless I wanted obvious rock-star posing, I needed to keep him distracted. "I do work for him, but not as a photographer in the field. Working in his lab is one of my jobs," I said.

"*One* of? How many do you have?"

I wanted to keep him talking, so I answered, "I'm working three jobs at the moment. I attempted four, but scheduling was a nightmare."

"Three jobs! Why doesn't your uncle pay you more? Or help you out some other way if he's such a big-shot editor?" His eyes were warmer. Liquid-looking. Beautiful.

"It's fine. We're doing great." *Click. Click. Click.*

"Who's 'we'?"

"Me and my brother. Relax your hand."

He did. "I can't believe your uncle won't help. That's rubbish. *I'll* hire you just because I like you and because I've never had a cowgirl in my—posse! Get it, Willa? You could be my literal posse. You want to come work for me?"

I laughed. "Nah, I'm good. This isn't forever." I didn't want him to have a bad opinion of my uncle, so I kept handing out personal details. "Uncle Ken wants to help, but I don't want handouts. He also wants to hire me to be a photographer for the magazine, which would definitely pay more than I make now. He keeps asking, and I keep putting him off. It's harder to say no to Hope."

"Why do you keep saying no? It must be better than working in the lab."

"I like working in the lab. If I'm going to do more, I have to earn a spot. Once I do, I'll work one job and make more than enough for Toby and me."

"Can't your brother work?"

I sighed. "He's disabled. Can you stop talking for a minute?"

He could not. "Disabled how?"

I hopped on the bed to get his attention. "I'm not telling you another thing until you pretend you're asleep."

His face went blank and smooth in a second. Gorgeous. When I stopped to check the pictures, he said, "I'm an artist. I can't tolerate being bored. Anyway, this is research about actual Americans, and I like your accent because it's ridiculous. Tell me what's wrong with your brother."

"Nothing is wrong with him. We're all set here. These are great."

Jimmy sat up and extended a hand for me to hold as I jumped off the bed.

I summarized for him while he pulled his shirt on and checked his hair in Hope's vanity mirror. I was five when Toby was born. He had retinoblastoma, a cancer in his eyes, when he was a baby. It wasn't diagnosed soon enough to save his left eye, which was removed when he was two years old. Kids with retinoblastoma have a higher incidence of other childhood cancers, and Toby didn't dodge that bullet, either. When he was a teenager, he needed surgery for osteogenic sarcoma; his right leg was amputated.

"Oh dear." Jimmy's voice was mournful. "He's blind, and he can't walk?"

"His other eye works fine, and he gets around great on his prosthetic." Everything happened when Toby was young. He was mostly as independent as any other eighteen-year-old boy.

"Except he can't work?" Jimmy asked.

"He does some IT freelance stuff from home, but he can't drive, which limits him."

"Does he have an accent like yours? A matching set of adorable American southerners. I should hire you both. Can't your parents take care of him?"

At the same time I was trying to keep up with his conversation, I was guessing what would come next in the day of a legend. Since it wasn't "go to work," I didn't have a clue. "What would you do now?"

"I'd eat breakfast, Willa. Is it not what you do? Do Americans not—"

"Oh, right. Good idea. Come on." I headed for the kitchen. "Let's go have your pretend breakfast."

Hope's house was great for a photo shoot. Her breakfast bar was spotless like it was waiting for a magazine spread. It was this breakfast bar's lucky day.

Jimmy opened the fridge and stared inside.

"Grab anything," I said. "You're not going to eat it anyway."

He held out a can of whipped cream.

"Not that. Something breakfast-y."

"It's the only thing in her refrigerator. Who only has whipped cream in her fridge? Weird, right?"

"It's odd." I checked her pantry. Nothing there but a jar of spaghetti sauce. "Okay, get a coffee mug. We can make it work."

He gasped in horror when he opened a cupboard, then stepped aside so I could see.

It was just mugs. "What's the matter?" I asked

"As I thought," he said after he'd looked in more of her cupboards. "She has only matching mugs, Willa. It's so sad!"

"I'm not following you, but okay. Hop up onto the stool, and…"
I spotted the coffee I'd brought. Hope already drank two of them, and I
was going to have to sacrifice the third.

I positioned the take-out cup so the logo faced the camera. Some
free advertising for Broadway Bean. Maybe my boss, Jenny, would give
me a bonus. "Try to look a bit rougher. These are first-thing-in-the-
morning pictures, and I know you didn't wake up like this."

"I did wake up like this, as a matter of fact." He obliged me
anyway by slumping over and nailing an impression of a man who'd
been out all night making bad choices. He tasted the coffee. "Mm. This
is delicious." He held it out to me to share. It was getting cold, but it was
still good. I make a great coffee.

I gave it back to him and put my camera back to my eye to study
him through the lens. The light was perfect, but he was conscious of the
camera again.

"You never answered my question from before," he said. "Why
don't your parents take care of your brother?"

Of course I hadn't answered; I didn't want to. On the other hand,
when he was listening, he wasn't thinking about the camera, and when
he wasn't thinking about the camera, we were getting some perfect shots.

"My dad died a couple years ago." I took several steps closer to
him and tightened the focus.

"Oh, poor Willa. What about your mom?"

"No mom," I said shortly, making use of the moments when he
was distracted. It wasn't as difficult as I'd thought it would be, anyway.
The camera was a buffer, and I was safe behind it. I kneeled on a barstool
for a higher perspective.

He drooped onto the counter. "Poor, poor Willa. All alone with
an ailing brother."

I laughed and climbed down. "You're not even close. Hold still.
I'm going to move around you."

"Did they take Toby to a workhouse and force him to work
around the clock for minimal pay until he got consumption?"

"Um, no, since we're not in a Charles Dickens novel. Haven't
you ever been to America?"

He sipped coffee and made an affirmative sound. "But as a rock
star, darling. Nobody tells me anything unpleasant. From my visits here,
I would assume America is full of gorgeous people who all want to sleep
with me."

I climbed on the counter next to him and continued to snap
photos while I talked. "Nobody took Toby, but it was tricky for me to
keep custody since he was a minor and I was barely an adult. It's fine

14

now. He's eighteen, and nobody can take him from me." I took a couple more frames and then rested my camera in my lap. "Okay. What happens after breakfast?"

"Depends on the day and who I'm with."

"Pretend it's today, and you're not with anyone."

His smile was clearly meant to humor me. "I'll play along. If I wasn't already with someone, I'd be getting ready to meet someone. I don't," he made air quotes with his fingers, "'spend time alone.'"

"So you would…do your hair?"

He patted my knee. "Silly girl. My hair is already perfect."

It was true.

"Makeup?" His face was bare, but he was a musician and obviously theatrical. It was worth a shot.

He spun on the stool to face me. "Yes. This is an extraordinary idea. I bet I'm going to be good at putting on makeup, Willa. Let's go check what Hope has."

I followed him down the hall and waited while he rummaged through Hope's makeup drawers. It quickly became apparent that his confidence when it came to cosmetics was completely unearned. I let him go on longer than it should have before I set my camera carefully on the counter. "All of it off," I said, gesturing to his face. "This is a disaster."

When I found makeup remover and a washcloth, I handed them to Jimmy. He gave them back to me and closed his eyes, waiting.

It was less work than arguing, so I wiped the makeup off his face.

"Hope is lonely."

I snorted.

His eyes were closed, but his lips curled up. "You even snort with an accent."

"I don't have an accent, you do, and you're wrong. Hope meets the best people, and everyone loves her. She's the opposite of lonely."

"Clearly she meets a lot of people. It's obvious from the prominently placed pictures." He jerked his head to his right, where there was a framed photo of Hope with some woman with a guitar.

"How much eyeliner did you put on? I can't get it off. Stop squirming."

He ignored me. "I'm extraordinarily intuitive, and this feels off. Like a set design, not a home. Those mugs, Willa! Nobody normal has matching mugs."

"That doesn't make sense."

"Like, not a *single* joke mug? People love to give joke mugs.

Like, 'Reporters Do it in the Newsroom?' I'd get that one for her. Or, like 'Death Before Decaf?' or 'World's Best Aunt?' *Nothing*? You know who has sets of matching mugs, Willa? Serial killers. Do you reckon—"

"No, I don't reckon Hope is a serial killer, actually. Stop talking for a minute. I'm almost done here."

"Mm. You smell like bubble gum, just like I'd have guessed."

"It's because I'm chewing bubble gum," I said.

He hummed. "It's the smell of American girls."

"It can't be that since I'm a woman. Stop talking."

His mouth finally stopped moving long enough for me to finish. "Finally. There. Now let's start over."

He handed me a black eyeliner pencil. I reached up but couldn't get the right leverage for a steady hand. It wasn't going to work. "I thought all Americans were tall," he said. "It's like your schtick."

"True, *most* of us are seven feet tall and smell like bubble gum, but not all of us. Here, let's switch places." I sat on the counter, and he stood between my knees.

"Your hair is so shiny, Willa. You look like a commercial for girl vitamins."

"Close your eyes."

"In a second."

I frowned at him. "Stop staring at me." It was one thing when I was taking his picture. It was something entirely different when I wasn't.

"You do have freckles. When you came in, I thought, 'the only way this creature could be even more appealing is if she had freckles.' Why are you covering them?"

"Close your eyes." When he did, I said, "Freckles make people think I'm younger than I am. Believe it or not, some people already assume I'm a girl, not a woman." I paused for a pointed beat.

"You shouldn't hide them, they're perfect. You should strive to look *more* like yourself, not less."

"Stop talking. You're moving your face too much."

He whispered instead. "Next time I see you, leave your freckles out. Promise?"

"You're not going to see me again."

"Yes, I am." He was still whispering. "So promise."

"Promise." I was sure it wouldn't matter.

I mulled over what he'd said about Hope.

"Out loud," Jimmy said. "What's going on in your head?"

"You're wrong. Hope has everything she wants. Her job is pretty much unheard of. Nobody gets to do what she does. I mean, like you said. These pictures of her with her idols, laughing with her, chumming it up. People love her, and she's such a good writer. She can put anybody at ease and get any scoop she sets her mind on."

"That much is true. I don't even remember how I got here. We were supposed to be meeting at my hotel with my assistant there to keep me on track. Then my assistant opted for a nap instead, and I found myself on Hope's couch, telling the story of how I lost my virginity, and she hadn't even asked me about my virginity." He paused for a breath. "It really is a good story. Do you want me to tell you?"

I laughed. "I'm good, thanks. But you see what I mean. Hope has an effect on people. Everyone loves her."

"Of course everyone loves her. She's amazing. I love her, and we just met."

"Exactly."

He wasn't done. "But I was only with her for a few hours. Even if I show off by sending her a chair or something, I won't interact with her again until my next album, if ever. An interview—even a good one—isn't a relationship. It's a job. It doesn't mean she's not lonely."

A twinge of discomfort momentarily rattled me. "I'm sure you're wrong. Hope loves her life." I hopped off the counter and handed him the eyeliner. "Now pretend you're doing this yourself." I angled myself behind him.

When we finished in the bathroom, he suggested we do a "party-aftermath" scene, but we hit a snag. "We could have you passed out in a tub. I'll get empty bottles from Hope's recycling bin and scatter them around. It's gonna be great. All we need is some beard scruff on you."

"Yeah. Grand idea. Sadly, I can't grow hair on demand. I would if I could."

I didn't have a ton of experience with men's facial hair, but Toby usually had some scruff by the end of the day. "Maybe you'll have some in a few hours?"

Jimmy nodded. "Probably. I'm going to try."

"Should we sleep in the meantime?" I suggested hopefully.

He brightened. "I call pink velvet chaise!"

"Of course you do."

He went back into the other room and nestled into the chaise, punching the pillows until he was comfortable. "This is going to be great. Tuck me in, Willa."

I covered him with a blanket, dimmed the lights, and got settled on the couch. Then I sat straight up. "Shit!"

"What's the matter?"

I was digging for my phone. "Toby's probably worried sick. I should have been home already."

"I should call my assistant, but I'm not going to. She doesn't take my calls anymore anyway. She's a rubbish assistant. I can't even complain because Oliver and Eric told me she would be, but I didn't listen." He sighed forlornly. "I have to keep pretending she's much better than she is. Saving face is important, Willa, even amongst your best mates."

I called Toby five or six times before he answered. "Don't worry," I said hastily when he answered. "Everything is fine. I'm working on a project for Hope. I'll be home later. Is everything okay?"

He muttered something sleepily into the phone and disconnected.

"All right, Willa?" Jimmy asked.

"Yeah. He worries." I stuffed my phone back into my pocket and snuggled back into the couch.

"Hm. It sounded like you woke him."

"Are you concentrating on growing your beard in? It seems like you aren't."

"Are we napping?" he countered. "Or haranguing? Because I'm feeling quite harangued right now. My beard will not grow in if it feels bullied, Willa."

I smothered a smile. What an irritating, charming man.

Chapter Three

I fell asleep harder than I meant to and didn't wake until the sun came up. Jimmy and I were both disappointed in his complete lack of facial hair.

"Can American men grow hair on command? No. Don't say. I can't, which is all that matters. I'm not a lumberjack, darling; I am a songwriter."

We did the best we could with the bathtub/empty beer bottle scene anyway, then I downloaded the images and emailed them to Hope, who had evidently pulled an all-nighter at the office.

He called for a ride as I packed my camera. Before he left, he asked, "Willa, can I hug you?"

I wasn't big on hugs, so I was surprised to want a hug from Jimmy. I was even more surprised when I was a little reluctant to let go. He smiled warmly at me, still holding onto my arms. "Thank you for taking pictures of me and for telling me your stories and for being lovely."

"Thanks for letting me take your picture." I smiled at him. "You're my favorite pop star I've ever met."

He wrinkled his nose. "I hope the sentiment stays true even when you've met a second one. Give me your number. If we come through anywhere near here on our tour, I'll get you on the list. Will you come visit?"

"Of course," I said. I even meant it. Concerts weren't my thing, but I liked the idea of seeing him again. I put my number in his phone.

After he left, I locked Hope's house and drove to my next job with a lighter heart than usual. The time with Jimmy had been a good night's work. I could add to my portfolio, thanks to Hope.

I made it through my shift at the coffee shop with no major disasters. All I wanted when I got home was a shower, my bed, and six to eight hours of unconsciousness. I opened the door, dropped my keys into the chipped pottery bowl on the table by the entry, and started down the hall before I noticed Toby on the saggy plaid couch, evidently waiting for me. The always-present knot of worry in my stomach got a little tighter. It didn't take long for me to realize he was all right. His body language was tense and stiff, which meant he was nervous, not in pain. If he was hurting, he'd be pale and focused on acting normal.

I ruffled his brown wavy hair, surreptitiously checking for a fever, but he wasn't warm. "How was your day? You want me to fix you something to eat?"

"I made dinner. There's some soup in the kitchen for you if you're hungry."

My breath caught in my throat. "What's wrong?"

His smile wasn't reflected in his dark eyes. "I can't make you dinner without... Have a seat. We need to talk."

I dropped onto the recliner across from him. "What's wrong? Does something hurt? Do we need to—"

He shook his head. "No. Listen to me for a minute."

I folded my hands in my lap and waited.

"I want to go to college."

I let myself digest it for a minute before I transitioned into planning mode. "All right. I can probably pick up a few more shifts at the coffee shop. I'll have to find a way to get you there in the morning, and it would depend on your class schedule—"

"I'm not done, Willa. Please listen to me."

"Sorry. I'm listening. You want to go to school. The community college?"

He frowned. "Why do you assume that? You assume I couldn't get in anywhere better?"

"Wow. Thanks. It's where I went, if you recall."

"You didn't start there," he reminded me as if I'd forgotten. He crossed his arms over his chest and frowned. This was a sore point. "You went away to Carson-Newman on a scholarship, then quit and came back home because of Cancer, Part Two."

Not entirely false, but not the whole truth, either. "I came home because I love you and wanted to be here in case you needed me."

"You came home because Dad couldn't cook and never took notes at the doctor visits."

He wasn't completely wrong. Dad had done the best he could, but he missed a lot.

I didn't blame him; I just thought it would be best if there were two of us handling things and if one of them was me. It was a good thing it worked out that way, because when Dad suffered a heart attack two years later, I was already home. Toby had been only seventeen, but I'd been able to keep him with me as long as we had regular visits from a social worker.

"Everything is fine, Toby. I love being here. We're good."

His jaw was clenched. He flexed his hands and shook his head. "Is it fine, Willa? What are your plans for next year? The year after? I can't sit here playing video games forever. I have to *do* something."

I didn't have an answer for him. All I needed him to do was stay well. "If CC is such bullshit, where are you going?"

"I'm starting at CC, like you. I'll get my first classes there and maybe transfer to a university later."

"How are we going to pay for it?" I was proud of how calm and rational I was being.

He lifted his chin and said, "Mom is going to pay for it."

It was like he'd dumped ice water over me. "Who?"

"Mom." He waited for my reaction.

"You *talked* to her?"

His gaze slid away from mine.

I got to my feet. "Toby? Answer me."

"Yes, I called her, okay? I called our mom."

"You asked her to pay for you to go to school."

"She owes us, right?"

A semi-hysterical laugh escaped me. "Uh, yeah. You could say that." I needed to get away. I didn't want to have this conversation. I wasn't sure what would come out of my mouth.

"Listen to me," Toby pleaded. "Don't be like this. She's our mom."

I flinched when he said it. "No. Maybe she's *your* mom if you're okay with what she's done. She's nothing to me."

"This is a big deal, Will. Can't you be happy for me?"

There was no chance of that, but maybe I owed it to him to fake it. "When were you going to tell me you'd registered?"

He picked at a hole in the leg of his jeans. "Not until I was sure. I knew you weren't going to like it."

"Of course I like it." I lied. "I'm proud of you. I'm strategizing about how we're going to make it work. Even if tuition is covered, we'll need a way for me to get you there every day."

He wouldn't meet my eye. "I bought a car. I used the rest of my share of Dad's insurance money."

I blinked at him. "You can't drive," I said stupidly.

Belatedly, I remembered there was a strange car parked in front. I'd assumed Toby had a friend over, then I'd forgotten about it in the upheaval of everything that followed.

Evidently, it was his car.

"I took classes. I got my license. I wanted to surprise you."

Mission accomplished. I was surprised.

"Willa?"

I went to the kitchen for a glass of water. After I drank it, I stared unseeingly at our small, untended backyard, my hands gripping the edge of the counter.

When Toby came in behind me, I cleared my throat and said, "Well, you've been busy. Reestablishing your relationship with the absentee mom. You registered for school, bought a car, learned how to drive. I guess you have lots of time to be doing things like this, what with me being at work. Or at my other work. Or at my other work. Or doing our shopping or running our errands. I'm glad you've made such good use of free time I don't have."

I needed something to do with my hands. I turned the faucet back on and filled the sink with hot soapy water.

He stood next to me. "Willa. I don't ask you—"

"That's the point," I said, sliding dirty dishes into the sink with unsteady hands. Hot water sloshed over the edge and onto the floor. I ignored it. "You don't *have* to ask me. I'm your sister. We're family. This is what I do. I take care of things." I blinked away tears. "You've been sneaking around and keeping things from me."

"Of *course* I've been keeping things from you," he said, sounding angry again. "Look at how you're reacting!"

"Like I'm surprised? I *am* surprised! I had no idea any of this was going on!" I tossed the dishrag in the sink, splashing more suds. I dried my hands jerkily.

We were off track, but I didn't know how to walk it back. I wanted to start over. I wanted it to have never happened. I wanted to go back to yesterday.

"Willa, I told you I wanted to go to school. I told you I wanted to get a job. All you ever say is you'll handle things."

"I *will* handle things! You don't need to do this!"

"I don't want you to handle things!" he yelled. "I'm eighteen years old! I don't need to be taken care of!"

His words hit me like a slap.

There was more.

"I don't need you to be my mom. Can't you be my sister? Can't you let me make decisions for myself?"

I left the kitchen and went toward my room, my only objective to get away.

"Oh, don't do this," he said, sounding disgusted now. "Please don't be a martyr, Willa."

"I'm not a martyr."

"Then don't—"

I spun to face him. "And you don't have to tell me I'm not our mom. Obviously I'm not because I'm here. I have always been here. She's showing up with her checkbook now? Where was she when you were in the hospital? Oh, right, with her *boyfriend*. Where was she when Dad died? With her new family. I'm the one who's *here*."

His bravado wavered. "I'm just going to school. Like every other eighteen-year-old."

I shook my head, and it was out of my mouth before I could stop it. "You aren't like every other eighteen-year-old."

I meant...*you're my eighteen-year-old. You're my baby brother. You're the reason I do what I do.* It's not what I said, though, and there wasn't a chance to fix it.

He got up and snatched the keys for his new car on his way out the door. I listened to the sound of him driving away from me.

~ * ~

I was in bed later when my phone rang, but I ignored it until it stopped. I didn't want to wake up anyway. Toby must have come home at some point because music was coming from his room. I started to get up to check on him before I stopped myself.

He didn't need me.

I turned over and yanked the blankets over my head.

My phone rang again.

I ignored it again until it stopped.

After a moment, it started ringing again.

I grabbed it. "*What?*"

"Oh, thank God you're there. Thank God! Willa! I need help!"

I recognized the accent and the voice because of course I did, but it didn't make sense. This was officially the first time a famous musician had called me at—I glanced at the clock—one in the morning, on what had been an extremely difficult day.

To be fair, it was the first time a famous musician had called me at any time, on any kind of day.

"Are you there? Oh God, say something, and make it something I can understand. I am surrounded by Americans speaking gibberish, and I can't take it. I'm locked in my room. Josette has left for good, and I can't get hold of her even if I wanted to, which I don't, and I am alone. There's no food. I can't remember my email password, and I don't want to call Hawk because—"

"Who's Hawk?"

"My manager, obviously. Once he finds out Josette is gone—"

"Who's Josette?"

"My assistant!"

"Where is she?"

"*Please* keep up, darling," Jimmy said. "I had an assistant called Josette. She quit and left me because she is very French and very over me. Does she care that she's left me stranded and afraid? No, she does not. Eric and Oliver are on the other side of the fucking world, so they're no use to me. I am alone on foreign ground. You're my only hope."

I ran a hand over my face, struggling to wake up enough to keep pace with him. "Where are you?"

"Kentucky. I know you're not going to leave me stranded because we have a connection, you and me. I said to myself, *I met a lovely girl who likes taking care of people and has nice freckles, and she's Willa.* You must come."

I was silent for a beat, and he practically screeched my name. "*Willa*! Why do you keep not talking while my world is falling apart?" He must have shifted the phone because his voice was muffled as he muttered. "She's probably hung up on me. Someone will find me here, months later. Headlines like *World's prettiest legend of a rock star found abandoned and dead in a hotel room in the American South.*"

"Take a deep breath, Jimmy. I don't understand how I can help. Can I call someone for you?"

"I'm going to say it again, darling, but do pay attention. I need you to come be my assistant. Please." He added, "Starting immediately."

"You hadn't said that, actually."

"Is it possible you missed the implication? That's a discouraging sign. Well, you're new. I'm sure you'll be a better assistant soon."

"I have no idea how to be an assistant, but I can help you find someone qualified." I regretted saying it immediately. How would I find him an assistant? I'd call Hope and go from there, I guessed.

"It's an incredibly vital but simple job. You'll love it. You'll make my day sheets. Do the shopping. Coordinate with Tucker." He paused. "You should also do my makeup because fucking hell. Hope emailed me proofs of those pictures we did, and I look good. Even for me. This is a thing now. I'm entering a makeup phase. It was inevitable, I suppose. I sent a picture to Eric, and he said he wants makeup too when he gets here. Oliver says he's fine, but he always says he's fine. Tucker's would be fine, only she has no idea where to take me tomorrow because we don't have day sheets, and I can't get into my email."

"Who's Tucker?"

"Tucker is my driver. Did you imagine I was driving myself around this massive country?"

"Who's Eric?"

"Who's—Willa, I told you! He's my guitar player. You're going to need to start taking notes."

The music in Toby's room went silent, replaced by the rumble of his voice. He was probably on the phone with a friend, telling them about how excited he was to be starting his new life and finally getting out from under the thumb of his oppressive big sister.

Big man who didn't need his sister anymore.

Jimmy was being ridiculous. It was definitely a ludicrous idea. At the same time...

The wheels slowly started turning. "You'd have to pay me," I said to Jimmy.

"Oh, is that how it works when you hire someone to do a job? Yes, Willa. I would pay you. I will pay you whatever I was paying her if you can help me find out what it was. We'll get it sorted."

Toby's door opened. "Willa?" he called from the hall. "You all right?"

I ignored him. Obviously, I wasn't. Would I seriously be considering this move if I was all right? "How long would I be gone?" I asked Jimmy.

"Ideally for the whole tour, but it's a stretch, considering my track record. Until you get sick of me and leave me stranded in the middle of nowhere, I guess."

Ludicrous or not, I dove in. "You'd have to pay me more than you were paying the other one because I'll be much better at it. I want to work on my photography portfolio while I'm there. I can build my body of work, maybe sell some freelance stuff." Uncle Ken wouldn't have to hire me as a charity case. He'd hire me because my photography would speak for itself.

In the meantime, I'd let Jimmy pay me to babysit him. It was crazy, but maybe crazy was good. The universe was obviously driving me into making a change.

"Yes. Photos, portfolio, whatever you need. If you get in a car right now. How far are you from where I am?"

"Where are you?"

His sigh came across the line loud and clear. "This is the kind of thing you're going to have to learn to be better at, darling. You should always know where I am. That's, like, Being an Assistant 101."

"Maybe I can take some online courses on how to take care of a pop starlet. I'll Google it."

"You mispronounced Rock God." He was starting to sound calmer. "Are you in the car yet?"

I got out of bed and flipped on the light. I started a mental inventory of what I'd bring with me. "It'll be morning. I have to pack, quit my other jobs, make arrangements—"

I dug an old duffle bag from the bottom of my closet. I couldn't believe I was actually going to do it. But after all, why the hell not? One job would be easier than three.

I wasn't needed at home, anyway.

I gave the limited clean clothes hanging in my closet a skeptical glance. They were serviceable for coffee shops and other part-time jobs, but maybe not right for being a personal assistant.

Jimmy sweetened the pot. "I won't be able to sleep until you get here. I'll buy you new everything if you hurry. Only don't tell Eric because he says I'm impulsive, and I don't want to bolster that particular opinion. Don't tell my *next* assistant either because I probably won't want to do it for them, but I'm more desperate than usual, and shopping is fun. If you ever stop talking, you can hang up and call a ride, Willa, honestly."

"There'll be a notepad or a folio or something in your room with the hotel's address on it. Take a picture and send it to me. I'll call a car and text you with an ETA when I'm on my way."

I could sense his smile across the line. "It was clever of me to call you. Bring smelling salts. I'll have fainted from hunger before you get here."

Chapter Four

I threw a few things together, despite Jimmy's promise to buy me "new everything." I was double-checking my old canvas photo bag when Toby walked in.

"What are you doing up?" I asked him.

"I couldn't sleep after our fight. Wondering what I could do to make it all right."

I didn't want to discuss it. "I accepted a new job," I announced abruptly. I zipped my camera bag closed and set it by the door.

"What? Just now?"

I shoved a few more things into my bag, trying to keep my hands busy. "Just now. I'm going to work for a guy named Jimmy. Hope introduced me to him. I'm going to be his assistant. I'll work on my photography portfolio at the same time, make a real go of it. You've inspired me to start something new." I sounded sarcastic and shitty, but I couldn't make myself stop. "We'll be on the road, I guess. I'm not sure when I'll be back."

He shook his head, confused. "Whoa. Slow down."

My smile felt brittle. "No time. I have to go."

"You can't leave like this, Willa."

"I absolutely can. You've got everything here handled, as you said. You're on it."

Toby groaned. "Don't do this. Let's talk in the morning, okay? Get some sleep, and we'll talk again when we're both calm."

I shrugged and finally let myself look at him. "I'm gonna go, Toby." I was determined not to cry. "Maybe it's time for you to spread your wings a bit. Maybe it'll be good for us both. You can call me if you need to. Call Uncle Ken if you need anyone closer." I couldn't help adding, "Or call your mom."

He rolled his eyes at that, but didn't bother to comment on it. "This isn't like you at all. I don't want you to go when you're mad."

"You don't want me to stay, either." I gave myself a moment to collect my thoughts, then said, "If you need a relationship with your mom, I can't stop you. I'm just going to remind you not to trust her. Don't be a sucker."

He sat on my bed and patted the spot next to him. "Stop for a minute and talk to me. You don't have to leave right this second."

My phone buzzed in my pocket, my ride announcing itself from the driveway. "I'm leaving now." My voice was unsteady. "You were so young; you don't remember. Dad and I were there to distract you, and you got past it. You have this idealized version of who she should be—and that's not who she is."

I put my hair into a high ponytail and twisted it into a bun. I straightened the alarm clock and reading lamp on my nightstand.

"It was a long time ago. People change."

"No they don't, Toby. She's a person who leaves when things are hard. That's who she was when we needed her, and it's who she's always going to be. Don't count on her. Call me if you need me, and I will come home. Okay?"

"Are you really leaving?"

"Call me if you need me," I said again. "I will come back if you ask me to."

"It's you I'm worried about. I'll be fine."

Toby assumed it was going to be easy, but he didn't really have any idea what it was like to be alone. We'd only been apart once. I went away and left him with Dad, and it was such a disaster that I'd come right back. I put my camera bag over one shoulder and a duffel over the other. "All right, I'm going. Wish me luck. This guy is going to be a handful. I'll text you when I get there."

"Are you mad?"

It was tempting to smooth over it. Even a day ago, I would have, but if he was feeling like such an adult, he needed to understand his actions impacted other people. "Yeah. I'm mad and hurt." I paused. "It'll be fine."

When I left my room, I came right back. "Don't forget you have a doctor's appointment on Tuesday."

I went back toward the front door. then reversed course again and went back to my room. "And make sure you get insurance for your stupid car. Get full coverage if you can afford it. Make sure the deductible isn't more than you can handle if something happens. Goodbye."

The next time I made it to the front door. "Send your tuition check in on time, or you'll have late fees," I yelled.

"I love you, Willa!" he called.

It's important to let people know when they've let you down, so I slammed the door on the way out.

Then I yanked it back open. "I love you, too. Lock this behind me."

I used my commute time to take care of some business. Leaving a message with the computer lab didn't even give me a twinge of guilt. It was the easiest job in the world; they'd have no trouble replacing me.

I texted Jenny. The coffee shop wouldn't be open for another few hours, and I hoped she'd be sleeping. No such luck. My phone rang seconds later. I explained what was going on and apologized for not being able to give her notice. "This guy is a wreck, Jenny, and he needs help now. It can't wait."

"You're going to be an assistant. To Jimmy Standish. From Corporate." Her voice was flat.

"Right. They're a band from England."

"I'm aware of who Corporate is, Willa. I don't live under a rock." Ouch. "The next time you want to quit a job and leave someone high and dry right before morning rush, you need a more plausible lie."

"What? No, I—"

"Thanks a lot, Willa. Enjoy your time with 'Corporate.'" She disconnected. I glared at my phone and made a mental note to send her a picture of me with Jimmy. She'd feel like an ass.

Uncle Ken probably wouldn't be awake yet, so I tapped an email to him. I was a few sentences in when my phone rang. "I was just emailing you, Uncle Ken."

"Toby called. He's worried. What are you doing?"

"I'm going to build a portfolio so I can work for you for real. You don't need me as your photo-retouch girl. Anybody can do what I do."

"Is this because you and Toby got in a fight? Did he tell you he was going to school?"

My stomach turned. "He told you?"

"We met for lunch the other day," Uncle Ken said gently. "He wasn't sure how he should bring it up."

"He probably could have done better than he did."

"Is it why you're leaving?"

"No." I was watching the scenery flash by the window. I didn't recognize anything. I was already a bit at sea, and I hadn't even left Tennessee.

"Talk to me," Uncle Ken said.

"The opportunity fell in my lap, and I decided to take it. That's it. I'm tired of overthinking everything. Nobody needs me at home. Jimmy needs me wherever he is, and it sounds like an easy job. I can take pictures whenever he doesn't need me. There's no downside. I thought you'd be glad for me," I added. "I'm chasing my dreams or whatever."

He sounded tired. "I am happy you're taking advantage of a new opportunity. I am. I'm not sure I love your reasoning for doing it is all. You don't need to prove anything to me. I know you're talented. I already offered you a job. Many, many times."

"I don't want a charity job."

"It's not charity," he said, his usual response. "I could help you, Willa. I have money. It's what your dad would want me to do. It's what I want to do."

I understood he wanted to help me. By giving me money, or paying the bills, or giving me a job—but I wanted to earn what I had. I wanted to take care of Toby myself. We'd had this conversation a hundred times. We didn't need to have it again.

He sounded resigned when he spoke again. "Be careful, Willa. Jimmy Standish is…a lot. His world isn't like your world."

I scoffed. "My world isn't great right now, so that sounds like a pretty good thing to me."

"Be careful," he repeated.

"I love you. I'll call you in a few days."

I disconnected and put my phone back in my pocket. I stood up straight and squared my shoulders. What I was doing was out of character, but surely it was healthy to turn over a new leaf. This was going to be a great opportunity and I was proud of myself for going for it.

That didn't mean I wasn't nervous.

I wasn't the kind of person who made spontaneous decisions. My decisions had all been made around Toby.

A voice in the back of my head told me this one was because of him, too, but this time the momentum was away from him rather than toward him.

I told the voice to be quiet. New opportunities. New job. Brand new Willa, coming right up, for better or for worse.

It was time for what was next.

"What was next" hadn't literally fainted by the time I got to him a few hours later, but he wasn't far from it.

I nearly fainted when the car dropped me off at the most glamorous hotel I'd ever seen. I could have been in a movie.

I tapped on the door. "Hey. Jimmy. It's me."

He swung open the door, closed his fingers around my wrist, and drew me in. "Thank God you're here. Did you bring me food?"

I brandished a pizza box at him, which I had picked up at a pizza joint I'd spotted near the hotel.

He beamed. "You're a brilliant assistant already. Put your stuff down, and let's eat. Did it go okay leaving your brother? Your room is next door. Or you can sleep in here with me if you want to. I wasn't sure if you were a sleeps-alone type or a likes-the-company-of-sleeping-with-a-friend type."

"I'm a sleeps-alone type." I opened the adjoining door and dropped off my stuff. He was already well into the pizza when I rejoined him.

"Did you bring clothes? I told you don't bring clothes! We'll shop tomorrow. You need to be in aesthetic anyway, darling, and for example, what you have on isn't."

I glanced down at myself. "What's wrong with how I'm dressed?" It was my favorite shirt. This topped the list of my limited options.

"Nothing, when you weren't with me. Now you *are* with me, and, um… we don't wear colors."

I inspected his ensemble—black sweater, black jeans. I wouldn't even bother photographing him in color. The rich tones of black and white would suit him perfectly. Unless his tattoos were out, there was no color anyway.

"Black, white, or gray," he continued. "All natural fibers. Your pretty, young skin needs to breathe. It's fine. Stop worrying. We'll get it sorted in the morning."

"I'm not worried," I said cheerfully. "If you can afford to buy me a new wardrobe, knock yourself out."

He leaned back in his chair. "I can afford it. Now listen. You need to help me. We have to get into my email. I have to tell Hawk to stop paying Josette, first of all, and I don't know where I'm supposed to be tomorrow. It's all in there."

"'Kay," I agreed. "Let's log in."

"Right. Only I don't remember my password." He stared at his open laptop and shrugged. "It could be anything. I told it to Josette, then poof. Gone from my mind. How good are you at hacking?"

Toby could probably get us in if I needed him to, but I didn't want to call him. "Let's see if I can guess it."

He pushed the computer to me, and I made a guess. Presto.

"You clever girl! How did you know?"

"It's JimmyJimmy. Your name, but twice. That's—"

"The best password ever, right? Don't forget it because we'll need it again. Write it on your hand."

"I'm pretty sure I won't forget it. Do you want to talk about what happened with Josette?"

"No, Willa, I do not. Because it doesn't matter."

I wasn't sure if I was supposed to encourage him to tell me more or if he legitimately didn't want to discuss it, so I waited.

"Because if it mattered, she would not be gone," he said.

"Got it."

"Willa, listen." He put a hand on my arm. "She's gone, so she's gone. The end. I don't mean I don't want to talk about it right now. I don't want to talk about it *ever*."

It made sense to me. If someone leaves you, they're gone. I covered his hand with mine. "It's cool. I already forgot who we're not talking about."

"Josette!" he cried. I gave him a minute. "Oh, right. You were doing a thing. I got you now." He tapped the side of his nose and winked. "You should probably dive right in, Willa. Figure out where we're supposed to be. But a warning—it's probably for the best if you don't open attachments. Sometimes fans send me things you might not like to see. Best to err on the side of caution, right? Mark those with a star, and I'll get to them later."

He found something on the television and zoned out. I opened his email, and he was not wrong. There were hundreds of unread messages. I started one list for schedule updates, one list for other band business, and, after one jarring mistake, carefully avoided his fan mail. Once I'd made us an agenda for the next few days, I felt less scattered.

Our first day together flew by. After dark, I went into my adjoining room and flipped on the lights. I was stunned all over again by how different his world was. My room was as extravagant as his. The plush carpet was spotless. A floor-to-ceiling window overlooked the city. I opened the curtains, turned off the room lights, and took in the city lights while I daydreamed about what my photography career would be like when I went back home.

Uncle Ken paged through my portfolio, full of gorgeous, glossy prints in a fancy leather binder.

"Willa! My God! This is brilliant!"

"I do like to imagine I have a style of my own. Charlie has been your head photographer for years, and I'd never dream—"

"Charlie who? My only question is which of these I should choose for our next cover! Listen, I need you to get these to the lab right away. Ask someone to scan these in. No retouching! It's flawless."

We were interrupted by Hope barging into Ken's office, the other reporters close on her heels, clamoring to hire me for their next story.

I snuggled into the cozy bed, more optimistic than I had been in a long time. The celebrity photography world was waiting for someone like me. Once I was working as a photographer and making more money, Toby and I wouldn't have to worry. Our missing maternal figure wouldn't have to pay Toby's tuition because I would do it myself. I'd renovate the house when I was between wonderful photo excursions.

Things were definitely going to be changing for me.

Chapter Five

I'd hoped a benefit of my new job was going to be the ability to sleep in. No such luck. Maybe the bed was a bit too comfortable, or maybe it was the habit of early starts. I was awake before daylight.

Since I was up anyway, I decided to do some research. I opened a search engine on my phone and entered "Corporate." Before I got anywhere, my phone buzzed in my hand.

Jimmy: *911 911 911*

I rushed into his room. "Are you okay? What's the matter? Are you hurt?"

He was propped up in bed with the room service menu. "Good morning, my American friend. Breakfast is on the way!" When he looked at me, the color drained from his face. "Good Christ, Willa. What is happening there?"

"'911' means emergency, Jimmy. Is something wrong?"

"It is now! What in the unholy fuck are you wearing?"

"What?" It was just a nightgown. Like all nightgowns, I imagine. White. Short sleeves. Knee-length. If we're being honest, it did have some fussy lace trim around the sleeves and the hem, but it was comfortable.

"Is this what you sleep in?"

"Uh, yeah."

"Wow. Okay. Don't panic." He took a deep breath. "It might have worked for your old life, although I can't imagine how there's *any* life it would work in, but it won't work for this one. Is it polyester? Never mind. Don't tell me. My nan has the same nightgown, Willa. I imagine. I've never seen her in her sleepwear, but I bet you she does."

"Jimmy."

"Oliver's nan doesn't, I can promise you. He hates to have it mentioned, but she's quite fit, actually, for a woman approaching ninety. Very spry. Oh, hold on, speak of the devil, just got a text. Oliver, not his nan. I'll call him."

"Sounds good. Since there was *not* an emergency and you totally abused 911 privileges, I'm going back to my room."

"Absolutely not, darling, it's time to be up. No, not you, Oliver. I was talking to Willa. She came to my rescue last night like I told you she would. Remember? You said, 'Don't be absurd, why would you hire a photographer who's actually a barista to be your assistant,' but I overruled you because my instincts are never wrong, apart from when they are, and this wasn't one of those times. You want to talk to her?"

I waved my hands in the international symbol for "I don't want to talk on the phone," but maybe it wasn't international after all because Jimmy presented me with the phone, beaming. "Say hi to Oliver!"

I crossed to the bed and took the phone. "Um, hi. Hello. I'm Willa Reynolds. I'm here with Jimmy."

"Hello, Willa Reynolds. How's your second day? Please say it isn't going to be your last day."

His accent was similar to Jimmy's, but thicker somehow, like the vowels were bigger. His voice, though—it wasn't like any other voice I'd ever heard. It was deep and smooth, and it made me think of things that taste good. The auditory equivalent of chocolate or espresso. Warm and rich.

"You there?"

"Hi! Yes. Sorry. I'm here. He's a lot, but I can handle him. Are the rest of you a little lower key? Please say yes."

Oliver laughed, and my stomach did a funny flip. I figured I must be hungrier than I realized. "On a scale from subdued to Jimmy, Eric is in the middle, and you'll be able to handle me with no problem."

Jimmy held out his hand. "Okay, enough. Focus on me, both of you." He took the phone back. "Oliver, this has been a lovely chat, but I must go. I'm having a real nightie emergency here, and it can't wait. Oh. Well, what did you want? Right. I'll ask Willa to email it to you. I have no idea where it is. Cheers, mate."

He disconnected. "We need to start making setlists, Willa. Oliver is on fire to have one right away. I started one, but it's somewhere in my damn laptop, and I have no idea where. Where were we? Oh, yes, right, we were talking about how you shouldn't worry because you won't ever have to sleep in that nasty thing again. Also, listen. I ordered breakfast since you were having a massive lie-in. I got you oatmeal."

"I don't want oatmeal. Gross." Just because I was wearing granny pajammies didn't mean I wanted granny breakfast.

"Oatmeal is healthy so I ordered it for both of us, but I got myself a couple other choices in case I change my mind. First things first, darling. We need to call Hawk. Don't panic."

He waited expectantly, but when I remained calm, he said, "All right, some panic is called for, maybe. It's highly unlikely this will go well."

I shrugged. It would be fine. Surely their manager's job was to keep the talent happy. It was my job now, too. This Hawk, whoever he was... he and I were a team.

Jimmy wasn't as calm. "All right, Willa. You definitely should panic. I am straight up panicking, and you should always follow my lead."

A knock on the door announced our breakfast. "Hold that thought," I said. I opened the door to a young woman with a cart piled high with food. She stopped dead at the sight of Jimmy in the bed and made choking noises like she had something lodged in her throat. I put a gentle hand on her back. "Are you all right? Can I call someone for you?"

"It's Jimmy Standish," she whispered.

"'Course not, love," Jimmy said, accent ringing out loud and clear. "Jimmy Standish is English, isn't he? Kentucky born and bred, me. I must be the spit of him because you're not the first one to say it, is she, wifey?" He winked at me.

I wrested the receipt from her and signed it before I hustled her back out the door.

He uncovered plates, utterly unbothered as if women choked on their own tongues around him every day. Maybe they did.

"Sit." He slid a bowl of oatmeal to me.

He looked over his own order—in addition to the oatmeal, there was an omelet, hash browns, three eggs over easy, three orders of bacon, a side of sausage, biscuits and gravy, and two pieces of cheesecake.

When he caught me staring, he said, "They don't even serve cheesecake this early. I played the English card. I told them it's tradition for my people."

"Next time, tell them it's tradition for both our people."

"What is breakfast tradition for people like you?" he asked curiously. Then he brightened. "Oh! Grits. Please tell me it's grits."

"Grits. For every meal."

"I knew it. With moonshine, right?"

"Obviously. Now let's talk about this conversation we have to have with Hawk."

His head fell back on his shoulders. "Ah, Christ, don't remind me when I'm eating." He set down his fork with a clatter.

"Hawk is your manager, right?"

"Right."

I took advantage of his obvious distress and snagged a plate of cheesecake. "We need to tell him you've hired me?" I prompted.

He made an expression like *sort of.*

"Jimmy?"

"Mostly. There is just this tiny technicality. I don't have the actual authority to hire you."

I sighed. "This is information I'd have loved to have before I came all the way here, but okay, we'll treat it as, what? An interview?"

"Right. Only, it'll be the tiniest thing, but first, we better tell him the other one's gone. I don't expect him to be thrilled about it, either."

"Why not? Didn't she leave you? It's not your fault."

He pointed at me. "Good girl. Exactly. It's not my fault, but let's gloss over it anyway. He'll rage a bit, then he'll say he's going to send us a new contract. We'll sign it, you'll send him your banking information, and there you go, all taken care of."

"It sounds like you've done this before."

He ignored me. "Let's get it over with. When we're done, we'll reward ourselves with some vigorous shopping. Sound good?"

"Sounds great."

I went back to my room to get dressed, and then we sat in front of Jimmy's computer at the desk. After he fidgeted around nervously for a few minutes, he placed the call.

Right after he hit dial, he said quickly, "You do the talking because it's your job as my new assistant, and it's a great way to impress him. Go."

When we connected, his manager was sitting in a leather chair/throne behind a giant desk, piles of paperwork visible to the side, the wall behind him covered with framed shiny records.

He barely gave us a glance. The first thing he said was, "Jesus Christ, Jimmy. Please don't tell me you've gone off another assistant already. I'm a busy man, and I do not have the time to deal with personnel changes based on your love life. Where the fuck is what's-her-name, and who is this? For once in your career, would it be possible for you to have a platonic relationship with someone you hire? So they could do the fucking job I hired them for?"

It was clear why Jimmy was more than a bit nervous. Hawk was one of the few people Jimmy couldn't charm. He didn't pay enough attention for it to penetrate.

Also, he was intimidating. Like, really intimidating. He was attractive in an older-guy-who's-seen-it-all way. Smile lines fanned out from his eyes, although I couldn't imagine how they got there because it was impossible to envision him smiling. Maybe they were rage lines, not smile lines. I'd do a super-tight close-up photograph of him if given the chance. Context wasn't needed for Hawk. His face said everything that needed to be said, and one of the things it said was my daydream of being on the same team was only a fantasy.

He made an impatient sound. "Let's have it. I've got a lot going on today."

Jimmy gestured for me to take over.

I leaned toward the screen. "Willa Reynolds, Jimmy's new assistant. It's nice to meet you."

He glowered. "Don't get too comfortable, girl. I have no reason to hope you'll last. Tell me what your qualifications are. Go."

"I'm a photographer, and a lab assistant, and a barista. I've been a caregiver to my brother for the past several years, and I've nannied for twin girls."

"Nanny and caregiver sound promising. You can take care of this one and Eric. Oliver can sort himself out. It's a pretty major position for someone who has no experience, though, and I'm done letting this guy choose his own staff. What else you got?"

"Um… I used to work in a barbershop, so I can, uh, keep him presentable."

"She's great at makeup," Jimmy chimed in. "And I'm going through a makeup phase."

"I used to work the Clinique counter at the mall." It was mostly old ladies—and exactly zero rock stars—but I didn't mention that.

Hawk grimaced. "Fucking hell, you sound like such an American. It's not doing much to build confidence, if I'm honest."

I stopped being intimated and got annoyed. "Makes sense since I'm American. Listen. He called me in a panic less than twelve hours ago. I got here, fed him, calmed him down, and I have his schedule set for the day. I can make sure he's where he needs to be, help him with whatever he needs, run their social media, and handle the other two when they get here. Feeling more confident yet?"

He was quiet for a moment, then said, "You're a photographer?"

"Yes."

"Any good?"

"Very good."

"Fine, we'll give it a go," he said decisively. "Fix their Instagram account. Jesus Christ, what a mess. No more nudes. Jimmy, I'm not going to say it again. Proper promo shit."

Jimmy leaned forward with a response, but Hawk pointed at the camera and said, "No."

Jimmy slumped back in his chair muttering, and Hawk gave his attention back to me. "When he goes to an interview, you go with him. Stop him from saying anything stupid. Jimmy, keep your eye on her, and if she's giving you a sign to stop talking, stop talking. We'll see how it goes. I'm not doing this again. I'm going to make a revision to the contract. Read it. Both of you. Wendy—"

"Willa."

"Willy," he settled on, "I'll email it. Get me a digitally signed copy by the end of the day."

"Will do, Howard."

"It's Hawk," he said, and maybe I was kidding myself, but I was pretty sure he nearly smiled. "Give her the band phone, Jimmy." He leaned forward and ended the video chat.

Jimmy's email chimed a few minutes later. I sat at the desk to read the contract.

"You don't need to read it, darling," he said. "Let's just sign it. Hawk fancies himself a real business mogul, but I guarantee you all he did was copy some boilerplate bullshit off the internet."

I scrolled in silence for a few moments. "There's a clause in here forbidding 'any relationship of a romantic nature between band employees and band members.' How have you gotten around it?"

Jimmy collapsed onto the bed and put an arm across his face. "*Fuck* me. It was bound to occur to him eventually."

"This is new? That must be what he meant."

"I'm sorry, Willa." He was staring at the ceiling and sounded morose. "I can imagine how devastated you must be, but—"

"Nah." I was still reading. "It's fine."

"What?"

Belatedly, I realized I might have hurt his feelings. I swiveled my chair to face him. He was propped up on his elbows, a stunned expression on his face. I hurried into damage-control mode. "I mean, I can live with it, Jimmy. Rules are rules!"

He shook his head sadly, his brown eyes more solemn than I'd ever seen them. "No, listen. No 'romance' means no sex. When he says none, he means, like, ever. Of any kind."

"Yeah. I got it. It's cool."

He was giving me an I'm-very-serious face. "Willa. I'm saying he's nixing *all of it*. We will never, ever have any kind of sex with each other. Not even oral! Nothing at all! Look at me, and consider what you're sacrificing."

I paused to give the impression I was weighing my options, then I said, "You're attractive, but—"

"Yes, this is what I'm saying, Willa. You are also attractive. We are two attractive people, and biology is science. So."

"I just don't have a sex vibe for you."

His eyes went wide, and he seemed to lose the power of speech, but only momentarily. "I figured it must be a slow burn situation." He was befuddled. "Like, a *very* slow burn because we've been together for three days already. Now you're telling me... there's nothing at all?"

"Not a drop."

"So strange," he said, a frown creasing his brow. "I'm not attracted to you either. Which is odd because I'm at least a little attracted to practically everyone."

I shrugged. "It does happen, Jimmy. You can't have chemistry with the whole world."

He wasn't convinced. I sensed that in order to win this one, I was going to have to make it his idea. "What should we do? I'm going to be good at this job, and it's not like you have anyone else waiting in the wings."

He sat quietly for a minute, then slapped a hand on the desk. "Got it. Let's kiss. It's the only way we can be sure."

"Do we have to?"

"Yes," he said briskly. "I do. It's possible the attraction is... what's the word? Latent. We have to be sure. It's either/or, Willa. You can be my assistant, or we can be lovers, but we can't be both. We need all the information before we decide which it'll be. We owe it to ourselves to do our due diligence."

I wasn't having the same trepidation he was having. "Even if I did want to be your lover, which I don't, I need the work, Jimmy. My choice is already made."

"You sound very confident, but let me ask you this. Between the two of us, which one has more sexual experience?"

I rolled my eyes.

"I'm going to take your eloquent expression as an acknowledgment that I have so far surpassed you. If I'm saying I'm not sure, you should be cautious. The only thing for it is to kiss, Willa. You should never swear off having sex with someone if you haven't even kissed them. Stitch in time, bird in the hand, all that. Are you ready?"

"Neither of those cliches work here, but okay. But fine. If we must."

"Let's get it settled." He clenched and unclenched his hands. "I'm finding myself oddly resistant, so let's hurry."

I cocked my head. "Is this your usual approach? If you don't want to do something, you should hurry and do it?"

He must have imagined he was being patient with me. "If cooler heads are in danger of prevailing, you should go faster. Like if you're starting to get drunk, but you want another drink, you have to drink it fast. You have so much to learn from me. I'm kind of excited for you."

"Oh, gosh. So am I." But this clearly mattered to him, and I was a tiny bit curious. "I guess we can test it."

He got to his feet. "All right, Willa. Stand." We stood at the end of the bed, facing each other. "One two three go."

Our lips touched.

We didn't even close our eyes. It was… utterly uninspiring. It wasn't revolting, but it wasn't exciting. I didn't want more.

He drew away with raised eyebrows. "What?" he whispered.

"It wasn't very good, right?" It was a rhetorical question; it was clear from his expression he was as unimpressed as I was.

"But …you're so pretty! And, to state the obvious, I'm all this. It seems like the inevitable would follow, but I do not feel you."

"I don't feel you either!" I said cheerfully.

"It's odd. Unless…"

"Unless what?"

"Unless the universe is telling us that even though we're both pretty, we mean more to each other than sex. Is it possible?"

I nodded.

He rested his hands on my shoulders and put his face close to mine, and said quietly, "I mean… more than sex. I don't think you're letting that sink in."

"It already sank in. Maybe we're meant to be friends."

"This is astonishing. Friends who are…more than sex." Based on his expression, I honestly believed he'd never encountered anything like it. "It must be a metaphysical bond. It's the only explanation."

"Right. Not romantic, but close to each other differently. It does happen."

"I assumed it was an urban legend, but I have to be honest with you. I have no desire whatsoever to have sex with you, Willa."

"Same."

"So odd," he said again. "I guess on the bright side, you can sign the contract and take the job!" He shrugged, already over it. "This is going to be brand new. An assistant who I don't sleep with. Might be fun!"

"It hasn't ever occurred to you as an option? Because it sounds like sleeping with assistants causes you a lot of problems."

"Sometimes I don't even mean to, but when you're constantly with each other, sex happens."

I'd have to take him at his word. "Why don't you hire men if this has been such a thing?"

He gave me a sweet smile. "Men aren't any better at resisting me than women are. You are a complete outlier."

"It really isn't strange." I went back to scanning the contract. "It happens all the time that people aren't attracted to each other."

"Please don't take this as arrogance—"

"Never," I said.

"Do you think I don't understand sarcasm? British people have sarcasm too. We had it first."

I continued reading. Confidentiality, blah blah blah. Housing and food covered by the band—great news.

Then it fell apart. I got to the dealbreaker. Hopefully Toby hadn't already repurposed my room or sold any of my stuff.

"What's wrong?" Jimmy asked.

This is what happened when I was spontaneous. Of course this wasn't going to work out. I closed the laptop. "It says any photos I take while I work for you belong to the band."

He got up and reached over my shoulder to open it back up. I tapped on the screen, pointing out the offending clause.

"Oh, that." He waved a hand dismissively.

"Yeah, *that*. Jimmy, I told you. This is why I wanted to do this. Partly why, anyway. I need to take pictures, and I need the rights. How else can I work on my portfolio?"

"It doesn't matter, Willa."

"It does matter. I wanted this for the photography. I want to be more than your Girl Friday. I wanted to be working toward something for myself."

I imagined going back home to Toby. Rushing back home from this even faster than I'd bailed on college.

It was humiliating.

It wasn't *fair*.

I had Jimmy's full attention. He held both my hands. "Sweetheart, you can take all the pictures you want! Pictures of me, the lads when they get here, anyone else we run across. I bump into loads of famous people. This is going to be great. Please stop with that heartbroken face."

"If I don't own the pictures, I can't use them. I was hoping to make a body of work and maybe even sell some on a freelance basis. I can't only have the images; I need the photo credit."

"Don't worry, Willa. Just sign it and send Hawk back his stupid contract. I don't want to poke at him anymore right now because he's in a Mood. Later, we'll get him to 'x' it out, initial it, and file it. It's not a big deal. The other thing matters to him because it's on his radar, and it's new. He probably doesn't even remember this thing is in there. Trust me. I'll handle it."

A cautious spark of hope flickered, but I hesitated. I hadn't known Jimmy long, but it seemed likely he wasn't completely reliable, no matter how much it seemed like he meant what he was saying.

I had to take the gamble. I was a grown woman, and all I had to show for it was the ability to make a great cup of coffee, a legacy of taking care of a kid/man who didn't need me anymore, and a portfolio that only existed in my mind.

Counting on Jimmy to keep his word, or even to remember he'd given it, was risky, but maybe taking some risks would be good for me.

Chapter Six

Jimmy spun around in the office chair and clapped. "We are going to be adorable in our matching robes! Willa, order these for us and have them delivered to the next hotel. They'll hold them for us. Get them monogrammed. I'm not going to wear an unmonogrammed robe like an animal."

I balked at the dollar amount. "Jimmy, those are..." I couldn't even bring myself to mention the number.

"Perfect, right? I will definitely be nude under mine, so be warned. Cashmere should touch as much of your skin as possible."

"I was going to say expensive, actually. You're spending so much money. Should we talk about it?"

He made an impatient sound and rubbed his forehead. "Right. We're going to have the money conversation, but this is the only time."

I waited.

Standing to face me, he put his hands on my shoulders. "I don't want you to talk to me anymore about money."

I couldn't stop myself. "The way you spend money is crazy! I mean, this hotel, for example. We could definitely spend less money on hotels."

"Of course we could, but we certainly will not. Have you ever spent weeks on end using crunchy towels and sleeping on cheap sheets? It's not for me. And another thing, while we're on this distasteful topic. You have to stop trying to talk me out of ordering my food. It's absurd."

"I'm not telling you to starve! Just order *one* entrée per meal. Order a burger *or* the lasagna *or* the brisket. You don't need three full dinners."

He shook his head. "You're being silly. I'm good at a lot of things, but I am not a mind reader. I can't magically predict what I'm going to want to eat."

"That doesn't... you'd just have... Jimmy, you'd only have to read your own mind. You would just have to ask your brain what you feel like eating and order that."

"I do ask my brain what it feels like eating, but it's never sure until the moment is upon us. Now listen to me because I'm getting bored with this." He sighed heavily. "I'm rich."

"But—"

"No. Enough. I'm rich. I want the robe, and it'll be cuter if we both have them, because we'll be like matching salt and pepper shakers except much posher and more comfortable. I don't have to decide what I want to eat before I order it because I am incredibly wealthy. It's crass for you to make me mention it, but here we are. I'm worth..." He paused dramatically. "Well, I don't have any idea, actually, but loads. Your job is to help me get what I tell you I want. I gave you a nice shiny credit card—use it. The bills go right to Hawk, and he takes care of them, and everything is fine. Of all the things there are to worry about in the world, this is not one."

He paused. "For example, in your shoes, I might be worrying right now that those cashmere robes are going to sell out while I waste my time worrying over nothing. Should we get the black or the gray?"

Money is only boring if you have a lot, lot, lot of it. So, duly noted. I ordered the robes in black *and* gray. When he decided the clothes he'd already bought me weren't enough and we needed to shop for more, I didn't try to dissuade him.

~ * ~

Those first few weeks, we learned each other's rhythms and habits. Well, mostly it was me learning Jimmy's. His main compromise was to agree not to text me *911* unless it was an actual emergency. For me, it was more intense. I learned a certain facial expression meant he needed his notebook because a song idea was taking shape in his mind. They wrote the music together, but the lyrics mainly came from him. I learned how to tell when he was bitchy because he was hungry or when I needed to get him back to the room to decompress. Even the most extroverted extrovert needs quiet time occasionally, and everything went much more smoothly when he got it.

We developed a non-verbal shorthand for interviews. He'd raise his left eyebrow at me when he wanted me to redirect an interviewer into a different topic. He'd start bouncing a knee when he wanted me to cut an interview short. When he wasn't sure if he should answer a question, a headshake from me would usually convince him to sidestep it. Even Hawk couldn't find much reason to complain.

So when a radio morning show wanted Jimmy to perform live, I assumed I knew what to expect. I got the guitar he told me he wanted, got him out the door on time, brought him in, made the introductions, then got out of the way.

When they staged it all out, he asked for some adjustments. "Sorry, love," he said to the DJ. "We need to rearrange a bit." He asked the woman operating the camera to switch to his other side and asked me to stay in his line of vision, just off-camera. "Okay, that's better. Thanks, everyone."

They said they'd be live in five minutes, so I went back to him to adjust his hair and fuss over him a bit like he liked. "You good?" I asked.

"Stage fright."

"What? Really?"

He shook his head impatiently. "This isn't just a chat. This is a performance, and it matters. I'm representing the whole band. Of course I'm nervous. A performance isn't smoke and mirrors. This is the real thing now."

Once the microphones and cameras were live, nobody would have been able to tell he was nervous. He was witty, charming, and exactly the right amount of outrageous.

Then he started singing.

I was blown away by his voice. Smooth, then just a hint of gravel to it, then easy again. I felt pain, and sex, and love, and loss, and I wasn't even paying attention to the words. His voice conveyed those things and more. He mesmerized everyone in the room, and it wasn't based on him being pretty or funny or outlandish. It was pure, raw talent, and I'd never seen anything like it. He disappeared into the song, and it was somehow personal and universal at the same time. Even I fell a bit in love with him when he sang.

When the music stopped, the lights flipped off and the cameras stopped rolling, everything had shifted. I would never look at him the same way again.

"Jimmy. Wow, I didn't know—"

"Don't, Willa." Hurt flashed in his eyes. "That was very clear. You don't need to point it out."

We went back to the hotel in silence.

I was an asshole. It hadn't occurred to me he'd be as talented as he was. He was pretty and funny with a big personality, and I'd assumed there was nothing more to him. Even worse, he knew it.

In the hotel later, he was quiet. Normally, he was bouncing off the walls, ready for whatever was next.

Not that night.

I decided to tackle it directly. "I'm sorry, Jimmy."

He gave me a one-shoulder shrug.

"Hey." I put myself into his line of vision. "I mean it. I'm sorry. You have every right to be hurt or angry, or however you feel. I didn't expect your performance to hit me like that."

He wouldn't give me eye contact. "Obviously," he said. "You haven't even made an attempt to learn my music. You've never even *listened*. I'm good at what I do. I work at it. I'm not a joke."

"Please come here and talk to me." I was sitting on the bed, leaning against the headboard with my legs stretched in front of me. I patted the bed.

He set down the book he wasn't reading, got in next to me, and put his head in my lap. It seemed like a good sign that he wanted contact, so I continued, "I made a mistake. I assumed someone who has such a big personality wouldn't also be talented, and it was shitty." I paused. It made me remember something I'd heard. "Hey, do you know the story about Marilyn Monroe, when she was out with a friend?"

He shook his head. I stroked his hair as I talked. "Marilyn Monroe was a stage name. Her real name was Norma Jean. I don't remember the exact context, but she was with a friend downtown somewhere, just Norma Jean and a pal. She was already famous by then, but no one recognized her. She wore a scarf over her hair and regular clothes, and she blended in. After a while, she said to her friend, 'You want me to become her?' Just like that, she became Marilyn. It was how she held her body, how she walked. She turned into Marilyn Monroe. She put on the persona, became a star, and was thronged."

"Her wiggle," he said. "Her wiggle probably had something to do with it."

"Probably. She had a great wiggle."

"Preach."

"You're like her," I said.

The bed shook when he laughed. "I don't wiggle," he said.

"When you're Marilyn, you're incandescent, and nobody can take their eyes off you. That doesn't mean charisma is all you have. I underestimated you because of your appearance, and I hope you'll forgive me for it. Your song was brilliant, and you're an absolutely heartbreaking performer, and I'm blown away by you. Being beautiful didn't make Marilyn who she was. She was incredibly talented. Part of her gift was making it seem easy."

He sat with his legs crossed, facing me. "You apologize quite prettily, Willa, but you should know better than to judge someone based only on their looks. You of *all* people."

He'd lost me. "Wait, what? Why me of all people? I mean, I

shouldn't have, but why should it have been more obvious to me?"

"Because you're so cute and little, but I didn't do it to you! I never even commented on your appearance! I never do. You waltz around being attractive in such a wholesome way, but I don't comment on it or act like it defines you."

"What? You literally called me cute, little, and a girl on the first day we met! You said, I quote, 'Willa, you are cute and little!'"

"Stop making this about me," he said. "We're talking about you. Anyway, I don't remember saying it; therefore, it's like I didn't."

"No, that's not how it works."

He was quiet for a few moments and shifted back to serious and thoughtful. "I do it intentionally," he said eventually. "Flash the Marilyn. People love that version of me."

"How could they help it? I'm telling you, you can be Norma Jean with me, okay? Relax sometimes. Power down. Have a snack and a cuddle. Read a book. We don't have to be doing something every moment, okay? You don't have to charm me. I'm already here."

"For now," he said.

I didn't respond. He was right. Eventually, I would leave. It wasn't like when my mom left—the musician/assistant bond was not the same thing as a mother/child bond. Nevertheless, I was starting to have an inkling that when I left, it would hurt. I was already in too deep to come out unscathed.

"It's scary, Willa. People love Marilyn, not Norma Jean."

"*I* love Norma Jean. I love her even *more*."

He gave me a tight hug. "What a gorgeous apology. I forgive you utterly. But fuck's *sake*. Listen to my music occasionally. You're probably the only person your age in the whole country who's never heard it."

We watched television for a bit, but I was edgy. Restless. He had his songs. His incredible, out-of-this-world talent. My job was to be there to smooth the way for it. Seeing him as an artist, as a creative genius, changed things. I wasn't answering his emails and washing his clothes only because he was rich.

I was facilitating things for him in order to make room for the gift he brought the world. I loved doing it. I did. What did it mean about me, I wondered. Was I invisible?

I helped smooth the path for his art, but what about mine?

Why didn't I prioritize my own work? It had been buried underneath caring for Toby. Now I was burying it underneath taking care of Jimmy, which wasn't going to get me anywhere. The least I could do was work with what I had.

"Jimmy, let's go take pictures," I said, tapping his back.

He shook his head. "I'm comfortable. Let's stay in. We'll do it tomorrow."

"It's perfect light!" I nudged him again. "I'll put pretty pictures of you on Instagram, and later we can scroll through them and read the comments." It was a temptation he couldn't resist.

"People will recognize me." It was half-hearted; I'd already won.

"I bet I can break your previous record for likes," I said. "I'm feeling lucky. Come on. We won't go far. It'll be fine. Nobody will recognize you here."

It was the second time I misjudged things in one day.

I got a couple good shots with the band phone. I was getting my proper camera ready when it went off the rails. He was recognized and definitely generated some attention. I mean, it wasn't like he was The Beatles, but we did not stay off the fan radar.

When we were back in our room with the door safely closed behind us, he raised a brow at me.

"All right. Yes, I get it. You're talented *and* famous. I assumed you could go unnoticed and, um, you didn't."

"As much as I hate to say I told you so, I sure as fuck did! I told you, 'If we go out there, people will recognize me, and it'll go to shit.' But you refused to listen. You said, 'Y'all ain't that famous, come on outside.'"

I'd been putting my camera away, but I stopped and faced him. "What did you just do right now?"

"Your accent." He smiled smugly, evidently convinced he'd nailed it. He was pleased with himself.

"No. No, Jimmy, you did not. I didn't say y'all, and I never say ain't."

"I wish you would. What is the point of having my own cowgirl if you don't say 'y'all?'"

"There are so many things wrong here I don't even know—I'm not your anything, I'm not a cowgirl, and I do sometimes say 'y'all,' just not often."

"Can you say it more?" he pleaded.

"If you're good."

Chapter Seven

I hadn't talked much to Toby since I left. It was fine, I told myself. It was great. I was giving him some space because I understood and respected that he needed it.

And because he wouldn't answer his phone.

Jimmy jumped, startled when I slammed my phone down in frustration after leaving Toby a fourth voicemail.

I flopped back on the bed dramatically.

He peered down at me. "Are you worried? Should you call your uncle?"

I sat up and shook my head. "He's fine. He's dodging me."

"But—"

I showed him my phone display. "He's at Broadway Bean."

"Your coffee shop? How do you—Willa, did you install stalker-ware on your brother's phone?"

"Shh," I said. "I'm going to call there."

My former boss answered. "Hi, Jenny, it's Willa. I'm curious, is my brother there?"

Jenny gave me a frosty silence, then she said, "Oh, hi, Willa. Aren't you busy with your buddy Jimmy Standish?"

"Jenny, please. Is Toby there?"

"She won't help you?" Jimmy asked, sitting on the bed next to me. "Give me the phone."

I decided she absolutely deserved what she was going to get for being such a cow to me when I was only worried about my brother. I handed him the phone.

"Jenny, is it? Hi, my name is Jimmy Standish. My friend Willa needs help, darling, and she tells me you're the only person she can count on. We're wondering if her brother is there. Could you possibly check for us?" He gave me a wink. "He is? Yeah? Back at his favorite table with the usual suspects, she says," he said to me. "Jenny, I can't thank you enough. Willa told me you would get it sorted, and now you have. Oh, yes, please do. Cheers."

He disconnected. One second later, my phone dinged. Jenny sent a picture of Toby, sitting at a table in the back with a group of people I didn't recognize. He was laughing. He was completely fine.

I burst into tears.

"Oh shit!" Jimmy gathered me into his arms. "Shit. What is it? Should I call her back? Tell me what I can do."

"I didn't even know where he waaaaaaas," I sobbed. "He's my Toby, and I'm not there, I'm here, and I miss him and I was worried, and he could have been *anywhere*."

He rubbed my back. "You had him pinpointed, darling, thanks to your stalker app. Anyway, he'd call you if anything was wrong, right?"

"I don't know!" I cried. "Maybe he'd have called our fucking mom."

"I thought your mom—"

"Was a leaver? She is."

"I had the impression she was out of the picture," Jimmy said. "From what you said before."

I took some deep, calming breaths. I used my sleeves to wipe the tears, then I finally answered him. "She was. She *is*, for me. I guess Toby has a relationship with her now. That's fine. It's his decision."

"Oh, Willa," he said. "It hurts, right? Because you're the one who takes care of Toby."

My eyes filled with tears again, and I shrugged. "I used to be. I guess I'm not anymore."

His eyes were suspiciously shiny.

"Jimmy, are you crying?"

"You are breaking my heart, Willa. I've never heard a woman cry with a southern accent, and it's devastating!"

Now I put my arms around him. "I'm okay." I sniffed. "I'm just sad because Toby doesn't need me anymore. I don't... taking care of my brother is what I do. I'm not sure who I am without it."

"You're the person who takes care of me, and that's not nothing, right? Anyway, a bit of rebellion is normal for a teenager, yeah? He's becoming his own man. It doesn't mean he loves you any less." He paused but couldn't help adding, "And you had eyes on him because you are illegally stalking him."

"It's not like, illegal-illegal." I was exhausted from my emotional outburst. I rearranged the pillows on the bed, then settled in. "It's a gray area."

"Did you get into bed with your socks on?" he asked. "You'll bring us bad luck!"

"Ridiculous superstition," I said. "It's not bad luck. It's bad luck for me to take them off because my feet get cold."

"Stop distracting me. I'm treading carefully because I don't want you to start weeping again, but does Toby know you put that app on his phone?"

I wished he'd phrased the question differently, so I helped. "Do you mean is Toby aware I sometimes use creative means to make sure he's okay? It doesn't matter. I only use my powers for good, so stop with the judgmental face."

"It seems like it's crossing a line. To take your blind brother's phone—"

"He's not blind. He has one perfectly good eye. What does that have to do with it anyway?"

"No matter how many eyes he has, it seems like an invasion of privacy." He got up and crawled under the blankets on the other side of the bed. He disappeared under the covers for a minute and tugged my socks off. He tossed them over me onto the floor, then rolled to face me.

I yawned. "Okay, good talk. I'm going to go to sleep now."

"This talk is not over," he said ominously.

"Is your phone ringing? Maybe it's the woman you met earlier at the bar."

He dug for his phone but then caught on. "You should be ashamed of yourself, but I can see you're not. Did you put anything on my phone?" He eyed it suspiciously.

I scoffed. "Um, no. Why on earth would I need to? The only place you're ever without me is the bathroom."

"Give me the band phone for a minute." He held out his hand. "No reason."

"You don't need it. If there ever comes a time when we are apart, I will answer if you call me. Promise."

"I want to make sure you're safe, darling. What if you get kidnapped? Someone could hold you for ransom."

"You wouldn't pay it?"

"I definitely would not. It would play right into their hands."

"You'd abandon me?"

"Never! I would find a handsome, down-on-his-luck detective. Probably someone who'd recently been fired from the force because he was a recovering alcoholic and slipped up one time, and someone died. Probably a kid. He's so scarred by it. Lucky for him, he's about to get a second chance, thanks to me and my plucky sidekick. I reckon he's played by Denzel Washington."

"Aw, Jimmy, you're the best," I said. "You would hire a fired, alcoholic, kid-killing detective for me. See, you don't need any high-tech tools. Apps like these are for amateurs."

"I could handle a ransom situation, obviously, but what if you get roofied and leave with some guy? You'd need me to come save you, but how could I if I didn't know where you were?"

"Where are we going that I'll get—no, never mind." I handed him my phone. "It's fine. I don't even care if you put it on there." Mostly because I was pretty sure he wouldn't be able to do it.

"Let's install it on Eric and Oliver's phones when they get here," he said, logging into the phone and frowning at it.

A few minutes later, he handed me a fully stalker-wared phone. I set it on the nightstand, then he gestured for my personal phone. I gave it to him and waited as he doctored it.

"There. Safe and sound. Now stop being ridiculous. If you get lost, I'll find you." His voice gentled. "Everything is fine. Anyway, if you need to fuss over someone, you might start with me. For example. Does my skin seem moisturized to you? It feels parched."

"Parched is a bit extreme," I said, "but you don't look fully moisturized. Maybe we should do masks."

"Agreed. We should do a hot towel shave on me too."

"Sure. If you ever grow a beard, we definitely will."

By the time we'd done masks and conditioning treatments, it was time to order dinner. I had to double-check the schedule for tomorrow and make sure he didn't have any new emails. I also needed to update their Instagram, tweet something, and order him some new notebooks since his songwriting book was almost filled.

He'd done it on purpose, the whole thing with the masks and the detective story. He wanted to distract me.

That made it even sweeter.

Chapter Eight

I'd thought I would never get used to the luxury of Jimmy's world, but I did adjust pretty quickly to our way of travel. Tucker drove us everywhere in a big cushy car. She never talked, never interacted with us at all, and it was like Jimmy and I were in a pod of privacy. We talked for hours.

If he was working on writing a song or he fell asleep, I'd stare out the window and absorb everything. I'd never really traveled at all, and now it was a whirlwind. In a different state every few days. After our first few trips, I left my camera bag in the trunk. I couldn't imagine asking Tucker to stop to give me some time to photograph anything other than Jimmy, and I certainly didn't have a shortage of pictures of him as it was.

I'd given up much hope of working on my portfolio, and I assumed he had forgotten about it until we were in New Orleans. He announced we were going out for the night. "Wear something delicious, Willa, because I'm sure we'll be photographed together. It should be something you can work in, because Jimmy Who Loves You got you a press pass for The Regrets concert tonight!"

My mouth dropped open. "You did not."

"I did! Are you happy with me? I called Hawk and pulled strings for you!"

I'd have been even happier with him if he'd taken care of the photo clause, but it would have been ungracious to mention it, so I didn't. I jumped up and gave him a hug, then packed my camera bag.

Jimmy chose our outfits as I researched The Regrets online and learned what I could. I didn't have much experience—okay, any experience—doing onstage photos, but I trusted myself to learn on the fly.

"Oh, look!" He was holding some mysterious leather studded rings. "I forgot we bought these! You should wear these tonight."

"I have no idea what those are," I said absently.

"Garters, Willa. Remember? In the cool store in… wherever we were. I don't remember. I said we should get you these in case something awesome came our way. You said, 'Whatever you want, Jimmy, because you yourself have so much style and panache, and I'm lucky to have your guidance.'"

"Mmhm. Sounds like me. I say 'panache' a lot."

"I got you those cute stockings to go with them! You *have* to wear these tonight. They'll peek out and be so cute! This leather is badass. I'll wear my leather jacket! We'll be perfect together. We should have gotten a matching one for you, but there's no time now."

"Yes," I said.

"Willa, are you listening to me?"

"Mmhm. You betcha."

"What should I wear other than my jacket? I don't want to look like I'm trying too hard."

"Okay, Jimmy." I didn't have a flash powerful enough to do any good; I would have to do the best I could with ambient lighting.

I'd probably use my 50 mm fixed lens, but I threw in a zoom lens just in case. What the hell, I'd pack my flash. My bag was going to be heavy, but I didn't want to need something I didn't have.

I lost track of time as I packed, unpacked, and repacked my bag, but some time later, I surfaced when his pants rang. *Trousers, Willa,* I imagined him correcting me. He wasn't in the room, and the shower was running.

I dug through the pile of clothes he left on the floor and patted around until I found his phone. I checked the display. "Hi, Oliver, this is Willa. Jimmy's in the shower. Can I have him call you back?"

"Oh! It's you. The American. Wow, hi."

My lips curved into a smile. His voice sounded startled but every bit as delicious as last time. "You're surprised I'm here." I went to where I'd been sitting at the desk and dropped back into the chair.

"Noooo, I just… yeah. Yes, I'm surprised you're still there. Good on ya."

"Mmhm. Want me to have him call you when he gets out, ye of little faith?"

"Maybe it's you I need anyway. I can't get into Insta. I called Eric, and he can't either. He said he called the band phone, and nobody answered, so…"

I glanced back at my camera bag. "Sorry. I was distracted. Yeah, I changed the password."

"Right, what is it?"

"Sorry. No way."

He hesitated. "'Sorry, no way,' like, one word? Any caps?"

"'Sorry, no way,' as in sorry, there's no way I'm giving you the password, Oliver." *No matter how lovely your voice is, and despite the fact I'm already pretty sure I can trust you more than Jimmy.*

"What? You're not going to give me the password... to my own band's Instagram account?"

"Right."

"I just want to post—"

"I've already fallen for that. Jimmy 'just wanted to post' something, so I gave him the password then had to take down a nude, which wasn't as tasteful as he seemed to believe, and reset it again."

"I want to—"

"Out of the question."

"Willa, be reasonable. I'm not Jimmy." The way he said my name was a purr.

Thank goodness I was unmoved by it. "Maybe you're as bad as he is. How would I know?"

"Google me. I'm considered the reasonable one."

"Have you ever dealt with Hawk when he's disappointed?"

He gave a startled laugh. "Um, yes. I've probably done it a fair bit more than you have at this point."

He didn't need this job the way I did, though, and *he* wasn't expendable. "Send me whatever you want posted, and I'll be happy to do it for you right away as I do for him, and I'll do for Eric." I paused. "I mean, not, like, *do* it for you. Or for him. Or Eric. I meant I'd post the pic—you know what I mean. Don't make it weird."

"Not the one making it weird." There was music in his voice like he was smiling. "I'll send it to you in a minute. Tell Jimmy hi for me."

I ended the call and dropped Jimmy's phone back onto his clothes pile. I glimpsed myself in the mirror on the way back to the desk. I was flushed, and my eyes were sparkling. I shook my head to clear it.

It would have been easier to keep him in the employer zone if he'd sent me a different picture for their feed.

I opened the message when my phone buzzed. *Let me know if this is okay or if you want Eric to retake.*

I tapped back a response. *It's fine. I'll post now.*

It was a close-up of his hands. Black and white, loosely holding drumsticks. It was a perfectly drummer-y picture.

His fingers were perfect. Long, but strong. Not pretty—callused and roughened from all the hours I imagined he spent practicing.

It was a good thing I was aware of how stupid it would be to get a crush on someone based only on their voice and hands, or I might have been tempted to believe I was getting a crush.

What a relief that I was a grown-ass woman, not a getting-crushes-on-musicians-teenager.

Maybe I should Google him. Seeing him might snap me out of whatever this was. I opened a tab to search for him, but then Jimmy rejoined me. We got into a debate over what I should wear when we went out, and the phone sat neglected on the desk.

~ * ~

The concert in Louisiana was something special. The Regrets were on the cusp of making it huge, the air was electric, and I was relieved to be back behind the camera. If Jimmy kept his word and fixed my contract, I'd be able to sell these pictures—with my name attached. This would go a long way toward proving myself to Uncle Ken. Or proving myself to myself since from my Uncle Ken's point of view, being related to him was qualification enough. It was a huge night for this band, and I was there to capture it. I'd be part of music history as more than the Woman Who Made Sandwiches for Jimmy Standish.

After the show, I jostled my way through a mass of happy, sweaty bodies and went to find him.

He was at the back of the bar at a tall table, talking to someone. It took me a minute before I realized who it was.

It was Benny Walker.

Benny. Walker. The lead singer of Apostolic.

My mouth went dry, and my heart pounded. All the noise and chatter surrounding me faded away. Jimmy gestured me over when I caught his eye, but I was locked in place. When I didn't move, he said something to Benny and then came to me. "Willa! Benny Walker is here, and he's lovely! Come meet him!"

I hid my face against Jimmy's shoulder. "We have to go."

He tried to jiggle me loose. "I can't hear you from there."

I raised my head. "It's Benny Walker."

"Right. I just said that. Are you paying attention to me? He's so nice! We have loads in common. I told him everything about you. Come meet him."

I stared at him like he was insane. "I can't talk to Benny Walker." I shifted so Jimmy blocked my eye line to the Man. "Oh God. Benny Walker Benny Walker."

He held my face in his hands. "Willa, what are you doing right now?"

"I love him so bad. I need to go."

Like Jimmy, Benny was wearing leather pants and a leather

jacket. Unlike Jimmy, he was Benny Walker. I wanted to reach for my camera, but the Benny Walkerness of him kept me paralyzed.

If I had pictures of him, I didn't even *care* if I wouldn't be able to sell them. I would keep them for myself. I would line my bedroom walls with them.

If I could sell pictures of him, it could be a career-maker. Any music magazine with a photo budget would buy them in a heartbeat.

It was moot anyway. I wasn't mobile enough to operate my camera.

Jimmy, unable to honor the moment, was still talking. "I want you to help me understand this. You woke up with all this, and you experienced nothing at all." He gestured at himself. "No stirring in your nether regions."

It was enough to interrupt my hysteria for a moment. "Please never, ever say 'nether regions' again. Do not."

"There was nothing. No spark. No longing. No sweet, sweet ache that could only be soothed by—"

"Not a thing."

"That guy—"

I yanked his arm. "Don't point at him!"

"Benny does it for you."

I closed my eyes. "Oh God. He does it so hard for me."

"You have odd taste in men, Willa," Jimmy said. "I mean, he is lovely, but he's at least twice your age."

"Is he looking over here?"

"I'm sure he is. I'm Jimmy Motherfucking Standish, darling. He probably can't take his eyes off me."

"He probably already forgot about you," I said. "I can't breathe. I need to go."

Jimmy's eyes were wide. "Holy shit. What is happening to you right now?"

I took a deep breath and fanned my face. "Oh, God. It's so hot in here. I feel weird. My stomach dropped out. I want to lick his teeth. Or, like, squeeze him. What's happening?"

He leaned down to look more closely at me, then smiled broadly. "Well, hello there, Willa's libido! There you are! I was starting to wonder if you even existed, and here you are, announcing yourself with such drama." He put his hands on my shoulders. "Do not panic. When a woman has special feelings for a man, her body goes through chemical reactions to prepare her to receive him. This is perfectly natural. It's biology, darling. Don't be afraid. Trust your body. Listen to your nether regions."

"I need a drink. I need air. I need to go. I need to eat... his entire... self." I frantically searched for a waiter who could bring me a drink.

Without another word, Jimmy led me toward the back of the bar, closer to Benny Walker. "You're going to meet Benny Walker, and if you eat him, we'll handle that when it happens. One thing at a time."

He dragged me to Benny's table, and they talked. I don't know. Words words words. I have no idea. Their mouths were moving.

Benny said, "Are you hiding a girl behind you?"

"She's not a girl," Jimmy said. "She's a small woman, and I'm not sure what she's doing. Willa, come here."

I couldn't.

He yanked me forward and said, "This is my Willa."

Benny. Smiled. At me. "Hello there, Willa."

We were frozen in a tableau: rocks stars and the regular woman.

With an exasperated sound, Jimmy pulled my arm up and held my hand out to Benny. "Shake his hand, darling. There you go."

Benny drew me into a hug. My face landed between his neck and shoulder. He smelled like cloves and heat. I swayed when he released me.

Oh God. I had to speak. "Big fan," I said. "I am one. I love you I mean your music. Songs, voice."

He laughed but in a nice way. "Your girl likes me."

I shook my head emphatically. "Not his girl. My own girl. Woman."

"What?"

Jimmy frowned with worry. "She used to be quite articulate. Did you break her?"

"She's cute. I like your garters, sweetheart," he said to me. "Badass and sexy at the same time."

"Thank you," I whispered. I hid behind Jimmy again.

"Let me order a round," Benny said. "What are you guys drinking?"

"We have to go," I whispered to Jimmy's back. "I can't do this."

"Bourbon for us. Neat for me, rocks for Willa." He whispered to me, "Listen to your nether regions."

Jimmy and Benny talked and drank, besties already. They had a lot in common, and they both had the swagger that comes from knowing the world finds you captivating. I couldn't deny the only thing more magnetic than either of them alone was both of them together. It was the opportunity of a lifetime.

"Hey," I said like it was just occurring to me. "How about a few pictures together?"

"Willa! What a great idea. Isn't it a great idea, Benny? Her camera is right here. When she's not with me, she works for *Offstage Magazine*. She's a professional."

"Oh, *Offstage*? Have you met Hope Harper?"

"I have."

Benny leaned close. I imagined licking his face but stifled the urge—barely. "She hates me," he confided.

"Who? What?"

"Hope Harper," he said. "She loathes me."

It was a fact. She did. "I'm sure you're imagining it," I said.

"I'm not. Did you read her review of my new album? It was brutal. Let's do this, gorgeous. *Offstage* owes me some good press. Can we go somewhere more private?"

We discovered we were staying at the same hotel. Benny gave us his room number.

I imagined telling eighteen-year-old Willa that Present Willa had Benny Walker's room number and did a fangirl scream, but only in my head.

~ * ~

I woke up in the morning back in our own hotel room, hungover to the point I thought I might die. I groaned.

Jimmy stirred next to me. "Are you finally awake?"

"My head hurts, Jimmy. And my everything else."

He turned to face me, then winced. "Wow. Okay. I'm don't say this to be rude, but hungover Willa is a real fright. I've never even… this is not your best moment. What is happening on your head? Your hair is shocking right now. I'm nearly at a loss for words. Do you feel as bad as you look? Not that you look terrible, but—yeah, no, you look terrible. You're pasty but green at the same time. I've never seen this particular color on a person."

I closed my eyes again. "I will give you a million dollars if you stop talking."

"I already have a million dollars," he said, "and I know for a fact that you do not."

"Hurts," I groaned.

"Poor Willa. I hope it was worth it. Benny is not gentle, right? My lips are bruised. No one has ever gone at my mouth the way he did."

I shot to a sitting position, knocking him off me. My head ached like it would split open, so I carefully lowered myself back down. "What happened last night?"

"Don't tell me you don't remember!" He was horrified.

I frowned. "Bits and pieces. It gets foggy. Did I get pictures? I got pictures, right?"

He ignored my question. "You're welcome for getting him primed for you. It was only a special favor. Don't expect me to do it every time we come across a man you fancy. This was a special exception, brought on by my inability to help myself."

"I am begging you to tell me what happened."

"It's disappointing you don't remember. Maybe it'll come back? It certainly seemed like you were enjoying it, and I'd hate your memory of it to be totally gone."

I put a hand over my eyes. "Can you please just tell me what happened?"

"You drank a bit more, and you made out with Benny Walker."

"Nothing else?"

"Nothing else."

I relaxed. "Okay. Well, that's fine."

"Not *much* else, anyway."

"What!"

"You *mostly* just kissed. His girlfriend wasn't thrilled to find you on him when she came in, but it was a massive overreaction. It barely would count as a cheat since everyone was fully dressed. You were, anyway, and he and I had pants on. Here, let's check your camera to see. I took some pictures." He rustled around until he found my camera, then flipped through the pictures.

He frowned.

"What's the matter?"

"Hm? Oh, nothing. These pictures of The Regrets are good, Willa."

"Yeah?"

"Yeah. You see things differently than I do," he said. "These are like... I thought it was maybe only down to me why your pictures were so good. These are great, and I'm not even in them."

It was an odd compliment, but that didn't make it any less significant. My headache lifted a bit.

He kept going through the images on the camera until he said, "Okay, here. These are the ones from Benny's room."

Out of the hundred or so pictures he captured, more than half were self-portraits, but Benny and I were visible in the background of some. I didn't even like having my picture taken; I much preferred being on the other side of the lens. Since I'd been too nervous/drunk to mind, at least I had these souvenirs. It was better than nothing.

As he scrolled through, it got better. He'd taken a few photos of

Benny and me that were more than accidents.

"Aw, check this one out," Jimmy said.

It was shot from the side. I was perched on the shiny black surface of his hotel room bar. Benny was standing in front of me, one hand on my thigh, the other holding a glass of whiskey. I was leaning down toward him, the curtain of my hair shielding our faces.

"So punk rock and *cute*. You could be Sid and Nancy! Or you could be Nancy, and Benny could be, like, Sid's dad. Oh, and look at this one! His fingers are just inching up under your skirt. You made the right call with that outfit for sure." Pregnant pause. "Willa, right?" When I still didn't answer, he made an impatient sound. "I mean *I* did since I dressed you. Aren't you lucky to have my advice?"

He kept flipping through the pictures. "Where are the pictures you took? Yours are probably—oh, here we go."

The first one was charged but pretty innocent, comparatively. Jimmy and Benny both wore leather pants and no shirts, with guitars strapped on. They were facing each other, hands on guitars, forehead-to-forehead. They were backlit and in silhouette. The next one was closer; they were making eye contact. The third in the series showed them tilting their heads, pre-kiss. Objectively, it was a beautiful photograph. I didn't remember taking it, so I could evaluate it as a neutral third party.

There was one taken pointing down at Jimmy and Benny on the floor. My legs were in the foreground. Jimmy's arm snaked up between my legs, his hand resting on my thigh. The tightest focus was on his nails with their chipped black nail polish, digging into the bare skin above my garter. Jimmy and Benny were in softer focus. My stockinged feet were resting on the inside of Benny's thigh. His hand was tangled in Jimmy's hair, tilting him to the right angle, and his bottom lip was between Benny's teeth.

I swore quietly. Being a photographer was what I'd always wanted. It was a way to be present but not seen. It was a drive, a coping mechanism, and an art. I loved it, but I hadn't known if I was good. I couldn't tell if I was successfully conveying what I hoped to show, or if I possessed that impossible to define quality, an "eye" for photography.

Now I knew. These were *good*. They were beautiful because of the subjects, composition, and lighting, but they were also visual explorations of visual persona and the ways we present ourselves. I'd done what I'd hoped I could do.

I clicked to the next image.

Jimmy had Benny pinned against a full-length mirror. He was making a perfect pain/pleasure face, and Jimmy was kissing his shoulder. My reflection was in the mirror, the flash making a star effect next to them.

In the next one, they were facing each other again, Benny with a fistful of Jimmy's hair, pulling his head back and licking his throat. His mouth was slightly open, and the image jogged my memory. It all rushed back—his sharp, startled sound. The way Benny growled. Suddenly, it wasn't about the pictures anymore. They were kissing for real, and the sound and sight of it were so overwhelming I put my camera down. Right on the nightstand. I left it there, unused.

I'd failed to capture it. It was the opportunity of a lifetime, and rather than capturing it in art, I'd chosen to be present in the moment. I could have kicked myself, but at the same time, I knew I was lucky to have experienced it without the camera mitigating the experience. The way Benny backed Jimmy against the wall, and his groan... it was locked in my mind in a way I wouldn't have to share with the world.

"Oh my God," I said.

"It's coming back to you?"

I remembered being on the bed with Benny. Jimmy was there, and it everything was happening fast and in slow motion at the same time until the door opened with a bang. It took us longer than it should have, but eventually, Jimmy and I determined the furious woman must be Benny's girlfriend.

I turned to Jimmy. "You screamed like a woman in a horror flick."

He didn't deny it. "Okay, but two things. If I didn't distract her, she was maybe going to kill you. The least she'd have done is rip out your pretty hair, and imagine how silly I'd look with you then." He shuddered. "It doesn't fit our aesthetic at all. If you were totally bald, I could work with it." He paused thoughtfully. "In fact, should we shave your head, Willa? That might—"

"What's the other thing?"

He paused long enough to make it clear he didn't appreciate being interrupted, then continued, "Well, I was scared. I haven't been caught in bed with someone's boyfriend in months, and, based on the way she shrieked and was reaching her claws toward my eyes, I gathered she wasn't cool with it. I could have used you as a human shield, but I chose to save us both instead."

It came flooding back to my mind. Jimmy screamed and yanked me off Benny. We ran around the bed and snagged my camera by the strap on the way out. My shoes and Jimmy's shirt were a loss. We raced out the door, then ducked into an internal stairwell and waited to make sure she hadn't followed us. When we were sure the coast was clear, we went back to our room and locked ourselves in.

We must have collapsed because we were both in our clothes from the night before.

Later, in the shower, I concluded it wasn't only my artistic side I'd neglected for the past few years. The time with Benny was like a fever dream. I'd been carried away, I'd been drunk, I'd been torn between taking pictures or not, but it didn't change the fact that I'd been in a long dry spell. At the first spark, I'd burst into flames. I needed to be more careful. I'd have regretted it if things had gone further. Probably. Okay, maybe.

I'd been touch-deprived when I got to Jimmy. He was refilling the well, no question about it. He was sensual, although with me, it wasn't sexual. He loved to touch and be touched, and once I got used to it, I became addicted to it. It's nice to have another warm body with you in a bed, even if it's platonic. We would occasionally fall asleep with the television on, and when we did, I didn't get up and go to my own room.

His speculation about my libido, as ridiculous as it was, wasn't entirely off the mark. I wondered if I'd been so determined to prove I wouldn't be driven by a romantic relationship like my mom was that I'd completely shut down. I didn't have to let sex be the only thing I was driven by, but maybe I didn't need to totally rule it out, either.

Chapter Nine

Jimmy drank all night, ignoring my whispered suggestions and throat-slashing cut-off motions. Their album had cracked the top ten in the US, and he wanted to celebrate with champagne. And whiskey. Then more champagne. Then some shots of something blue. We'd been at the bar with some fans and several reporters.

Attention brings out the absolute best in him—he was charming, adorable, and beyond drunk. "Another round, everyone! Let's drink to me!"

He dropped into bed the minute we were back in our room. I got him out of his shoes and jeans, maneuvered him under the blankets, turned off the lights, and prepared myself for bed. I washed my face, brushed my teeth, combed my hair, put on my favorite pajamas, and tiptoed back into the room.

Jimmy flipped the light on. "Let's go back out! I want one more drink." He was already headed for the door in a T-shirt, boxers, and socks.

"No sir. Back to bed."

He blinked at me. "What? No. Why? I want to go back out. You made us leave so early. There's more partying to be done and drinks to be had."

"To start with, the bar is closed. Secondly, you're already drunk. Also, you're not wearing pants."

"*Trousers!* And neither are you."

"True. Back to bed, Jimmy."

"Willlllllllllaaaaaaa. I can't sleep. Let's go back out."

"If you get into bed, I'll tell you a story." I hoped I'd be able to lull him to sleep, but I also wanted to make sure he didn't drunkenly sneak out.

"I will, but it's under protest," he said. "Under hardcore protest. Let's get in your bed. Mine smells like cigarettes. Disgusting."

I didn't bother to say it was Jimmy himself who smelled like cigarettes. I fluffed the pillows and tipped him into the bed, then went around the other side and climbed in next to him.

He burrowed under the covers with a lot of sighing and then sat up again. "Socks, Willa! My socks are on!"

"Take them off then, Jimmy."

"Can't reach."

Planning to insist on a raise in the morning, I burrowed under the covers and took his socks off.

He frowned at me when I came back up. "Tell me a story or take me back to the bar where I belong," he demanded.

"Once upon a time, there was a beautiful, beautiful, patient princess and an obnoxious boy."

Jimmy snuggled in. "Was he a prince?"

"Nope. Just a selfish boy. Talented, lovely, and selfish."

"Did he have good hair?"

"He had glorious hair," I said, intentionally making my voice soothing and quiet. "It was the envy of the whole kingdom. Which was entirely due to the princess because she made sure he had a proper hair-care protocol, and she styled it beautifully every single day, and it was allowed to shine in all its glory."

"What happened next?"

"One night, the boy got extremely drunk. The princess warned him he should have stopped after the third round of shots, but he carried on far into the night."

He was starting to sound sleepy when he said, "He sounds fun. Maybe the princess is a party pooper. Did she ever consider that?"

"She's definitely not; she only wanted to help a friend make good decisions. Eventually, even the boy was forced to admit she was talking sense, and he was being ridiculous. He was sweetly silent, and went right to sleep, and they lived happily ever after, but first, the princess got a raise."

He laughed quietly. "You're a bad storyteller. Someday I'll write you a song and show you how to do it properly."

"Sounds great, but for right now, let's play the quiet game. Next one to talk loses."

"A trick from your nanny days? Did it ever actually work?"

I didn't answer.

"Ugh! I lost, right, Willa?"

"Yes, Jimmy."

"Ha! Now you lost. Shit! Now I lost."

"Good night," I whispered.

"Night. Mother*fucker*! I lost again."

I was smiling when I fell asleep.

Hours later, I woke to the familiar warmth of Jimmy nestled behind me.

I nestled into my delicious-smelling, warm, smooth pillow. I sighed happily. Best pillow ever.

"I can't get comfortable," Jimmy complained. "Scooch *over*."

"Me?" my pillow asked. "Or whoever this is?" The delicious voice rumbled under my ear.

"Oliver! When did you get here?" Jimmy's voice was gleeful.

"Couple hours ago."

"Is Eric here?"

"Not yet," our new companion said. "He came in on a later flight. He'll be here by morning."

"I've missed you, and we're top ten! But also, I'm drunk as shit."

"Missed you too, mate. Who's this girl?"

"It's Willa!" Jimmy said.

"Of course." Pause. "Hello, Willa. Nice to finally meet you in the flesh."

"My name is Willoughby, actually," I said.

It was a strange thing to say, given the circumstances. Really, it was a miracle I could speak at all.

I wanted to finally get a glimpse of him, but no matter how my eyes strained, there wasn't enough light.

"Willoughby!" Jimmy exclaimed. "You never told me!" He nudged me with his knees. "What other things are you hiding, Willoughby? Apart from your *name*?"

"I'm not hiding it. Hawk knows."

"Oh great! Now you're telling Hawk personal things you haven't even told me?" He half-rose and spoke over me. "Be careful, Oliver. She's a woman. Don't call her a girl; she hates it. She's a raging feminist."

"I am not. You're parroting the patriarchal agenda you grew up immersed in because you're so intellectually lazy. You don't even realize how ridiculous you are."

"Whatever, Elizabeth Cady Stanton."

"Nice one." I was impressed.

"Right? I'm drunk, even. I had it right at the front of my brain anyway."

"How about if we go back to sleep?" the voice under me suggested. "We can battle the patriarchal agenda in the morning."

"I'll get off you," I said to Oliver.

Jimmy sighed dramatically. "It doesn't have to be so complicated. Everyone turn toward the window. Willa, you be middle spoon." We shuffled around, then Jimmy said, "Perfect! All tucked in. No, your feet are freezing; put them on him, not me. I'm glad I'm not alone anymore and don't have to carry this entire load by myself. She's cute but high maintenance. You'll see."

"Sorry," I whispered to the back in front of me. "I didn't realize... I was sleeping."

"I know. You're fine."

"How did you get in here?" I asked him.

"They gave me a card at the front desk."

"They just gave you one?"

"I'm famous. They recognized me."

Even his whisper sounded deep. Being together in the dark, our voices hushed and close, bordered on intimate.

"We have two beds. The other one is empty," I said.

"Jimmy likes to sleep by the door, so I guessed this one would be open."

"Yeah, but he and are I in this one."

"Yes. Here you both are." He was complacent about the whole thing. They probably did this kind of thing a lot, to be fair.

"It's pretty crowded," I said. I couldn't figure out what to do with my arms. I settled for tucking them against my chest. Not comfortable, but less weird than any of the other options.

"Three is a lot," he said around a yawn. "You're quite talkative for the middle of the night."

"Only when I wake up on a stranger. The other bed is empty is what I'm getting at."

"Is it? I can't be sure. Sometimes, a bed you assume is empty ends up having a chatty woman with a funny accent in it. I'll stay right here. You can trust me, Willoughby."

"You can call me Willa. Everyone calls me Willa."

Jimmy sighed heavily. "Fuck's *sake*. My head is going to split open. You can become properly acquainted in the morning. Right now, you must go to sleep."

I half turned. "Do you need me to get you some—"

"All I need you to get me is some not-talking."

It was worth mentioning, so I said, "I did tell you to stop drinking last night."

"Yeah, but you didn't get me to stop because you are the worst assistant in the world."

"Should I move to the empty bed?" I asked hopefully.

"No," they both said.

"Should I?" my new friend asked.

"Absolutely. It smells like cigarettes, but—"

"Oh no. Dealbreaker. I hate cigarettes."

Jimmy sighed again. "Let's play the quiet game, guys. Next one to talk loses."

Oliver's chest rumbled with a laugh.

~ * ~

The next time I woke, Jimmy was eating breakfast, the lights were on, and there was another man in the room. He was leaning over the bed, studying me.

I was back on top of Oliver. I was resting my face on his chest, with both hands resting on him. One on his chest and one on his nice, hard stomach. "She's fine," he was saying. "She'll wake up eventually."

I wasn't ready for it. I kept my eyes closed.

"She won't." Jimmy was cheerful. "This one will sleep forever if you let her. She once slept for three days straight through," he lied. "I was sure she was dead. I nearly called a coroner."

"She peeked at me!" said the new guy. Process of elimination told me it was Eric.

"Oatmeal time, Willa!" Jimmy sang. "It's getting cold! Boys, I got us all oatmeal along with some pancakes and sausage and bacon and cheesecake. And hash browns, waffles, biscuits, and honey."

"Jimmy," I grumbled, not willing to come fully awake. "I'm not eating oatmeal unless you are. If one of us needs to monitor his cholesterol, it's not me."

"All right. We'll order oatmeal again tomorrow. One of these mornings, we're bound to make a good decision."

I still sensed someone's stare. Reluctantly, I opened my eyes.

"There she is!" Eric turned to Jimmy. "Is she even old enough? Do Americans age differently? You found her in Nashville? Are we going to get in trouble for kidnapping or something? Does she talk like a cowgirl?"

What was with these British boys and their preoccupation with cowgirls? "He didn't find me; I found him, and I don't talk like a cowgirl."

Eric wasn't as gorgeous as Jimmy because few people are, but he was close. He had light brown hair, short on the sides and an artful tangle on top. Bright green eyes and gorgeous bone structure. His cheekbones were high, his jaw was square, and he had a dimple in his chin. Unlike Jimmy, even at the height of his efforts, Eric had perfect beard scruff.

He tilted his head. "You kinda do. I'm just being honest. Not trying to be racist."

"You sound a bit like Mary Poppins," I said. "Not trying to be racist."

He laughed. "She's a sassy cowgirl, Jimmy! Good find."

Jimmy poured himself some coffee. "Her freckles make her look younger than she is."

Oliver's voice rumbled under me. "Do you have freckles? I love freckles."

"You're going to have to get up, darlings," Jimmy said to those of us in bed. "We have loads to do. You can't sprawl on my band all day, Willa."

I sat up and stretched, then peeked over my shoulder.

I liked the physical reality of Oliver.

A lot.

His dark hair was thick and wavy, and his eyes were a deep, dark brown. His bottom lip was slightly fuller than his top lip. I tried not to imagine what it would be like to bite it. His left arm was covered in a full tattoo sleeve, which went over his shoulder and partway down his chest. I promised myself I could study his tattoos more later if I could stop gawking at him now.

He didn't seem to mind. He was looking at me, too. "You're different than I expected," he said.

I couldn't read his expression. Different good? Or different bad? Or different who-cares-she's-just-the-assistant? "Don't tell me," I said. "You were expecting a cowboy hat."

When he smiled, his eyes scrunched up, and there was flash of dimples.

He could have looked like a troll—with that voice, I was already in trouble. But he did *not* look like a troll, and it was game over for me. I didn't stand a chance.

"I wouldn't have been surprised to see a cowboy hat," he said.

"She doesn't even *own* one," Jimmy said disgustedly. "Or boots! She's very half-assed at being a cowgirl."

I crawled out of bed, sneaking another peek at Oliver's abs on my way out. "Please tell me there's coffee left, Jimmy."

Oliver made it to the table in a couple strides. I stopped in my tracks. The tattoo sleeve went partway down his shoulder. His back was strong, his legs were long, and his ass was amazing.

I obviously needed coffee to clear my mind so I could stop leering at a man who was technically one of my bosses.

"I need the coffee," Oliver said.

Jimmy held the coffee away from him. "Believe me, we'll be sorry if she doesn't have coffee. She is mean when the caffeine withdrawals start."

I took the mug he poured me, then went to the phone to order more coffee.

When I turned back around, he screamed. "Willa! What are you wearing?"

I smiled at him. "My pajamas."

"I bought you tons of cute pajamas. Why are you wearing this ratty old thing?" He held out his hand, palm up. "Let me have it right now," he insisted. "This garment is not getting on the bus with us. I've told you! I cannot be exposed to polyester. It gives me hives. I refuse it, Willa. Never again."

"It's not that bad," Oliver said.

"Don't defend her," Jimmy said. "She does it intentionally to upset me. I'm docking your pay, Willa. I'm fining you. Every time you wear synthetic fiber, I'm fining you two hundred pounds."

"All right. Call Hawk and tell him to take money from my paycheck because you don't like my nightgown. He won't do it because he loves me. Are you going to finish the biscuits?"

"Eat whatever you want," he said. "You've put me right off my food. And you're deluding yourself. Just because Hawk finds you less distasteful than he finds the rest of us does not mean he 'loves' you."

He was right—I was bluffing. I actually had no idea what Hawk thought of me. I was so intimidated by him that we'd never had a real conversation, and the fact he could never remember my name didn't feel like a particularly good sign.

"Aw, Jimmy," I said, "Don't be mad." I stood behind him and wrapped my arms around his shoulders.

"I will not hug someone who is intentionally cruel. You're aging me by even touching me with that appalling thing."

I kissed the top of his head then released him and sat in the chair across from him. "If you hadn't been drunk, you could have stopped this in progress. It's your punishment. It's aversion therapy."

"It's tremendous overkill," he said. "Ridiculous behavior." He paused. "It'll probably work. Will you agree never to wear it again unless I'm as drunk as I was last night?"

"Deal," I said. "If I agree not to wear this again, will you wear whatever pajamas I pick for you? Even if they have unicorns on them?"

"Deal," he agreed. "But don't think because you won, I don't realize how manipulative you are. Because I do realize it."

"Got it. If you want the first shower, you should get in there now.

I'll pack your stuff and make you a day sheet. Oh! Three day sheets, now. Coming right up."

When the door closed behind Jimmy, Oliver and Eric stood in front of me.

They loomed over me. Feeling at a height disadvantage, I got to my feet.

I was still at a height disadvantage. I crossed my arms across my chest and briefly regretted my nightwear choice. It wasn't easy to be authoritative in a nightie.

Eric was probably only around six inches taller than me. Oliver had close to a foot on me. He was only wearing black boxer briefs, and he seemed much more comfortable with that than I was.

Eric launched into it. "Listen. This thing you're doing with Jimmy—"

I figured my best bet was to come out swinging. "This thing? You mean this job he hired me to do? Which I'm doing per my contract? That 'thing'?"

Eric looked at Oliver, who shook his head and said, "Listen, you might have pulled it over on Jimmy, but—"

I scoffed. "I didn't pull anything over on Jimmy. He begged me to come save him. Getting away from home suited me, so I agreed. I figure if I can handle him, I can handle you guys." I shrugged. "I'm not off to a good start with you two like I was with him, so maybe not."

Eric gave me a big smile. "I like her, Oliver. She's not impressed by him at all."

"I don't think she's particularly impressed by any of us," Oliver murmured. To me, he said, "You're a bit self-righteous for someone who was sleeping in his bed."

"Code word there is sleeping, champ," I said. "I practically sat on him to keep him from going back to the bar, and then we fell asleep."

"That's how it is?" he asked.

"It's none of your business, but yes. That's how it is."

Eric leaned forward. "We're doing bad-cop-bad-cop," he whispered. "Hang in there." To Oliver, he said, "Listen, mate. Maybe Jimmy found a mythical creature—someone who doesn't want to sleep with him. This is a massive win."

Oliver almost pulled off the intimidation routine, with his stiff posture and clenched jaw, but the sparkle in his eyes gave him away. "We're bullying you so if you're bad for Jimmy, we can get rid of you now."

"I don't think she is," Eric said to him.

"I don't think she is either," Oliver said, without taking his eyes off me. "Are you, Willa?"

"Am I intimidated? Or bad for Jimmy?"

"Either," Eric said.

"Neither. You're not intimidating, and I'm not bad for Jimmy." Even as I said it, I questioned if it was entirely true.

Eventually, I was going to have to leave, like however many assistants before me. The reason he refused to consider it was because it caused him pain.

"I like this job, I like him, and I need the money." I paused. "Whether or not I like *you* guys remains to be seen."

They were silent, and then both laughed.

The tension was broken, and it was okay.

For now.

Oliver extended a hand, and we shook on it. Eric gave me a hug. When he released me, he put his hands on my shoulders. "Willa. Listen. Can we talk about eyeliner? Because Jimmy says you put eyeliner on him, and you should also do it for me."

"I will," I said.

"Tell me this. How did you win Hawk over? Because I've worked with him for years, and I haven't managed it."

Jimmy came out of the bathroom with one towel wrapped around his waist, one around his neck, one turbaned around his head, and he was using one to dry his face. "Willa loves Hawk," he said, joining right in. "She reckons he looks like a sexy pirate. You want to walk his plank, right, Willa? I can tell by the face she makes when we talk about him. Hey, where's the leave-in conditioner? I can't find it." He rustled through my suitcase. He paused and noted the way we were facing off. "Oh. They've done bad-cop-bad-cop already, eh? I already told you guys; Willa is different. That will never work on her."

"Did you use every single clean towel?" I asked. "Again?"

He reluctantly unwound the towel wrapped around his hair and tossed it to me.

"Does anyone mind if I take the next shower?" I asked.

Oliver gestured me toward the bathroom.

I heard Jimmy's start talking as I closed the bathroom door behind me. "So, what's the verdict? How did she do? Not that I even care because I've made my decision, and it's done."

I turned the water on right away, hoping to drown out their conversation. I needed a break from Oliver's voice to regain my equilibrium.

I probably should have done my research on him before he got here so I could have braced for the impact. I must have seen him on television or in a magazine or something before, but it hadn't registered. Pretty rock stars are easy to ignore until you find yourself on top of them. I'd have to shield against his power, that's all. I could do it. Starting right now. I didn't need more distractions, and I didn't need more ties. It was going to be hard enough to leave Jimmy without getting more embedded.

Also, I was Willa Reynolds. I wasn't the type of woman who made a habit of almost-threesomes in spite of my recent behavior. *Head in the game,* I told myself. *Eyes on the prize.* I didn't want to leave here with nothing to show for it but a laundry list of things I'd done for Jimmy—like his laundry.

The problem was that my "prize" of a growing portfolio was useless if it was filled with things I didn't own. I needed a way to motivate him to get my contract fixed. It was my best hope.

Chapter Ten

After a couple interviews in the morning, we made our way to the tour bus. I was seriously impressed by our new accommodations. A tour bus was a nice way to travel.

Jimmy told me that in the past, their bus was packed with roadies and sometimes an opening act or two, but this tour was "an evening with," so there was no opener. A small road crew would follow in their own bus. They could afford to travel by themselves now, and Eric wanted the space and privacy so it would be easier for them to write new songs. He was already planning for their next album and wanted to build as much new material as they could during the tour.

Jimmy showed me around the bus. First was the front lounge, with a kitchenette booth, a mini-fridge, a sink, a microwave, and a small range. I followed him to the front, where he opened the curtains to a bunk above the driver's seat. "This is Tucker's. This will be the last time we ever witness it. We never ever go up there, and if her curtains are closed, talk quietly, and use headphones if you have anything with sound. We need her to be rested because she keeps us safe."

"Got it," I said.

"We don't want her listening to us," Eric said. "Loose lips sink ships."

Oliver filled in the blanks. "There's no way Hawk would know everything he does without eyes on the inside," he said. "There's only one person it could be."

"She, like, tattles on you?"

"Your skepticism is noted," Jimmy said, "but it's the only thing that makes sense. I had a cigarette once, and he sent me an email the next day with horror stories of musicians who'd ruined their voices and careers by smoking."

Eric chimed in, "I referred to him as a rotting old twat one time—just once!—and my royalty checks unexpectedly stopped for a while."

"Jimmy and Eric got in a fight over a woman once, and he called in the middle of it and told me to get rid of the girl and put them both in time out," Oliver said.

We continued exploring the bus. Behind the front lounge, there were four bunks. "Me and Oliver already called all-time bottom bunk ages ago. You'll be on top." Jimmy patted a hand on the top right bunk. "You sleep above Oliver, and Eric will sleep above me." He held my face in his hands. "Now I have to tell you something important, Willa. When you're up in your bunk and you close the curtains, that's privacy."

"Are they soundproof?"

"Utterly."

"Not at all," Oliver said. "But this is tour bus étiquette. You have to act as if sound doesn't go out and it doesn't come in."

"If your curtains are closed, sound doesn't come through from the outside. If we're talking about boy stuff, you can't hear it," Jimmy said, still holding my face.

"You'll be able to hear it," Oliver said. "You have to pretend you can't."

"If you're talking about *boy stuff*? Is there anything you ever don't say out of respect for me being a woman?" I asked Jimmy. "Seriously. I'm asking. Have you ever had a thought and then decided, 'No. I won't say this one'?"

"I'm keeping a thought to myself right now," he said haughtily, "and it's that you're being rude."

I paused to let it sink in. "You see what you did there? How you—"

"You're not concentrating, and this is important." He finally released me. "Do you understand? Curtains. It's the most important part of tour bus living. Otherwise, we'd probably kill each other. You have to have privacy, even if it's only imaginary." He opened the curtains to the bunk he'd claimed. "See? If my curtains are like this, you can be all, 'Hello, Jimmy, you ravishing man. Do you want a sandwich?'" He yanked them shut. "Then like this," he shook his head, "there's nothing. Not a peep. Even if there is."

"Got it," I said. "What else?"

He guided me by the elbow past the bunks into a bigger space in the back. "This is the lounge. This is our hang-out spot."

I plopped onto the couch and spread my arms across the back. "I love this. It's going to be great. Like camping, but better."

They all smiled at each other. "She's not even kidding," Jimmy said. "She has the weirdest ideas."

Eric said, "After a few days, you're going to want to smother us in our sleep, Willa. Everything is magnified on a bus. Sound, smell. Everyone's bad habits."

"It's harder to live on a bus than you think," Oliver said.

"Nah," I said. "It'll be great." This glorified RV was more my style than fancy hotel rooms anyway.

~ * ~

"Hey, Jimmy, is there really nothing going on between you and Willa?"

"Um, there's tons going on between Willa and me. We understand each other on a metaphysical level, Eric. We are of one mind. Our souls can communicate without words because—"

"I mean sexually. There's no sex?"

We were on the bus, a couple shows into their tour. Tour bus bunks might have been too small for Oliver, a fact he'd mentioned grumpily more than once, but they were perfect for me. I was snuggled in, contemplating how strange it was to be so at ease on a bus with men I'd just met, when Eric's voice distracted me.

He knew the answer to the question. For one thing, I'd already told him. Secondly, the four of us were always together. The only time I was alone was when they were on stage. Even for soundcheck—I was there. Jimmy loved having an entourage dressed in band aesthetic, even if it was a small entourage. He couldn't resist it. He would strut into the venue holding my hand, purely for the joy of being seen with his coordinating American Barbie.

In addition to all that, the demands on my time had only increased since Eric and Oliver joined us. More laundry, more groceries, more coffee to make and food to prepare. More luggage to organize. More speakers to monitor in interviews. I didn't mind the time it didn't leave for sex—it was good to be needed. I was in my element.

There's no way Jimmy and I could be hooking up, even if we wanted to. There was never time for it.

He sighed. "Oh, Eric. I'm disappointed in you. You should be able to tell things are much more profound between Willa and me, but I guess you have no experience with something like this."

"You've *never* fucked her? Not even a tiny bit?"

"Never."

"Sexist," I chimed in from my bunk. "Fucking is a mutual activity. It's not an act performed upon a woman."

"We can't hear you out here, Gloria Steinem," Jimmy said. "Your curtains are closed."

"Isn't the person who penetrates the one who's fucking?" Eric asked. "I'm pretty sure that's the way it works, Willa. The person penetrating is the fucker, and the person who gets penetrated gets fucked."

"Absolutely not."

"Yeah, pretty sure you're wrong about this," he said.

"If I'm on top and controlling the pace, I'd say I'm fucking you, wouldn't you?" Picturing Oliver in the bunk under me, I wished I could take the words back. The idea of him hearing that made me itchy.

Eric wasn't convinced. "I guess." Like he was talking to himself, he said, "The blonde with the tattoos fucked me." He paused. "Mm, no. I don't think people say it that way."

"Think about it, Eric," I said. "I promise you she went back to her friends and said, 'I fucked Eric Rockwell,' not 'Eric Rockwell fucked me.' To say it the other way takes away her agency. It makes her sound passive."

"She might say, 'Me and Eric Rockwell fucked,'" Jimmy offered. "Yeah? That's even better. Then they could be co-agents in their fucking."

"I hope she would say 'Eric Rockwell and I fucked,'" Eric said. "Grammar matters, doesn't it? Anyway, I'm surprised you and Willa aren't being intimate in a mutually satisfying balance of power and agency. Better, Willa?"

I smiled. "'A' for effort."

I heard him shift to talk toward Jimmy's bunk. "You *always* have sex with your assistants. She's appealing, Jimmy. You have to admit it. She's like a beautiful, three-quarter sized woman."

"I don't know," Jimmy said doubtfully. "Three-fifths sized, maybe. Or even... you know, I'd say four-sevenths."

I opened my curtains. Eric gave me a big smile from the bunk across from me. "Oh, hello, love. What have you been up to?"

"Researching modern English men and their outdated sexual attitudes toward women."

"Willa and I don't have a sex vibe for each other," Jimmy said to Eric. "Right, Willa? We even tested it. Not there."

"Right, Jimmy." If I was lucky, Oliver was wearing headphones, missing this whole conversation.

Jimmy talked to the bunk above him. "I don't expect you to understand it. Maybe someday you'll have a relationship like this with a woman, but probably not. You're not evolved enough."

"If I can jump in here," I said to Eric, "the reason Jimmy's not attracted to me is because I'm not his type."

Eric shook his head dismissively. "Jimmy doesn't have a type. He loves everyone."

"His type is anyone who's attracted to him."

Jimmy leaned out of his bunk and glared at me. "Willa, are you slut-shaming me?"

"No! I'm not judging you. I'm saying you don't have a body type or a hair color or whatever. It's a person's opinion of you that you're drawn to. The high of being wanted."

"Isn't everyone drawn to that?"

"Maybe. I'm not being critical. It's sweet."

"You have no idea what you're talking about. You've never seen me with anyone other than Benny, and he was an exception."

Eric perked up. "Who's Benny, and how was Willa involved?"

I didn't want to go into it with Oliver there. Jimmy didn't have the same reservations.

"Benny Walker from Apostolic. Remember I told you we met him? We met him, met him. Like… we met him hard, right, Willa? We both did. Don't let her calm demeanor fool you, Eric. She is quite capable of going for it when she wants to."

He raised his brows. "Tell me this story."

"We have pictures! Willa, where are the pictures? Did you download them onto the laptop?"

"I downloaded them, but we never got Benny to sign the photo release," I reminded him. Then I said more pointedly, "Not that the photo release matters, since I don't own the copyright to them."

He groaned. "I will *fix* it, Willa. I just have to wait for Hawk to be in the right mood."

Hawk seemed to have only one mood—ornery. I wondered what magic would have to happen for Jimmy to feel like the time was right.

He moved on. "Anyway, Eric, Benny's girlfriend got there and chased us out. She was a scary surprise."

"How compromised were you?" Eric asked.

I shrugged. "His girlfriend wasn't happy, but we weren't *very* compromised."

"Willa was more compromised than I was," Jimmy said. "Barely. The only reason I wasn't fully gone was because Willa jumped on the grenade for me. Literally, if you imagine Benny's cock as a grenade."

"I didn't jump on it."

He made a negative noise. "You did, darling. There's no shame in it. Nobody could blame you, and I hate to imagine what would have happened if you hadn't." He paused. "I don't really hate to imagine it. I spend a lot of time imagining it, if I'm honest."

I'd hit my limit. "It's late. Can we go to sleep now?"

"You could go to sleep if you'd close your curtains," Eric said. "It's quiet in there."

"I'm not tired," Jimmy said.

"Hey, Oliver?" I said.

"Can't hear you, love. My curtains are closed."

So much for him wearing headphones.

"Since we're awake anyway," I said, "let's talk about tomorrow. I need you to be awake no later than seven-thirty—"

Jimmy and Eric's curtains closed with a jerk.

I flipped off my bunk light. I rolled over and fluffed my pillow and enjoyed the silence. It was fine if Oliver heard everything. It wasn't any different than talking to Eric or Jimmy.

I kept repeating it to myself until I fell asleep.

Chapter Eleven

My buzzing phone woke me before my alarm. It was a text from Hope: *How is Nashville's own Annie Leibowitz? Whatcha been working on? Send me something. Distract me from this article I'm procrastinating on.*

My head throbbed. I imitated her chipper tone and texted back. *Fun stuff in progress! I'll have photos to share soon.*

Can't wait! Keep me posted. Their Instagram is fantastic, Willa. Great work there!

I sent her back a string of happy emojis and swore quietly. She was right. Their Instagram was great, but I wasn't going to ever be able to take credit for it.

When Jimmy shifted in bed, I peered down at him.

"All right, Willa? You're a bit peaky."

"Just claustrophobic," I said.

It wasn't so much claustrophobia as anxiety over letting this time go by me while I accomplished nothing because I was trapped by one clause in my contract, but I didn't want to get into it.

I climbed out of my bunk, got some clothes from my bag, and went to the back to get dressed.

"Where are you going?"

"Out."

He sat up. "What? You can't go by yourself."

"I'm going to take pictures." I put on jeans, a heavy sweater, and then dug through my bag for clean socks. "Because I'm a grown-ass woman, and I'm a photographer, a fact everyone except Hope Harper seems to have forgotten. Including me."

"Hope remembers you're a grown-ass woman? Or a photographer? I've lost the thread."

I declined to respond.

Jimmy rubbed a hand over his face. "I'll come with you. Give me a minute."

"I don't need a nanny. I *am* the nanny."

"Take the phone and call Tucker if you need a ride." He wisely retreated back into his bunk.

Oliver got up. "Okay if I tag along, Willa? I could use some air."

I cursed silently as I left the bus, Oliver behind me. If Jimmy had joined me, it would have been the second-to-last thing I needed.

Having Oliver along was the last-last thing I needed.

He was in a hoodie and athletic pants, a baseball cap over his hair. With his hat on and his tattoos covered, he was pretty much incognito.

Seeing him in public like a regular guy made me wistful. If Oliver hadn't been *Oliver Everett from Corporate*, maybe things could have been different, and maybe different would have been good. Telling myself it didn't matter wasn't doing a whole lot to make it not matter.

I walked in silence, stopping to take pictures of buildings, trees, a shaft of light bouncing off a window, anything that struck me. He was quiet company, and eventually, I realized I was more relaxed. My camera's familiar weight, the combination of invisibility and power I felt when I made images… it worked together to lift my spirits.

Pictures of buildings weren't what I wanted. I turned my camera toward him and raised my eyebrows, asking if it was okay. He gave a small shrug and an even smaller smile but allowed it. We wandered through the town. He'd stop when I stopped, letting me set the pace.

I took a close-up of his hands on a bridge railing. A profile lit from the side by the early morning sun over his shoulder. One of him sitting on a bench, his hands laced together behind his head, his face tilted toward the sun. It was easier to use the lens as a filter. It was more intimate and safer at the same time.

My tension and foul mood evaporated.

"I need coffee," I announced. "You need coffee?"

He nodded, and we ducked into the next coffee shop we came to. It was called The Roaming Gnome. It was the opposite of the clean lines and modern style of Broadway Bean back home. This one had fifties-style diner booths and shelves filled with a bursting-at-the-seams collection of gnome figurines.

We ordered coffee—chocolate espresso for me—and slid into a booth. I studied his hands on the table, then reached out and turned them over. He had calluses on his palms and fingers. He looked down and smiled.

"Drummer hands," he said.

I traced his fingers lightly with my fingertips and then snatched my hands back. He left his hands on the table for a minute, open, waiting for what I'd do next.

"Sorry." I sat on my hands. "That was weird."

He smiled again and shook his head. "It's not weird." He cupped his hands around his coffee cup. "You can touch me, Willa. You feeling better than you were this morning?"

I kept my hands safely tucked away. "Yeah. I said I was claustrophobic, but that's not exactly it." I struggled to find the right words. "There's a big distance between where I expected to be and where I am. It makes me panicky sometimes."

"What helps when you're panicky?"

"Taking pictures. It helps to do something with intent. Like I'm *choosing* something."

"Didn't you choose to be with Jimmy?"

Did anyone ever make their own choices with Jimmy? "I did, yeah. Mostly. Now it feels like I'm caught in his wake. You know?"

He smiled. "Are you asking me if I know what it's like to be swept up and carried along with Jimmy? 'Cause yeah, I do. How did it happen for you? How'd you meet him?"

"I took his picture for *Offstage* magazine."

His eyebrows shot up. "The 'day in the life' article was your work? Those were *good*."

I grinned at him. "Don't sound surprised. I *am* good." I had another drink of coffee. "Do articles like that bother you?"

"No. Why would it?"

"It was just Jimmy, not the three of you. Do you and Eric mind?"

"Oh, no," he said easily. Then he was quiet for a moment, his brow creased with a frown. "Well, I don't. It might grate on Eric sometimes. I don't want to speak for him. If it does, he hasn't said."

"It doesn't bother you?"

"I don't need the attention. Jimmy does. He loves it."

"He's lucky to have you, Oliver. A friend who understands him and makes room for what he needs. Not everyone has that."

His eyes darkened. "I like the way you say my name," he said. "With your accent. 'Aahliver.'"

When he held my gaze... it was hard to remember we were coworkers. I gulped my coffee and made myself break eye contact.

He brought the conversation back around. "This isn't the career path you'd mapped for yourself? Musician's assistant?"

I smiled. "My only plan for years has been 'make enough money to get by.' I thought I'd be taking care of my brother, but then he made it clear he doesn't want me to anymore." It sounded pathetic, so I rushed on. "I want him to be independent. I do. But it's been a long time since I imagined what I'd do if I wasn't taking care of Toby. He released me— or shoved me away, depending on who you ask, then Jimmy called me in full-blown Jimmy-panic, and I came."

"Just like that."

I shrugged. "Toby didn't need me. Jimmy did."

His gaze was on me, but I couldn't quite meet his eyes. "What is it you wanted?"

"To take pictures." I slumped. "When I first went to school, I did have a plan. I was going to get a Fine Arts degree with an emphasis in photography and take the art world by storm with my brilliant, innovative portrait photography. I wanted to do an exhibition with a theme. How our stories are mapped on our faces and what you can learn from how time molds someone. It seems naïve now—assuming someone would give me the space and time for an exhibition." I shrugged. "I wanted to work for *Offstage* and revolutionize the way we photograph and view celebrities. Once I'd built the credibility."

"Why are you here with us, then? Not that I'm complaining." Oliver paused, and I chanced a look back at his eyes. "I'm glad you're here with us."

My face warmed. "I just… it didn't happen. Dreams like that don't really come true. Not for people like me." I shook my head impatiently. "I sound like I'm whining. I'm not. We all make choices. I chose Toby, and I needed money to take care of him."

"You chose that over your own dream?" he asked. There was no judgment in his tone; he was just asking.

"He's my family. Of course I chose him," I said. "But things change. Now my plan is to build a portfolio strong enough my uncle would hire me even if he'd never met me. People will assume it's nepotism no matter what. I'll know I wasn't, and that's what matters."

"Makes sense to me," he said. "You're well on your way, right?"

I made a see-saw motion with my hand. "In a way. I am taking pictures, but I'm not building my portfolio. Hawk has a thing in the contract. He might be hot, but he's kind of an asshole, right?"

Oliver winced. "Did you have a bad connection when you video chatted with him? Like a *really* bad one? Like no connection? Was it a blank screen?"

"Oh, I had a very good look at him. It's a shame someone with such great smile lines is such a shit. Any pictures I take when I'm working for you guys are owned by the band. Even those pictures I took this morning, no matter how good they are—and they're really good, actually—don't belong to me. They belong to you. So that's backfiring."

I was glummer by the moment. "It's great for right now. You guys are fun, and the photography is good practice, even if it's not going anywhere. But soon, this is going to be over. I'll go back to Toby, who doesn't need me, and away from Jimmy, who does, and it's going to suck because I like him so much. I'll have to go back to doing the jobs I was doing before I came here, and it's a dead-end if I can't legitimately earn a job with the magazine."

I sucked in a breath. "God in Heaven, please make me stop talking."

His dimples made an appearance, and I was hit with an endorphin rush. "I could listen to you talk all day," he said. "It's the cutest thing I've ever heard. You looked happier when you were taking pictures and not being asked to analyze everything. I'm sorry. I didn't mean to make you sad, Willoughby."

"Ah, I'm not sad. How could I be? I'm having coffee with the famous Oliver-whatever-your-last-name-is."

"Everett!" He laughed.

I was ridiculously pleased with myself for getting him to laugh. "I told you my whole story. Tell me yours. Are you seeing someone?" It had just occurred to me, honestly. Holy shit. What if he was?

He gave me a slow smile. "Completely single at the moment."

"Really?"

"Really."

I pressed my lips together, trying to hold in a smile.

"Now you," he said. "Do you have someone back home? A boyfriend you left waiting?"

"Nope!" I sounded cheerful. I couldn't help it. "I sure don't. Tell me how you met Jimmy and Eric."

He gave a startled laugh and shook his head. "Do you really not know?"

"Maybe I do!" I didn't. "Maybe I'm making conversation."

"Are you?"

"I could be."

His right dimple was a tiny, tiny bit deeper than his left dimple. I wanted to lick them both.

I tugged my sweater sleeves down to my fingertips and held my coffee, more from nerves than because I was cold.

He was close enough for me to touch most of the time, but we didn't usually make this much eye contact. It was more intimate.

The bell on the door jingled as someone else came into the coffee shop, and the sound broke the spell.

I cleared my throat. "Um, you're going to tell me just for fun because, naturally, I'm familiar with the story of how you guys met."

"All right," he said. "I'll play. I met Jimmy and Eric when I was eight years old. I moved to their school. I was small for my age. My accent was wrong, my clothes were wrong, everything. I was lonely, I missed my home, I was totally... adrift. They adopted me."

"Those sweet boys."

"They were. Are. Jimmy was pretty much the same then as he is now. He's always had the swagger. Eric was his right-hand man. He was intense. When the other kids took the piss out of me, Jimmy and Eric ended it. I don't know why." He smiled. "It never occurred to me to ask them. They brought me in, and that was that. Later, when my mum died, Eric's family pretty much became mine."

"How old were you when your mom died?" I asked him.

"Seventeen."

"So young."

"Jimmy said you were young when your dad died. I imagine you know more about it than most."

I nodded.

"I had the lads. With most groups, the band comes first, then the bond if they're lucky. It was the other way round for us. I only learned to play drums because they needed a drummer. If they'd needed a goalkeeper, I'd be a football player. Whatever they asked, I'd have done it." He paused. "I'm glad it was drums. I'd be a shit keeper."

"See, I'm glad I asked you instead of searching for it! Now I know you guys are together because you love each other, not for the money and easy sex. I also learned what an enormous mushball you are."

"I'm not a mushball," he protested.

"You definitely are. It's adorable." I patted my pocket for my phone. "I should probably text Jimmy to check if he needs anything."

There were seventeen messages from him. Most were versions of *Willa, are you okay*? or *Where are you and when are you coming back?*

They ended with *YOU ARE AN IMPOSSIBLE GIRL. I SAID GIRL INSTEAD OF WOMAN ON PURPOSE BECAUSE YOU'RE BEING EXTREMELY IMMATURE TO IGNORE MY MESSAGES. I'M TEXTING OLIVER.*

Oliver was texting Jimmy back by the time I finished scrolling through them. "I told him we're fine," he said, "but we better get you back."

"Why is Jimmy so weird about being left? Eric's there with him. It's not like he's been abandoned."

Oliver hesitated, then shook his head. "Not my story to tell. He just… doesn't like it.

We took our time on the way back. I had the sense he wasn't in any more of a hurry to bring our time together to an end than I was.

I waved him in when we got back and grabbed a few minutes of privacy to call Toby.

To my surprise, he answered. "Toby!"

He laughed. "Were you expecting someone else to answer?"

"I wasn't expecting anyone to answer. How are you?"

"Buried under homework. How are you? How's the new job? How's your rock star boy toy?"

"How are you feeling?"

"It took under three seconds." His exasperation was clear. "Can we please talk about something that won't turn into a welfare check?"

"Um, okay… How's school?"

He laughed. "All right, good enough. We can talk about school. It's better than health. Actually, school is harder than I expected. It's kicking my ass, but I like the challenge. I haven't had to use my brain like this for a while. What about you? Do you like your job?"

"I do, actually." I was probably even more surprised to admit it than Toby was to hear it. "We have to get this photo thing straightened out, but I love what I'm doing."

"I listened to their new album. It's not my thing, but I have to admit they're talented. My school friends are awed when I tell them my big sister is touring with them."

It was strange to imagine him talking about me to his friends. Evidently, he hadn't totally forgotten me.

We chatted for a few more minutes, but Jimmy was staring at me from the bus window. "I gotta get back to work. Say hey to Uncle Ken for me. Take care of yourself."

"Yeah, yeah. Love you, Willa."

I disconnected, smiling. That was different than me checking on Toby. It had been Toby and me checking on each other.

Jimmy was sullen when I got on the bus. "Oh, here you are. If it's not inconvenient, maybe you and I could get some work done today?"

"What's the matter?" I asked. "What did I miss? We don't have any interviews, and you don't have to be at soundcheck for hours."

"Right, but… well, there's loads to do. I'm not paying you to strut around whatever this town is. I'm starving, for one thing," he said. "You probably do not realize it, but I haven't even eaten breakfast."

I made him some food and then sat next to him while they made their setlist for the night, and eventually, his bad mood evaporated.

When I glanced up, Oliver's eyes were on me. My cheeks got warm. It might have been a terrible idea to spend time alone with him. It was also exactly what I'd needed.

Chapter Twelve

I smoothed Jimmy's hair and checked his makeup. "You're good. You have your phone? Gum, wallet, condoms? Call Tucker half an hour before you need her in case traffic is bad. Or you know what? She should stay. Ask her to stay, okay? Then if you need to leave in a hurry, she's right there. Don't be out late. Wake me up when you get in and tell me you're here. You have early soundcheck tomorrow—don't forget."

Somehow I'd convinced him he could do without me for the night since he'd have Eric. I was about to settle into a hard-earned night in. I assumed Oliver was going to join them, but he passed.

"You boys have fun," he'd said. "I'm going to stay in and watch a movie."

Jimmy kissed me on the cheek. "'Night, Willa!"

I turned my attention to Eric. "All set?"

"How do I look?"

"Delicious. Keep an eye on Jimmy, okay?"

"Do I need more eyeliner?"

"No, you're perfect as always. Have a good time. Make good choices."

Peace settled over the bus when they left. I took my book and a blanket off my bunk, poured myself a glass of wine, and curled up on the couch.

Book, blanket, wine for relaxation, Oliver for eye candy. Perfect night.

"What are you reading?" he asked.

I showed him the book.

"Did you not just read it?"

"It was a couple books ago. I want it again."

"How much *Jane Eyre* do you need?"

"More," I said. "Always more."

He stretched out next to me with his laptop on his stomach. After a few minutes, he scooted closer and propped himself against my legs. "All right?"

"All right," I confirmed.

I savored his warmth against me until he shut his laptop. "You don't do that with me," he said. "Why not?" I tried to focus on his words, not the sensation of his voice rumbling through me.

"I don't do what with you?"

"The thing you do with Jimmy. The way you take baby him."

"Do you need it?" I was surprised. "I can do it for you. What do you need? You want me to rub your head? You want me to make you something to eat? You need a facial, Oliver?"

He shook his head. "This is enough for now."

He was quiet for a bit, but it wasn't exactly a companionable silence. More like a loaded one. I knew there would be more, and there was. "You're different with Eric than you are with Jimmy."

"Well, Eric doesn't need to be babied, does he?"

"No, Eric worries he disappears next to Jimmy, so you flirt with him." He sat up and faced me. "You don't flirt with me."

I closed my book. "Do you want me to flirt with you?"

"Maybe sometimes."

"It'd be different if I flirted with you, though." We probably should have had this conversation before I was most of the way through my wine because maybe I was being a bit too honest.

"Is that why you don't?"

"Yes. Jimmy needs to be babied, so I baby him. Eric likes to flirt, and it's harmless."

"Why would it be different if you flirted with me?"

He must have already known the answer. I said it anyway. "I'd mean it differently."

He smiled. "Good."

"Is it?"

"Yes. I've noticed you're... adaptable."

"What do you mean?"

"There are lots of Willas. Mommy Willa, Flirtatious Willa, Efficient Willa, Bossy Willa. Sleepy Willa is a cute one. The Willa you are when we're being interviewed, and you don't like the questions? Authoritative Willa is impressive."

It wasn't something I did consciously, but he was right. I did vary based on what was called for. "Are you saying I'm fake?"

"Not fake. Strategic. You read people, and you give them what they need. You're like Jimmy but more subtle. He is always angling for whatever will benefit him at the moment. You're usually trying to get something for him, or for us, or Toby."

"What do I try to give you?" I asked him.

"I don't think you do it with me, do you?"

"No."

"Why not, Willa?"

"Maybe I'm not trying to get anything from you?"

"Or maybe you can tell I like Just Willa better than any other Willa. Maybe you're giving me exactly what I want."

"You like Just Willa the best?"

"I do. Authoritative Willa is hot, but Just Willa is my favorite. Willa with a book and a blanket, and no objective. She's the one I like the most."

I smiled. "It might be the nicest thing anyone has ever said to me."

"Ah, surely not. Jimmy said only this morning you're his favorite person in the world." Oliver showed me his dimples, and his sunny smile made what was already an excellent night even better.

"He did, yeah. He also said I'm the meanest and worst personal assistant he's ever heard of, so those cancel each other out."

He turned away from me again and settled in. "As you were, so I can use you as my pillow. Maybe rub my head. Let's test drive it."

I held my book with one hand and stroked his hair away from his forehead. He sighed. "S'nice."

I never let myself touch him like this. The only time I made contact with him was when I was getting him ready for a show or a photo shoot. Never casually, and never just because I wanted to. I put my book down. His movie was playing again, but he wasn't paying attention to it. His lashes lowered as his eyes drifted closed.

Eventually, he said my name.

"Hm?"

"I don't want you to stop." His voice was deep and quiet.

"All right."

"So you better stop."

"Don't wanna." I continued to play with his hair.

He let me go for a few more minutes before he said, "Yeah, the thing is, if you don't stop, something else could happen. Which would be bad, right?"

"Depends on what it is," I said. My voice was as hushed as his. I didn't want to break the spell.

"I want to kiss you. It's getting worse and worse."

"Oh," I said.

"I'm pretty sure I wouldn't want to stop there, either. Because this isn't a harmless experiment anymore. Now I know."

"Know what?"

"Touching you more isn't going to help me build an immunity."

"Immunity to what?" I asked.

"To how I feel about you."

"Oh no," I said. "I have a certain kind of feeling for you too. This is a problem."

"Is it?" He captured my hand and kissed my palm. It tingled all the way through me.

"Of course it is." It sounded more breathless than I intended it to.

Oliver brought my hand back to his mouth and kissed my knuckles. He bit my middle finger, just the pad of my fingertip, then soothed it with his tongue.

"Oh no," I said.

He didn't turn to face me. "What's the matter?"

It was like we were attempting to navigate on a tightrope, but I'd already fallen off.

"You shouldn't have done that," I said.

"Let's pretend I didn't, then," he said.

"All right. While we're pretending, let's imagine I didn't do this either." I tilted his head up and leaned over and kissed him. It wasn't ideal, as first kisses go. We were upside down from each other, and I was bent awkwardly. He was surprised, and we were both aware we were going over a line we couldn't un-cross.

It wasn't ideal... but it was perfect.

Our lips brushed together. It was nice, so we did it again. When I moved my tongue against his, the jolt of heat shocked me. I jumped back.

His gaze was on mine, intense. "Oh, fuck."

"Yeah," I breathed. "Fuck. Now look at what you did."

He smiled at me. "I didn't do it."

"You opened your mouth. I wouldn't have gone in if you hadn't."

"You're really going with 'he was asking for it'?"

"You were," I said. "You were *definitely* asking for it."

"Gagging for it," he admitted. "Oh, Willa." He let out a deep breath and then turned to face me, serious now. He took both my hands in his. "You have to—we have to—it can't happen again. Not unless you mean it for real."

"I can't mean it for real right now. Because job. Jimmy. Tour bus. You're Oliver. He's Jimmy, and I'm me. Still. *Wow.*"

He laughed. "You're you, and I'm me, and he's Jimmy. All true. Still. *Wow.* It would probably have been better to wonder instead of know, but now we know."

"Right," I agreed. "What do we know, exactly?"

"There's a heat."

"There is. There's a heat." An inconvenient heat, but I wasn't even going to pretend to myself I didn't want more.

I definitely wanted more.

Oliver was attempting a stern expression. It was adorable. "Let's not do that again unless there comes a time when we really mean it. If there's a next time, it'll be for real. We won't be just checking."

It made good sense. "I'm with you one hundred percent, but can I check one more time first? Because maybe it was a fluke."

His gaze found my mouth. "You make a good point. It might have been a fluke. Because it was basically an upside-down Spider-man kiss, which would obviously be hot. Maybe if we kiss when we're both right-side-up, it might not be a big deal."

"Then we wouldn't have to worry." I agreed. "We wouldn't have to waste our energy imagining there's this big issue."

He put a hand on the back of my neck and pulled me to him. He kissed me. It was not gentle, and it sure as hell was not without heat.

I got on my knees to get closer to him and buried my hands in his hair again. He shoved his laptop off the couch onto the floor and then laid back, gathering me closer to him.

When his hands slid under my shirt and touched the skin of my back, I knew I was going to lose the ability to stop myself in about another two seconds. I made myself stand and take one big step back.

His eyes were dark, and his breath came faster. I made myself take another step back rather than letting myself do what we both wanted. "Shit. Fuck. God damn it," I muttered.

"Willa."

"Don't say my name. Oh my God."

"Come back here," he said, inviting me in his sex voice. "Please."

I swayed toward him, but the fans who were outside the bus got louder, a signal that they'd spotted Jimmy and Eric.

It was like being caught by your dad making out, but worse. I backed out of the lounge, scrambled into my bunk, and yanked the curtains closed. I fumbled for my phone and texted Oliver: *Pretend it never happened!*

He answered me immediately: *Not possible.*

Don't tell Jimmy!

I waited for his reply, but he didn't answer me before Jimmy and Eric came on.

"Hey, where's Willa?" Jimmy asked.

"Sleeping," Oliver said easily. Nobody would guess he'd turned my insides into lava mere moments ago.

"You're flushed," Eric said. "You feeling okay?"

I mentally high-fived myself. Go *Willa*. He was flushed.

"I'm fine," Oliver said. "It's warm in here."

"Crack a window open," Jimmy said. "Tucker, we're ready!" he called to the front of the bus. "Now," he said to the boys, "I've been keeping a lot of things in because Willa is a delicate flower, and I don't want to offend her with sex talk. Now we have an opportunity, let me tell you—"

I scrambled for my earbuds and crammed them into my ears.

When Oliver got into bed a couple hours later, the movement jarred me awake. My phone buzzed when he answered my text from earlier: *I'm not going to tell Jimmy. Obviously.*

I sent him three thumbs-up emojis.

Another text bubble popped up: *I won't tell him about it the next time, either.*

I didn't have a response, so I sent him a gif of a kitten sleeping.

He laughed softly, and a giddy warmth spread through me. It was a long time before I fell asleep.

Chapter Thirteen

The first US "mob scene" happened when we were leaving a restaurant and going back to the venue for soundcheck. We were close to the car before the group of girls spotted them, but once they did, everything happened at once. We were surrounded, and they were screaming and reaching for Jimmy with grabby hands.

He tucked his head down and covered his face, but there were so many of them. I put my body between him and the girls. I felt something hit me, but the pain didn't register. Oliver closed the back, and Eric broke a path to the car. It was over in moments, but it unfolded in slow motion.

As soon as we were in the car, Tucker drove away.

Oliver said, "All right, Willa?"

Jimmy made an indignant noise. "Did you mean to ask if *I'm* all right? They were rushing me, not *Willa*."

Oliver sounded angry. "The reason you're fine is because Willa protected you with her body, and when she was doing it, she got hit in the face. Which is why I'm asking about her."

Jimmy blanched. "Willa! Shit! I'm sorry. Are you hurt?"

"I'm fine. Everything is fine."

"You're shaking!" He leaned forward to inspect me and gasped. "Your lip!"

"It hurts a little," I admitted. "Is there a mark?"

"Look away, Eric," Oliver said sharply.

He was a second too late. Eric was already making gagging sounds. "Oh my God. Oh, God. Willa. Blood."

"Put your head between your knees," Oliver said.

"Me?" I asked.

"No, Eric. You have a scrape, and Eric faints if he sees blood," he said.

"Willa! You're bleeding!" Jimmy went full Jimmy Standish. He ripped his shirt over his head and dabbed carefully at my lip with it. "Oh,

Willa. Poor baby." He held me close to him. "We should take you to a hospital. Tucker, we need to take my Willa to a hospital! She's gushing blood!"

Eric gagged with more energy.

I tried to sit up, but Jimmy's arm was locked around me. "I'm fine—"

"Get her to a hospital, Tucker," Eric chimed in, his voice muffled. "She might have a concussion. Or the scrape could get infected, and her whole face could go. Gangrene, maybe. Her looks could be ruined. Oh Jesus. I'm gonna blackout."

"Oh my God, Willa!" Jimmy cried. "You probably have a concussion. Are you having double-vision? What's my middle name? Tell me what we ate for breakfast this morning, darling, can you remember?"

"You attempted to force-feed me oatmeal like you do every morning. I'm okay. It just startled me."

Jimmy appealed to Oliver. "Shouldn't she go?"

"If you let go of her for a minute, I could check," Oliver said. "Eric, get it together. Deep breaths, mate. Come here, Willa."

Jimmy unwound his arm, and I leaned forward. Oliver held my chin in his hand and tilted my head.

"It hurts?" he asked me quietly.

I didn't trust my voice. I nodded.

"Oh, Willa." Jimmy rubbed my back. "Poor baby. I'm going to call the police. I'm going to cancel tonight's show. Tucker, hospital!"

"Do you want to go to a hospital?" Oliver asked me.

"Absolutely not. Stop staring at me, you guys. I'm fine."

"Let's get her back to the bus," he said. "We'll get some ice on it. I think she's fine."

"Poor Willa," Jimmy crooned, holding me with both arms now. "Rest now. We'll get you back and settled in your bed, you poor baby." He stroked my hair and hummed to me. It was ridiculous. A massive overreaction to a tiny bump to the face.

It was kind of nice to be pampered. I leaned into him.

"Is Eric okay?" I asked. "Does he need anything?"

Oliver sighed. "He passed out."

~ * ~

Jimmy insisted I stay in bed through soundcheck. He let me work on his hair before the show, but then he sweetly tucked me back in. After he gave me a dozen kisses and made me promise I'd call him if I needed anything, they left.

When Oliver came in after the show, he said, "First, Jimmy

made me promise to tell you this: he has a pierced, pretty brunette for the night, but if you need him, you should call, and even if he's mid-coitus, he will rush back to you."

"Got it," I said.

"He was particularly attached to the phrase 'mid-coitus.' He said it at least three times." He dumped the contents of a bag on my bunk. "We gave Tucker a shopping list, and here are our offerings. From Jimmy: jellybeans and a teddy bear. He also wanted to get you diamond earrings because he said it would distract people from staring at your injury and making you self-conscious, but drug stores don't carry diamonds, and he said fake diamonds would make everything worse. From Eric, an ace bandage. He encourages you to wrap it completely around your face in case you start bleeding again." He stopped to roll his eyes. "Also from Eric, a mouth guard for you to wear the next time we're near teenage girls, just in case. From me, frozen peas to ice the swelling, teething gel to numb it, and Red Vines because you love it."

"You guys are the sweetest," I said, absurdly touched by a bag of drug store goodies. "How did you know Red Vines is my favorite?"

"Because when fans bring Jimmy candy, it's the only one you don't make him throw away." He cupped my chin with his big hand and tilted my face. "Your poor pretty mouth," he said quietly. "You're such a badass, Willoughby Reynolds."

"Hurts," I said.

"Want me to take your mind off it?"

My eyes dipped down to view his mouth.

He went still.

My gaze went back to his.

He raised his eyebrows.

I back-peddled immediately. "Oh no. Don't."

"Don't what?"

"Nothing, sorry. Nothing."

"Willa?"

"Nothing! I'm just tired, and my mouth hurts."

He studied me. "Is that all?"

"Yes! Yes. That's all."

He gave me a moment, maybe hoping I'd change my mind, then said, "Those crazy girls. What are they hoping to accomplish with that nonsense?"

"It's not their fault they love him so hard. It's not easy to be a teenage girl, Oliver."

"It's not easy to be me right now, either," he said.

"Why not?"

"Do you want me to answer?"

My heart was racing, and I momentarily forgot what we were talking about. "Maybe not."

"All right. We can leave it unspoken for now, but don't think it isn't there."

When I didn't respond, he continued, "The other thing is I hate that they hurt you."

"It hurts. Poor me, right?"

"Poor you," he echoed. "Don't do it again. I'm bigger than you are. I can shield."

I shrugged. "It was automatic."

"Yeah, well, it's definitely not included in your job description. Are you going to stay in bed?"

"I'll come down. I need to do the dishes anyway. Have you eaten? You want me to make you something?"

"I'll do the dishes. You officially have the night off, so find something to do other than dishes or cooking. Hey, you want to show me some pictures? Show me what you took the other day when we went out."

I couldn't remember a time anyone other than Hope Harper asked about my work. Even Toby never asked.

I plugged my camera into my laptop and downloaded what was on the card while he did the dishes. When he was done, I moved over to make room for him. He slid in next to me and studied my face. "I didn't take you seriously enough in the beginning. You're the first assistant of Jimmy's who actually takes care of him. He's lucky to have you."

"It's all right. You didn't know me."

"I should have been able to read you faster. It probably would have been easier if I hadn't been thrown off by waking up with you draped over me."

I grinned at him. "I flustered you, right?"

"You did." He wasn't smiling. "You do."

"Oh," I said. "Sorry?"

"Are you?"

"Am I? What are we talking about?"

"What it feels like to be under you."

We'd been inching toward each other as we talked. When a car door slammed outside, I jumped back. "Shit! Sorry!"

"Stop apologizing. You didn't do anything."

"I did inside my head," I said.

"If you knew what was in my thoughts, you'd—" He cut himself off, then gave his head a quick shake like he was redirecting his mind.

"Pictures. Show me your work."

I hesitated. I didn't remember a time when I wasn't planning on being a photographer, but if I showed my work to Oliver and he didn't like it or he didn't get it, it would sting in a different way than if I'd emailed them to Ken or Hope.

He seemed to guess what was going through my mind. "Come on, Willa," he urged. "You'll have to get used to sharing your work with the whole world. Right now, it's just me."

I loved that he said it like it was a foregone conclusion that I'd be successful. I turned the laptop toward him.

He began with the photos from the first day I'd met Jimmy. Oliver was quiet, moving through them. He'd occasionally stop and comment or laugh at something, but mostly he was silent.

I got progressively more and more uncomfortable and tried to take the computer back from him at one point. "No," he said, deflecting me. "Don't. Let me see."

"You're making me nervous!"

"Don't be nervous. These pictures of Jimmy—these are different than any I've ever seen. These capture who he really is. Even these, where he's putting makeup on, and the whole thing is staged. This is how he looks to Eric and me."

I was more than mollified. "Yes! That's exactly what I'm going for!" Now I was excited. I took the laptop from him and flipped through the images to the ones of The Regrets. "Like, these? Boring, right?"

He studied them for a few moments and shook his head. "No, not boring. The lighting is good, the framing. They're different, though."

"Because these are just the show itself. It's a picture of a performance being a performance. These pictures of Jimmy, or even— here, this one of Benny Walker. No, don't look at the rest; it'll get weird. Just this one. This is what's interesting to me. When you can get under or around someone's persona. Benny is smoldering and giving me those sex eyes, but it's camp. He's in a costume, putting on an act, but you get a glimpse of the real him in spite of it. He's staring into the lens, but he's also indirectly looking at you, the viewer, with a sort of wink. He knows you know it's an act. Do you see what I mean?"

Oliver turned back to the computer. "Show me the pictures you took of me when we were out together."

As I was scrambling for a reason not to show him, Jimmy and Eric came crashing in. Relieved, I went to close my computer, but Oliver blocked me from it.

"Hi, boys," I said brightly. "Did you have a good night?"

"Did you get our presents, Wil—" Jimmy cut himself off with a scream and then covered his mouth with his hand. "Oh, hello, darling. You're healing nicely, and you don't look gruesome at all. Oliver, could I please speak to you over here for a minute? Eric, save yourself. God in heaven, man, avert your eyes."

Oliver said, "Get ahold of yourself, Jimmy. It's swelling before it heals, but she'll make a complete recovery, I promise."

"Her face is ruined." Eric groaned. "God, this is exactly what I was afraid of. Do we even offer benefits? American healthcare is completely fucked. Call Hawk, Jimmy. She's going to need some sort of compensation. What's the financial value of a non-ruined face? We'll have to find out and then pay her that."

"We'll call Hawk tomorrow," Jimmy stalled, heading off what he must have known I'd suggest he could talk to Hawk about. "What are you guys doing?"

"We were going to go through the pictures Willa took the other day," Oliver said.

Jimmy crawled over the back of the booth bench and wormed his way between Oliver and me. "Lemme see."

I turned the screen toward them with a sick feeling in the pit of my stomach. My feelings for Oliver were written across the photos in flashing neon lights. I didn't want to share them.

The way I photographed him was different than how I'd ever photographed anyone else. There was a quiet intimacy that was more about me than him, in a way. The light caressed him like I wished I could. On the other side of my lens, he glowed. In the few images where he was looking directly at the camera, he had the same expression he always had when he looked at me: like a warm smile lurked right below the surface. It was in his eyes and the way the corners of his lips were barely lifted.

Eric broke the charged silence. "These are solid, Willa," he said cheerfully. "You should put the picture of him on the bench on our Insta feed."

"No, don't," Jimmy said. "We don't need to publicize his going-out-unrecognized clothes." He was subdued when he said it, and I breathed a little easier. Maybe it wasn't as obvious as I'd feared.

It was wishful thinking. He shifted his attention from the photographs to me. He looked at me for what seemed like an eternity before he shifted his gaze to Oliver. Then he closed my computer and pushed it away from him.

We were quiet for a beat.

Eric bailed us out again. "I'm overdue for my turn, Willa. Tomorrow let's do me. If, uh, your face is up to it. We'll restore some balance to our social media world. I'm not only the brains of this operation, you know." He yawned loudly. "I'm exhausted. Calling it a night."

When I got into bed and drew my curtains closed, I was rattled. *They're just pictures. There's nothing more to it.*

It wasn't true, and we all knew it.

Chapter Fourteen

Oliver and I were awake first and were having coffee at the table on the bus. We were hours from our next destination, watching the scenery go by, talking quietly. "You make a good coffee, Willa," he said, sipping from his "Save a Drum, Bang a Drummer" mug.

"All you drink is black. It's not difficult."

"Black coffee is hardest to do right," he said. "You can't hide behind anything. It's got to be a good, pure cup of coffee."

I wanted to touch him. To give myself something else to do, I grabbed our half-full mugs and slid out of the booth to refill them.

I collided with Jimmy and gasped when coffee sloshed onto my hand. Thankfully, it wasn't hot enough to burn.

"Good morning, my Willa! Did you burn your hand, darling? Here." He took the cups from me and ran some unnecessary cold water over my not-burned hand. He dried it carefully with a towel and kissed it. "There you go, good as new. Don't worry, Oliver," he said around me, "I've got it sorted, she's fine. What's our schedule today?" he asked me.

I got another mug for Jimmy. He beat me to the table and sat next to Oliver. I sat across from them. "Um, we don't have much scheduled for today," I said. "I checked in with Tucker this morning. We have at least five hours until we get to the venue, so... just hanging out. I'm going to take pictures of Eric at some point and then trim Oliver's hair. You're getting shaggy." I leaned across the table and brushed his hair out of his eyes.

"His hair is great," Jimmy said, without even giving him a glance. "I have a better idea. Let's deep condition our hair, and then you can paint my nails. How about that, Willa?"

He didn't wait for an answer. He sipped his coffee. "It's true; you do make good coffee. It's probably because of the French press I got you."

"Or it could be because she used to be a barista," Oliver said.

Jimmy gave a one-shouldered shrug. "Maybe both things."

Later, when the bus parked at the venue, Eric asked if I could take some pictures of him for Instagram, and Jimmy agreed to release me "very briefly."

Eric suggested we go inside. "This is a gorgeous old theater, and it'll be a nice change of pace."

He was right. It was beautiful. Ornate decorations, warm gold and red tones. I framed the shots to bring in the environment and his place in the midst of the theatricality. Normally for a portrait, you keep the background in soft focus to direct attention to the subject. For Eric, everything in the scene was part of him. Amps, extra guitars on stands, keyboards, Oliver's shiny drum set, microphone stands, the flashy atmosphere... those things illustrated who Eric was and what mattered to him. I made sure the light was perfect on his face, then I let everything else remain part of the visual conversation.

The only sounds were my camera's seductive clicking and the gentle strum of him playing an unplugged guitar. Behind my camera, I couldn't misstep. Everything I did was right, and the only person I had to answer to was myself.

We worked together quietly until Eric said, "Do you ever think about how your relationship with each of us is different, Willa?"

"Hm?" I zoomed in tighter on his face. His expression was thoughtful. Subdued. Rock Star Eric in makeup and costume was dynamic and appealing, but quiet, reflective Eric was beautiful in a different way.

He continued, "You're like a sister to me, in a way, because I adore you, and I'm also protective of you, and I need you to keep those things in mind while we have a difficult conversation."

"Mmhm," I murmured. I found a chair to stand on for another angle. Tight focus on his hands on the guitar, everything else in a lovely soft focus.

"You're a mom figure to Jimmy, but also his platonic lover, the way you guys are enmeshed. It's a weird dynamic." He shrugged. "It works. Jimmy is a lot. It's easy to view him as a caricature, but you don't fall for it. Hey, are you listening to me?"

"I will be in a minute. Look down. Play something." *Click. Click. Click.* "No, sit straighter. Not quite that straight. Perfect!" *Click. Click.*

I stepped off the chair and slid it across from him, turned it around, and straddled it. I set my camera carefully on the floor next to me. "Those are nice, Eric. You're going to like them. But go on. I'm Jimmy's mommy and not-lover, you were saying, as my sort-of brother.

What's on your mind?"

"It's not my business, but I'm referring to the way you and Oliver are dancing around each other."

All right. He was going to dive right in. I wasn't sure how to answer. "It isn't what you think. I mean, there's nothing to hide. I'm not... there's not a... it's not like there's this secret affair or anything." A couple stolen kisses and a few flirty text messages were hardly a relationship. Anything more was purely in my head. I didn't know what, if anything, it meant to Oliver.

"Not my business," Eric said again. He put the guitar back in its stand and then leaned toward me, his hands clasped loosely between his knees. "Listen for a minute. You're a lot of things to Jimmy, and I care about you, too, partly because of who you are to him and partly because of who you are. So take this in the spirit it's intended: We belong to Jimmy."

I shook my head. "I understand you three have this bond, and I'm happy for you because it's uncommon and special. I'm not part of that."

"You are, whether you want to believe it or not." He paused like he was debating with himself how to go on. "I'm going to tell you a story about Jimmy. Maybe I shouldn't, but you need to hear it."

I wasn't sure I wanted to.

The silence stretched on until he said, "We used to be a foursome." He was waiting for my reaction. "You didn't know?"

"No."

He sighed. "Yeah. You don't read about us, and he pretends it never happened. Okay. Here we go. Once upon a time, there was a bass player."

"What does he have to do with—"

"Her name was Claire."

It startled me into silence.

"Jimmy loved her. Maybe it was reciprocal, maybe not. Right before things took off for the band, Claire quit. She said she couldn't 'hang out playing rock band' with us. She needed 'the kind of job an adult would have,' she said. She went to university, met and married a doctor, and now she works somewhere in accounting. Oliver and I keep in touch with her, but Jimmy hasn't spoken to her since the day she left."

"Shit."

"As close as he is to Oliver and me? To you? He was that close to Claire. He never forgave her, and he's not over her. When you talk about being a photographer after this, when Jimmy worries you might be getting closer to someone else... I understand you wouldn't hurt him intentionally, and you have every right to want what you want. I'm just asking you to be careful. You're poking at his soft spots. You understand what I'm telling you?"

"I understand," I said, my voice wavering.

I got up quickly. I put the chair back where I'd gotten it from side-stage. I took my camera off from around my neck, removed the lens, and put the body cap back on, then tucked everything securely into separate compartments. Safe and sound, everything in its place.

Eric moved the stool back to where it had been and put away everything else we'd rearranged. I followed him back to the bus with a heavy heart. No matter what might be happening with Oliver, I was in deep with them all. There was no way it wasn't going to hurt when it ended—and it *would* end.

When I left, it would give him Claire flashbacks. Maybe I couldn't stop it from happening, but I could be good to him until then. He needed my attention because he was hurting. When people needed you the most, that's not when you abandoned them.

Unless you happened to be my mother, and I wasn't.

~ * ~

The first night Oliver and I were alone after my talk with Eric, I was waiting for him on the couch in the back lounge.

The bus smelled like the cookies I'd made for their after-the-show snack. The lights were dim and warm, giving the place a homey glow. I plugged in my laptop and worked on some photo editing to keep my mind occupied. *Eyes on the prize, Willa. You need to focus on your photography career and causing Jimmy as little damage as possible because you love him, and it's the least you can do. Stop mooning over warm cookies and hot Oliver. Have some discipline.*

Despite my pep talk, when Oliver came through the door, my whole body tensed. He rustled around in the kitchen and came to sit next to me on the couch. "Hey, Willa." He was munching on a cookie. "These are good."

I practically launched myself at him. It didn't take more than a second for him to catch up to me. He shifted us so my body was under him, and he worked an arm under me to hold me tightly against him while he kissed me. I arched into him, and my hands went to the warm skin of his back. When my laptop clattered to the floor, I came back to my senses. I wriggled out from under him, and we both sat up.

I brushed my hair away from my face with both hands and steadied my breath.

He gave a low whistle. "Whoa. Wow. Okay. Hi, Willa!"

A hysterical giggle escaped me. "Sorry! I'm sorry. God."

"You should be sorry," he said solemnly. "Come back here and tell me through kissing how sorry you are. It's the only thing I can understand."

I closed my laptop and put it safely on the side table. "You have to understand my words," I said. "No more kissing."

"Does not compute," he said, reaching for me again.

I scrambled back to the opposite end of the couch. "You keep your delicious mouth to yourself. I'm working."

He looked pointedly at my closed laptop. I snatched it back off the table and opened it.

"All right, all right," he said. "What are you working on?"

I was working on keeping myself off him was the real answer. "Editing for Ken."

"Your own stuff? The Regrets?"

"Hm? No. Someone else's stuff. Another cover for Hope. I'm going to concentrate, so quit distracting me with your hotness."

When Jimmy and Eric came back to the bus, I was on one end of the couch, and Oliver was on the other, sleeping with his headphones on, an unwatched movie flickering on his own laptop.

Jimmy's gaze flicked between Oliver and me. He should have been reassured by how much space was between us, but he didn't look it.

I patted the couch next to me. "Come tell me about your night."

He sat next to me and leaned his head on my shoulder. His hair tickled my cheek when he peered at my screen. "Did you take those?"

"No, I'm just editing them."

"Been a while since you've done much of your own work. We should find you something to shoot next time we have a day off. Maybe you and I could go out."

"Sounds good. Did you guys eat? Can I make you anything?"

"Do I smell cookies?" he asked hopefully.

"Yep, let me get you some. Hang on."

"Not yet," he said. "Sit with me for a minute." He nestled against my shoulder and released a long breath.

"You all right?" I asked.

"Yes," he said. "You?"

"I'm okay."

It was obvious there were things neither of us were saying.

~ * ~

I got the guys ready for the next night's show largely uneventfully. Not entirely uneventfully, because anytime I touched Oliver, it was An Event. He didn't wear makeup like the other two, and he chose his own clothes and took care of himself. He let me do his hair, which put me close to him. Heat radiated from his body; I could smell him, sense the rhythm of his breath.

Once they were finally gone, I sank into the back couch and relished the quiet. I eyed my camera bag. Maybe some creative time would give me back some of the energy I was missing lately, but instead of taking my camera out, I put the still-zipped bag back onto the floor. With a twinge of resentment, I hooked a laundry basket with my foot and dragged it closer to me, tackling the now-familiar task of sorting their clothes into three piles, folding them, and putting them away in the tiny drawers that served as dressers on a tour bus.

When the basket was almost empty, my personal phone rang. I checked the number and got to my feet, tipping over a Jimmy pile of black jeans. "Hey, Uncle Ken. Everything okay?"

"Toby is fine," he said right away. Uncle Ken knew how my mind worked.

I sat back down, putting him on speaker to leave my hands free to continue folding. "Oh, okay then. Hi! What's up?"

"I had an interesting call with Apostolic's manager earlier. They're headlining the Summer Fest."

"Cool. What's Summer Fest?"

"Benny's new idea for a music festival. His eventual plan is to pick a different city and different headliner every summer, but the inaugural show will be here in Nashville, with Apostolic in the headliner spot. His manager called to tell me they want *Offstage* to be the media sponsor, but she said the deal stands only if you're the photographer for it."

At first, the only thing in my mind was *Benny Walker Benny Walker Benny Walker*. I let myself have a moment to revel in the unbelievable: he'd asked for me. No, he'd demanded me. Benny Walker said, "It has to be Willa Reynolds." OhmyGod.

Photographing a festival, Apostolic, *Offstage*... this career opportunity could give me the opening I needed, and it wasn't because my uncle was throwing me a bone. I'd been requested. As a photographer, not a glorified babysitter.

I didn't realize I hadn't answered Uncle Ken until he said, "Yes or no, kid? Come on, I'm on deadline."

"Yes! Yes. Thank you, yes."

He gave me the details. It was in a week and a half. A full day of music, two stages, with Apostolic closing on the main stage. All of Uncle Ken's reporters would be on deck, but Hope would be lead, and he'd give me more details when I got back to town.

After our call ended, I jumped to my feet and danced around the bus. This was exactly what I needed! A short break to refill my creative well. I'd get a chance to do some professional photographs, spend time with Toby, have a break in my routine. It was going to be *great*.

Plus Benny Walker.

Once I'd danced myself out, I paced around the room and worked through the details. There was no way I could have said no to it, and I didn't regret saying yes.

However, it was not without problems.

Jimmy and I hadn't ever talked about me having a day off. This would be four or five days with travel time. I wasn't sure how he'd react.

There was a good chance he'd react poorly.

Even worse, once I got there, what did my contract mean for photographs I took on my personal time? Technically, I was still "employed by the band," so anything I shot might not even belong to me.

I didn't have a lot of time to make it happen, and I was going to have to pick my timing carefully.

Chapter Fifteen

We were in the venue's green room in a large prep area with counters and mirrors lining three walls. I could do their makeup and hair on the bus when we needed to, but it was nice to have more space, and Jimmy loved being able to see so many angles of himself. He was in a salon-style chair, relaxed while I massaged a curl-enhancing product into his hair from the roots to the ends. This was his favorite pre-show ritual. He said it calmed his nerves.

I wished for something to calm my nerves. I'd been bouncing off the walls, picturing myself at this festival. Camera around my neck, new, multi-pocketed leather messenger-style camera bag taking the place of my old beat-up canvas backpack. A big, laminated pass hung on a lanyard around my neck, printed with MEDIA PASS in authoritative block letters across the bottom.

The more the hours ticked by without me getting permission from Jimmy to go, the more the mental image faded, crowded out by to-do lists, shopping lists, day sheets, and a mountain of boy laundry.

I'd been waiting for the perfect moment to have the conversation, but there wasn't going to be one. I took the plunge. "Jimmy, I need a couple days off to go to Nashville to shoot a music festival for my uncle's magazine," I blurted.

Pause.

"I...um...also need you to get my contract amended so I can publish the pictures in *Offstage* magazine."

Pause.

"Okay?"

I wasn't sure if he'd answered me, and I'd missed it because of how my heart was thundering in my ears or if he was sitting there in silence.

"When?" he finally asked.

"A week from this Friday. I'll leave on Thursday and be back by the next Tuesday at the latest."

He relaxed. I hoped it meant he was reassured by how short it was, and he was about to say yes.

He wasn't.

"Oh no. I can't possibly spare you right then. That's Red Rocks. It's an iconic venue. I'm definitely going to need you to be with me. I'll be a wreck."

I arranged the brushes and makeup we'd need, my hands shaking. "Eric and Oliver will be with you," I reminded him. "It's not like I'm leaving you alone."

"Yeah, but Red Rocks! First of all—elevation. What if it strains my voice? I need you to follow me with hot tea. This show is going to be totally different. We're part on a double bill, and I suppose now is a good a time to tell you about a particularly difficult situation." He paused.

"What is it, Jimmy?" I asked dutifully. I wiped my hands clean on a towel and unscrewed the lid of our makeup primer. I spread it across his face with my fingertips.

"The other band is Geronimo. They're a Swedish dance fusion duo. Very trendy right now, and the keyboard player is hotttttttt. He and I have a bit of a past. Do you know what I mean?"

Of course I did.

"A *sexual* past."

"Got it."

"We had sex, and it was good."

"Okay. Maybe you can have good sex with him again. It's nothing to do with me." I put the top back on the primer and dipped a brush into the powder.

"I'm not finished, darling. I had *exceptionally* good sex with the vocalist. Sex is never a contest because all sex is good, but if it was a contest, she would have beat him. She was sublime."

"Okay, then—"

"Where it gets tricky is neither is sure I've been with the other one, although they must suspect it."

"Maybe it would be better to steer clear," I said, getting drawn into his story. "You might have to do without either of them."

"They're married, Willa."

I set down the makeup brush. Okay, he was right. It was a sticky situation.

He smiled. "So I had a great idea: You could pretend to be my girlfriend! We'll be adorable together, and neither of them will make a scene in front of my new lover. Problem solved."

It would have been fun if it was any other night. I could dress up, play rock-star girlfriend, keep Jimmy safe, make him happy... it was checking a lot of good boxes for me.

There would always be a reason I'd want to stay. Fixing things for him couldn't be the only thing that mattered to me. "You'll have to come up with something else. I can't miss this opportunity. You understand, right?" *Please, please let him understand. Let it matter.*

"Do my eyes next, Willa." He closed them and waited and continued talking. "I know it's bad timing, and I'm sorry. I'll find you another chance. Isn't Lollapalooza next month? I could talk to Hawk, get you in there. Yeah, that's even better! You could get more bands. Maybe the timing will work so we can go together. I've never been, believe it or not."

I tilted his chin up and lined his lids with an onyx pencil. "I'd love to go to Lollapalooza. That'll be great. I still need to go home for this one anyway. Benny specifically asked for me. His manager told Ken they'll pull the media sponsorship if Ken doesn't have me there to photograph them."

Jimmy smiled. "Benny must have liked you a lot. I'm sorry you'll have to miss him."

I dragged another salon chair in front of him. The loud metal-against-tile scraping sound was jarring. I sat so we were eye to eye and put my hands on his knees. "Pay attention. I need you to listen to me right now."

He opened his eyes. "I always listen to you."

I struggled to keep my voice even. "I'm not really an assistant. This job is temporary for me. I need to be preparing for what's next, and that's hopefully going to be photography."

"Obviously you're not just an assistant. You're assistant *extraordinaire* to the greatest rock star in the world, and I *do* make room for your art; I'm just telling you no for this one weekend when I need you to do the job I hired you to do. I'm not being unreasonable."

What he was asking for wasn't unreasonable on the surface. It *was* my job, and I was good at it. I got a thrill from being indispensable to him. It was seductive.

But what about what I wanted? This could be a long road littered with this kind of temptation. He wasn't forcing me to stay. He was making it almost impossible for me to want to leave.

Maybe I was a good photographer. Maybe I'd be successful.

Maybe not.

Taking care of these guys, though? I was good at it. I was the *best* at it. Was it enough? Could I get by on that?

I tried again. "Jimmy, I need you to compromise this time. I work hard for you. I haven't asked you for a day off yet, right?"

"Right, but—"

"I want to take this assignment. I miss Toby, for one thing, but this isn't only about me. Uncle Ken can't lose this sponsorship. The festival is in his backyard. He's my family. Even if I didn't need to do this for me, I need to do it for him."

His dark eyes shone with understanding, and once again, I thought, for a moment, it was going to work out. Then he said, "Of course you're disappointed. I'm sure I can get you into Lolla. Then when we go to England, I can get you into Glastonbury! Glastonbury is huge, Willa. You could sell tons of images from there."

Next month. Next year.

My hands were still on his knees. I gave him a squeeze and stood. My purse was on the counter. I dug through it for the band phone and set it on the towel next to the makeup brushes. I took his credit card from my wallet and placed it next to the phone.

"What are you doing?" he asked me.

I kissed him on the forehead and walked out.

He was on my heels. "Willa? Where are you going?"

I didn't let myself turn around. He needed me, and I was leaving him anyway. I couldn't think much about it, or I'd go running back.

Eric was on the couch in the lounge area. "Hey." I waited until he looked up from his phone. "Take care of him."

"Where are you going?"

"Keep him here. There are already kids outside. Don't let him make a scene, or it'll end up online."

"Willa," Jimmy said again. "What are you doing? I'm not even ready for the show!"

I was almost to the door.

"Stop! You absolutely can't leave right now." He didn't sound angry; he sounded scared.

If I stopped now, I wouldn't leave.

I made myself leave the building, then I strode across the parking lot as fast as I could without running. All I'd need from the bus was my camera and my laptop. I wouldn't take the clothes. Technically, he owned them anyway.

Keep going. I'd made a decision, and now I was going to follow through. If I let myself dwell on the panic in his voice or how he'd probably be remembering now what he'd gone through when Claire left him—no. *Focus. New leather camera bag. Magazine covers. Press passes. Toby and Ken. Benny. Go, go, go.*

Oliver wasn't on the bus, thank God. If I had to face him right now, I wasn't sure what would happen. If I touched him, I'd stop moving. If I stopped moving, I wouldn't go.

I shoved my computer and my mouse into my backpack. I crawled under the table to unplug the power cord, but it was tangled around the chair legs, so I cut my losses. There was no time to wrestle with it. I slid my backpack on, grabbed my camera bag, and secured my purse straps over my shoulder. I stopped rushing for a minute and stood in the small kitchen, indecisive.

I should leave him a note.

What would I say?

I don't want to go, but I have to go. How would that make anything better?

A lump rose in my throat, but I swallowed it. The sun hit me in the eyes when I stepped off the bus, and it took me a minute to adjust.

"Hey, you." His voice startled me as it rolled through me like the first time I heard it, setting fire to my insides and overcoming my common sense and good intentions. "Where are you headed?" He raised the hem of his shirt and used it to wipe the sweat off his face, waiting for me to answer.

Don't touch him, I said to myself, even as I closed the space between us.

I put my hands in his hair and got on my tiptoes to kiss him. He made a surprised sound, but his arms wound around me, and he kissed me back.

I told myself to move away, but when he captured my bottom lip with his teeth and gave a gentle tug, I couldn't.

He slipped a warm hand under my sweater and pressed it against my bare back, pulling me more tightly against him. He was hard against me, and I'd never wanted anyone more in my life.

He bent his knees, hooked his hands behind the backs of my thighs, and lifted me off my feet. I wrapped my legs around his waist and held on.

I was doomed to mimic my mom one way or another. I was about to become either a leaver, or a woman who gave in to lust or romance or whatever it was, and let a man take things off her shoulders.

The giving in to lust option was getting more likely—and more appealing—by the moment.

I couldn't give in to it. I made myself let him go. When he set me back on my feet, I put distance between us, and cold surrounded me.

"Willa?"

I gathered my bags, which I'd carelessly dropped. He said my name one more time, but I turned away.

The only sound was the quiet crunch of gravel under my feet as I walked away.

Chapter Sixteen

I joined Hope and Uncle Ken in the Summer Fest media tent. We gathered around a round high-top table to plan our day. A dozen tables like ours were under the white canvas tent, all filled with other reporters and photographers. He kept his voice low because he was paranoid about someone spying on his "media strategy." Given that his strategy was mostly "get good pictures," I wasn't sure it was groundbreaking enough to warrant spying, but maybe it was the rookie in me.

"I can't even hear you," I said. "Hang on."

I climbed down awkwardly from my tall chair. The big plastic media pass hanging from the lanyard around my neck was caught by a gust of wind and hit me in the face. I pushed it away and struggled to pull my chair closer to the table, but it kept getting caught on the uneven grass, and my new camera bag hanging over the back made it even more unwieldy. I finally got the chair where I wanted it and scrambled back into it. I'd somehow managed to get my lanyard hooked around my knee in the process and nearly hung myself on the stupid thing before I got untangled again.

"You doing all right?" Uncle Ken asked me.

"I'm great."

Hope smiled. "Nervous, Willa?"

"Not at all." She was the picture of rock-and-roll confidence. "I just don't know why they make these damn cords so long," I said. Although both Hope and Uncle Ken were doing fine in theirs. Theirs must be custom-made, I thought.

He leaned forward again and lowered his voice. "Okay. Listen. Hope, you and I will switch off between the main stage and the second stage. Willa, you can be wherever you want until Apostolic's set, then I need you in front. Make sure Benny sees you and get as many photos of him as you can. Other than that, get a few candids of the bands backstage, or watching other bands. Charlie will be at the second stage, and Margo will be back and forth." He checked his notes. "No pressure, Willa, but I'd like to put Apostolic on the cover, so get me a strong vertical. If you get a strong horizontal, we could do a three-quarters spread on the inside."

I wasn't worried. Onstage photographs weren't my sweet spot, but it was difficult to get a bad photo of Benny, with or without Jimm—other people—as window dressing.

"I got it." I slid back out of my chair, put my camera bag on the table, and unzipped it, checking for the twentieth time that everything was where I'd put it.

When an arm went around my shoulders, I recognized the scent of cloves. My involuntary response was to blush. Benny pulled me into his arms for a close hug. I glanced over his shoulder for his girlfriend.

"She's not here," he whispered in my ear, sending tingles down my spine. In a normal tone, he said, "I didn't get to say goodbye to you last time we were together." He gave me an inside-joke-between-the-two-or-three-of-us sort of grin.

I fought the urge to fan my face. "Hi, Benny. It's good to see you again."

"Where's Jimmy? I wasn't sure he'd let you come at all, but I was sure he'd have you on a short leash if he did."

I glared at him. "He didn't 'let' me come."

He raised his eyebrows. "Did you go rogue?"

"I didn't have to go rogue since I don't have to ask his permission for anything." I didn't have to ask Oliver's permission either, so it was annoying as hell to have images of him on a permanent loop of guilt and restlessness.

"Oh, right." Benny snapped his fingers. "Now I remember. You're your own Willa. You mentioned that." I wasn't sure if he was being sarcastic. He probably was, but either way—he was right. I was my own Willa, now more than ever.

He reached behind me and tugged on a plastic adjuster, shortening my lanyard to a more comfortable length, and adjusted the clip on the badge so it laid flat.

"I don't work for him anymore." It sounded like I was stating a simple fact. Nobody would sense my second thoughts about what I'd given up and who I'd hurt to do it.

I had taken charge of my own life. I wasn't going to fall back on old habits of putting everyone else first. I told myself that defaulting to caregiving was self-sabotage. I made enough noise about being my own woman; now it was time to act like it. Did I miss the guys? Yes. Yes, I did. It didn't change anything. I'd done what I'd had to do. When forced to choose between what they wanted and what I needed, I chose myself.

Jimmy had made it clear: There was no middle ground. Now I was like Josette to him. I was gone, so I was gone. Now it was just Toby and me. Toby didn't need me like he used to… but surely it was better for him to have me nearby.

I wanted to call Oliver every single day, but I couldn't let myself give in. There was no gain on that play. I wasn't going back. There was nothing to say.

Maybe I was also a tiny bit scared of what he'd say to me.

I made a deliberate effort to bring myself back to the moment. To my dream career, which was coming into focus right now.

Benny tilted his head, all fake sympathy. "Aw, Willa. Trouble in paradise? The two of you seemed so close. You and Jimmy were open to sharing everyone—I mean everything."

I widened my eyes at him, trying to get him to cool it with the threesome jokes in front of my uncle, but he wasn't sorry. He waggled his eyebrows at me. Then he asked, "Are you looking for a job?"

"Why, are you going to hire me?" I joked.

Before he could respond, Uncle Ken chimed in. "Pleased to meet you. I'm Ken Pilkington from *Offstage*. Willa works for me."

Benny made small talk with Uncle Ken for a few minutes, then gave me another hug. "Find me later, Willa," he said into my ear. Then he was gone.

~ * ~

I wished I'd been able to take more joy in the rest of the day because it was something I could only fantasize about a few short months earlier. The Regrets were on the second stage, and I'd gotten some great images of them. I'd been in front of the barrier for Apostolic. Benny played it up for my camera. My memory card was filled with cover-worthy images by the time I was done.

When Apostolic finished their set and took their bows, he made eye contact with me and jerked his head toward the side of the stage, gesturing toward the VIP tent. I debated with myself. Spending time with Benny Walker wasn't just cool—it was a professional opportunity I couldn't allow myself to miss.

I allowed myself to miss it anyway. I didn't have the heart for it. I texted Uncle Ken and Hope: *Got great stuff! Will show you tomorrow. Gonna call it a night.*

I drove home with the stereo off, soaking in the quiet after a day of being under sonic bombardment. I let myself in the dark house, closed the door with my foot, and dropped my keys in the dish. I made my way to the kitchen and opened the fridge—nothing more than Chinese take-out I was pretty sure was from before I left and a single, lonely Coke can.

I snagged the Coke.

I sat at the kitchen table, seeing the room with fresh eyes.

The kitchen cupboards used to be a cheerful yellow but were dingy now. The counters were dusty, and the faucet was dripping. I stared at the harvest gold fridge, not sure if I should laugh or cry. I hadn't really *seen* it in years. There was a painting held by magnets. It was a picture of me that Toby drew in second or third grade. I had disproportionate arms and legs, with a serious face and braids on either side of my head. Apart from the fact that I'd only ever dreamed of having long legs, it was a decent likeness of who I'd been then. Now the edges of the paper were yellowed and curling, but my face was just as unsmiling at the moment.

I snatched the painting off the fridge, throwing it and the magnets in the trash.

I reconsidered and took the painting back out. I put it under the old phone book on top of the fridge. There. Progress! I did a thing.

Maybe tomorrow I'd do another thing.

This was going to be my home again. I supposed it was time to make it more mine. Mine and Toby's. I could work on a couple projects. Do a search for how to fix the faucet. Paint the cupboards, maybe.

I looked at the refrigerator door again, and a scrap of paper held by a magnet from the local pizza place caught my eye. "Mom" was written in vaguely familiar handwriting above a phone number.

"Mom." Psh. Hell with her. I didn't intend to talk to her any time soon, but if I ever did, I would call her by her damn name. I wasn't ever going to call that woman "mom" again. She'd be Susan, or even better, she'd be nothing because I wouldn't have to talk to her.

~ * ~

It was good to have a project in the weeks after Summer Fest. Toby was gone most of the time. He'd embraced his new life, and I felt guilty for having doubted him. He'd thrown himself into it. A lot of nights, he didn't come home at all, deciding to stay and crash at a friend's house after a late night of homework.

I worked in the lab, stretching it to ten hours or even more if I could. I met my uncle for dinner a few times. I went to the bar for drinks with Hope. I still had too much empty time.

This was good, I reminded myself. I'd continue to put in my lab time while the assignments gradually increased in frequency and status. There was no glass ceiling for me at the magazine because Hope Harper already shattered it. If I was willing to put in the work and the time—and

I was—there was no limit to how high I could go. Head photographer, photo editor, anything was possible.

All my dreams were coming true, so why did I feel hollow? I must be hungry, I decided. Not unhappy. Not unfulfilled.

I was thinking about what to make for dinner when Toby came in. I was surprised and relieved he was there. Now I could concentrate on something else. "Toby! Hi! Hey! I'm glad you're home! Have you eaten? Can I make you something?"

He shook his head. "I don't need you to make me any food."

"Are you sure? Because I'm not busy!"

"I'm sure. We need to talk."

My head dropped forward. Conversations that opened with "we need to talk" were never good.

Toby laughed. "Everything is fine. Don't be such a doomsday diva."

"A 'doomsday diva'? That's a new one, college boy." I followed him into the living room and sat on the couch. He sat in Dad's chair.

I got back up and got him a glass of water. Toby was never drinking enough water. He was chronically dehydrated.

"Thanks." He set it on the side table next to him. "Listen, what are your long-term goals with the house?"

Perched on the arm of the couch, I glanced around, liking what I saw. It was more modern, looked more lived-in. I'd found a cool throw rug at an estate sale last weekend, and the black and gray tones brought a hint of chic to the room. I'd covered the brown plaid couch in a crisp white slipcover and added some playful black and white polka-dotted throw pillows.

Maybe Toby was sentimental. This was our childhood home, after all. "Does it bother you? I was trying to freshen things a bit. Make it more modern."

"We should sell it."

So much for sentimental.

"Sell it? Are you crazy? No. It just occurred to me we haven't done anything with it since Dad died, and it was time. I'm not going to sell it."

"Why are we keeping it, Willa?"

I blinked at him for a few moments and then launched myself off the couch. "I have to go to work. I forgot a thing I need to do with a thing."

Toby stood and caught my arm before I could get away. "This conversation isn't going to be any easier for you tomorrow than it is right now. Sit down, and let's do it."

"No, I really have to—" I trailed off when he shook his head. He wasn't going to let me off the hook. I dropped onto the couch. Toby was chock-full of surprises lately, and they weren't all good. "I don't want to sell our home. I just want to update it a bit." I gestured at Dad's old chair. Even when Toby got up, the seat would show a permanent dent in the shape of Dad's butt. "We might even want to save for some new furniture, for example. You are sitting in the chair dad literally died in. Doesn't it bother you?"

He looked at the chair with horror. "Ugh. Well, yeah. Now it does. Thanks a lot." He dragged a chair in from the kitchen and sat in that, facing me. "Nice attempt to distract me, but it won't work. Let's go. Why shouldn't we sell the house?"

"Um, because we live here?" I suggested with overblown sarcasm.

He was unfazed. "Sort of. I'm at school most of the time, and when I'm not, I crash with Chelsea. I've been coming home every few days because you're here, but it'd be a lot easier for me to get an apartment near school."

"Who is Chelsea?"

"She's my girlfriend." He grinned. "You probably could have puzzled it through when I said I'm sleeping at her place."

"But—but—you said you were studying."

"Sometimes we study." He grinned. "Sometimes we do other things."

I frowned at him. "I mean, like at the library. I didn't know you had a girlfriend."

"I do. Her name is Chelsea."

"Congratulations. I'm happy for you. I would love to meet her," I said, lowering myself into the pit of lies I was digging. In reality, there was only one woman in the entire world I was less interested in hanging out with, and that was our mom. Well, and Benny Walker's girlfriend. "So you only live here part-time. Okay. I live here."

He smiled at me again. "I'm glad you brought this up," he said. "Since you've been back, it's seemed like you don't want to talk about what happened or what your plans are. I'm glad you're ready to share. I'm ready to listen, sis."

I couldn't help it. I laughed. He got comfortable in his chair, folded his hands over his stomach, and watched me with a smile. "Go on," he said when I stopped laughing. "I'm all ears. Why did you leave your dream job? Are you just working for Uncle Ken now? What happened with your rock and roll bros? Why did you leave them? Are you going back?"

"I'm not going back, it wasn't my dream job, and they're not bros. Ridiculous on every level."

"I'm listening."

I explained it to him. Jimmy wouldn't let me come home to do this, my contract didn't allow me to work on my portfolio, and I never planned on it being forever anyway. "It was an intermission," I said. "It wasn't ever going to be a career. Now I'm getting the cover from Summer Fest, and Hope has given me some small assignments. I got some good ones of another band the other night. I'm easing my way into working for the magazine more." I attempted a cheerful smile. "Yay!"

He studied me with narrowed eyes. "What's going on? It's what you *used* to want, but you obviously aren't happy now you're getting it. Why?"

I hadn't spent so much time with Jimmy without learning a few tricks. I didn't want to think about what Toby was asking me, so I didn't. I kept talking instead. "Anyway, I'm already making enough money selling photos here that I only have to work one other job. Soon photography will be all I do. It'll be great. We can go back to the way things were."

Even as I said the words, I knew they weren't true.

We weren't going to go back to the way things were.

Goddamn Chelsea, for one thing. She was a complication I hadn't foreseen. Toby didn't date much in high school and never seriously. This hadn't even been on my radar.

Toby ran a hand through his hair, a sign he was stalling. I waited.

"Willa, here's what I need you to understand," he said. "I don't need you to take care of me."

"Toby—"

"No, please listen to me. I used to need you to, and you did. I'm grateful for it." He sniffed and cleared his throat. "When I decided to go to school, I didn't handle it gracefully, and I hurt you. I'm sorry." He paused, then said, "Don't talk yet. I'm not finished."

I mimed zipping my lips.

He sipped the water I'd brought him, then put the glass back on the table. "When Mom left, and I had my surgery, when I lost my leg… you're what got me through those things. It should have been Mom, but she was gone. Or it should have been Dad, but he didn't have the strength to do it. You're the one who raised me, and you shouldn't have had to. I never realized how much I depended on you until you went to college, and Dad and I couldn't hack it. I'm sorry. I'm sorry we needed you to come back home. You put everything on hold for me, and I never said thank you." He took a breath. "So, you know. Thank you."

My vision blurred. I hugged a pillow and stared at the ceiling until I was sure I could speak without crying. "Being there for you is the only thing I've done that I'm proud of, Toby. I wouldn't change it for anything. Being your sister, taking care of you—those are the things I am."

He shook his head. His voice was gentle when he spoke. "I don't need you to be a caregiver anymore. You were forced into that role too young. Thank God you took it on because Dad and I were lost without you, but this isn't going to be our home anymore. Not yours and mine. This was Dad's house. It's time to let it go."

I focused on the easy part. "I'm not selling the house." I kept going when he tried to interrupt me. "Even if I wanted to, it wouldn't matter. We have two mortgages on it. We owe more than we could get for it. Anyway, even if I travel some, like Hope does, I'll need a home base. You can go if you need to. It's okay. Get an apartment. If you change your mind, or if you need to come home, it'll be here. Okay? It's fine."

"No, I don't like it. Even if it doesn't make sense financially to sell it, this isn't healthy for you. You're crippled by it."

"Don't say crippled," I said, correcting him automatically.

He laughed, and I joined him. It was teary, but it was a laugh. "I'm serious, Willa," he said. "Things have changed. You have to... the way you took care of me? You need to do that for yourself now."

I picked at the seam of the pillow. "I am taking care of myself. I'm here, and I'm pursuing a career. I'm making it happen."

He drained his water, then took the glass to the kitchen and came back. He headed for the recliner before he changed course and sat with me on the couch instead. "I can't tell you what to do. I just want to say when you were with those guys, there was a spark and an energy in your voice that had never been there before, and now it's gone. You sounded like a different person over the phone, calling from wherever you happened to be. I don't think this is what you want. Not anymore."

"Yes, it is," I said. "This is what I've always wanted."

"Are you sure?"

"I'm positive." I was making a living working for the magazine. I was building a portfolio. I had connections like Benny Walker, for fuck's sake.

Toby put his hand on my knee for a minute and gave it a gentle shake. "Okay. If you're happy, I'm happy. Consider what I said about the house. You don't need this. If you're staying, get a condo or something." He stood. "Now I gotta go. I'm late for a date with my lady. We're going to 'study.'" He winked at me.

"Ew," I said.

He gave me a hand and helped me up from the couch into a hug. He rested his cheek on top of my head. "You okay?"

"I'm great." I reached to ruffle his hair. He bowed his head to let me. "It's time for you to stop with this inspirational business," I said. "You're the Karate Kid in this relationship. *I'm* the Mr. Miyagi."

"You're usually the Miyagi. Today it's me!"

"Hey, how about you stay home this weekend to help me paint those kitchen cupboards. They're super gross."

He wrinkled his nose. "We have a bad connection. I didn't catch that last part. I gotta go." He opened the door and paused, one hand on the door frame. "For real, we gotta lose the death chair."

I sat back on the couch and hugged a pillow to my chest as I replayed our conversation in my mind.

It was weird he couldn't tell how happy I was. Of course I was happy! How could I miss my former life as a babysitter when I was here at home, fully enmeshed in the life I'd fought for?

What would it mean if my dreams were coming true, but I wasn't content because I didn't have anyone to take care of?

What kind of woman *needed* to be a caregiver?

That would be sad and weird. I was glad I didn't have to worry since I was not that kind of woman.

I went to my bedroom, powered on my laptop, and sat cross-legged on my bed, clicking through the latest photos I'd downloaded. I wasn't sure if Uncle Ken would want anything from these, but I'd get the best of them edited and ready.

I was focused and ambitious. Maybe the tiniest bit lonely, but it would pass. I just had to stay busy.

Chapter Seventeen

When Hope called me into her office, she greeted me with a huge, glowing smile. "Hi, Willa. I want to get your opinion on this cover before I send the proof to your uncle. Can you take a look, please?"

Her office was as stylish as everything else about her. One whole wall was a window overlooking downtown Nashville. The walls were a soft aqua, and there was a bright pink area rug under her enormous desk. A shelf lined the wall behind her, with oversized coffee-table books about music alternating with framed, autographed photos.

A white leather couch in the corner was occupied by a bald man with a long gray beard. He was snoring loudly.

She noticed where my attention had drifted. "Don't worry about him. He needs to sleep off his hangover before I can interview him. He's an absolute ass when he's hungover."

He looked suspiciously like one of classic rock's most notorious guitarists. I might not have recognized Jimmy, but this guy I knew—my dad had been a huge fan. "Hope, is that—"

"Yes. Don't tell Ken he's in here. I sort of... kidnapped him from the bar. Well, *kidnapped* is a misnomer since he's like a hundred years old." She waved me over impatiently. "Enough about him. Come here, come here!"

I went behind her and... there it was on her screen, larger than life.

My first cover.

The cover of *Offstage* Magazine. A photo of Benny Walker.

By me.

"Fuuuuuuuuuuck," I whispered.

Hope bounced in her chair and clapped her hands. "Right? This is gorgeous! I mean, I do wish it was someone else, if I'm honest. He has an air of drunken dickishness, don't you think?"

"Um, no," I said. "He has an air of super sexy awesomeness."

She made a gagging sound. "Disgusting, Willa. Still, there is no getting around it—this is a great cover."

The neon green *Offstage* banner was splashed across my photograph. Benny was holding the microphone with both hands, staring into my lens with a rock-and-roll snarl, his guitar hanging loosely around his body. The cuffs of his leather jacket were rolled up, revealing glimpses of tattoos.

He was sweaty, happy, and absolutely in his element. Beautiful. I'd tilted the camera to make the angle more dynamic, a bit dangerous. The sense of movement suited him. He'd love it. More importantly to me right now, *I* loved it.

"So, how's this work?" I asked. "Do you have to get his approval or anything?"

She snorted. "Uh, no. I don't care if he likes it, although he'd be crazy not to. I don't care about him; I care about you. Are you excited?"

I smiled at her. "So excited."

We high-fived. "Things are taking off for you, girl. No more nanny jobs for you! Not for kids, not for rock stars. Welcome to life as a music journalist!"

Hope Harper was acknowledging me as… maybe not an equal, but someone like her. A grown-up. A professional. Even a few short months ago, it would have been a dream come true.

Was it still a dream come true, though? I thought of Hope's schedule, her hectic lifestyle, her temporary connections with so many people. My perspective had shifted a little. Now I thought about an uncomfortable chair and a cupboard full of matching mugs.

"You all right, Willa?"

"Oh, yeah! Great."

She studied me. "This is what you want. Right?"

"Absolutely!"

Her expression softened. "Honey, it's okay if you don't. You don't have to—"

"Nope, I'm great! Thanks a lot, Hope."

"Well, if you say so. Go back to the lab before Ken comes searching for you and discovers—" She jerked her head to the man on the couch.

When I got to the door, she said, "Oh. Hang on. I forgot. This came for you last week or the week before. I don't know why he sent it to me. No message, just the attachment. Let me find it."

She scrolled her mouse, then clicked a couple times. "There," she said. "I sent it to print. Some paperwork from Jimmy. Probably putting an end date on your contract for your files."

I winced. "Yeah. Okay. Great to have that taken care of." Now he could pretend I'd never happened. Like Josette, Claire, and everyone else who'd let him down.

I nabbed the papers off the printer on my way back to the lab. I folded them and stuffed them into my back pocket. I refused to dwell on whatever it was. I was focusing on myself, and this cover was a milestone in my career. Not just a milestone, a steppingstone. A major piece for my portfolio! Maybe I'd failed as an assistant/caregiver, but I was gaining ground in my career. I'd made huge progress, and it deserved my focus.

~ * ~

I invited Toby to dinner to celebrate. He brought his girlfriend, Chelsea.

Probably because I'd have said no, he hadn't asked me if he could bring her. He waltzed in, holding her hand.

I couldn't deny she was charming in a nerd-chic way. She had a high blonde ponytail and black frame glasses and was wearing a white button-up under a black sweater with boyfriend jeans and white canvas sneakers. He gazed at her adoringly. More importantly to me, she mooned over him at least as much.

"I hope you don't mind I'm here," she said. "Toby's so proud of you. He can't stop bragging about how talented you are. I hoped you might be willing to show me some of your work."

Well, hell. It was going to be difficult to stay mad at her if she was going to keep being nice. "Let's eat while the pizza's hot." I glared at him when she wasn't paying attention, but he smiled at me. He knew he'd already won.

We chatted through dinner, getting-to-know-you small-talk. She was easy and natural, and I kept forgetting I didn't like her. Chelsea loved photography, especially portrait photography. We bonded over Julia Margaret Cameron and her groundbreaking photographs of women and discussed the connection to the more modern work of Cindy Sherman. We laughed about how Toby couldn't cook. We discussed how much we loved old movies. She even loved Marilyn Monroe. Once we finished the pizza and moved on to the cake they'd brought, she asked me about the guys from Corporate.

He cleared his throat and made a slashing motion.

She flushed. "I'm sorry. Toby said you wouldn't want to talk about it. I got carried away because you're so easy to talk to."

I made myself smile. "No, it's fine. What are you curious about?"

She bit her lip. "Um… if it's not weird… I'm a big fan. A huge fan. Probably their biggest fan in the entire literal world. Can you tell me something about what it's like when they're not in the public eye and they're just hanging out together? I promise I won't tell anyone."

I didn't want to access that bank of memories because I was trying to keep them under lock and key. Then I reconsidered. What if I was giving them too much power? Maybe I needed to be able to casually mention them. This would be a chance to practice.

I said, "When there are no cameras or fans, they're …pretty much the same. They love having an audience—especially Jimmy. But they're just as happy in each other's company."

So far, so good. I cut Toby another piece of cake. I raised my eyebrows at Chelsea, asking if she wanted one, but she shook her head and put her hand over her plate. "They spend a lot of time writing music and then working on perfecting it. Jimmy always has a lyric book going, and Eric's usually playing a real instrument or some version of it on his laptop."

"Eric's my favorite," she whispered.

I smiled at her. "He's nice. Like, big-brother nice."

"I don't have big brother vibes for him at all." She and I laughed. Toby rolled his eyes.

"Anyway, yeah. Jimmy writes lyrics whenever something inspires him. He gets this dazed expression and reaches for his notebook. Then Eric puts a melody to it. If they like where it's going, they'll work on it during soundchecks."

"It must be magical to witness it happening in real-time," she said.

It hadn't seemed magical at the time, but it did when she said it. I nodded. "Yeah. Pretty much."

"Wow," she breathed.

I panicked for a moment. Did Jimmy know where his notebook was? The last time I'd seen it, it was in the back lounge, but what if an idea hit him and he couldn't—no. Not my problem to solve.

Her smile was full of awe. "I can't believe it. What a great job. Like, a real dream come true."

I gave a tight smile. "Sometimes. Should I make coffee?"

Chelsea covered my hand with hers. "I'm sorry. I'm sure it wasn't pure dream job. I'm sure it was a ton of work. People only think about the good things." She then cleared away the dishes like she'd been in our kitchen her whole life.

I *knew* I'd be better off not meeting her. She was so delightful she'd totally ruined all my distrust and resentment. Damn it.

I puttered around the kitchen when they left, wiping counters and sweeping the floor. That had been a side of Toby I'd never seen—a comfortable, sociable, cheerful Toby. He was thriving, and I was proud of him.

I was proud of myself too. I'd been able to talk about my past with Corporate. Although I'd only mentioned two of them. The one I didn't mention was every bit as integral to the songwriting process. The tempo was all him, and I'd seen him change a song's direction entirely by changing the pace. Anything they were working on was a rough draft until he got to it. I hadn't been able to bring myself to say his name, but I'd get there. I'd try it another time when I missed him less.

In the meantime, there was something I was going to have to do. Seeing the way Toby was thriving made it clearer than ever—I needed to make a call I didn't want to make. He was what mattered, and if someone else played a role in his happiness, no matter how goddamn minor it may have been and how *late it was in coming,* I was going to have to be the bigger person and acknowledge it.

I stared at the number on the refrigerator door and stalked out in a huff. I was going to take a shower. I would worry about it later.

Later, I needed to vacuum. I didn't want to make a call when the floor was filthy, for God's sake.

By the time I vacuumed, dusted, re-caulked around the tub, and painted the mailbox, it was getting late. Probably too late to call. I looked at the clock hopefully.

It was only 8:30.

Fine. Fine. *Fine!* I would call her. I put her number into my phone, marched to my room, and sat on the floor with my legs crossed, back against my bed, before I hit the call button.

She answered on the second ring. So much for my prayers for voicemail.

I cleared my throat nervously. "Hello, I'm calling for Susan."

"This is Susan." There was a pause, and then, "Willa?"

I was startled. I hadn't expected her to recognize my voice and had already been strategizing a way to back out. I'd been about to offer her a special one-time deal on a magazine subscription when she threw me off by saying my name.

"Um, yes. This is Willa."

"I, um, you caught me off guard. I'm not sure how to—uh, hi. It's nice to hear from you."

I picked at a spot on the hardwood floor of my room. Old nail polish spilled God knew how many years ago.

The silence stretched over the line until she said, "Is there something you wanted to talk to me about?"

This was a bad idea. Her voice was tearing me up.

After she left, I used to worry I'd bump into her. She'd relocated northwest of town, but it was always a possibility we could have ended up in the same store or something. Well into my teens, it lingered in my mind. What would I say if I ran into her? We hadn't crossed paths, but I'd never stopped listening for the sound of her voice. Kind of like how lately, any time I heard music, I braced myself in case Jimmy's voice came at me.

My own voice is low, a little hoarse. Dad used to say it's because I screamed so much as a baby, but I don't know if that's true or a story. My mom's voice was soft. Melodic. Comforting. At least, it used to be comforting until it went silent. For me, at least.

"I wanted to formally thank you for paying for Toby to go to school. It means a lot to him. I could have paid for it, of course." I paused and then admitted, "No, I couldn't have paid for it. I couldn't have made it happen for him by myself. He wanted to go, and he's happy. So, I wanted to thank you."

Another long pause—she was rattled. Finally, she said, "It was the least I could do."

I wrapped the anger around myself and felt safer. "Oh, not the least. The least you could have done was not abandon your baby when he was having surgery for cancer in his eye. That's probably the least you could have done, Susan. You could have *stayed*."

When I heard her indrawn breath, I cursed myself.

"Shit," I muttered. I let my head drop back against my headboard. I stared at the ceiling. "I'm sorry. I didn't call you to be an asshole, believe it or not. I really did want to say thank you."

"You have every right to be angry. If it matters, I kept in touch with your dad. He kept me up to date on how you were doing."

I laughed. "I wasn't okay. I'm still not. All I wanted was to tell you you're doing a good thing by helping Toby with school. I'm sorry for the other thing I said. I don't need to rehash anything with you."

She hesitated. I figured she was figuring this out as she went, and I wasn't making it easy for her. "I'm happy to help him. I'm happy to be building a relationship with him now. It's late, and not what it should have been, or could have been, but more than nothing. You've done a good job raising him, Willa. You should be proud."

"I am proud." I steadied my voice so she wouldn't be able to tell I was crying. "I'm proud of myself, and Toby, and Dad. We did fine. Before we go another twenty years without speaking, I want to ask one thing."

"All right."

"Why didn't you ever visit us after you left? You weren't even far. You could have—"

"I did come!" she said. "I was there so many times. You refused to have anything to do with me."

"Me?" I was surprised. "No, I didn't."

"Don't you remember? When I came to the house, you wouldn't even leave your room. Your dad forced you to get in my car once, but the way you screamed, we were afraid you were going to make yourself sick. We tried having me stay at the house and having your dad go somewhere else, but you locked yourself in the bathroom and refused to come out or even speak. You stayed in there until your dad got home."

"I don't remember that," I said suspiciously.

There was a memory teasing at the back of my mind, though. Falling asleep on the bathroom floor, then waking up and listening with my ear pressed against the door. Had I been in there to avoid her? I couldn't swear it hadn't happened.

"Why didn't you spend time with Toby?" I asked. "If your story is true, and I'm not saying I believe it, why did you punish him?"

"I didn't. Those years, when you were in second and third grade, I came over to get him when you were in school."

"Then you stopped?"

"I did," she said after a long pause. "He didn't like coming with me. He'd cry and ask for you, and I—yes. I stopped. He didn't want me, and your dad and I agreed it was probably doing more harm than good. So, we stopped."

"What about when Dad died? We never heard a word from you. You didn't even come to his *funeral*."

Her voice was gentle. "Did you want me to? I worried my being there would make it worse for you and your brother. Was I wrong?"

"I don't know!" I got up and paced. "Why are you asking me for answers? I don't understand why you—why you—how you could—we were *babies*."

I paused and swept my hair back away from my face. My voice was raw when I spoke again. "You were his mom. He asked for you in the hospital. Over and over. He was scared, and it hurt. He didn't understand what was happening, and you weren't there. I was terrified. I didn't want to leave him, but I didn't know how to make it better, and Dad was shattered. Why did you leave?"

Her breath caught. "There isn't anything I can say to make it okay for you," she said eventually.

"Try," I demanded.

I sensed her hesitation. I was asking the impossible, but I didn't care. I waited until she spoke. "When Toby got sick... I wasn't strong enough to handle it. I didn't have what it took. Moms are supposed to be able to fix everything, and I couldn't. I felt like such a failure, and I was scared all the time. And Bob was there, and I ... he didn't look to me to do the impossible. He made me feel like I was enough, like I was safe. When everything came apart—I couldn't do it. You guys needed me, but I wasn't strong enough, and I left. I wish I had a better answer for you, but that's the truth. It's that simple and that ugly. I couldn't cope, so I didn't."

"I don't forgive you," I whispered. "We needed you, and you left."

I hadn't forgiven myself, either, but that was different.

Her voice was uneven when she said, "I'm not asking you to forgive me. But if it's ever a possibility... I would like to see you."

"There's no reason for it. You weren't there when I needed you, and I don't need you now."

"Okay."

"Thank you for paying Toby's tuition. That's what I called for. Goodbye."

After I ended the call, I crawled into bed and curled up under my blankets with a pillow over my head.

I wanted to call Eric. He'd be able to reason through it with me.

Jimmy would say something outrageous and make me laugh.

Oliver could hold me.

Before I drifted off to sleep, it occurred to me that I'd claimed I couldn't understand how my mom could leave us. I'd said if she loved us, she'd have stayed... but sometimes maybe it wasn't completely black and white.

I told myself my situation was different. I wasn't like my mom. Jimmy wasn't my child. I left him, but it wasn't the same thing as a mother abandoning her children.

He was probably fine.

I reached for my phone. I'd just check. I'd skim their Twitter or Instagram, and—

No. I set my phone screen-down back on my nightstand.

I'd left. It was over. I was going to focus on my own life now, and everything was great.

Chapter Eighteen

A terrible chore awaited me the next morning: paying bills. To make it even worse, I hadn't been exactly organized. Some paperwork was in my room, there were stacks on the kitchen counter, random things crammed in pockets, and a pile of unopened mail on the table by the front door. I made a stack on the kitchen table, poured myself a whiskey for courage, and settled in at the table for a marathon session. I promised myself a second whiskey when I made it through the pile.

I sorted receipts to record and bills to pay. When I got to the folded-up paper, I flattened it and started skimming it before I realized what it was: the contract Jimmy sent Hope. I skimmed the document for a void stamp or an end date, but there wasn't one. I flipped through the pages until I came to the photo clause. It had a big "X" drawn through it. "Clause voided per Jimmy Standish," it said, with Hawk's initials. It was backdated to my first day with Jimmy.

I stared at it, processing what it could mean. Jimmy would probably have sworn to himself never to mention my name or think about me again, yet he did this for me. It felt like an apology.

I hadn't finished processing it when my phone buzzed with a text.

It was from Hope. *Go check your email. Then CALL ME.*

I powered up my laptop and opened the email Hope forwarded me, with the subject line: "FW: Photo Release for Willa Reynolds." The scanned attachments were standard releases, signed by Jimmy Standish and Benny Walker, making it even more explicit that I could sell the images I'd taken of the two of them together. Hope's message above was brief: *What do you have???*

I sent back an email with a few of the best images. About three seconds after I hit send, my phone rang.

"Holy fucking shit. How long have you had these? Do you realize what you've been sitting on?"

"Hi, Hope."

"Are you crying?"

I cleared my throat. "I'm fine."

"There's a Benny Walker story you haven't told me," she said. "I'm no leg expert, but I suspect those are your thighs those boys are between. Am I right?"

I felt my cheeks get warm. "Does it matter?"

"Not to me. You should come in and meet with Ken. I'm not the one who told you this but aim high. If he doesn't make you a good offer, shop them somewhere else. You have more?"

"Yeah. I have a lot."

"More of Jimmy?"

"More of all three of them. Jimmy, Eric. Oliver." I started to tell her I didn't have the right to those photos, then I realized I did. The contract was backdated—I owned the pictures I'd taken.

I owned every one of them.

"This is just off the top of my head," Hope said, "but Ken might want to run a feature on it. 'On the Road with Corporate,' or something. Pitch it to him. Aim for a special off-cycle edition, but don't settle for less than an eight-page insert." The dollar amount she named made my throat go dry.

I tossed back my whiskey when we hung up, then emailed Uncle Ken and scheduled a time to meet with him. Head spinning, I returned my attention to my bills and statements.

Then I got yet another shock.

My statements for the house, my second mortgage, both credit cards, and my car all showed lump payments and a zero balance. On top of that, my bank statement showed continuing weekly payments from Corporate. There must be a mistake because there were only the regular, smaller bills to pay—our phones, the electric bill, water, wireless internet. Even after I'd paid them, I was going to have a balance.

All those loans were through the same bank. They must have had a systems failure. The devil on my shoulder told me to run with it, but I wouldn't have any peace if I did. I was going to have to call and get it fixed, no matter how much I didn't want to.

Twenty minutes later, I had an answer. Sort of. It wasn't a mistake. Every cent of debt was paid. The guy I talked to on the phone wasn't able to tell me who, but he said I could come in next week and meet with the manager, who could possibly give me more information.

There was no need to meet with the manager. I had a pretty good idea of what had happened.

I did the math. It would be near the close of business hours in

England. I searched for the number and dialed before I lost my nerve. I needed to tell Hawk to stop paying me, first of all. Jimmy must not have hired a new assistant yet to take care of those details.

When he answered, I said, "Hawk, it's Willa Reynolds. I need to tell you—"

"Hello, love. Feeling a bit better, are you?"

I was wrong-footed already. "Uh, yes?"

"I've been worried sick." He was oozing sarcasm. "You might want to get yourself checked out. It's unusual to get dysentery on a tour of the United States. Crabs, maybe. Herpes is a guarantee. Dysentery is a first."

"Oh. Um—"

"Imagine how worried I was when Jimmy said you'd been hit so hard with it," he said. "Every time I called, you were back in the toilet."

I decided not to mention the salary; it seemed safest to play along for now. "Crazy, right? All kinds of things are coming back now that people don't vaccinate, ha ha."

"Why did you call?"

"I wanted to thank you for updating my contract."

"Mmhm." The skepticism was thick in his voice. "It's a bad idea, and I didn't want to do it, but Jimmy wouldn't shut up until I did. Whatever you kids are up to, get it sorted. I'll talk to you tomorrow."

I had no idea what was happening tomorrow, but my only strategy now was to get off the damn phone as fast as I could. "Have a great day, Hawk, byeeeee!"

I hung up before he could say anything else.

Leave it. Let it go. I didn't last for even a full minute.

I opened my laptop and went to their Instagram, ignoring the bills that slid off the table and onto the floor. I needed to see the boys. I expected to find the kind of casual, candid things they took with their phones. I wasn't prepared for what I found.

The first picture loaded slowly. There was Eric, in a mirror putting his own makeup on, in what must have been a deliberate recreation of the picture I'd taken of Jimmy in Hope's bathroom. Then I saw it: on the inside of Eric's wrist reflected in the mirror, printed in tiny backward letters: "Willa."

The next one was Jimmy at the table with a disposable white coffee cup. Once I could take my gaze off him, I noticed my name written on the cup. What the hell? What did it mean? Were they sending me a message? If so, what was the message? Writing my name was a weird way to prove they'd forgotten about me.

The next picture was Oliver. It was a close-up of him giving the camera side-eye and embodying the word "ornery." My name was nowhere to be seen. Okay. Whatever the message was, he was abstaining. Maybe he was angry. Or maybe not even. Oliver and I weren't from the same world. Not even the same universe. Our few stolen kisses meant a lot to me, but I had to be honest with myself. There was a lot less kissing in my past than his. What loomed large in my world might barely register in his. I couldn't tell what hurt more—him being angry with me or the idea that he didn't even care enough to be angry.

Next photo: Jimmy onstage with his arms open, embracing the crowd. His shirt was gaping open, hanging off his shoulders. "Willa" in large letters on his stomach.

There was one of the three of them sitting on a couch for an interview. Through the ripped-out hole of Eric's jeans, I spied my name written on his knee.

I kept scrolling. There were about twenty pictures of them with my name written on Jimmy or Eric or on something in the scene.

There were zero pictures of Oliver with my name anywhere near him. I didn't want to take it as a sign, but… it definitely felt like a sign.

It was a relief to get my eyes on them, but pictures weren't enough. I opened a search engine and clicked on a link to a news article announcing their social media was nominated for a major, well-publicized internet award, with me named as head artist. I was too frantic to react, but I stored it away. This award would get my name in front of industry people.

I found a headline that said they were going to be on a late-night show tomorrow in New York. I clicked on a link to an interview they'd done to promote it.

They were sitting in a row, wearing black jeans and shirts I recognized from having washed and folded them many times myself.

"I understand you guys are huge overseas," the reporter was saying. "Tell me how long you've been together and how you got—"

Jimmy took the microphone from her. "Listen, Mary," he said. "Can I call you Mary? Let's not worry about those boilerplate questions. Everyone already knows that anyway. Let's chat about whatever is on our minds. I'll go first. Hm, let's see. Oh, here's something. Have you ever met someone, like a new friend, say, and told them that once you make a decision, you never go back on it? Maybe she sees you write off a relationship completely and without regret, and then she reckons she can predict how you'll react in the future if the two of you have a row and get separated?"

"Um—"

Eric was to Jimmy's left, following along and nodding. Oliver was to his right, arms over his chest, eyes focused on something offscreen. I leaned closer to my screen.

"And *maybe*," Jimmy continued, elbowing Eric in the side, "maybe one of your best mates told her you'd write her off if things went wrong, even though he was not right to speak on your behalf about metaphysical connections he doesn't understand. Maybe he even took it upon himself to tell this new friend something from your past that has nothing to do with anything and was better off buried with everything else you don't like to think about."

Eric leaned toward the microphone. "I underestimated someone's 'personal growth.'" He didn't physically make air quotes, but they were implied.

Oliver hadn't moved apart from a twitch in his jaw.

Jimmy continued, "Perhaps the permanent break with a certain Frenchwoman who used to be your assistant only happened because she wasn't important to you *anyway*, and it was different because it was only sexual in nature and utterly trivial. Perhaps with this new person, this grown-ass woman who d*oesn't belong to you, and you know that*, you may have taken advantage of her, and put yourself first and refused to listen when she was trying to tell you something important. If all that happened, you might understand now that you were an absolute selfish shit. Maybe you're infinitely sorry, but you're *struggling not to use the stalkerware on her phone* to track her down because you mean to show her you're a new man who won't even attempt to control her, and also those apps smack of desperation, don't they? You shouldn't even use them on your siblings, in my personal opinion, which I have expressed previously. But if this friend wanted to *call you*, like *right away please God*, she should know she's very, very welcome to. Immediately upon seeing this interview, or any other interviews with similar content, because no matter how hard you're trying to respect her, give her the room to be her own grown-ass woman, you miss her *terribly* and won't be able to hold out forever. She could consider herself literally begged, at this point, to please, please call so you can apologize to her properly."

Mary blinked at him.

"Anyway, back to you. Yes, darling. Like you said. Massive in England, breaking in here in the States. Thanks so much for asking." He dazzled her with a smile, handed the microphone back to her, and mimed "call me" into the camera. Oliver gave a tiny sigh before the clip ended.

I immediately dialed my brother. When he answered, I said in a rush, "I want to go back. Do you mind, and can you check the house at least every few days? I'm going to fly out tonight if I can get a flight—"

"Whoa, whoa. Slow down. What is happening?"

I told him everything. Amended contract. Publishable, sellable photos. Money in the bank. Apologetic Jimmy. "They haven't even fired me. He's treading water with Hawk, hoping I'll come back, and I *want* to go back. I miss them, and he needs me. He hasn't even shaved his own face since I left. He has visible facial hair, Toby, and it takes him like three weeks to grow a five o'clock shadow, even. He's a wreck."

"Who?"

"Jimmy!" I shrieked.

"Okay, okay! What about your career?" he asked. "One job, photography, all that?"

"I don't know! I'll figure something out later," I promised. "Eric and Jimmy want me back! I need you to tell me you'll be okay if I go," I said. "Because—"

"That's two. What about the third?"

Oh, yes. The third.

The tall, gorgeous one with arms crossed over his chest, his expression stony.

I'd spent enough time studying Oliver's body language to read what he was trying to hide—he was furious. Absolutely seething. The clenched jaw, the tense muscles, his hands curled into fists. He couldn't even bring himself to be nice to the interviewer, and he was always nice to strangers.

Maybe I'd exaggerated what was between us. Maybe it mattered more to me than it did to him.

Or maybe it did matter to him—so much that he couldn't even bring himself to play nice for an interview on national television. It was an awful lot of anger for a woman who didn't mean anything to you.

"I'm not sure yet, but I'll handle it. I'm going, okay?"

"Yes. Yes. Go if you want to. I'll watch the house. Go." Toby paused. "If you're sure it's what you want. It's a real about-face, Willa. You've been so impulsive lately."

He was wrong. I'd been the *opposite* of impulsive. I'd been trying to convince myself to want what I thought I should want, and I'd almost missed this chance.

They weren't even my family. Why did taking care of them seem like the most important thing in the world?

I shrugged mentally. I didn't *know* why it did.

It just did.

"I'm sure, Toby," I said. "I'm sure, sure, sure. This is what I need to do."

"Okay, then. Get it. I'll keep an eye on the house. Call me when you get there."

I was shoving things in a bag while we talked. Just the basics because I'd left almost everything there.

I left as soon as I got off the phone with Toby. I was in a car on my way to the airport before I dialed the number for the band phone.

"Hello?"

My heart stopped. It was Oliver. That *voice*.

"Hi, um… it's me."

There was a long pause. "Who?"

"Willa."

Nothing.

"Willa Reynolds." He was an obnoxious man, and I couldn't believe I'd made it this long without his beautiful voice in my ear.

Sounding bored, he said, "Jimmy's not here."

"Oh, um, I was going to… where is he? Should I call his phone?"

"No. He's doing interviews. Then we're in rehearsals tonight. He won't be able to talk."

"Will you stop talking to me like this?"

"Like what?"

"Like you don't know me."

He made a scoffing sound. "I *don't* know you. I was wrong when I imagined I did."

"You weren't. You weren't wrong."

"It's fine. Not the first time I've misread someone. Not a mistake I'll make again, at least not with the same person."

It felt like a slap. It occurred to me maybe there was such a thing as too angry. Like, angry meant he cared. Then again, what if he wouldn't give me a chance to try to fix it? "I'm coming back. I'll be there before you go on tomorrow. I promise."

Silence.

He had hung up.

On me.

Oh, hell no. He wasn't going to shut me out. Maybe I'd—okay, for sure I'd made a mistake by walking away from him. I had to fix it. I needed to put myself in front of him. *Try to avoid me when I'm standing right there, Oliver.*

I wasn't sure he heard me say I was on my way, but I wasn't going to risk calling him again. I considered texting Jimmy, but it was probably better to show up. I was afraid he might have changed his mind.

If he didn't want me, I'd deal with it when I got there. I was going to face this head-on because I wasn't my mom. When things got hard, I would work to fix them instead of disappearing.

Everyone and their favorite inspirational throw pillow said the key was to "follow your dreams," and I had. I'd dreamed of being a photographer, and I'd set everything aside to make it happen. Now I was on my way. My work was going to be on the cover of a major magazine. I was probably going to get an insert or a special edition. I could take a job with Uncle Ken now because I'd proved myself to myself.

It wasn't enough.

I wanted to be an artist, and I wanted to take care of those boys. Was I going to be able to juggle it all? Maybe not. I hadn't managed it yet. I was going to give it a shot anyway. My work mattered to me. So did they. I'd built something with them that mattered, and I was going to go pick it back up if they'd let me.

First, I had to get there.

Drive faster.

~ * ~

When you need get somewhere immediately, you have to take whatever flights they can get you on. The first flight was fine, but when I got to the airport, my second flight was delayed.

Then delayed again.

It was delayed a third time. I sat in an uncomfortable airport chair, drinking sugary soda and doing the math in my head. If I was on a plane within twenty-five minutes and took the world's fastest cab and there was no New York traffic, I'd make it.

Finally, my plane was boarding. I rushed to the bathroom to pee one more time before getting on, and that's when it happened. As I was zipping my jeans, a splash came from behind me.

Oh God no. Please no.

I looked down.

At my phone.

In the toilet.

I almost went in after it; I really did. Then I decided I'd rather not have my fictional dysentery become real dysentery contracted from an airport toilet.

I got on the plane with no phone and only a long shot at making it to New York in time to keep my word to Oliver and start making things up to him.

Poor Jimmy was out there, probably assuming I'd seen those interviews, and I was ignoring him.

I crammed into a seat against the inside of the airplane wall. Not a window seat because people who get on last-minute flights don't get window seats.

The young woman who dropped into the seat next to me could have been nineteen, maybe, or twenty. She had blue hair, a triple-pierced nose, and a pink leather jacket. She also had a phone, because hers wasn't in a toilet.

"Hi." I gave her a hopeful smile. "This is going to sound weird from a random stranger, but I wonder if you could help me. I need directions for how to get somewhere when we land, and I dropped my phone in the—I mean, my phone doesn't have a charge. Could I possibly trouble you for a favor?"

She gave me a bland stare. "I know who you are. That's why I traded seats with the guy who was going to sit here."

"Um, what?"

"You're Jimmy Standish's assistant and Oliver Everett's girlfriend."

"Um, okay, this is weird. You're right about the first one. I'm Jimmy's assistant, but—"

"I'm right about both." Something about the way she chewed her gum came across as reproachful. "I saw you guys making out by the tour bus in the middle of the day. He'd been running and was sweaty but still gorgeous. He was wearing gray athletic pants, black Adidas, and a tour shirt from the tour before last. You were... there. Ringing a bell?"

"My name is Willa. It's nice to meet you, and also, it's rude to spy on someone's private moments."

She tilted her head and closed one eye. "Is it private? The outside of a tour bus?"

I needed her on my side. "Fair point."

"So tell me what happened. Why are you here instead of there?"

"It's complicated." I dropped my head back on the seat.

She made a point of checking the time. "We aren't going anywhere soon."

"If I tell you, will you let me borrow your phone?"

"I could maybe be persuaded if it's a good enough story," she said.

"You'd have to keep it to yourself."

"You'll have to trust me. The one with the cellphone is the one with the power." She waved her phone at me.

So I unloaded my tale of woe. When I got to the part about having to leave, I kept it high level. The last thing I needed was for the fandom to decide I'd betrayed Jimmy. There was nothing they wouldn't do for him. I didn't want to tell her anything to put him in a bad light. We deserve to keep our heroes pure in our minds. Or spectacularly impure, but in a good way.

When I was done, she held her hand out to shake. "I'm Zoe," she said, "and I'm happy to meet you, even though you must be insane. I can't believe you left the most brilliant songwriter of our generation, and I don't say that just because he's hot."

"Don't tell him this because his ego will get even more swollen than it already is, but he's luminous. He practically glows."

"It's true." She studied me for what seemed like a *very* long time, then said decisively, "I like you. Nobody's more surprised than I am, but there it is. I'm going to find someone who can pick you up at the airport because you'll never make it in a cab. I assume you're going to the studio where they're filming the Late Show, right?"

"How did you—"

"Number one fan. Of course I know where they are."

"Yeah, it's getting creepy again."

"So creepy you don't want me to help you?"

I shook my head. "No. Nope, not that creepy."

As soon as we landed and could reconnect to cell service, she went to work. I waited, impressed.

"Okay," she said when she surfaced. "A guy named Finn is going to meet you at baggage check. He'll take you to his girlfriend's car. She's Cate. She's going to rush you to the building. Seriously, you're going to have to haul ass. They go on in like fifty minutes. When you get there, they're not going to let you in just because you say you're Jimmy's assistant. Believe me, I've attempted it. But we found a guy who works there. Cate will take you to the back entrance, and he'll meet you there with a pass."

I put my hand on her arm. "Thank you so much. What strangely organized fans they have."

"Best fandom in the business," she said.

When we landed, she called out, "I got a puker back here, guys. Get her off the plane before she hurls."

I tried to look green as I shouldered my way to the front and dashed out in search of a guy named Finn and his girlfriend, Cate, who were going to take me to some rando at the back entrance of a venue in New York.

What could go wrong?

Chapter Nineteen

As promised, Finn met me at baggage check, and once he verified I was the correct desperate assistant, he rushed me to Cate's car. He and Cate drove me through the loud, congested New York traffic right to the venue's back door. There, a guy who introduced himself as Leon hustled me in after answering the door to what seemed like a needlessly complicated code knock.

He clipped a pass on my jacket, then took me through a maze of dim corridors to a green room door with a paper sign that said "Corporate." Before I processed that I was finally going to face the music, a voice came from behind Leon. "There she is, the woman herself! Wanda, we meet in the flesh. Finally."

I turned to face an attractive older man in a charcoal suit. Hawk.

"Oh, hello," I said, in a tone I hoped was nonchalant. "I was gone for a second doing a thing. No big deal. Got me a bit winded, but I'm fine. I need more cardio, I guess." Based on his stunned expression, I'd overshot nonchalant. I took a calming breath and tried again. "It's nice to meet you in person, Harvey."

We shook hands, and I opened the door in what I hoped was a confident manner, but I was afraid it was more like a weird robot.

The boys were on a dark blue sectional couch that dominated the room. Oliver was on the chaise section, head leaned back, tapping a beat on his leg. "Just leave it, Jimmy," he was saying. "There's no time to worry about it now, anyway."

He hadn't shaved in the past few days, at least, and it made him look different. Dangerous and—even though it was probably not his intent—hotter than normal.

His face was neutral when his eyes met mine. He didn't even flinch. It takes a lot of anger to have the discipline to show no reaction at all.

Jimmy was sitting between Oliver and Eric, holding his head in his hands. Eric was rubbing his back. "I don't understand," Jimmy said. "That useless app is giving me nothing. Did she take it off her phone? Is she sending me a message by going dark? Or maybe she's hurt! What if someone took her?"

"How would her being hurt or taken impact the app, mate?" Eric asked. "Think about what you're saying."

Oliver said, "She's right—"

Jimmy interrupted him with a groan. "I *promised* her if she was ever kidnapped, I'd get a down-on-his-luck—"

Oliver sat forward, touched Jimmy on the arm, and said, "Hello, Hawk, glad to see you." There was a pause before he could force himself to say my name. "Willa. Finally back from your... smoke break?"

Jimmy and I stared at each other for several beats. He leaped up, threw his arms around me, and clenched me tightly. "Oh, thank God."

I held on to him. He smelled like leather and our favorite hair product, and the familiarity of it was making it even harder not to cry.

His voice was muffled. "I'm sorry. I'm the worst. I'll do whatever it takes, Willa. I can fix it."

"What in the bloody hell—" Hawk started.

"Pull it together," Oliver said sharply to Jimmy.

Eric gave a hearty laugh. "She just went for a smoke break! Joined at the hip, these two," he said to Hawk. "You can't imagine the drama. They're like this all the time. Big emotional reunion after every parting. Come on, mate, time to be getting ready," he said to Jimmy. He gave Hawk an enthusiastic handshake and a clap on the back. "Glad you could join us."

I clung to Jimmy for another moment before I let him go. I tried to act like I had only been away for a few minutes, and everything was fine-just-fine. "Let's get your makeup finished, Jimmy," I said loudly. "I wasn't quite done."

It was already perfect, but we needed to step away from Hawk before we gave the whole thing away.

Jimmy led me to a counter with a big, lighted mirror. I perched on the counter, and he shoved a makeup brush in my hand. I peered over his shoulder and gave Eric a big smile. Still talking to Hawk, Eric gave me a thumbs-up and a wink. I stole another glance at the lovely, dead-eyed Oliver, then gave my full attention back to Jimmy.

He spoke quietly as I stroked the empty brush over his face.

"Did you see my interviews? Were you able to decode my secret messages to you? What took you so long to come back? Do you hate me now? Are you going to quit in person in a rage, or can you forgive me and work again? Did you get the contract and releases I sent Hope? Why did you take the stalker app off your phone? It disappeared, and I've been going mad trying to find you without it! Did you like our Instagram feed? Did you see you're nominated for a Webby award? Is Toby doing okay? Did you meet up with Benny? Did you sleep with him in spite of the fact we had an implied agreement that neither of us would have him without the other? If you did, was he as good as I frequently imagine he is? Were you working at the magazine again? Willa, why aren't you answering me?"

I laughed and held his face in my hands, resting my forehead against his. "Because you won't stop talking. Be quiet for a minute." When he was, I said, "I didn't come to quit in a rage, and I'm sorry I went dark on you, and I want to work with y'all, but we need to make some changes. You need to get ready for this performance right now, and we'll talk later, okay?" I gave him another squeeze. "I missed you all."

"Fucking hell, I missed you so much. Eric did too." I noted the omission and the implication that one of them hadn't missed me, but now wasn't the time to go into it. "Now the three of us are going to go charm America," Jimmy continued. "You stay back here and do assistant-y things in case Hawk is paying attention, because guess what, Willa? As far as he's concerned, you've been with me the whole time. Wait until you hear how cleverly I arranged it. If he found out you were gone, he'd make me hire someone else, but I didn't want someone else if there was a chance I could have you again. I do have one particular boy who was a distant plan B, but now you're here, it doesn't matter. It's for the best anyway because he's madly in love with me, and I never realized until you the benefits of an assistant who isn't."

"I do love you," I said.

He kissed my cheek. "I love you, darling, to a zillion infinity. But we're not in love, thank God."

"What time are they going to call you to go onstage?" I asked.

"I don't know, ask my assistant. Only she won't have an answer either," he said, raising his voice to be overheard, "because she has been outside, smoking like a chimney! Disgusting, Willa. It'll ruin your pretty teeth. Prematurely aging, as well. Your body is a temple, and you are defiling it."

He clapped his hands. "Ready, lads? They should be ready for us any—" There was a knock on the door. "Right this second," he amended. "Hawk, come watch us! Willa's going to stay here and get our stuff together. She's got makeup and hair products scattered everywhere. She's good at what she does, but she's messy."

I sank onto the couch when the door closed behind them. If there was a polar opposite to the empty quiet at my dad's house, it was wherever Jimmy Standish was. I was going to have to rebuild my sensory calluses.

I needed to have a conversation with him about boundaries, and it wasn't going to be easy—but it would be worth it.

I'd be able to handle him. I was more worried about Oliver. I tidied the green room, happy to have the familiar task to keep me busy.

Judging by everyone's moods after they came back off stage, the performance must have gone well. The boys were pleased, and Hawk's vibe was less angry than normal. I was half-afraid he was going to come back to the bus with us, but he had no interest whatsoever in hanging out. He congratulated them on their performance and then called a cab to get him to his hotel.

As the adrenaline of our reunion faded, the lack of sleep caught up with me. I was half-asleep by the time we made it back to the bus. Jimmy said, "Eric, you should let Willa have your bunk tonight. You can sleep on the back couch."

"Why?" Eric asked.

"Her bunk is trashed," Jimmy said. "It's filled with everyone's stuff, and she's too tired to clean it off tonight."

I yawned.

"See?" he appealed to Eric.

"It's filled with all *your* stuff," he said.

Jimmy didn't deny it. "I can't do anything about that, Eric. Be reasonable."

"She can have mine," Oliver said.

"Thank you," I said.

He shrugged. "I'd rather have the space anyway."

So much for the kind gesture. When I got settled into his bed, sleep didn't come right away. Jimmy and Eric's bunks were in total disorder, but Oliver's was neat. Sheets and blankets tucked in, pillow just so.

It was the best bunk in the house, but the delicious Oliver smell was distracting.

I had pictured him in this bed every night I'd been gone. Had he been thinking about me? Had there been room for anything other than anger?

Had he missed me?

He was only feet away from me, radiating angry vibes. He was close in distance but completely unreachable.

~ * ~

I was sure I'd never fall asleep, which was my last thought until morning.

"Willa!" Jimmy whispered loudly. "Wake up!"

"Not yet. In an hour. Promise."

"Willaaaaaaaaaaa."

I gave up and opened my eyes.

He was stretched out on his side, giving me mournful eyes. "You're probably going to give me a bollocking, Willa. I'm prepared. I deserve it. Go ahead."

"What on earth is a bollocking?"

"A *bollocking*," he said again.

"I don't—"

Eric jerked open his curtains. "A scolding! He means you can tear into him, and he's going to say he's sorry, and then we can get on with our lives. Just get it over with, Jimmy. You've definitely got this coming."

I leaned out of bed, hoping for a glimpse of Oliver in the back of the bus. There was less rage pulsing from back there, so he must have still been sleeping. I sighed and returned my attention to Jimmy. "All right. Let me get dressed. Are my clothes still in the—"

He grabbed his phone and pretended to be absorbed by something on it. "Hm? Oh, let's go get you some new things, Willa! For no reason at all. It'll be fun."

"We don't need to shop. I left everything here."

"Oh, um, well, maybe for a special treat, we could buy you more everything! For no real reason at all, there's nothing we need to discuss."

"Jimmy, did you throw away my clothes?"

"I was upset! Maybe I wept over them, and they're ruined from the salt of my tears. Or maybe I threw every single thing out the windows of the bus somewhere in America's heartland. The particulars aren't important."

"We haven't reconciled yet. We have to have a real talk. Soon."

I definitely didn't want to have that talk in front of Oliver. I got to work cleaning, avoiding the back of the bus completely, apart from a quick peek to check if he was awake.

He must have sensed my gaze because he turned away from me and put a pillow over his head. I had to give credit where it was due. The man was good at a nonverbal "fuck you."

Eric caught my eye and gave me a sympathetic smile. "You've got some messes to clean, Willa."

He meant more than the state of the bus.

Chapter Twenty

When we got to the arena, Eric said to Oliver, "Should we go in? Knock about and get a feel for the place?" I wasn't sure if Eric was trying to give Jimmy and me space to talk or if he intended to give Oliver space from me.

I chanced a peek at him and immediately wished I hadn't. Before I'd left, Oliver always had an adorable almost smile for me, like it made him happy to put his eyes on me. Now whenever I accidentally caught his eye, he grimaced a bit, like I was something distasteful but not quite gross enough to get really riled up about. It was a specific, unpleasant expression to be on the receiving end of.

"Yeah, I got it," I said to him under my breath. He made a "pshh" sound like I was speaking gibberish he couldn't be bothered to decipher.

One thing at a time. First, the easiest one. I put a hand on Eric's arm before he left. "Hey, are we cool?"

His green eyes met mine, and he gave me a reassuring smile. "Oh yeah. I missed you. I'm glad you're back." He leaned closer and whispered, "Good luck with the other two."

It was going to take longer to fix things with Jimmy, but he was sorry and adorable, and I was pretty sure we'd get there. When the door closed behind Eric and Oliver, I poured two mugs of coffee and set them on the table. "Let's talk, Jimmy."

His shoulders slumped, then he squared them. "All right. Time for the bollocking. I will face it, Willa! Bravely, like I do everything, and also because I owe you this." We sat facing each other.

"We need to have a conversation about what happened so we can make sure it doesn't ever happen again."

"Can I go first?" When I nodded, he said, "I'm sorry I acted like I did. I didn't realize how terrible it was until you left, and it's inexcusable. It would have been wrong if I was only your employer. I owed you time off, and I'd promised to fix your contract and never did.

But I'm not just your employer. I'm your friend. As a friend, what I did was even worse. I made it impossible for you to stay with us and pursue your own goals at the same time after you'd been patient with me. I wanted you at Red Rocks, so I tried to bully you into it and keep you from something important to you, and that was some spoiled-toddler-level shit. There's no excuse for it. I owed you better."

He paused to drink his coffee. He scooted my mug toward me.

I was speechless, so he continued, his voice uneven. "I will fuck up again, Willa. I'm not good at relationships. Eric and Oliver are the only two healthy friendships I've ever had, and my track record with them is not flawless, but I can do better. I thought I'd ruined this relationship forever. I'm well-aware of lucky I am to have you back here to give me another chance."

He stopped again and peered at me over his mug. "Are you going to participate in this at all, darling?"

"Um, you're doing quite a good job on your own, truth be told."

"That's all I have for now. I love you. I'm sorry. I've only ever been close to one other woman, Willa, besides my mum, and things did not end well with her. I want to do better with you."

I took a moment to gather my thoughts. I presumed I was going to have to steer this conversation, and now I was off track. I should have known Jimmy wouldn't be predictable.

Finally, I said, "I took this job with you because I needed the money, I needed a change, and I wanted to work on my portfolio." I smiled at him. "And I really liked you, right away. The more time we spent together, the more I realized... I love taking care of you. I want to be an artist, and I have things to say and things I want to do that have nothing to do with you. That's true, but I missed this job, and I missed you guys."

I studied my hands and considered how to proceed. "You let me down, Jimmy. You blocked me intentionally from a great opportunity. That's not just a shitty thing to do as my 'boss.' It hurt so much because, like you said, we're friends."

He covered my hands with his and, surprisingly, didn't interrupt. "It's a difficult dynamic," I said. "But it's worth it. How about if we put our cards on the table, establish some boundaries, and give it another shot?"

His smile was radiant. "Yes, cards on the table. Go." He set his mug to the side and gave me his full attention.

"I want to work with you for now."

"Back home, too? After the States, we have a few more shows in England. Even after the tour, I'll still need an assistant, won't I?"

"I could finish this tour like we initially said. But I won't do this forever," I said. "This isn't my long-term goal."

He nodded. "You have your own dreams, and they're more than working with us."

"This is what I want for right now, if we can do it in a healthier way."

"We can," he said confidently. "I'll be good at boundaries once I set my mind to it. I've just never tried. Name your terms."

"Okay. I've thought about it a lot, and this is what I need. I get time off for myself, every single day. At least four hours, and it belongs to me."

He slapped a hand on the table. "Done. What else?"

I sat straighter. "I don't owe you this. If you treat me like that again, I will leave. As much as I care about you, I'm not obligated to give you anything other than the work you're paying me for."

"Right."

"If there comes another time when I need time off for something, I'm going to need you to be a whole lot more open to it than you were this time."

"Got it," he said. "What else?"

This was a lot easier than I'd expected. I was running out of demands. "Now you. Tell me something you need."

"I want you to be honest with me," he said.

"I am honest with you!"

He raised his eyebrows. "Oh, good. Let's go. Are you in love with Oliver?"

"I—"

"Are you going to be honest with me now? I'm asking you as your friend, not the person you work for."

I was asking a lot of Jimmy. He was only asking me to be honest with him.

To do that, I was going to have to be honest with myself.

I let out a breath. "Yes. Maybe. Probably. Or maybe not. It's more than a strong like, at least. I didn't mean for it to happen, but it did."

"I know that how you feel about someone else isn't my business, on the one hand. I get it. But he's my best friend, and you're my Willa. You guys both shut me out."

I hadn't considered it from that angle. "I can understand why it would hurt you to have one or both of us keep something from you. I was focused on convincing myself I wasn't falling for him, though. So I didn't want to talk about it."

He started to speak a few times, then cut himself off, searching for the right words. It made sense—this was new to us. We were discussing things I'd hardly been able to acknowledge in the privacy of my own mind.

He got up to make us both more coffee. When he sat again, he said, "I know it's hard. We were careful to not talk about this, and it's partly how we got here. We have to push past it. Whatever you guys are, it happened right under my nose. You both kept secrets from me."

I squirmed. He was partly right—but only partly. "My love life and my theoretical sex life are none of your business. That's a boundary. We're going to put some in place. Unless you're the one I'm having sex with, the whole topic is off-limits."

He wrinkled his nose. "Ew, Willa. Now you've crossed my boundaries. I don't want to have sex with you, but I don't want you to have sex with Oliver because then you'll both love each other more than you love me."

"Jimmy, I'm eventually, hopefully, going to have sex with someone. It isn't going to make me care any less about you. Those two things are totally separate from each other."

He glanced out the window. "I understand I have to accept it, but also I hate it."

"No, look at me," I insisted. "Listen, because this matters. You and I aren't ever going to be that for each other, right?"

He rolled his eyes, like *yeah, I know.*

"So you can't begrudge me having a romantic relationship with someone else. It's the same theme. You don't want me to do photography because you want all my attention and time. You don't want me to fall in love with someone else because of what it would mean to *you.* This can't work that way."

He slumped back in his seat, defeated but frustrated. "You're right. I want you to be happy, and it's not up to me to draw lines around it."

I smiled at him. "Good job, Jimmy. Now another thing. Sometimes I'm going to wear colors. I love colors."

He gasped and put a hand on his heart. "Willa! You are killing me, but fine. Colors, if you must. Unless we're on band business, then you have to be in aesthetic. Okay?"

"Deal!" I said.

"Ugh. What's next?"

"Less touching."

"What? No! I'm a physical person, Willa! With everyone. I don't do it to impose myself on you. I had no idea you minded."

"No, I don't! It doesn't bother me, Jimmy. You're a nice snuggler. Nevertheless, now that there's a man in the vicinity with whom I might eventually—"

He held up his hands to stop me. "All right! Don't keep saying it. Duly noted. Not quite as much touching. I guess I can occasionally shake your hand. Or perhaps a high-five on Tuesdays and Thursdays?"

"Stop. I'm just saying, like, less kissing, and let's not sleep together anymore."

"I like sleeping with you," he said mournfully. "You're so soft and warm."

"I love to sleep with you, but it's probably weird. I don't have any other friends I sleep with."

"You don't have any other friends like me, so that's a useless point. But listen." He gave me a conspiratorial grin. "I'm going to tell you something that's not my business or yours. Oliver hates it when I sleep with you," he said, somewhat giddily.

"He doesn't mind," I disagreed.

"Oh yes, he certainly does!" Jimmy said. "He haaaaaaaaaates it. He hides it from you, but he has this expression like, 'Get off my girl, mate,' which is funny since you're not his girl. Except in his mind, you are. Or you were. Maybe not now."

"Is he mad?"

"Certainly not. He's not that far gone. He's entirely sane."

"I mean pissed."

Jimmy shook his head. "It's morning. He hasn't had a drop to drink."

"I mean angry!"

"I'm only kidding, Willa. I've gotten good at interpreting your Americanisms. Yeah, he's angry. Good luck bringing him around. If you even want to! It's none of my business. Let's change the subject."

"Gladly." I took our mugs to the sink.

He sat on the counter next to me and kept me company as I washed our mugs and tackled the backlog of dishes. Jimmy brought me up to speed on the Red Rocks debacle. He hadn't lost his voice and hadn't slept with the keyboard player *or* the vocalist, but it was "a very close call," whatever that meant.

"After we go shopping, I'll do bills." I put the last of the dishes on the strainer and dried my hands. "I assume you haven't—oh! One more thing! I logged in to my bank account, and—"

"Oh, wow." He hopped off the counter and pointed out the window. "The sun is coming out."

I tugged on his arm until he returned his attention to me. "Jimmy.

Did you pay off my… everything?"

"Do we have to discuss this?"

"Yes."

"I don't want to, darling. Let's not. What should I wear when we go shopping?" He rifled through the clothes piled at the foot of his bunk. "Should I wear these jeans?"

"They're identical to your other black jeans, and they're fine. Talk to me." I sat on his bed.

"Are you going to be weird? Don't waste your time. I did it, and it's done."

"We have to talk about this. Sit down."

He sat on Oliver's bunk, facing me. "I'll sit, but there's not much to say. I wanted to, so I did. The end."

"Not the end," I insisted. "It was a lot of money, and it's going to take me a long time to pay you back, but I will."

"You most definitely will not!"

"Jimmy—"

"No, Willa. Stop it. I have compromised a lot this morning."

"Yeah, but I can't allow you to—"

"I can't allow you to not allow me to. I can afford it. It's done."

"But I—"

He leaned forward and put a hand on my knee. "Do you like not being in debt?"

"Uh, yeah. But—"

"Good. Can you please drop it?"

I could not drop it. I needed to know the answer. "Did you think you needed to buy me?."

He captured my hands and held them. "I bought myself the peace of mind of knowing if you're with me, it's because you want to be, not because you can't afford not to be. If we have another fight, not that we'll have another big one because I'm sure we won't, but if we did and you left, at least I wouldn't have to imagine you and Toby losing your house or declaring bankruptcy or something. I did it purely to soothe my own conscience and to make it easier for me not to worry. Completely selfish like everything else I do. Don't make more of it than it is."

I swallowed past the lump in my throat and squeezed his hands. "You paid off every red cent of my debt because you're selfish."

"That's it exactly!" he said cheerfully. "It's about me."

My eyes filled with tears. "I think you did it because you love me, and you wanted to help me even when you couldn't find me."

He gave me his fake-amazed expression. "Then wouldn't you be an ungrateful cow to suggest you're going to pay me back? Appalling.

The only proper thing to do would be to say thank you and drop it forever." He shook his head. "Now stop it. No crying. You're going to make me cry, and my eyes will get puffy."

I released his hands and wiped my face. "I won't cry, but listen."

"I'm listening, but you are crying."

"You can't imagine what it means to have the weight of it gone. Thank you."

"Well, don't get too carefree. I'm bringing you back to a challenging job with a trio of men who need a lot of attention. One of us is a diva, I won't say who, and one of us is going to make life difficult for you, at least for a bit—that one is Oliver. And seriously, this bus is disgusting. You're going to be busy, Willa. Those other two live like pigs when they don't have any supervision. Oh! The pictures!"

"The pictures!" I said. "Was that your idea?"

"It was Eric's. Did you sell them?"

"My uncle bought them, and they're doing a special insert. It's going to be amazing. I'm so excited!"

"What did you do with the money?"

"I opened a savings account!"

He slumped in disappointment. "A savings account isn't very glamorous."

"You don't understand, Jimmy. I'm in the black. That has never been the case in my entire life."

He brightened and smiled at me. "How's it feel?"

"Good!" I said. "So, so good."

~ * ~

Jimmy was a new man.

Sort of. A lot of the time.

He tried.

I needed to remind him sometimes. Like the time I met with Hope for drinks in Boston, and he followed me "in disguise." I reminded him I was on my four-hour break and sent him back to the bus.

When we were in Florida, I did a photo shoot with a folky, acoustic band called County Fair. They were playing in a brewery with an event barn. It was Uncle Ken's idea. At best, it'd be a small review article. Still, it wasn't nothing, and I needed these opportunities to keep my foot in the door.

Jimmy attempted to stop me. "Willa, I know we agreed you could work on other things sometimes, but we couldn't have foreseen you'd get a gig… on a night I… on a night I had a migraine coming on."

"You're not getting a migraine," I said.

"He could be," Eric said. "He's quite accomplished at getting inconvenient disorders."

"Giving them, too. I say that as someone he's assigned dysentery to."

From the back of the bus, Oliver made a sound that sounded suspiciously like a laugh.

We were frozen with surprise for a moment. When I came back to myself, I said to Jimmy, "Remember we agreed? Sometimes you're going to need to let me do things even when you don't want to."

"I'll take some ibuprofen," he said glumly. "Have a good time."

"Drink some water, and call me if it gets worse."

It wasn't perfect, but he was doing his best. Like any other relationship worth having, we had to work at it.

The Oliver situation, on the other hand, wasn't getting better. He completely shut me out. He didn't even talk to me when I did his hair and makeup. He sat there like a big, pretty, angry statue. A warm, fragrant, super-hot, angry statue.

"Willa, I love Oliver," Eric said, dropping on the couch next to me. "I do."

We were in the green room, and I'd just gotten Oliver ready. He'd stalked out the second I was finished, and I sank into the couch, dejected.

I sighed. "Everybody does. Because he's the most lovable of anyone."

"I hate that he's struggling," Eric continued.

"So do I! I want to apologize, but he won't even let me get started. I'm at a complete loss."

"Jimmy, c'mere, help me out," Eric said.

Jimmy stopped admiring himself in the mirror and sat at my other side. "Willa needs to force Oliver's hand," Eric said to him, talking over my head. "This is getting ridiculous. He's being stubborn, and now he's hurting both of them with it."

Jimmy shrugged. "It is none of my business at all, Eric. I don't even have an opinion on it. Boundaries. Right, Willa?"

"Yes!" I said. "Nicely done, Jimmy."

He pointed at me and winked. "See? I'm learning."

"Yes," I said, fidgeting with the hem of my shirt. "Yes, you are, and I appreciate it." I paused. "It's only that in this particular circumstance, I'm at a loss, and—"

He dropped his head back on his shoulders and blew out a gusty sigh. "Oh my God, I thought you were never going to ask me. Who knows Oliver better than Eric and me? Nobody. Literally. Not even his own mother. We are uniquely qualified to give you advice, and I have been absolutely dying for you to ask. You could have already bagged that if you'd only asked sooner. Right, Eric? Because Oliver is gagging for it. Gagging. For. It. He needs the right shove so you guys can get past this and be together, and you'll both be happy. So will I, and I know that's not the point, but this is much worse than when you were both dancing around it. I woke up this morning, sure I was suffocating, and then I realized, no, I'm only choking on sexual tension. You could *fix this* if you would *focus*, Willa!"

I blinked. "Wow. Okay, one, we're not talking about anyone gagging or bagging. I just want him to *talk* to me. Two, you are vastly overestimating his opinion of me. Three, we agreed you had enough coffee for the day."

"I just finished what was in the pot, and there was hardly any in there. Focus, darling." He patted my knee. "You've come to Uncle Jimmy and Uncle Eric for advice, and now we're going to give it to you."

I shook my head. "Well, now I'm reconsider—"

Jimmy covered my mouth with his hand. "No take-backs. Quickly, Eric. Go."

"More short skirts, Will. He definitely noticed your black skirt the other day. We need him to look at you in spite of how determined he is not to. You need to get under his skin."

Jimmy was impressed. With himself. "All your talk about choosing your own clothes, but who was it who chose the skirt? Was it you? No. It was not. Let's keep going. Wear your leather pants. Oliver loves leather pants."

"They're kind of uncomfortable—"

"Oh, sorry," he interrupted. "I thought we were discussing how to help you help Oliver stop being miserable! Are we talking comfort? Get your granny nightgown back on then, darling. By all means. Wait. Only you can't because I threw it away when you were gone! It was the first thing out the mother*fucking* window, Willa, and I regret nothing!" He paused. "All right. That was a bit much. Why didn't you dump the rest of the coffee? I'm always going to drink it if you leave it there. This is on you."

Eric said, "Maybe walk with a bit more wiggle. Or, like, flip your hair around? Drop something and spend a long time leaning over to pick it up? I don't know what tricks girls—I mean women—get up to. Just do whatever you can do to catch his eye. He stares at you when you're not paying attention. Maximize that."

"Right! Channel your inner Marilyn, Willa." Jimmy said. "He's as good at being stubborn as he is at everything else. The only thing that can override him is himself. You need to rouse his animal nature. You know how to do it."

I was struggling to keep up. "Yes? I do?"

"Why are you saying it like you're asking?" Jimmy frowned at me. "It's not a question. Yes, you do."

"Okay?"

"Definitely!" he insisted.

I fiddled with my shirt some more. "All right."

"Why are you acting like you have no idea what to do? Do what you did to Benny Walker."

"I didn't do anything! Benny wanted you. I was the equivalent of slop on the pool table."

"Other way round, darling," Jimmy said. "I was the slop. And believe me, it was a first."

"False. You were the target."

He smiled at me. "You're adorable, because you're clueless. It's good you have Eric and me, yeah?"

"Is it? I'm not sure any of this is helpful, actually."

He gave me a disapproving frown. "You need to loosen up. For a cowgirl, you're incredibly uptight. That's all I'm saying."

"I doubt very much it's all you're saying," I said. "It never, ever is."

"How can you expect—"

"See?"

"—things to change if you're not going to do anything differently? You must understand that."

Oliver came in then, and when he noticed I was in the room, his face went blank. When he thought it was just the boys, his expression was neutral. When he saw me, he turned to stone.

Something snapped in me. It was the moment the guilt evaporated, and I decided to force his hand.

I didn't need advice from those two well-meaning, misguided boys.

I knew what Oliver liked, and it wasn't leather pants or wiggly walks.

It was Just Willa.

Chapter Twenty-One

Once I remembered what Oliver liked about me, I set a new strategy.

The next night when he came in, I was in the back lounge with a blanket, a glass of wine, and a book. I had washed my face clean; my hair was in a sloppy bun, and I wore a T-shirt and leggings.

He stopped in his tracks and stared at me for a moment. His face softened before he caught himself. He doubled down on his mean face, but he'd already tipped his hand. I was on the right track.

He stayed in his bunk with the curtains closed tightly, but it was fine. I could handle baby steps as long as they were in the right direction. On Wednesday, he did a double-take before Mean Face slammed down.

On Thursday, he actually sat on the couch next to me while I stared unseeingly at a book. His laptop was open, and he wasn't speaking to me, but he was there. He was skittish, but since I didn't make any sudden movements, he stayed there until I went to bed.

A few hours later, I was startled awake when the bus stopped. I peeked out the window, and I was confronted with a gorgeous, empty beach. Waves were crashing on the sand. It could have been a movie set.

"Where are we?" I whispered to Tucker.

"Rest stop," she muttered before climbing into her bunk. She was a woman of few words. I could respect that.

It certainly didn't look like any rest stop I'd ever seen, but if there was time, there was something I wanted to do. I dressed quickly and rushed outside.

I ran down the sand until I was close to the water, then sat to watch the way the moonlight's reflection swelled and scattered with every breaking wave. It was mesmerizing.

I felt more than heard the footsteps behind me: Oliver. Being on a moonlit beach with him would have been the most romantic thing in the world if things weren't painful and awkward between us.

He sat in the sand next to me.

"Did you ask Tucker to stop for me?" He was the only one who would have.

I'd told him about how it was when Toby was first diagnosed. We had a dream family vacation planned... Disney World and a week in an oceanfront condo. My parents started saving for it before Toby was born, but then he got sick, mom left, and everything in my family changed forever.

"Yes."

"Even though you're angry?"

His voice was chilly. "I'm not angry. Things have changed, that's all."

If it was true, it would have been even worse, but I didn't believe him.

He gave an exaggerated gesture toward the waves. "Don't you want to go in the water?"

I shook my head. "I'll just enjoy the view."

His voice had a new edge to it when he spoke again. "You've never been in the ocean, Willa. Don't you want to?"

I shrugged.

"You said you wanted to do it. Here you are. Now—what? Nothing? You're going to change your mind for no reason? Turn your back on what you said you wanted?"

"It's not for no reason," I said, stung. "I'm scared, but I'm here. I'm just not going all the way in."

"Being scared is a stupid excuse. Everybody's scared."

We weren't talking about the water anymore. "I'm sorry, Oliver. I know I hurt you by leaving, and I should have called or messaged you while I was gone." I crossed my legs and scooped small handfuls of sand, letting it run between my fingers as I talked. "I told myself that by making a clean break, I was respecting the relationship you have with Jimmy. Like, refusing to put you in the middle or make it awkward for you. Or that I was ripping the bandage off instead of letting things go on to be more painful later. I was just letting myself off the hook. The truth is I didn't call because I was afraid."

"Of me?"

"Of how I feel about you. Felt. Feel. Whatever." I paused. "I hate it when you look at me like you have been since I came back."

"Fine. I lied. I'm angry." His jaw clenched, and he stared at the water, giving me nothing, not even his mean face. "Why are you scared?"

I wrapped my arms around my knees and hugged my legs to my chest. "You don't know me in my real life. This thing I'm doing with you? This isn't how I am."

"Keep going," he said, his impatience obvious. "What does that mean?"

"I'm not like Jimmy. I don't bond with people like he does. I'm close to Toby. Somewhat close to my uncle. Hope Harper is my friend. That's it. I worked at the same coffee shop for years. I haven't thought about my coworkers once since I left there. It never even occurred to me to keep in touch with any of them."

"Nobody is like Jimmy. It's a ridiculous comparison."

"Fair. Okay, I'm a look-before-you-leap kind of girl. No, not even. I'm a don't-leap-at-all kind of girl."

"It sounds like there's a 'but.' If we're gonna have this conversation, keep going. Don't keep making me prompt you. I don't have the patience for it."

Uh, obviously. "I'm trying! I met Jimmy, and I loved him right away. I met Eric, and he was funny and sweet, and I liked him right away. With you it was… there wasn't time to process it. My emotions got too big too fast, and I haven't ever experienced anything like that. It didn't make sense. The more time I spent with you, the more overwhelmed I was. It was scary."

He turned my face toward him. He was intense and frustrated with me, but I wanted to lean into his hand. I wanted to crawl into his lap and show him how much I wanted to stop talking.

"I need you to tell me, Willa," he said.

"This is hard!"

"You know what else was hard? To let it sink in that you weren't coming back. It was hard to believe feeling the way we did—or I felt the way I did, at least—you could leave like you did when the situation was totally salvageable. You could have come back. He wanted you to come back. You took your sweet time, and you never called me, or texted, or emailed, or did anything to suggest I'd ever meant anything to you. So *keep fucking talking*. Why are you scared?"

I got to my feet. "Because this isn't a crush anymore! I'm not just attracted to the way you sound and your appearance and the way you are. I don't just want you. It's so much more. I'm calmer when you're with me. When you're not with me, I wish you were. When I wake up, you're in my head. That's what it's like when I'm here, and how it was when I was at home. Me and my mom—a thing happened, and it hurt, and I wanted you. That's more than an attraction. It feels a lot like falling in love, and I'm not brave enough to do that."

He stood, too, and stepped toward me. "This isn't how I am either, for the record. This angry, grudge-holding guy? This isn't me.

The lads had no idea what to do with me. I couldn't *believe* you were gone. I would never have left you without a word. I assumed what we had mattered to you because it mattered to me, but you bailed."

I stomped a foot in the sand. "It doesn't mean it wasn't real, or it didn't matter to me! It means you're *braver* than I am. That's all."

"No, it isn't all," he insisted. "Because brave implies a choice. I can't get you out of my head no matter what I do." He ran a hand through his hair, turned away from me, and then turned back. "When you were gone, I tried to force you from my mind. Even now you're back, I almost wish I could. Because this is terrible."

He walked away from me. The breaking waves echoed in the silence between us.

He cursed quietly to himself, and he came back to me. "This isn't done. I can't stop. I am constantly fighting to keep my mind off you. The whole day, I'm aware of exactly where you are and what you're doing. All night, you're right there. If you roll over in your bunk, I can feel it. If you sigh in your sleep, I can hear you, and I can't stop wondering what you're dreaming and if you're warm enough or want another pillow. I worry that your fucking feet are cold because Jimmy won't let you sleep with your socks on and you've stopped sleeping with him because you guys convinced yourselves I care. It's fucking ridiculous."

He clenched and unclenched his fists. When he spoke again, his voice was quieter but hoarse. "When you left the bus tonight, I promised myself I wasn't going to follow you, but I couldn't help it. Most of me doesn't want to let you back in, but I'm not sure I'm going to win the battle with myself. You're not the only one who's scared, Willa. I'm scared of what it means if I can't get you out of my head. I'm scared to take a chance on you when I'm not sure you're tough enough for it."

"I'm sorry," I said again. I put a hand on his arm. "I came back. Does that make a difference?"

He didn't shrug off my touch, which was a good sign. I let my hand run up his arm and back down. I captured his hand. He allowed it, but he didn't come closer, and he didn't touch me. All I got was the barest curling of his fingers around mine.

"You came back for Jimmy."

I shook my head. "I came back for me. It's what I wanted. I haven't ever had this kind of... I fit with you guys, differently and better than I fit anywhere else. I wanted that back, and I'm glad I have it. Even when you're twenty feet away, glaring at me ferociously, at least we're in the same room."

He dropped my hand and went to the surf and let the waves wash over his feet. Eventually, he came back to me and sat back in the sand again. "I didn't handle it well when you left. Drank a lot. Was a real prick to everyone. Eric said I should get laid. He said it the whole time you were gone."

My stomach churned. "Is that what you want to do?"

"Yes," he snapped. Then he sighed. He looked at the sky. "No. But it *would* be nice to stop thinking for a while."

"I hate Eric." The two-timing bastard.

The ghost of a smile. "You do not. He stopped saying it once I told him I'd talked to you anyway."

He was silent, watching the waves. "Even if you needed to go, you shouldn't have done it the way you did," he said. "You kissed me, in broad daylight, not a sneaky, stolen thing. You let me believe we were building something real, and then you disappeared. Why should I trust you now? If I even can."

Fair. I understood the need to close the door on someone who'd left you, but I wasn't ready to give up. "I'm going to stay for now, but this isn't my real life. My future isn't with you guys. I want to be a photographer, and I can't be if I'm tied to Corporate. The way I feel about you, whether it goes somewhere or not, it can't be permanent. Our worlds aren't the same. There are so many reasons this is a bad idea. But I... I like you. A lot."

He was turned away from me again, staring at the water.

I touched his arm. "Oliver."

"I wasn't asking you for forever, Willa. I wanted a right-then."

That brought us to the only important question. "Do you want a right-now?"

He didn't answer me. He stood and pulled off his shirt. "Come on."

"What?" I asked nervously.

He stepped out of his pants, and there he was in his only-wearing-boxer-briefs glory, and I was briefly distracted. Overwhelmed by the sight of his skin, and the shadows and curves of his muscles... it was getting harder to keep my mind clear, but a lot hinged on this moment.

He offered me a hand. "Let's go in the water."

"I'm scared," I said.

"I know you are. Do it anyway."

I wanted to take the hand Oliver was offering me. It was important. He was trusting me enough to do this with him. That didn't take the fear away. Ocean... big, scary, dark... those things were true.

"I want to," I said, willing him to understand. "I'm just not sure it's safe."

"What are you scared of?" he asked softly.

"I could get a cramp—"

"I'll hold on to you," he said. "I won't let you go under, Willa."

"You could get a cramp—"

"Then hold on to me. Don't let me go under."

"A shark could come—"

"We'll punch it."

"A jellyfish could sting me."

"I'll kiss it better."

I perked up a bit. "Really?"

His lips curved. "Promise."

I covered my face with my hands. "Oh God. I don't want to say no to you when you're being nice and mostly naked."

"Come in with me, Willa. Don't miss this chance."

He waited with his hand outstretched.

When I put my hand in his, he pulled me to my feet. "We're going to do this?" he asked.

"We're going to do this." I took my shirt off.

Of all the lingerie I'd bought with Jimmy's money, this simple black bra was probably the tamest. Judging by Oliver's heated gaze, it was good enough.

I unsnapped and unzipped my shorts and shimmied out of them.

His gaze was hot on my body. "I like your tattoo," he said.

"Thank you."

"I mean, I like it a *lot*."

I glanced at the black, blue, and purple flowers blooming across my hip. He ran his fingers over it, giving me shivers.

I grabbed his left hand and turned it palm up so I could see the big tattoo on the inside of his forearm. "This is my favorite one," I said, putting my other hand over it. It was a bare, twisty tree with roots stretching toward his wrist.

"Yeah?" he said.

"Mmhm."

We'd been moving closer as we talked, our voices softer and more intimate.

"Come with me, Willa."

I followed him to the water. I gasped when the first wave hit us. It was cold. It didn't smell like I'd expected, either. I imagined it would smell like salt and coconut or something. Now that I was in it, it smelled primal, like living things. I froze, digging my heels into the wet sand.

Oliver waited in the surf. "I'm not going to force you. You have to go in on your own, but I'll be right here with you."

I hesitated, then stepped into the water.

"Good. Come on. Now we have to run," he said.

"Wait! No, slowly. Let's ease in."

He shook his head. "That makes it harder. If you're going to do a thing, do the thing. Dive into it."

Holding on to each other, we rushed into the water until it was higher than my waist. We both went underwater and came back up, facing each other. The waves were strong enough to come up to my chin. I smiled at him, grateful we could have any kind of interaction at all. His hair was wet and slicked back, and the waterdrops on his eyelashes were reflecting the moonlight.

"You're beautiful," I said.

He finally graced me with his dimples. "I need you to stop being gorgeous and so adorably earnest, Willa. It's getting harder to stay angry."

"You could stop being angry," I suggested. "I am really sorry. If you stop being such a dick, we could go back to having nice peaceful nights."

"Would you rub my head again if we were having peaceful nights?"

"I would toooootally rub your head. I would do it every single night." I waggled my fingers at him.

He laughed—actually laughed. "You sound so American. You would 'toooooootally rub my head.' You're cute." He traced my cheek and chin with a finger. "How do you like being in the ocean, you gorgeous thing?"

"I'm still scared."

"Does it feel good anyway?"

A bigger wave came and lifted me off my feet. It set me down closer to Oliver. Then again. "It feels good," I said.

He stood his ground while the tide brought me closer until we were touching.

"Hey," he said quietly.

"Hey."

"I'm scared too." He tucked a wet lock of hair behind my ear. "You hurt me a lot. If I let you back in, you might hurt me again."

"I don't want to hurt you, but is there any option *other* than pain for both of us? If we do this, and it's good, it's gonna hurt because it'll end."

When the wave made me sway against him, he put his arms around me. "All relationships end eventually. We go into ours knowing from the beginning that our end date is when you need to stop doing this job and go back to the rest of your life. You have to decide if it's worth the good it would be for now. For me, I guess the answer is yes."

"I like you so much, Oliver. I don't want to miss this opportunity."

His voice was a soft murmur. "Don't miss it, then."

We kissed until my head spun. He held the back of my neck with one hand, his other arm around me, and I forgot to worry about our past or our future. The rhythm of the waves and the electricity of contact with his skin were the only things that mattered.

Then the bus's engine roared to life.

He groaned.

I swore.

"Can we pretend we don't hear her?" I asked.

"Better not. If she has to honk or call us, it'll wake up Jimmy and Eric, and then it'll be a whole thing. Let's just keep it between the two of us."

I made a frustrated sound, but he was right. He set me back on my feet, and we held hands as we walked back to the sand. "I like us together like this. I like it a lot. I may not have mentioned it, Oliver, but you're hot. Like, pretty much the hottest person I've ever seen."

"Hotter than Benny Walker?" he teased.

"Benny who?"

He laughed. "Good answer, Willa. When we get home, can I take you on a proper date?"

"Um, yeah. Yes, you can."

He kissed me again. "I can't wait," he said when he pulled back. "It's only a few weeks. We can make out like teenagers if there is ever, ever, ever a time when you and Jimmy aren't in each other's pockets. When we get home, I will take you on the best date of your life."

When we were back at the bus, he caught me by the arm and gave me one more kiss. "Up you go. That was just an until-later kiss."

I went back to the lounge in the dark and took off my wet bra and underwear. I got back into my pajamas and crawled into my bunk.

My entire body was zinging with excitement.

I'd been in the ocean.

I'd kissed a guy I liked.

He was going to take me on a perfect date.

Things were looking up for Willa Reynolds.

Chapter Twenty-Two

The band's favorite places to eat were truck-stop diners. Not only were there enormous amounts of greasy food, but there also wasn't much chance they'd be recognized in a truck stop. Jimmy also claimed truck stop breakfasts were the "quintessential American experience," although I'm not sure what made him qualified to judge.

We were around a table enjoying a peaceful, artery-destroying breakfast when Oliver said, "You should watch us on stage tonight, Willa." For a moment, the only sounds were the clatter of silverware and the oldies tunes piped in over the speakers.

Jimmy lit up and slapped his hand emphatically on the table. "Oliver! This is a great idea! Watch us, Willa."

Eric added a fourth sugar packet into his third coffee. "Yesssss," he said. "You're in for a treat. This show has been sold out for weeks."

"Oh, no." I poured more syrup on my waffles. "No, I can't."

"Why not?" he asked.

"It's the only time I have to myself. The quiet time keeps me sane."

Jimmy scoffed. "That excuse doesn't hold water anymore now that you take your 'personal time' every day. You have *loads* of quiet time to yourself. If you factor in the time we're on stage, you're practically only working part-time."

"If you factor in how many times you wake me up each night, I'm working like time and three-quarters." I helped myself to Oliver's home fries.

Jimmy said, "It's hardly my fault the air on the bus is dry. I have to stay hydrated to protect my vocal cords."

"Here's an idea for you. Bring a bottle of water in there with you instead of calling me from six feet away to get you a water. You're like a toddler."

The waitress brought a second round of cinnamon rolls with

extra frosting. His was covered with extra-extra frosting. Maybe they had been recognized after all. Or maybe he'd just charmed her. "Thanks, love. Should we get walkie-talkies, Willa? That might work better for when we're all right here."

"You would rather order walkie-talkies than get your own water?"

"We could learn the codes! Like... 'Ten-four, good buddy.' I'd be really good at that."

"Good idea." I slid my plate closer to Oliver, who was eyeballing what was left of my waffles. "You can learn the code for 'I'm a diva who refuses to get my own drinks, help me.'"

"Why don't you remember to get him water before you get in your own bunk?" Eric suggested. "It would save you the trip down. Are those good?" he asked Oliver. "Maybe we should order another plate."

"We're getting off-track," he said, leaning across the table into my eye-line. "I want you to watch us. Will you, please?"

"Why?"

"Why don't you want to?" To Eric, he said, "They are, yeah. Maybe order another couple of plates."

"Oliver, I don't want to think of y'all—"

Jimmy gasped. Eric clapped his hands. Oliver smiled at me.

"I want to kiss that accent right off your face every time you say 'y'all,' Willa. I won't because Oliver is giving me a *very* stormy expression for having said it." He wasn't. "For crying out loud, Oliver, settle down," Jimmy said to a perfectly calm Oliver. "I'm not going to kiss your girl even though she's *my* Willa." He rolled his eyes. "Ever since y'all started having sex, he's such a caveman."

It was funny in so many ways. Not funny ha-ha, more like funny in a when-was-I-ever-going-to-get-to-have-sex-with-my-own-boyfriend kind of way. It wasn't going to happen when we were living together on a bus, but it seemed like forever until we left for London.

Oh, London. Wherefore art thou taking so fucking long, London.

It did double-duty as a metaphor for how cockblocked I was in my career. I wasn't making any more progress on that than I was on getting Oliver into bed. I had a lot of pictures of him, but unless someone wanted to publish a book called *One Hundred Pictures of How Beautiful Oliver Everett Is*, it wasn't going to do me much good.

Then again, I'd buy that book.

"I will come to a performance sometime. I promise." I batted away the straw wrapper Eric blew at me. "I can't tonight. I've got some photos I need to edit before I send them to Uncle Ken."

Oliver glanced at his phone. "You've got... eleven hours before we go on. Plenty of time to do a favor for your uncle."

"But—"

He put his hand over mine and stroked my knuckles with his thumb. "Willa. You don't need to stay on the bus with your Brontë films. Come to a show, sweetheart. This is our last one in America. It's special."

Trying to tune out the buzz I always got when his skin was on mine, I said, "What if the reason we work well together is because I don't pay attention to that side of you? You're regular guys to me. What if that changes? What if I get starstruck or something and ruin it?"

"You've seen me perform and survived it," Jimmy reminded me.

Oliver took a different approach. "I love seeing your pictures. I like sharing what's important to you. I want you to witness me doing something I love, something I'm good at."

Probably there was nothing I wouldn't have done for him at that moment. Anyway, if I was honest with myself, I did want to see this part of his life. A zillion fans were better acquainted with his musician persona than I was.

Jimmy put his hand on my other hand and shook it vigorously. "It's settled. Nobody can resist Oliver when he's like this, and I'm not saying it's my decision, because of course it isn't up to me what you wear, except for when it is, like now, since you might be photographed with us, and that's our deal. I'll pick something for you while you work on your photos. This is going to be fun."

~ * ~

It wasn't even three songs in before I realized I'd been right to avoid their live performances. I simultaneously wished I'd attended every single one. Every night of my life. As enormous as Jimmy's ego was, and even though I'd already seen how talented he was when he performed at the radio station—I wasn't prepared for the power of seeing them in their element in front of twenty thousand fans. Nothing could have prepared me for it because there isn't anything like it.

Eric was amazing. He was in complete command of whatever instrument he played at every moment. The whole time, Jimmy and Oliver kept one eye on Eric. When Jimmy's improvisation was on the verge of going too far, it was Eric who reeled him in and made sure they walked the line. Eric was who Oliver watched to get the feel for what they were going to do next. Jimmy was the frontman, but Eric was the brains. I wasn't ever attracted to him, but watching from the side of the stage, believe me, I *got* it. There's a pretty fine line between music and sex. He erases it.

Then there was Oliver. God, Oliver. Back there holding it

together, steady, even, and completely in control, driving a beat that was the only thing that mattered. Eric and Jimmy pranced across the stage, chasing the spotlight, but my gaze kept returning to Oliver's quiet, solid gravity. He'd wanted me to see him doing something he loved, something he was good at. He loved it so much he radiated joy, and "good at it" didn't even begin to hint at his abilities. All three of them are brilliant musicians, but Oliver's heart holds it together.

After an instrumental break, Eric and Jimmy both turned toward Oliver. In spite of the thousands of screaming fans, it was like the three of them were in their own world, performing for and with each other for the pure joy of it. The charisma, the heat, the noise, the screaming, the drama, the pheromones, none of it mattered. If it disappeared or had never happened, they would be doing the exact same thing for each other in a garage somewhere.

When Jimmy turned back to the audience, he did a little head jerk to acknowledge Oliver, and the audience went wild. He let it wash over him. Then he turned his attention to me for a moment, and he was *mine*, at least for right then. The reasons I was afraid to be with him suddenly seemed contrived. I wasn't like my mom. I wasn't going to let my attraction for him derail me or lead me to abandon everyone else. I was done denying my emotions. It wasn't going to hurt anyone for us to be together.

There was no reason to keep waiting.

They came rushing off before the encore, and Jimmy lifted me off my feet. He was sweaty and exultant. "You love us, right, Willa? Are we so fucking talented you can hardly stand it?"

"So fucking talented. You're amazing." I hugged him and grasped hands with Eric while Jimmy held me up.

He set me down in front of Oliver, who smiled at me and came closer. "Hey, Willa."

"Oh, hi, Oliver."

He pulled his sweaty shirt over his head. "What do you think of Corporate now?"

I ran my fingernails lightly over his abs and relished how the muscles contracted. I couldn't hear his indrawn breath, but I could sense it. "I am… impressed. Could you sense me watching you?"

His eyes were glued to my face. "This was a bad idea."

I smiled at him and bit my lip.

"I gotta do another few songs," he said, not moving.

"Hurry. Then let's go to the green room. Just you and me."

"What about those two?"

"Don't care. They can go back to the bus."

He kissed me until my muscles went liquid. When he released me, I wasn't sure I'd be able to remain standing.

"Hurry," I said again.

His laugh had an edge of desperation. "Believe me, I will. Go back there and wait for me."

I shook my head.

"I'm wound too tight. I feel your eyes. You're gonna fuck me up."

"You'll figure it out." I gave him a gentle nudge toward the stage.

Jimmy and Eric were already back on stage, and the crowd's roar was a physical thing. Oliver walked backward onto the stage, into view of the audience, his hot gaze on me. He smiled. Everyone saw him, but that expression wasn't for any of them. It was only for me.

When they came off, I grabbed his hand, and we rushed toward the room they'd used to get ready.

"Oh no," Eric said.

Jimmy clucked his tongue. "I knew this would happen. I did warn you, Oliver."

"He and I have to talk privately right now, you guys," I said. "Important, grown-up things. Go back to the bus or something."

Oliver and I hurried down the corridor into the small dressing room area, and I slammed the door and pushed Oliver back against it. I was frantic for him. Nothing was happening fast enough. I was pulling at the buckle on his pants but getting nowhere and trying to reach up for a kiss and not able to make that happen, either. He chuckled shakily, then lifted me and turned to hold me against the door. Finally, finally, finally, I was getting his mouth, and he was kissing me with pent-up desperation. I was making slow progress with his belt until his hand slipped between us to help me. Then the wheels came off.

"So it's true. What in the *hell* is going on?"

Oliver froze.

When he let me go, I slid down between his body and the door and ended up in a forlorn pile, eye to eye with what remained trapped behind his zipper. I sent it comforting thoughts through the fabric barrier.

"What the fuck. This isn't the first time I've come across one of them in the throes after a show," Hawk said to me. "If it was with anyone else, I'd let Oliver blow off some steam since he's usually the level-headed one."

"Stop it," Oliver said. "That's not what this is." His voice was quiet but no less threatening for it.

Hawk ignored him. "So much for your detachment, eh, Willa? I hoped Tucker was misreading the situation, but she had it right. You're as bad as the rest of them; you just picked a different target. Just like all the rest of them, you'll get all sensitive because they don't 'respect' you, and you'll quit in a huff."

He wasn't wrong. He wasn't aware of it because they'd covered for me, but I already had quit in a huff. Nobody in their right mind would call me "professionally detached."

Oliver blocked me with his body. "I said stop. If you've got a complaint, bring it to me. Leave her alone."

Hawk's voice was cutting. "It's very gallant, Oliver, but my problem isn't with you. You're not the one who has a fucking contract forbidding this."

A tentative knock came on the door behind us. "Um, Willa?" Jimmy said. "The nice security woman out here said there's an angry man in there. Is it Hawk?"

I didn't bother getting up. I reached behind me and unlocked the door and scooted over on my butt so they could come in.

"All right, Willa?" Eric asked.

He gave me a hand up, and we kept our hands joined as we faced Hawk.

"Hawk, this is a surprise. Is something wrong?" Jimmy's voice was cold.

Oliver leaned against the wall, arms crossed over his chest. He hadn't put his shirt back on, and his belt was twisted around like the universe was taunting me.

Hawk crossed his arms, mirroring Oliver's pose. He faced the four of us but spoke to me. "Here I am again, playing couples counselor. Believe me, it's for the last time. For whatever reason, you're good with them. Their interviews are great. Their social media is breaking records. They're on time everywhere. There's a lot of upside to you, Willa Wright."

"Reynolds," Eric said. "Learn her name."

"Well, aren't you adorable with your united front. Listen, whatever her name is, she's under contract. I waived the photography clause, but everything else stands. I do not have time for this drama bullshit, and there is too much on the line."

"I signed an agreement I wouldn't hook up with Jimmy. I haven't, and I won't."

Jimmy was quick to back me up. "She's absolutely right. Willa and I are not—"

Hawk shook his head. "It says *no relationship of a romantic nature with any band member*. That," he gestured toward us, "definitely qualifies." He fixed a steely gaze on me. "I'm not flexible on this. You can have your pictures. That's it. I hope you choose to do your job according to our agreement. If you don't, you need to go. It's either-or."

Rage bubbled inside me. Why did it have to be either-or? These two things shouldn't be mutually exclusive. I could have a job and a lover. Everybody did!

My righteousness deflated a bit when I had to admit to myself that most people's lovers weren't their bosses. It was pretty commonly off-limits.

Hawk was watching me through narrowed eyes.

"I got it," I said. "Can I go?"

He waved me away. He wasn't upset; he'd already won.

"You three stay," he said to the boys. "We have some business to discuss."

Eric gave my hand a small squeeze before he let me go.

"You all right, Willa?" Oliver asked me, his voice tight.

"Yeah. I'll be back on the bus, folding laundry or something."

"I'll be there soon, darling," Jimmy said.

I closed the door behind me.

I let myself into the bus and closed the door behind me. I threw myself on Oliver's bunk and buried my face in his pillow. I focused on relaxing my tensed muscles and breathing evenly. By the time they came back to the bus, I could do a good impression of calm.

When they came in, the aura of defeat was impossible to ignore. Jimmy went straight to his bunk and flopped facedown. Eric's shoulders were slumped, and he followed Jimmy to the bunks.

Oliver's cheeks were flushed with anger. "Can I talk to you in the back?"

I followed him to the lounge.

"Hawk's not coming back, is he?" I asked.

"No," he said shortly. Oliver's hands were clenched on the table in front of him. He stared down at them.

"I'm sorry about this," I said.

He shook his head. "No. You don't have anything to be sorry for."

"I read every word of the stupid contract before I signed it, and I knew the no-sex clause was new. I thought of it in terms of Jimmy, then I forgot all about it."

"It wouldn't have mattered," Oliver said. "I wanted to be with you. I *do* want to be with you. I quit the band."

"What? Oliver, you can't! This isn't—"

"This isn't what, Willa?"

"I mean, it's not... it wasn't the kind of . . . you can't quit the band." *Especially not for something with no future* is what I didn't say.

He held my gaze.

"You can't quit," I said again. I couldn't believe it had even been an option. "They need you, and you need this. You can't *not* make music with them."

He rubbed his hands over his face. "You're right. I un-quit. The thing is, I think Jimmy and Eric would have allowed it. They're as furious as I am. But I can't do it. I'd leave anything else for you. For a shot at what this could be between you and me, even though it's temporary, even though we don't fit in each other's worlds—they're the only thing I can't give up." He sighed. "Not to mention, I can't do anything other than this. Drumming is the extent of my professional skill set."

I folded my legs up to my chest and wrapped my arms around myself. "Of course you can't leave the band, but I can't quit this job—"

"I'm not asking you to. Even if you were willing to, Jimmy wouldn't forgive me for it." After a pause, he said, "I tried to get them to fire Hawk. No-go on that, either."

"Firing Hawk would have been good. He deserves it."

"Maybe. He's an asshole, but he's the only one who gave us a chance in the beginning. We wouldn't be here without him. No matter how much mutual distaste there is, there's no denying we've done well for each other."

"Fucking Tucker," I grumbled. "She might not have much to say to me, but I guess she has a whole lot to say to Hawk. She ruined everything."

Oliver's smile didn't reach his eyes. "Yep," he agreed. "She ruined everything."

"I'm tired of choosing, Oliver," I said. "Having a job and a boyfriend isn't that much to ask for."

With a gentle hand, he moved my hair back from my face. "Say the word, Willa, and we can pick right back up where we left off. The contract means fuck-all to me. Jimmy and Eric would cover for us."

I was tempted.

Even if I was the kind of person who signed a contract and then went back on it, and I wasn't, we'd probably get caught by Tucker the Spy, and I didn't put it past Hawk to sue me for breach of contract. My new financial freedom would be lost, and Toby and I would be back in the same boat.

I couldn't let it happen.

Oliver smiled. "You don't have to answer. Your expression says it's a no-go."

"I can't risk it, Oliver."

"I didn't think so. My honest cowgirl."

I rested my forehead on my knees. "I guess it's for the best." My voice was muffled. "After the end of this tour, we're worlds apart, anyway."

"No, it isn't." He was still angry. "We may have to live with it, but it's not for the best."

He was right.

It wasn't for the best.

It was bullshit.

Chapter Twenty-Three

Our first night in London was a homecoming for them, but until we were in Eric's driveway, I hadn't even considered what it would be like to be apart. They weren't going to be far, but it was definitely farther than the next bunk down or over. He was out and in his own house before I could process it.

Then we were at Oliver's house. "I'll call you in the morning," he said. I wasn't sure which of us he was talking to.

I was bereft when he went into a house and closed the door behind him. The world was colder and too big. "You're all right," Jimmy said, his voice gentle. "They're not far, and you'll be with me."

When we got to Jimmy's, he opened the door and ushered me in. Following his example, I hung my jacket on a peg by the front door. We were in an enormous, open room. I took it all in: exposed brick walls, oversized, dramatic artwork, big leather furniture, and soft, plush area rugs. He pushed a button on a remote, and a fireplace came to life.

He smiled at me, released my hand, and spread his arms wide. "Welcome home, Willa." He dropped his bag next to the couch. "You have space for yourself upstairs. Office, bedroom, bathroom. We'll redecorate however you want once we're settled in. I'll even let you paint the walls a color since I love you."

I didn't have the heart to tell him he wouldn't need to redecorate it for me; I wouldn't be staying long enough to make it worth it. I should have remembered Jimmy could read my mind.

He made a negative sound. "I'm choosing to interpret your expression to mean you're overwhelmed and exhausted, not that you're already planning to leave me."

"Jimmy—"

"Nope, we're not talking about it today. This is a day of celebration! Go upstairs and get settled. I'll be right here if you need me, okay?" He kissed me on the forehead.

"Okay. Deal. We won't discuss it today, but we're going to have to—"

He clapped his hands over his ears. "La la la, I can't hear you. Go to bed, and we will talk about other things later, love you!"

I went up a flight of steep, open stairs and was tired enough for the lack of a barrier or a railing to make me nervous.

I unpacked, called Toby to tell him I got there safely, and had a long, hot soak in the gorgeous bathtub in my bathroom. There were things from being on the bus I'd miss. Sharing a closet-sized bathroom with a trio of boys was not on the list, and this tub was a definite upgrade from the bus shower.

After my bath, I was ready to sleep in a big, comfortable bed that wasn't driving down the road. I pictured Oliver finally able to stretch without hitting his head or feet against the ends of his bunk.

Keep your mind off Oliver, I instructed myself sternly. One of the benefits of having all this space now was surely the ability to concentrate on something—anything—other than Oliver.

It was ridiculous to be blue. The proximity was torture, anyway, since stupid Hawk had placed anything more firmly out of reach. So yes! More space, solitude, some emotional distance—these were good things.

Screw it. I texted him: *Is it dumb to say I miss you?*

His answer came seconds later. *Nope. I was picking up my phone to text you because I miss you. Remember, I'm not far, and I'm thinking about you.*

That helps. But I hope you're only thinking about me as a friend since that's all we can have.

The dots bounced until his response came through. *Okay, yeah. We can say that. I'm thinking about you as a friend that I'd love to be naked with.*

LOL

He responded with a drooling emoji.

I sensed the big dopey smile on my face. *Good night, Oliver. (I'm not thinking about you as a friend, either.)*

Night, Willa. Go to sleep. I'll be by tomorrow.

~ * ~

"Where are you going now?" Jimmy asked me. He looked up from where he and Oliver were shooting pool at the billiards table on one side of the great room.

"Out to photograph Castle." I checked my camera bag to make sure everything was where it belonged.

"Again? Did you not already do them?"

"Bran said he wanted some more, maybe for liner notes or

something."

Jimmy chalked the end of his cue stick and winked at me. "Oh, there's something Bran wants. It's not photos for liner notes."

"What's that supposed to mean?" My gaze flicked to Oliver.

"Are you kidding me right now?" Jimmy said.

"What?"

Oliver was leaning over the pool table, cue stick in position, eyes on Jimmy.

"Bran wants to spend time with you," he said with fake patience. I knew he'd discarded more vulgar ways of saying the same thing. I appreciated the effort.

I frowned. "Maybe he wants me to photograph him and his band because I am talented."

"You're incredibly talented, and word is getting around. Probably because you're never home anymore, you're always waltzing around town on assignment. The interesting thing to me here is Bran already has pictures with his band. He's asking you for photos of just him now. He wouldn't need any unless he was going solo, which would be a terrible mistake. He'd be useless on his own. My powers of deduction are telling me he wants something else from you. Since you didn't answer him when he asked you to a bar in Shoreditch, this is his next effort."

Oliver took his shot. The cue ball bounced off the pool table and landed at Jimmy's feet. "Easy, mate," he said to Oliver.

"Who told you Bran asked me for drinks?" I asked Jimmy.

"It was in your email, Willa," he said slowly like the answer was obvious.

"Um, I guess what I'm asking is why are you reading my private email?" And worse, summarizing it in front of Oliver.

"You left your laptop open right on the table with your email open. Is email yet another boundary?"

"It's *always* been a boundary. You can't read someone else's private messages."

He shrugged. "You read all mine."

"Surely you understand the difference, Jimmy. It's because in that case, you said, 'Willa, it's your job to answer my emails.' See how it's different?"

"Well, now I do. You better go, or you're going to be late. Did you tell Oliver about it?"

I hadn't. It hadn't come up. It seemed weird to give him a report of everything I was doing like I assumed he'd be jealous or something.

Jimmy put the white ball back on the table. "I'm only kidding.

Obviously you don't have to clear your plans with Oliver! You're your own Willa. Anyway, don't worry. Now he knows."

Oliver said to me, "Hey, can I talk to you in your office for a minute?"

"Of course." I glared at Jimmy on my way to the stairs. He smiled serenely at me.

Oliver closed the door behind us. "It's none of my business," he said. "I know."

"I'm just—"

"If you wanted to—"

"I don't," I said hastily.

"You will eventually, and I *hate* it."

I hadn't realized how close we'd gotten; I stepped back. "Sorry."

"For what?"

"For getting in your space. I don't mean to. I can't help it."

He made a frustrated sound. "I *want* you in my space. I wish... I want you to... fucking hell. *Fuck.* I want to tell you if you wanted to go out with Bran, I won't make it weird." It came out in a rush. He smiled. "Nah, I'll probably make it weird. I'll try not to, though. If you're going to date someone, part of me hopes it'll be Bran."

"What a strange thing to say."

He smiled at me. "You're not going to fall for a guy like him. He's no threat." He ran his thumb over my lower lip. "I bet he's rubbish in bed, anyway," he said before letting me go.

I licked my lip where his thumb had been. "Are we good?"

"As good as we're gonna get right now." He leaned down and rested his forehead against mine for a moment, then stepped aside and opened the door for me to pass. "I hate it," he said. "*Hate it.*"

"So do I," I whispered.

"What if we...?"

"He'd find out," I said miserably. It wasn't even far-fetched. Hawk would. Here in London, they couldn't even walk between each other's houses without fans taking pictures and posting it on social media.

Not to mention his distressing habit of showing up out of the blue "just to drop off some papers" or "grab a quick signature."

Oliver sighed. "I know you're right." He kissed me on the forehead and left.

~ * ~

I did decide to meet up with Bran. I settled in a window seat on the train while I digested what Jimmy said. He was right—I was doing a lot of my own photography lately, and it was good work. Maybe it was all the time I'd spent in Uncle Ken's lab correcting other photographers' lighting and composition, but those aspects of photography came easy to me. My technique was solid.

Technique was nothing more than nuts and bolts. There was something else I wanted. Something to set me apart from any other technically proficient photographer. I wanted to be *unique*. I wanted it to be clear that my work could only have been done by me, the way it was obvious that an Annie Leibovitz photo could only have been done by Annie Leibovitz.

I was confident I'd get there if I kept having so many opportunities. As much as it grated to admit it, one reason things were taking off for me was thanks to Hawk. He'd thrown himself behind my photography aspirations. Corporate was the biggest band he managed, but they weren't the only ones. For the other acts in his stable, he arranged for me to do a shoot for a cover and liner notes for a new album, update some press kits for a couple bands, and he even invited me to help set up the lighting for a video shoot.

When I got to Bran, it didn't take long to figure out two things. One, Jimmy had been right. Bran didn't really need any photographs. Two... Bran was an attractive guy, with a mop of curly hair and a charmingly crooked smile. If I'd met him at a different time, I didn't doubt I'd have been into him.

But I hadn't met him at a different time, and I was emphatically *not* interested. I navigated my way out of it and went back home as quickly as possible, even earlier than I'd committed to being back to go to an interview with the boys.

That was when my luck regarding Hawk ran out. He strolled into the studio, dapper but smarmy in a suit jacket and dark jeans. "You know you don't have to do their hair for radio, right, Winnie?" he said.

"I'm going to photograph it." I refused to let him bait me.

"For what?"

"Instagram, Twitter, and another project I'm kicking around."

"What project?" he asked.

"I'm working through the details. I'll send you a proposal when it's ready."

"Is it a book to go along with this tour?" he asked.

"Uh, yeah, actually. Something in time for the holiday season, if possible. Probably a glossy paperback format. Just photos and captions, no other text."

"I've been chatting with a publisher, and we could do a limited run. Charge fifty pounds a pop on their online merch shop," Hawk said.

"Maybe make a mini version for less," I added.

"Short run of autographed versions. Put it on the website, do a special distribution for industry people," he said.

I was startled into silence. Hawk and I were on the same page without even discussing it. Maybe my early fantasy of him and me on the same team wasn't out of reach after all. Maybe we could call some kind of truce and actually collaborate.

"How about it then?" He prompted me when I didn't answer him right away. "Should we make it happen?"

The boys were watching me silently.

"Yes," I said. "Let's."

He gave me a curt nod. "Come to my office Friday morning, and we'll start sorting through pictures. I want to talk to you about re-upping your contract. Last one was only through the end of this tour."

In some ways, this was the key to what I wanted.

I could stay with them. I could work on my photography.

The spark of hope in Oliver's eyes told me what was occurring to me had already occurred to him.

If I stayed and took what Hawk was offering me, I could work as a photographer; I could be published. I wouldn't have to leave.

But as long as I was under contract, I couldn't be with Oliver.

I wouldn't be with him if I went home to work for Uncle Ken, either, but at least there, I could be near Oliver. I saw him every day right now. It wasn't the same thing as being with him, but it was more than I was going to get from Nashville.

On the other hand, taking pictures of this band with the occasional outside assignment was a big improvement over working in a coffee shop and a computer lab.

There was no such thing as "having it all." Everyone made compromises.

~ * ~

The next night, things got even more complicated. We were at Jimmy's, and I was on my laptop at the breakfast bar while Jimmy, Eric, and Oliver sat around Jimmy's table playing back some of the songs they'd recorded when they were on tour, making notes about which ones should go on the next album.

I hadn't heard my phone ring over their music, but Jimmy reached for it with an obnoxious, "Oh, let me get your phone for you, Willa! I have nothing better to do than to run around acting as your—fuck me! It says Benny Walker! Answer your phone; it's Benny Walker. Maybe he's in town! Invite him here if he's in town. Oooh, the house is a mess. You lads are going to have to go home if Benny Walker is coming over," he said to Eric and Oliver. "She and I have some unfinished business there, don't we, Willa? Christ's sake, answer your phone, woman! Are there clean sheets on my bed? Or on your bed? Your bed is probably better; let's use yours if it comes to it, not saying it will, but of *course* it will. Don't let him go to voicemail. Don't mention this to Oliver, Eric, no reason to bring it up to him. He'll only be jealous, and there may or may not be a reason for it yet, and Willa, for the love of fuck, would you please answer your phone?"

"I'm right here, Jimmy," Oliver said. "Why is he always talking like I'm not here?" he asked Eric.

"He's flustered." He hit pause on the playback. "You know how he is with a crush."

"If you don't answer—here, I'll get it for you. Jesus, I have to do everything. Hi, Benny! It's Jimmy. I'm answering Willa's phone for her. How are you, mate?" Pause. "Yeah, glad to hear it. Are you in town, by chance? London." His face fell. "Oh. Hmm. Okay. Well, if you ever are, definitely call me. Or her. Or either of us. Both of us. Whatever you fancy. Yes, she's right here."

He put my phone on mute and set it on the table. "He's not in London. He wants to talk to you. I don't know why. Who even cares if he's not in touching distance? Find out what he wants, Willa. I can't be arsed."

"No problem. You don't need to be arsed since he called for me." I got up and snagged my phone. "I'll take it upstairs."

~ * ~

I didn't know what to say to Oliver about my talk with Benny, so I wasn't going to set foot downstairs until I was sure they were gone.

It would have worked if he hadn't come up and tapped on the door to my office.

I was slumped on the couch, staring into a cup of cooling tea.

"All right, Willa?" Oliver asked.

"Mmm," I said. I sipped my cold tea and grimaced before I set it on the end table. "I was on the phone with Toby."

"Everything okay?"

"Yes, he's fine. Good. With Chelsea, 'studying for finals.' You want to sit down?"

He sat in the chair across from me. "What's going on? Do you want to talk?" He was ready to listen if I needed him to, willing to let it go if I didn't. He was open, patient, and sweet. I wanted to curl up in his lap and cry.

"Benny offered me a job."

Oliver nodded. "It was just a matter of time. If not Benny, someone else. Jimmy is going to be angry. Are you going to take it?"

"I don't know much about it. It isn't as his assistant. I'd be a photographer in some capacity. I panicked and pretended we had a bad connection. He said he'd email me."

Oliver's expression was serious. "Why did you panic?"

I sipped my cold tea, then said, "Because if Benny Walker wants to offer me a job, it's probably a good one, and I'd be closer to my brother."

My first call had been to Toby. In characteristic younger brother fashion, he made it sound like I was panicking for nothing. "You have a great job now, and maybe you're going to get an even better one. What are you freaking out about?" Leave it to a brother to simplify it and to miss the point completely.

The problem was the stakes were so high. Any decision I made would cost something I wasn't willing to give up. Being near Toby. Career dreams. Being with Jimmy, Eric, and Oliver.

Oliver.

None of my options offered me all of it.

Toby said, "Don't take this the wrong way, Willa—"

"Whenever someone says *don't take this the wrong way,* there's never a good way to take it."

"—but I'm going to be fine either way. You don't need to come back to Nashville if you have a better offer. We can sell Dad's house. I can get an apartment. Pick what's best for you. It'll work out."

"What did you tell him?" Oliver asked after I rehashed the conversation for him.

"I said I wasn't sure yet what I was going to do." I didn't have answers for anyone. Not Toby, not Benny, not Oliver. Especially not myself.

"What should I do?" I asked him in a small voice.

Oliver rubbed a hand over his face. "Toby's right. You can't lose."

It wasn't funny, but I laughed. "No, it's the opposite. There isn't a way to win. Whatever I pick, I lose something I don't want to be without."

"If you have the opportunity to go be an artist, you have to take it, right? You are an artist. Not an assistant."

My frustration was bubbling over. "I don't want to leave you guys, but what does it mean if I stay? If I stay here, or if I go work for Benny, I'm away from Toby. If I'm not doing this for my family, what am I even doing it for? Beyond that, what is it going to mean for us? I don't want to be away from you, but what am I going to do? Just, like, be here, close enough to see and hear and smell you, but not have you?

Am I supposed to sit around until you date someone else? I can't—"

"I'm not the one debating about going out with Bran," he cut in.

"I'm not debating either! I told you I don't want to."

He got up to pace the length of my office. "I don't know how to do this. I'd rather be near you than not, but it's not my call. I'm going to listen to you, and I'm not going to attempt to sway you either way because these decisions are yours to make."

"I don't want to date someone else. Which leaves me with the only option of waiting here until you find someone else, and my heart splits open."

He made an impatient gesture. "I'm not dating. It's not even on the table for me."

Frustration was getting the best of me. "Yet. But we're not going to be together, and unless we're swearing to a life of celibacy, at least one of us is going to have to watch the other one be with someone else. I can't speak for you, but it's not something I'm really interested in doing."

"I'm not really interested in it either, Willa. What is it you want to know? If you're asking me if I'd rather have you with me but not be able to have you or have you not with me and not be able to have you, I'll choose having you here every single time. So don't ask me. I'm going to support you no matter what because this isn't about me or what I want. It's about you deciding what's best for you."

I put my head in my hands. "I'm confused."

He sat next to me and gently took hold of my hands. "If you go, we could be together."

"Uh, what? If I'm not here, that's the opposite of being together, Oliver."

"I could fly you to me," he said. "Wherever we are. When you're free."

"Wouldn't I be a groupie then? Like Hawk said?"

He narrowed his eyes. "No, it would make you my girlfriend, Willa. Jesus."

"Sorry." I put a hand on his arm. "I know it's not what you meant, but that's how it would feel to me. If I live in the States and you live here, I'm not your girlfriend. We'd just have a conjugal visit every now and then. Sporadic sex isn't a relationship."

"Sporadic sex is a lot more than we have right now."

I shook my head. "It's not. Even with the no-sex, we have a relationship. Don't we?"

After a moment, he nodded. "Yeah. We do. It's not enough. It's better than nothing, but it's not enough."

I threw up my hands. "It's hopeless. There isn't a solution."

"Not an easy one," he agreed. "Sleep on it. Maybe it'll come to you."

When he got to the door, he turned around to face me. He waited until I made eye contact with him. "I care about you so much, Willa. That'll be true if you stay or if you go."

I nearly melted into a puddle on the floor. How did he always say exactly the right thing, and why did it make everything even harder?

He closed the door behind him when he left.

I should feel lucky. My career opportunities were bigger than I'd ever dreamed they could be.

Oliver was more than I'd ever dared dream of, too.

Tomorrow. I'd sleep on it like he'd said, and I'd call Benny tomorrow. Maybe things would become clear.

Chapter Twenty-Four

Despite how much I'd wished for it, I didn't wake up with a magically clear mind and a clear-as-day path laid out ahead of me.

While I was waiting for clarity to come to me, I'd decided to do everything else on my to-do list. I'd stay busy. I was going to work on the proposal for Hawk, and I was going to review the job summary Benny promised to email me.

I should follow up with Toby. I'd been so upset the day before that I'd only focused on myself. I hadn't asked him about his health or school at all. Everything had been okay, but it was never a good idea to let my guard down completely.

Jimmy needed groceries, I had to get the dry cleaning, there were social media posts to get to, and an email from Hope I hadn't answered. Maybe if I kept busy enough, the right answer to the question of what I wanted to do with my life would pop into my mind. I dressed quickly and hurried to the stairs.

~ * ~

The next thing I was aware of was the sound of beeping monitors. "Toby!" I shot up in bed, panic rising in my throat.

"Shh, shh. Willa. Toby's fine; nothing's wrong. You hit your head, and we're in the hospital. Please lie back down, there you go, that's a good girl. Toby is fine, I promise. Relax." It was Jimmy.

I heard Oliver's warm voice as his hand slipped over mine. "You're all right, Willa. They've done some tests, and everything is going to be fine. Eric called Toby, so he knows you're here."

"I'll get the nurse." It was Eric.

"Why can't I see right?" The beeps from the heart monitor got closer together, but I didn't need the audio cue to tell me my heart was racing. I could see, but nothing was in focus.

The nurse asked me to explain.

"The light is big. Smeary."

"Halos? Do you see light rings?"

"Yes."

I heard the scratching of her pen and figured she was writing in my chart. "It's common with a concussion, and you have a corneal abrasion in your right eye. You're on painkillers now. As they wear off, pay attention to how much pain you have in that eye. We can get you some drops and put a patch on if you need it."

"Is it going to get better?" I asked.

"Eventually," she said. "It'll get worse before it gets better. You have several contusions, and your muscles are going to be sore, particularly your neck. I'm going to call your doctor and tell her you're awake. Your brothers can stay here with you until she gets here." She cast a skeptical eye on my "brothers." "Even though I don't understand how you're all the same age, you have different last names, and one of you is American."

Jimmy gave her a tired-but-still-charming smile. "Foster siblings, love. We already said. Thank you for taking care of our sister."

Oliver leaned over my bed. His eyes were shadowed, and lines were etched into his forehead. He was beautiful. "You scared us, sweetheart. I'm glad you're awake."

When the doctor got there, she did some brief tests and then echoed what the nurse said—it would get worse before it got better. Luckily, other than a sprained right wrist, I hadn't done much damage to anything other than my head and my eye.

I was mostly worried about my eyes. "What's going on with my vision?"

She referred to her clipboard. "You scratched your cornea, and concussions can cause vision problems too. Have you ever had a concussion before?" I told her I hadn't, but then Jimmy cleared his throat loudly. "Oh," I said. "That's right. It's possible. I didn't go to the doctor, but some of Jimmy's fans—I mean my brother's friends—jostled me around pretty good. I could have had a concussion after that.

She sounded concerned. "Post-concussion syndrome is more common after an initial concussion. It'll take longer for you to heal this time. You need to be patient. It could take several weeks before you see improvement, and your symptoms could be anything from fatigue, headaches, migraines, vision disturbances, tinnitus, anxiety, insomnia, and disturbances with your balance."

"We'll take care of her, doctor," Jimmy said, gripping my hand. "Willa, don't worry about *anything*."

I didn't remember anything after I decided to go downstairs. He filled me in. Evidently, I'd been right to be wary of those stupid barrierless stairs at Jimmy's.

"That wanker of an architect said those stairs were fashionable!" he said indignantly. "It's not fashionable at *all* to find your Willa at the bottom of them, completely unconscious and bleeding! I stayed completely calm, naturally." Behind Jimmy, Eric was shaking his head emphatically. "Very rationally and not screaming, I called Oliver first, then an ambulance. I knew not to move you after Oliver said, 'don't move her.' I sat next to you and held your hand until the ambulance got there. I insisted on riding with you, and I'll tell you, it's a tight squeeze in an ambulance, but I didn't want you to be alone if you woke up."

"Thank you for not leaving me, Jimmy. I would have been so scared to wake up alone in an ambulance."

He patted my hand. "Yes, well. Lots of people probably wouldn't have been so cool-headed, but I have nerves of steel." This time it was Oliver shaking his head.

Jimmy leaned toward me. "Listen, darling. Seriously. You can never get hurt again, in any way. You scared me half to death. I have to insist on this."

The doctor said I had to spend the rest of the night there. I told my "brothers" to go home, a suggestion they ignored. They stayed in my room with me until I was discharged—with a removable splint for my wrist, prescriptions for numbing eye drops and pain medications, and a follow-up appointment for next week.

When I woke several hours later at home on Jimmy's couch, I could confirm what they'd said at the hospital; the pain was getting worse, not better. I focused with my good eye and saw Jimmy sleeping on the other end of the couch I was on. Eric was on the second couch. Oliver was lying on the floor next to me.

He stirred. When he saw I was awake, he sat up. "What do you need?"

"I want to get up," I said.

He got to his feet and moved behind me, supporting my back and neck as I sat up carefully. He swung my feet around to the floor and helped me stand. "All right?"

I waited for the room to stop spinning. "All right."

"What do you need? Are you in pain?"

I hurt like I'd fallen from the top of the London Tower instead of partway down Jimmy's stairs. "It's not that bad," I said.

"How about a snack so you can take more medicine?"

"That sounds good," I said. I started toward the kitchen, but he said, "Sit down, Willa, I'll get it."

He rustled around in the kitchen, then joined me at the table with toast with jam and hot tea. He opened a prescription bottle and tipped out two pills, then set them on my plate, next to my toast.

"I hate this." I reached for the tea with my right hand, then changed course and used my left hand instead. I sloshed some tea over the rim onto my hand and slurped it off.

"Of course you do," he said. "Nobody likes to be hurting."

"Being helpless is even worse. I want to tell you I don't need you guys sleeping right here with me, except I obviously do since I couldn't even get up by myself."

He was annoyingly serene. "None of us mind being here, and it's important for you to rest."

"I'm not a baby," I grumbled.

When he smiled at me, I couldn't help smiling back. He was rumpled with sleep. His hair was sticking up, he had a pillow crease across one cheek, and his dimples were still, hands down, the most adorable thing I'd laid eyes on in any country.

"Let us take care of you for a bit. You scared us."

I made a "hmpf" sound, and his smile got bigger. "Eat your toast, baby, then we'll get you settled back on the couch."

I sighed. I wanted to tell him I'd been sleeping all day and I wasn't tired, but I was exhausted, but I wasn't inclined to argue with a delicious Oliver who called me "baby."

"I'm only going to do it because you're cute, and you want me to," I said.

"Fair enough. Do it for me. What your body needs right now is rest."

"I'm *only* doing this for your sake," I grumbled as I slipped right back into sleep.

~ * ~

Hours later, pounding on the door startled me awake.

Jimmy surfaced from under the blankets and fumbled for his phone. He checked the feed from the security camera at the front door, then sat up. "Oh *shit*." He rushed to the door and yanked it open.

A familiar voice said, "I know she's here because I tracked her phone here, and there's no way you're not Jimmy with that hair. Why the fuck isn't anyone answering their phones? Willa, are you in there? Where is she? WILLA!"

"Toby!" I struggled to a sitting position. "I'm okay! I'm here!"

He pushed past Jimmy. When he saw me, his whole body sagged with relief. He crushed me in a hug, then gentled when I cried out. "I'm okay. I'm fine."

"What happened? Why aren't you answering the phone? What

did the doctor say?"

Tears filled my eyes, and I leaned into him. "Toby. You came."

He sat next to me, careful not to jostle me. "All I knew was you'd fallen and were headed to the hospital, and they would call me back, but nobody did. I called the hospital, but when I said I was your brother, they said your room was already full of brothers, and they hung up on me! Are you okay? You look terrible," he said. "She looks terrible," he said accusingly to Jimmy, then turned to the other couch, where Oliver had joined Eric. "Which is which, Willa?"

I laughed weakly. "The frowning one is Oliver."

"They're both frowning," Toby said.

"Oliver on the left, and Eric on the right. Jimmy's the one with the hair."

Toby shook everyone's hands. "I'm sorry I barged in and didn't introduce myself."

Jimmy yawned and headed for the kitchen. "Coffee. We knew it was you, Toby," he said over his shoulder. "How many one-eyed, one-legged Americans would show up screaming for Willa? Figured it out, didn't we? Do you really have a stalking app on her phone? Am I the only one here who respects boundaries?"

"I'm sorry we didn't call you back," Eric said. "I think that was my job. We were relieved she was all right, and once we got her settled back here, we fell asleep."

Oliver took over. "She has a concussion, a lot of bruises, a scratch on her right eye, and she sprained her right wrist. She's got pain pills and a follow-up appointment next week. She can rest here unless the two of you decide something else."

"I'll make plans later." Toby was a real take-charge guy suddenly. "Thank you for getting her to the hospital."

"Can someone help me sit up?" I asked.

Oliver and Eric both got up, and Jimmy called, "Just let me get the coffee on, darling," but Toby leaned down and helped me. He gave me another hug. "I was so scared."

"I'm fine. Let's have coffee, then we can go talk in my office."

Oliver shook his head. "Absolutely not."

"Nope," Eric said. "Sorry, Willa."

Jimmy said the same thing but with more words, characteristically. "Willoughby Austen Reynolds, you must be out of your goddamn mind if you think you're setting one foot on those stairs. We'll bring everything to you. You are to remain safely on the first floor until I get the stairs Americanized for you."

I tried to stop Toby from asking, but I wasn't fast enough. He hadn't learned yet that sometimes when Jimmy says something, it's best to let it float away without responding to it.

"Americanized?" Toby echoed. "What does that mean?"

Jimmy set down a tray with the coffee pot, mugs, cream, and sugar on the table and gestured us over. "It must be why you fell, right, Willa? Because they're English stairs? I'll call a carpenter and ask him to make them American so it doesn't happen again."

"What makes a staircase American?" Toby asked. He helped me up again and held me carefully by the arm as I walked slowly to the table.

"Well, I don't know," Jimmy said. "I was hoping you would. She didn't go tumbling down any staircases when we were stateside, so something must be different here. She's normally reasonably nimble." He poured mugs of coffee and moved the cream and sugar closer to me. Toby got it first and fixed my coffee.

"Why did you fall, Willa?" Eric asked. "Do you remember?"

I sipped my coffee. "Not really. I remember stressing about everything I needed to do and walking to the stairs, but nothing else until I woke up at the hospital." I looked at Toby. "I heard the monitors first, and I flashed back to being there with you."

He made a sympathetic face. "Poor Willa. How scary."

"It was, but then I heard them, and I knew I was going to be okay."

Jimmy smiled at me from the other end of the table. "You will be okay, Willa. We're going to take care of you until you are."

Toby poured more coffee in my mug. "Maybe you should come home. I can bring my stuff back to Dad's."

Even a few months ago, I'd have agreed with him automatically. I was hurt, and things were hard. Home was a refuge, and it made sense to want to be there, but things had changed. Jimmy's was as much a refuge as my own home.

I was every bit as safe in London with them as I would back home with Toby.

Because these guys weren't my coworkers or my bosses.

They were my family.

I let the realization settle. Waited while it sank through my bones and became a truth I trusted.

They were my family. It changed things.

If they were my family…they didn't have to be my job.

If they weren't my job, something else could be.

If something else was my job, there could be an Oliver and me.

It changed everything.

They didn't want me to quit, but they'd support me if I did.

Oliver and I could be together, at least for as long as it took me to decide what I was going to do and where I was going to be.

I couldn't muster the courage to say anything, so I remained silent. I'd tackle it when I was better, I thought.

~ * ~

I learned being "taken care of" isn't necessarily what it's cracked up to be. Nobody would let me do a single thing for myself, much less anything for the rest of them. Every time I tried to do anything, a brood of mother hens intervened.

One of the final straws was when Jimmy brought me my laptop and announced he was going to help me "go through my correspondence."

"Absolutely not. Let's do yours. Bring me your computer, and I'll get started on it. You probably have hundreds of messages by now, and there might be something important in there."

"Has your vision improved? No more blurriness or anything?"

I didn't answer him because no, my vision wasn't better, and what started off as a concern was now low-grade panic. The doctor said it would resolve, but it wasn't.

Jimmy was watching me. He shook his head. "Stop. It's not time to worry yet. You have to be patient."

Toby came into the room. "Time to be worried about what?"

I stifled a groan. I loved him forever and more than anyone, but he was going overboard. You would guess I was on death's door based on his behavior. "I was upstairs cleaning off her desk."

He was talking to Jimmy, not me. I hadn't asked him to clean off my desk, but that didn't cross either of their minds. "What's wrong with her? What's she worried about?"

"I'm right here," I reminded them.

Jimmy answered him anyway. "She's worried about why her vision hasn't gone back to normal yet. The doctor said it would, and I'm sure it will, but she's sensitive to light, and she's having some blurry vision."

"Is that why she keeps squinting and frowning?"

"Must be. I'm going to help her with her email. Do you want to grab her pills? Later, when she falls asleep, should we play some cards?"

Toby smiled. "Sure. I'll play poker with you again. In just a few more rounds, I'll have enough money for my flight back."

"I'll pay for your flight back," I said.

"I've got it." Jimmy powered up my computer and began typing. "Concentrate on me helping you with your email now." He typed again, more forcefully. "Willa, it's not taking your password."

I heard Toby rustling around in the kitchen. I started to get up to help him, but Jimmy put a hand on my leg to keep me at the table. "He's got it. Bring her the daytime pill," he called. "She doesn't want a nap yet." To me, he said, "Still won't take the password." He shook it. "Is it broken? Did you fall on it? Were you carrying your laptop during The Incident, by chance?"

"You don't know my password." My patience was held by a frayed thread.

" JimmyJimmy, obviously."

"That's your password, not mine."

"Yeah, but—well, all right," he said, tapping on the keyboard again. "Not WillaWilla," he said to himself. "Fucking hell, it better not be OliverOliver." He typed it in. "Take my awesome password idea but use the name of another—it's not that either! What the hell is your password?"

I recited a string of letters, numbers, and characters.

"Are you kidding me? What kind of stupid password is that?"

"A secure one."

"Ugh. Say it again. Slowly."

I recited my password again, and Toby brought me my medicine, a cup of tea, and a scone. "Teatime, Willa! Take your medicine." He said it in a sing-songy voice like he was talking to a toddler.

"I'll have it later," I grumbled.

When Eric came in, he put the kettle back on and joined us at the table. "You should take it now. It gets worse if you wait. Stay on top of it; that's your best bet."

My phone buzzed, and Toby nabbed it and read the text message to me. "It's Oliver. It says *time for your pills, sweetheart.*"

"There, Willa," Jimmy patted my hand. "I've fixed your password for you. Now it's JimmyJimmy. It'll be an easy one to remember, a good thing, since your brain's not quite as sharp now you've concussed it. You're welcome, darling. Now let's go through your messages; here we go. Spam. Spam. Spam. Bran, delete, and fuck him anyway. He probably is going to say he needs even *more* pictures of himself, and there's one thing the world can do without. Spam. Hawk. Hawk. Hawk. Oh shit, did anyone tell Hawk she's hurt? Eric, can you call him, please? Ah, one from Hope Harper; I'll answer her in a bit. Oh! Benny Walker!"

He was silent as he read it.

Quietly to Toby, Eric said, "Call Oliver and tell him to come here right away. We have a family emergency. I forgot about this," he said to me. "I assume you hadn't told Jimmy?"

"There's nothing to tell, really. He said he wants to offer me a job. I don't know what it is, and I haven't committed to anything. And I hadn't told you, either."

"Oliver told me," Eric said, his eyes on Jimmy.

He groaned and put his head in his hands. "Everyone let me think!"

When Oliver came in, he joined us at the table. Jimmy read the email to himself again and then aloud to the rest of us.

"Willa, we had a suspiciously bad connection tonight. Give me a call tomorrow, and we'll try again. I have a job offer for you that will be good for us both. Talk soon. Love, Benny."

"Jimmy, will you please email him back to tell him I've been in an accident, and I'll get back to him soon?"

Jimmy didn't have hysterics. He didn't make jokes about threesomes. He just did exactly what I asked him to.

He wrote the message, then said solemnly, "He's probably going to offer you something you can't refuse."

The tension was a ball in my stomach. "It's possible. I'm nervous to talk to him."

Toby inserted himself again. "First, drink your tea and have your medicine."

I glared at him.

"Now, Willa."

I ignored him and turned back to Jimmy. "Don't be sad. Nothing has changed."

"Not yet, but it's only a matter of time. Benny wants you, and he's closer to home." He brightened. "Although Hawk does want you to renew your contract, so that's an option. You also have the book-of-us project. You were going to talk to him about that."

"Let's worry about it later."

"She's going to have to take a job closer to home," Toby said.

It pulled me up short. "Do you need me?"

"You might need *me*. I could get to you a lot faster if you were in New York."

"But—"

"Did you take your medicine?"

I slammed a hand on the table. "Stop telling me what to do and quit hovering like I'm going to break if you're not staring at me! I don't want my medicine, and I'm not taking it now!"

It didn't ruffle his feathers at all. "I'm helping you. Your head is obviously bothering you a lot, or you wouldn't be snapping at me like this."

I swore under my breath and got to my feet. "You're driving me crazy! I'm not an invalid; I just hurt my fucking head. I don't need you telling me what to do all the time." I spun on the rest of them. "Same goes for you all. I'm going to be fine, and I'll get there a lot faster if you stop hovering!"

"I'm taking care of you, god damn it!" Toby's temper gave out. "I want you to be okay because I love you. I'm sorry that's so much trouble for you. Jesus!"

"You can't make me better by staring at me and bossing me. I hurt myself. I'm not a child, so stop telling me what to do. You're being such a dick."

"You're being a dick!" He threw back.

"I can't be a dick." I put my hands on my hips. "Because I'm a girl."

"Woman," Jimmy said, correcting me.

"You're *kind* of being a dick, Willa," Eric chimed in.

"They're not wrong," Oliver said.

Toby and I were locked in a standoff until the absurdity hit us both at the same time. Our glares morphed into reluctant smiles, then we both laughed.

Eric shook his head sadly. "They've gone mad. Both of them, at the same time."

"Congenital, must be," Jimmy said.

Oliver smiled at us.

"How do you like it, Willa?" Toby asked.

"It's horrible!" It hurt my head to laugh, but it felt good at the same time. "I'm so sorry. I never realized what it would be like from your end, having caregiving shoved on you when you didn't need it."

He gave me a bear hug. "I never realized what it was like on your end, either. To love someone and want them to be okay and to be unable to fix it for them. It fucking sucks."

Jimmy stepped between us. "Will someone please explain to me what is going on?"

"They just realized what it's like to be in each other's shoes," Oliver said.

"Ohhhhhh. Because it's usually you smothering *Toby*," Jimmy said to me. "Now he's the one choking the life out of you!"

"You're all doing it, to be honest."

"Except me, right, Willa?" Jimmy asked.

"It's because we love you," Oliver said.

I went back to the table and took my pain pill, then drained my tea. "And I love you all, but you're driving me crazy. Let's watch a movie. I'll worry about everything else later."

"All right, darling," Jimmy said. "Not *Jane Eyre*. I veto it."

"Anything you want, Willa," Eric said.

"*Jane Eyre*," I announced. "The BBC version. I haven't seen it in months."

"Fucking hell," Toby said, sounding more British by the moment. "This is on you, Eric. I hope you didn't have any plans for like a million hours."

Eric shrugged. "If we're going to sit through *Jane Eyre* anyway, we might as well have a proper Rochester."

"He is much more sympathetic," Jimmy agreed. "Scoot over, Willa. Share the blanket."

Chapter Twenty-Five

The boys were sitting around Jimmy's dining room table, a big messy pile of poker chips in the middle. Oliver chomped on a candy cigar. Toby had found a visor, and Jimmy was wearing a cowboy hat and a leather vest. Eric was rocking a corset top and a black feather boa. Their trash-talking and laughter rang off the walls.

I picked up my camera and got off a couple shots before it even occurred to me to evaluate my vision. I was weak with relief when I realized it was fine.

That meant it was time for some difficult conversations. I didn't have a reason to stall anymore. The soreness was fading by the day, and now that I could use my camera again, there was no reason to keep treading water.

I left them playing and went to my room. Since the renovation was finished, I was allowed in my suite now. Turns out if you're willing to pay enough, you can get pretty much anything done as quickly as you want it. What used to be an open stairway was now completely enclosed, floor to ceiling, with a thick wall of glass. There were also sturdy rails on both sides, from top to bottom. Jimmy had been leaving piles of pillows on the floor at the bottom, though, and I had to kick them aside every time I came down. It was ridiculous, but he wanted to keep me safe because he loved me. Every time I came down the stairs, I felt cherished.

I called Hawk. He surprised me by asking about my health first. "You don't have to sound so shocked. I'm not a monster." He paused. "They're a business, Willa, and nothing matters more to my career than their success. Which means protecting it against everything, including you." He let it sink in for a moment before he continued. "It also means wanting the best for them, which includes you."

I was doodling on a pad of paper at my desk—mostly hearts and flowers. My artistic ability was definitely limited to photography. "I'm listening," I said.

"It might be time for you to have a bigger role. You could train someone else to be their assistant, and you could be the tour manager. It would give you more time to practice your hobby." I made an impatient sound, but I didn't interrupt him. I was curious where this was going. "When they're on tour or prepping for it, you'd work a lot of hours. When they're recording, you'd have more time to yourself." Then he added, "The clause against fraternizing would hold. If you're a band employee, you're keeping it professional."

I thanked him for the offer and told him I'd have to talk to my family. He told me to call and schedule some time with him when I was ready.

Benny was next.

"You okay now?" he asked. "Jimmy said you took a tumble."

"I'm getting there. Sorry I didn't get back to you right away."

"Are you also sorry you panicked and pretended there was something wrong with your phone?"

"I wasn't ready to talk to you."

"You're ready now?"

"I'm ready to listen to what you have to say." I tapped a rhythm on the desk with my pencil. "I'm not sure I'll have an answer for you yet."

He gave me the details. He'd written and was producing a theatrical musical, a rock opera. The production was in rehearsals now but, given who he was and his history of success, it was a safe bet it would land on Broadway. On top of that, Apostolic was going to launch a world tour to support their new album.

Benny wanted to hire me full-time as a photographer. I'd be paid an impressive salary to be his one-woman press corps. The PR for the theater production, and the program, advertising, and everything else involved. I would be a photographer. Not his assistant or his anything else. We'd negotiate rights to the photos, but apart from having first right of refusal to them, he was open to me selling what I could and taking pictures of whatever I wanted when he didn't need me.

"The no-fuck clause isn't industry-standard, Willa. In case you're curious." His voice was a dark purr.

"Why do you even *know* about that? It's not public or any of your business."

"That doesn't matter. I'm just saying I won't try to control you that way. Whatever you want, honey. If it's me, I'm up for it. If it's someone else in the band, no hard feelings."

"It'll be none of you."

I'd walked right into it. "Ah, you're so sure. Those rumors must be true too," he said. "Interesting. I wouldn't have picked a drummer for you."

My cheeks got hot. "We're not going to discuss that, but I'm sure your girlfriend will be glad that if I come to work for you, it'll be only to *work for you*."

"Interesting. There was a time when I'd have sworn you were into me," he said. "Remember when we were in my room together? Me, you, and Jimmy? When you knocked me back on my bed and ground your—"

"That was ages ago," I said.

He made a sound of disagreement. "It was just a few months ago, sweetheart. I guess time moves fast when you're young."

I bristled at the age comment. "I'm old enough to know that if that's why you want me to work with you—"

"It's not, but it would be a fun bonus."

"Well, I was starstruck, and I'm over it. If we're going to work together, it's not going to be like that."

He didn't miss a beat. "Fair enough. I won't bring it up again. If you change your mind—"

"I won't. Let's keep going. I have more questions. What's your manager like?"

"My manager is delightful. You'll love her."

"Will I get time off?"

"No, you have to work 24/7. Yes, Willa. You'll have time off. Jesus."

I chewed on my lip. "Can I think about it?"

"Sure. For a few days. Let me know either way by the end of the week. I'll have to hire someone else if it's not going to be you."

When I hung up with Benny, I sat in my office chair, watching a fat magpie hopping along the fence that divided Jimmy's garden from his back neighbor's. My window was cracked open for the fresh air, and the muffled sounds of kids playing danced through the air. Cars sent puddles splashing against the curb, and the soft, insistent rhythm of raindrops tapped against the window. The sounds of London.

Jimmy, Eric, and Oliver were playing a song downstairs, testing it out on Toby. The notes of their music and the timbre of their voices floated up the stairs, punctuated with bursts of laughter. The sounds of family.

I pictured being in New York with Benny. How long would it take me to adjust? Being on Broadway, working with actors—would I love it like I loved working with musicians?

This kind of opportunity wouldn't come to me twice, but I didn't know if I was willing to give up everything for it.

I heard footsteps on the stairs, and I turned in my chair as Toby came in. "Hey," he said. "What're you doing up here? Is your head okay?"

"Eh. Not bad. How're you feeling? Everything okay?"

His eyes sparkled when he grinned at me. "Touché. I'm fine, you're fine, nobody needs mothering. Come hang out with us. My trip is almost over. Jimmy wants to make us a big, belated Thanksgiving dinner tomorrow since we missed it, and then I have a late flight."

"Is he going to cook?" The rain was coming down harder, so I closed the window.

Toby grinned. "I guess so. He wants us to include our favorites from when we were kids."

I grimaced.

Toby was on the same page. "Yeah, I know. We didn't have many traditional Thanksgiving dinners. I didn't want to ruin it for him."

"Mom used to do a big dinner." I settled back into my chair. "You were too young to remember. For a few years there, we had the works. Turkey, stuffing, sweet potatoes, cranberry sauce, the whole thing. Ridiculous, since it was just the four of us." I was quiet for a moment, remembering. "I miss us being a family."

His gaze was serious. "I wish you'd heard these guys when they called me. Jimmy's drama is one thing, but this wasn't a schtick. He was genuinely panic-stricken. I didn't talk to him, but I overheard him talking to you in the background. A running monologue of reassuring chatter the whole time, and he sounded ragged. You hadn't woken up, but he and Oliver were taking turns talking to you next to your bed. Eric's the one who called me."

"Eric couldn't have been there," I said. "I bled. Eric can't be near blood."

"He was there. They were all there, and they were freaked the fuck out. I knew you guys had gotten close, but they were obviously more than coworkers or friends."

"They're my family now too," I said quietly.

Toby grinned. "Yep. They are. You have an imperfect, sloppy, loving family. Of rock stars. This is not what I would have predicted for you, Willa, but life is funny."

"I talked to Benny Walker," I blurted. "The job he wants to offer me is even better than I imagined it would be."

He laughed. "Could you have imagined a year ago where we'd be right now? Me back in school—"

"With a girlfriend."

"With a hot girlfriend, and you juggling a bunch of musicians?" He got up and kissed the top of my head. "Life is funny."

"Hilarious," I said glumly. Juggling musicians sounded like a lot more fun than it was. The fact was that I was going to let someone down. I knew that if I quit my job, I could just … be here. It's what Jimmy wanted. He would keep me. I could stay here and be Oliver's girlfriend and Eric's friend and Jimmy's…whatever it was. But settling for that would mean letting *myself* down. My mom had been content to go to Bob and just hand over the reins. That might have worked for her, but it wasn't what I wanted for myself. I wanted to create my art. I wanted to be heard.

"Go play with your new friends," I said to Toby. "I'm going to make Jimmy a grocery list, and I'm going to find some recipes online because he has no idea what he's getting himself into with this idea of a Thanksgiving dinner."

Eric poked his head around the doorway. "Come on, Toby. Let's play pool. Hey girl, you look good," he said to me. "You're feeling better; I can see it."

"Eric, did you come to the hospital when I fell?"

"Yes, I was there," he said carefully. "Do you not remember?"

"I do, but… I had some scrapes. Didn't I bleed?"

He blanched. "Oy. Don't remind me."

I gave him a tight hug. He didn't tower over me like Jimmy, Oliver, and Toby. He was taller than me, but it was a nice fit when I hugged him. "I love you, Eric."

He gave me a squeeze. "I love you too, Willa." When he released me, he held me at arm's length and gave me a stern frown. "I bet I'll also love American Thanksgiving food. Get to work on that list and stop mooning about."

"I'm on it."

He looked behind him and let out an exaggerated sigh. "So much for that. Here comes ya boy. Let's get out of here, Toby. It's getting crowded in here."

Oliver smiled at me and flopped on my couch. He adjusted a pillow behind his head and crossed his hands on his belly. "Hi, Willa."

"Make yourself at home."

"Don't mind if I do. Did you talk to Benny?"

"Yes."

He sat up and leaned forward, resting his arms on his knees. His gaze was steady on mine. "All right."

"Oliver—"

He held up a hand to stop me. His eyes appeared shiny, but he smiled at me anyway. "We can talk about it later. Let's implement a variation of don't-ask-don't-tell. If you don't tell me, I can't tell Jimmy when he asks—and you know he will."

I should have known Oliver would be able to tell I'd already made a decision. "It's only because—"

His smile was sweet. "I get it."

"I have to—"

"I know," he said again. "When?"

"Soon."

"All right. Let's table it until after Thanksgiving. In the meantime, I owe you a date. Let's do it."

My heart made a funny jump. "We can't."

"We can, actually. We're not talking about what we're not talking about, but what we're not talking about means we can."

"What'll we tell Jimmy?"

"That we're sneaking. He'll love it."

I was wavering, but Oliver leaned closer. "Let's do it, Willa. One perfect date before everything changes."

"But… what if it makes everything even worse?"

He scoffed. "How could it?"

It was a fair question.

He put a hand on my knee. "I want you to do what's best for you, whatever it means for you or for us. Before then, I want us to have gone out properly one time, so we'll always have that."

It was hard to think of a reason this was a bad idea. It was hard to think at all, actually, when he deployed his magic voice.

"Don't overanalyze it. What do you want right now?"

"To go out with you."

His smile lit up the room.

"*Willa!*" Jimmy bellowed from the bottom of the stairs. "Did you make a Thanksgiving foods list? Oliver, stop bamboozling her or whatever it is you're doing up there! I need her to focus."

Oliver captured my hands. "Come on, Willa. We can go right now. We'll be back here tomorrow in time for Jimmy's feast."

"Toby's here, and—"

"Jimmy wants to take him to the bar tonight anyway. They'll never miss us."

"Oh my God. I'm not sure I should allow that to happen. Poor Chelsea. If she only knew what goes on at a bar with Jimmy, she'd—"

"Willllllaaaaaaaa!" Jimmy shouted. "Don't make me come up there, you two!"

"Say yes," Oliver urged again.

"Yes."

He gave me a quick kiss. "You won't regret it. Go pack. I have to make a few calls."

Chapter Twenty-Six

I finished the grocery list and arranged for everything to be delivered so Jimmy could make his "one-man Thanksgiving dinner." I printed some recipes and took them downstairs to the breakfast bar, then ran back upstairs to get ready for my date with Oliver.

He wouldn't tell me where we were going, only that it was a "bit of a drive," I should bring an overnight bag, and to dress warmly.

He promised Jimmy we'd be back in time for dinner tomorrow and somehow sweet-talked or bullied him into letting me go. Toby promised he didn't mind, and Eric promised to supervise Jimmy, who imagined he was supervising Toby. For my own peace of mind, I asked him to keep a special eye on Eric. They were circularly taking care of each other and would be fine.

Oliver and I were cleared for take-off.

I didn't figure out where he was taking me until we got there. He pulled the car over and came around to my side to take my hand as we waded into the high grass. The wind was whipping my hair, and the clouds were coming in. The air smelled wild, the heather was growing, the grass was high, and he and I were hand in hand... walking across the moors.

Jane Eyre's moors. I'd spent God knew how many hours daydreaming about this place, and he'd brought me here.

He lifted my hand and kissed my fingers. I soaked up the sensation of being in such a beautiful, wild place, with someone who cared for me so much he would go to these lengths to make a dream come true for me. He'd promised me the best date of my life—it already was.

The smell of the air changed, became more electric. The storm rolled toward us from miles out. "We should go back to the car, sweetheart," he said.

"In a minute." The wind whipped my hair around. It smelled different than any air I'd ever smelled. I never wanted to leave.

"The clouds are getting pretty sinister," he said a few minutes later.

I turned toward the car, then glanced back. "Maybe one more minute."

Lightning flashed, and he laughed with me while stinging pellets of rain lashed at us.

I shouted over the storm. "Oliver!"

"Willa?"

"Best! Date! Ever!"

He swooped in to kiss me again. A slippery, rain-soaked, heated kiss that totally did justice to being in the middle of a storm on the moors.

My future was a question mark, but my present was a perfect exclamation point.

He cranked up the heater when we got in the car and drove for a few minutes before he turned off the road and followed an uneven two-track for a mile or two. By the time we got to the building, the rain was coming down so heavily I couldn't see much. He parked by a low stone wall, then got out to open a wooden gate. He drove in and parked, and we dashed to the door. When we got inside, I stopped in my tracks.

The interior was different because there were modern appliances in it now, but I recognized it immediately. The arched brick ceiling, the distinctive tile, the wood-burning stove. "You brought me to Jane Eyre's Moor House! From the best adaptation!"

"I did."

"Are we staying here?" I whispered, dropping onto the wooden bench in the entry.

"We are." He nodded and knelt at my feet to untie my muddy boots before standing and toeing off his own.

When he straightened, I leaped into his arms, wrapped legs my around him, and kissed all over his face. I'd become accustomed to not kissing him and always desperately wanting to; it was a luxury to be able to put my mouth on him every time I was moved to.

I was really, really moved to do so.

It was obvious we were on the same page. He held me up for a minute, then let me slide down his body until my feet were on the floor while he held me tightly against him. He didn't stop kissing me until I couldn't control a shiver.

He rested his forehead against mine as we caught our breath. "We need to get you warm. Go take off your wet things, and I'll get a fire going."

I squelched down the hall in my wet socks to the bathroom, where I found an enormous claw-footed tub next to windows overlooking the storm.

I filled the tub with hot water and poured in a generous amount of vanilla-scented bubble bath I found on the counter. Leaving my soggy clothes in the sink, I submerged myself in warm, fragrant bubbles. The storm beat against the windows, raindrops tracing uneven lines down the panes.

Oliver tapped on the door and called, "All right, Willa?"

"Come in here. You have to see this."

He opened the door and peered around the corner. His brown eyes were warm, and he showed me his dimples. "Oh, hi. You're right. Naked wet Willa is something I'm very happy to see."

I felt my cheeks get pink. I gestured him over. "Come here. You can watch the storm from here."

He sat on the tub's edge. "Beautiful," he said. I smiled, and he leaned down to kiss me. "I started a fire. By the time you come out, the chill should be out of the air."

"Aren't you cold?"

"A little." He traced one hand through the thick bubbles. "I was going to go get some dry clothes."

I captured his hand and tugged him closer. "It's a big tub."

His expression was serious, but his gaze dipped to my mouth and back up. "Are you sure?"

I let go of his hand and brought my knees to my chest to make room for him.

I faced the window, suddenly shy as Oliver shucked his wet clothes. Nobody was going to burst in and interrupt us, thrusting a contract or anything else between us. It was just him and me.

He got in slowly, careful not to spill the soapy water over the edge. He sat across from me and settled against the back of the tub. He leaned his head back. "Feels good in here. You're right."

I shifted my legs against his, relishing how his skin against mine. I sighed happily. "It's perfect, right?"

"It's perfect." His voice was a caress.

There was so much Oliver on display for me to feast my eyes on. I ran my fingers over the art on his body, tracing a path of bubbles along his warm skin, eventually settling my hand over his heart. I raised myself up to my knees and settled onto his lap. I tilted his face toward me and kissed him.

He shifted under me, his skin a warm, slippery slide. "Ah, Christ. Sorry. I need to stop. This is too—you're too—Willa." There was a tremor in his voice. My unflappable Oliver was definitely flapped. It made me more confident.

I kissed him again and slid my hand down his chest, over his stomach, under the scented water.

He drew in a ragged breath.

"Let's go to bed," I said.

He gently moved my hair back from my face with wet fingertips and waited for me to meet his eyes. "Are you sure?"

"I'm sure. Please." He kissed me, and this time I was the one who pulled back. "Yes?" I clarified.

"Yes," he confirmed, his voice hoarse.

We both stood at once, water streaming down our bodies. He stepped out first and lifted me out.

He worked on toweling us both off as I rifled through my toiletry bag for a condom. He snagged it from my fingers when I held one up, victorious, and then he leaned in and kissed me again. I couldn't get enough of the taste of him, the warmth of his lips, the perfect sting of his teeth, the buzz of his voice traveling through me when he groaned. I wanted to take my time and savor, but I couldn't get enough of him fast enough.

He hooked the towel behind my back and used it to pull me with him while he walked backward down the hall. I giggled as we made our clumsy way, our damp naked bodies colliding and tripping along. "Too slow," he muttered, lifting me off my feet again. He hauled me to the bedroom and dropped me on the bed.

His eyes were heated. "Beautiful," he whispered.

I held my arms out to him, and he covered me with his body.

I remember vivid flashes of the first time. Snapshots, like I photographed us with my brain. His hands gripping mine, knuckles white, holding us both steady. Slowly rocking into me. The sweet ache of it.

His brown eyes on mine. Right there with me.

The way he bit his lip as he forced himself to hold on, last longer, make it better for me.

How he wrapped his arms around me and kept me grounded.

The way he held me after, tracing circles on my back with his warm fingers as I nestled against his chest.

I sighed against his skin and kissed him again because I could. "Oliver, you know what's better than being on the moors?"

"Hmm?"

"Sex with you."

His laugh rumbled against me.

"You might have ruined me for all other sex forever." I was kidding, but not really. The whole higher ground stance, where he'd offered me a long-distance relationship, and I'd rejected a life of conjugal visits with him? My brain understood it was the right decision, but the rest of me wasn't sure anymore. "I'm not complaining. It was worth it."

"I'm glad you're happy," he said.

As my body cooled, second thoughts kicked in.

I pulled the blankets over our bodies, then nestled my head under his chin so I wouldn't have to face him. I hadn't been self-conscious in the heat of the moment. I'd been preoccupied with making it happen, but now that it *had* happened, what if he was underwhelmed? He was Oliver Everett. I was just Willa.

Now that I was coming down from the high, it occurred to me that Oliver had probably been with a lot of women. He'd certainly had more partners than I had. He'd probably slept with beautiful women all over the world. Women who were more experienced than I was, since there was hardly such a thing as less experienced. This was the first time I'd had sex straight from a bubble bath, but maybe he'd had dozens of sexing-in-bath-tubs adventures with women who had a much better idea of how to please a man. I mean, suggesting we get out of the tub? Was that weird? Was I lame? Maybe everybody knew bathtubs were way hotter than beds, and I'd ruined it. Then again, did condoms work in a tub? I had no idea.

When I moved away from him, he tightened his arms around me.

He shook his head. "Don't, Willa."

"Don't what?"

"Don't get up in your head. Stay here with me."

"It occurred to me—"

He kissed me, then murmured, "If you're thinking, I need to work harder."

"No, I mean—" I cut myself off with a yelp and then a groan as he made two things perfectly clear. He wasn't listening to me, and he definitely, definitely did not find me underwhelming.

~ * ~

We did get up eventually. I was pleasantly sore, my muscles noodles. Oliver had arranged to have dinner made ahead of time, so we put a dish of ravioli in the oven. He made a salad while I opened the wine and put plates and silverware on the weathered wood of the dining room table. It was domestic. It felt right, as if post-sex meals were something he and I should be enjoying much more of.

I made myself stop. I wouldn't taint the present by longing for a future I couldn't have.

When the ravioli came out of the oven, he put in a pan of bread pudding.

He read my skepticism. "Willa, no. Never make a face at bread pudding. Have you ever had it?"

"It's mushy bread, not pudding."

"Have I led you wrong yet?"

"Um, no. Not today."

"Not ever. You're going to love bread pudding."

I dropped into a battered wooden chair across from him. I felt a big dopey smile on my face.

He tried to frown at me. "Now listen. I'm going to talk to you seriously right now, so quit making your hazy post-orgasm face. You're distracting me."

"I am hazy and post-orgasmic." I sat up straighter. "Ooh! Maybe pre-orgasmic too!"

His eyes went a bit darker. "You're definitely also pre-orgasmic. Stop saying orgasmic. I'm not finished, and you're distracting me."

"I'm listening." I attacked my dinner with gusto.

"Okay. Pay attention. Two things. First, the horse has left the barn, as you would say, but there are two bedrooms. I need you to know I didn't assume we'd have sex."

I pointed at his plate with my fork. "Eat! You should eat this delicious meal. We need to refuel from moors and sex."

He smiled at me and took another bite of ravioli before he continued, "I want you to know that as wonderful as it was, and as glad I am it happened, and will happen again soon, I didn't expect it. Okay? That's important."

I nodded. "Got it. I expected it, though. I'd have been disappointed if you didn't put out, Oliver. I packed lingerie for you and everything. Also, when I got here and opened my overnight bag, I discovered that Jimmy had considerately packed about seventy condoms for us. A custom variety pack with colors, flavors, textures, everything. So I'm not the only one who expected it, not that it matters. We were overdue for it, right?"

"Well, I brought condoms myself, and seventy is maybe more than we'll need, but I like his optimism. Anyway, that's the first thing. Now listen to the second thing because it is also important."

"I am all ears."

"Are you?" he asked doubtfully. "It seems like you're mostly focused on eating and thinking about sex, and I need you to pay attention."

I put down my fork. "I'm listening."

"All right. It's not cool to say this right after sex, but I'm just pleased I didn't blurt it out it when I was inside you. I can't keep not saying it when you look at me with that face, Willa. Okay?"

I patted his hand encouragingly. "Of course! Only I don't know what you're talking about."

"I love you." He took my hand in his. "I'm in love with you. Completely."

I stared at him, delicious food and even more delicious sex forgotten for the moment.

He squeezed my hand. "It's not just that I like you because you're fun to hang out with, even though you are. It's not just because you're smart and funny and strong and confident and resilient and so fucking cool. It's not because the sight of you curled up with a book with your frowny reading face is the most adorable thing I've seen in my life. It's not just that I want you because you're gorgeous and because you have such a great ass. It's all those things and so much more. It's everything. All of you."

Why did Jimmy and Eric write the lyrics, I wondered, when Oliver was the most romantic and poetic man in the world?

"I'm not asking anything of you, Willa. Whatever you do next... whatever you need for yourself and your career, whatever you want for life, I'm not ever going to regret this. Every second with you has been worth how much it's going to hurt if you go. Okay? So don't... I don't want you to feel guilty. When you do what comes next, don't convince yourself I'd have done anything differently because I wouldn't have."

I hadn't done anything other than stare at him while everything else in the world stopped. He was so open and so beautiful and so Oliver my heart almost couldn't hold all of him.

I pushed my plate to the side and leaned toward him. "Oliver."

"Willa."

"Now you listen to me."

He reached across the table and threaded his fingers through mine.

"I love you."

His mouth did the super cute thing it did when he wanted to smile but was trying not to. "Yeah?"

"I'm not done. Keep listening. I love you so much. Your voice is the sexiest sound in the entire world. You're funny and thoughtful. You take care of everybody, and you laughed in the rain and took a bubble bath with me, and you just made me come, for like, a *really* long time. I know I keep mentioning it, but it bears repeating."

He tucked my hair behind my ears. "What else?" he whispered.

I was happy to keep going. "I loved you even when you were mad at me," I said. "I loved you when I was hiding from how I felt. I loved you when you waited for me. Whatever comes next for me... I refuse to regret falling in love with you. I'll always..." I trailed off, frustrated with myself. I couldn't find the words to say what I meant, but it was important. "I never knew people could love each other like this. I know you love me, and you want me, and you're going to let me go do what I need to do anyway. I haven't ever seen a relationship work this way. Thank you for being that for me."

The timer on the stove interrupted me.

"Bread pudding," he said, giving me a soft, Oliver-y smile.

With shaking hands but a great deal of determination, I carried our plates to the sink and found an oven mitt and removed the warm dessert from the oven. I set it aside and held out my hand.

"We have to eat it warm," he protested.

"I need to have you again first," I announced.

As it turned out, he wasn't opposed to letting the bread pudding wait.

~ * ~

The next morning was the second part of our date.

It was Haddon Hall, where *Jane Eyre* was filmed. Oliver arranged for a private tour, which we almost missed because it's difficult to get up when you're in bed with a warm, drowsy, aroused Oliver Everett. Luckily, he can be efficient and on-task when he needs to be.

He took a picture of me so I could text it to Jimmy. As soon as it went through, I called him. "Jimmy! Guess where I am!"

"Well, not on the road yet, which has me worried you're going to miss dinner. Are you guys keeping an eye on the time?"

"We won't miss dinner, but guess where I *am*!"

"Hang on, let me look at the picture again." I heard a muffled "fuck me!" and then he was back on the line. "Is that Rochester's study? I mean—I have no idea because how would I know? If you think I've re-watched *Jane Eyre* on my own because Toby Stephens, you are sadly mistaken. I'm very busy being a rock star. I don't have time to for movies, and even if I *did*, I only like action flicks."

I laughed. "Of course. But you're right! I'm in the real Haddon Hall!"

His voice was warm. "Is it the best date of your life, Willoughby?"

"*Yes*. Nothing else has even come close."

"I'm glad you're having a good time." He paused. "Are you proud of me for not asking if you're still a virgin of Oliver?"

"I'm so proud of you. Good job, Jimmy!"

"I know, right? My ability to change and grow surprises even me, and I hold myself to a high standard."

"Be home soon!" I made a kissing noise into the phone and disconnected.

Oliver kept my hand in his the whole drive back to London, only letting go when he needed both hands on the wheel, then threading his fingers back through mine as soon as he could.

When he parked the car back at Jimmy's, Oliver turned to me, held my face gently in his hands, and kissed me.

When we broke apart, that was it.

There would always be pre-moors and post-moors from now on.

But right now it was time for Thanksgiving dinner and for telling my family I'd made a decision.

I was going to go work with Benny.

It was the best opportunity I'd ever had. I'd worked for it and earned it. It wasn't just going to set me on the path to my career; it was going to full-on catapult me into the job and lifestyle I wanted. I had to take the job. Money enough to help take care of Toby if he needed it. The luxury of *one job* I loved.

My dreams were coming true, and my heart was breaking a little at the same time.

Chapter Twenty-Seven

The sight of the dining room table in the main room stopped me in my tracks and momentarily distracted me from my nerves.

It was like the cover of a *Better Homes and Gardens* magazine. The turkey was perfectly browned, sitting on a platter with herbs arranged artfully around it. I walked around the table, leaning over to smell the stuffing, running a finger around the rim of a glass of deep red wine. There was steam rising off the mashed potatoes. A pat of butter melting over the dish of green beans. There was even an apple pie waiting on the counter.

"Did you help with this?" I asked Toby. It was almost as difficult to imagine as Jimmy doing it himself.

Toby shook his head. "Not a bit. I wasn't allowed in the kitchen. I'm glad you guys are back from the date we're not allowed to mention in case it makes you emotional and ruins dinner."

Jimmy was a bit droopy, but he gave Toby a wink.

"Happy Thanksgiving!" Jimmy came to me with his arms open.

I gave him a hug. "You're the best. Thank you for doing this. I can't wait."

"You good?" he asked quietly.

I didn't quite trust my voice, so I nodded. He knew I was lying. He gave me another hug. "Oh, Willa."

I wanted to lean into him and weep, but I didn't give in to it. I made myself let go of him after a moment. "Let's eat, Jimmy. Everything is perfect. Thank you for making this feast."

I tried to keep my gaze off Oliver because looking at him triggered a physical memory. How he tasted. The thrill of his wet skin sliding against mine. The look on his face when he moved inside me. The joy in his expression when he watched me realize a dream come true by being on the moors. I willed myself to stay in the moment instead of being preoccupied with the recent past.

He seemed to be similarly preoccupied. Whenever I let myself look at him, his dark eyes were on me. He looked hungry for something other than the delicious feast in front of us.

Toby's bag was packed and at the front door, and I'd arranged for a car to pick him up. Jimmy, with typical generosity, had bought Toby a first-class ticket home. I wasn't ready for him to go, but I was going to be okay.

We finished dinner, and I cleared the table, made coffee, then cut the pie. When I sat back down, Jimmy clinked on his glass for attention. "Let's borrow a tradition from our American friends. We'll go around the table, and everyone say what you're thankful for. Other than this delicious dinner I made because obviously. If things fall apart for us—I kid, how could they—and I don't work as a model, I'll probably be a chef. What a blessing to the culinary world I'd be."

He was funny, adorable, and so Jimmy. I was lucky to be there, to have had the chance to get to know them. Leaving would be so painful only because I loved them and felt safe with them. I reminded myself to be thankful to have that, not sorrowful because things had to change.

He continued, "I'll go first. I'm thankful for everyone here. I'm thankful our album is better than anyone else's and is breaking records and holding at number one even though you'd think everyone had already bought it." I laughed, and the knot in my stomach eased. "I'm thankful we met Toby, even though he's complete shit at cards and only mediocre at pool. I'm thankful Willa gave me a second chance when I fucked up and that she's on the road to recovery." He squeezed my hand. "I'm thankful to Americans for this racially-problematic holiday, which they should reflect upon and maybe align with something less historically horrible, because it's given us a reason to eat delicious food. Eric, now you."

"I'm thankful to be in a band with my best friends and to have Toby and Willa here with us. Also thankful to learn that Jimmy can cook. I had no idea."

"Toby!" Jimmy directed.

"Thanks to all of you for taking care of my sister and for being such good hosts who are rich enough to not mind the amount of money I won off you at cards. To new friends." He held up his coffee cup in a toast.

"Oliver!"

"I'm thankful for you lot," he said. "For this. Every day."

"Now Willa!"

I swallowed around the lump in my throat. How could I say it? How would I express what these people meant to me and how grateful I was to be there with them? How could I articulate how thankful I was for what they'd taught me about the give-and-take of being in a true family? It wasn't just giving up everything else to take care of someone else. They'd taken care of me in return, and taught me how precious it was to have people who would always be there, would have your back with no hesitation.

I cleared my throat.

"I'm not even sure where to start. I have so much to thank y'all for. Toby, I'm thankful you're my brother. You came rushing out here to take care of me, and you showed me how we can be adults and friends. I'm lucky to be your sister."

I covered Jimmy's hand with mine. "Jimmy, I'm grateful to you for giving me a chance. You had no reason to believe I'd be good at this job, but you gave me a safe place to pour out every bit of nurturing I needed to give." My eyes filled. "I wouldn't have been able to articulate what I needed, but you gave me exactly what I needed to get through a rough time."

He smiled. "It has been a real sacrifice on my part to let you take care of me, Willa, but you're welcome."

"You're the best friend I've ever had," I said. "I don't know how to say thank you for that. You're also the prettiest friend I ever had. Thank you for that since it helped me get such great pictures of you and finally get some acknowledgment as a photographer."

I cleared my throat. "Eric, I'm thankful to you for being the wisdom of this group. You know when to talk and when to listen and when to wait it out or give a word or warning or encouragement. You're wise beyond your years and a brilliant musician. I added a hefty dose of a pain-in-the-ass factor into your band and your life, but you brought me in with open arms, and I'm thankful for your friendship."

He coughed. "Yeah, um, I'm thankful for you too. Jimmy saved his good decision-making about hiring and spent it all at once on you. We're lucky to have you with us, Willa."

I looked at Oliver, sitting across from me, gorgeous and steady. It would be easier to pretend what I felt for him was less intense than it was, but I wouldn't. "Oliver, I'm thankful for you for a hundred things. For being the best pillow in the world. For giving me a second chance when I ran. For understanding what it is I do as an artist and for believing in me. For supporting me even though what I'm going to do will make it hard for there to be a you-and-me. I am grateful for you every day, and whatever the future holds, that won't change."

I gave myself a minute to find the words to say what came next. Going to work for Benny was a great opportunity for me, and it didn't have to be an ending.

I'd spent so much time debating what I was willing to be without. Proximity to Toby? Time with Jimmy doing a job I loved, and he needed? My art? Credibility as a professional? A great salary? The man I loved? The give and take of a real family?

I wasn't willing to do without any of it.

I wanted all those things. I wanted everything.

Nobody was going to hand it to me, but I could take it. Everything was coming into focus. I'd spent years trying to prove I wasn't like my mom. In the process, I'd lost sight of who I was and what I wanted. I wanted to be a family with Toby and with these guys. I wanted to be an artist. I wanted to have a career.

I wanted to be with Oliver.

Some people would say it's outdated to want to take care of people, to want to be needed, to sacrifice things for a man. It wasn't like that. It wasn't a sacrifice to insist on having everything I wanted. It was the opposite of a sacrifice. I believed the people around this table loved me enough to give me room to make it happen, and it was time to find out.

"I have to make a phone call," I announced baldly. I pulled my phone from my pocket and dialed Hawk. When he answered, I said, "Hi, I quit."

"Hello, Willa," he said wryly.

At least he got my name right.

"I'm not going to work for you anymore. Not as their assistant." Oliver wasn't surprised by my announcement, but he was the only one who wasn't. Jimmy had paled. I stroked his arm, trying to reassure him.

My voice gained strength. "I'm ending my contract on today's date, Hawk. Thanks for giving me a chance and offering me that other job. I appreciate it. I'll come in and meet with you tomorrow because we should still do the book. 'Kay. Bye, Hawk. Happy Thanksgiving!"

Jimmy was the first to speak. "Did you just quit, Willa? Did you…. are you leaving me?"

"I did, and no. Not if you don't want me to."

"I don't understand you. Does anyone else have any idea what she's on about?"

I held up a finger. "I'm going to explain it all. Gotta make another call first."

When he answered, I said, "Hi, Benny. I accept your offer! I will work for you."

Eric winced. Jimmy's face fell even more. Oliver winked at me.

"Listen, I'll do it, and it's going to be great. Photos of you, publicity for the play, the program, all of it. Here are my terms: I'm going to split time between here and there. You can pay me seventy-five percent of what you offered, and I'll give you fifty percent of my time."

"Whoa, whoa, whoa. Fifty percent of your time? You're practically a rookie, kid. You're telling me you can do everything I need as a part-timer?"

My stomach clutched. *Could* I do it all? Was I taking too big of a gamble?

I rallied.

"You wouldn't have asked me to do this if you didn't know I could. You're a pretty photogenic guy, Benny, but my pictures of you are better than anyone else's. You can take what I'm offering, or you can make do with second-best. If you don't want me, I've got other offers lining up." That was not strictly true, but it would be.

He laughed. "Shit, girl. Look out, world. Willa's coming into her own. Okay, fine. We'll give it a try."

"I'll call you tomorrow with my start date." I couldn't keep the smile off my face. "Thanks! See you soon!"

When I ended the call, the men were staring at me. I didn't understand what they were waiting for. I'd just done it. I'd solved everything. Why didn't they understand? "What? What are you guys... aren't you glad?"

"Willa," Oliver said gently, "We're wondering what you're going to do with the other half of your time."

"Oh!" I beamed at them. "I'll be here with you! Take pictures of whatever comes up if it works, but mostly... be with you."

"This would be home base?" Jimmy asked.

"Yes! When I'm not in New York, I'll be in London," I said. "Except for when I'm in Nashville visiting Toby. Or, I don't know, on location somewhere."

"Clever girl," Oliver said quietly. I let him get away with the "girl" because of the admiration and fondness written all over his face.

"Willa!" Jimmy cried, perking right up. "We've found a way for you to do everything!"

"Everything, Jimmy. That's what I pick."

"Well *done*! If you're only giving us half your time, though, I hope you're not going to be running off to the moors with Oliver as often as you have been lately, or I'll never be with you. You're going to have to find me a new assistant and good luck finding someone who doesn't want to sleep with me. You have your work cut out for you there."

Compared to the problems I'd already solved... this was still formidable, but things were different now. I had confidence. I knew what

I was capable of.

I'd made my decision. I was going to take everything, and I had no doubt my family was going to support me.

We ate more pie, did more rounds of toasts. I couldn't stop smiling at them all. Way before I was ready, it was time to say goodbye to Toby. I walked him to the door.

"You're sure you're okay with this?" I asked. "One hundred percent positive, you promise?"

He smiled at me. "One hundred percent positive. I promise. As long as you sell Dad's house. It's time."

"All right, all right. We'll talk about it. Hey, um, listen. I want to say… like, I get it. When you were telling me I didn't need to take care of you—"

"—Willa, I'm sorry about how—"

"—no, just listen for a second. I get it. You needed me to trust you enough to make your own decisions. That's not the same thing as telling me you don't need me. You were asking me to let you have the room to make your own path."

He gave me another hug and held me tight for a minute. "It feels good to make your own path, right?"

"It sure does," I whispered. I cleared my throat and said, "Okay, go. I love you. Have a safe flight."

When the door closed behind Toby, Oliver was there with a hug. "All right?" he asked.

I brushed away tears. "I'm good. I just hate saying goodbye."

"He'll be back. And you can visit him in Nashville, right?"

"Right."

Eric handed me my wine, and we relocated to the living room. "That's the beauty of your new set-up, Will," he said. "You're going to be saying goodbye to everyone all the time, but never for long."

I liked the sound of that. Saying goodbye would be easier when I would be saying hello again soon. I was going to have the career I'd dreamed of, and I didn't have to surrender everything else I wanted in order to do it.

My heart was going to burst, but now it was because of how full it was. I could have everything I wanted if I kept it in balance. I didn't have to define myself as a caregiver, but I didn't have to deny it, either. It was part of who I was and what I loved, but so was my art and my career. The reason it hadn't worked when I tried to be on my own was the same reason it hadn't worked when I'd tried to lose myself in taking care of other people. I didn't want to choose one or the other.

For the first time, I trusted myself enough to believe I could do all of it, and I loved myself enough to know I deserved the perfect-for-me life I was building.

There was one more call to make. When the guys turned on a soccer game—*football*, I corrected myself mentally—I settled in an armchair next to the fire, searched through my call history, and dialed another number.

When my mom answered, I said, "Sorry to hit you up out of the blue. Do you have a minute to talk? It's Willa."

"Oh! Of course I do, hon—Willa. Is everything okay?"

"Yes. I know Toby told you I was hurt, and he's been sneaking you updates. I wanted to tell you myself I'm okay." I took the blanket off the back of the chair and wrapped it around myself.

Her voice was warm like she was smiling. "I'm so glad. I was worried about you. Your vision is clearing up? Headaches are better?"

"Getting there. I'm going to be okay. Toby came here to be with me, and everything is going to be fine. I thought... I thought you might like to hear it from me."

I kept my gaze on Oliver. He made me feel calmer. More peaceful.

"I was so worried. So was your brother. It means a lot to me that you called."

I stared at the fire and listened to the sounds of my boys trash-talking the television and each other. It sounded like home. "I don't like what you did," I said to her after a moment of silence. "Before. I hate that you left Toby and me. But I... sometimes when someone is faced with a difficult choice, even if they make a wrong decision because they're not strong enough to—"

I cut myself off. If I was going to do this, I owed it to myself to get it right. "No. That was all wrong. Let me have a do-over. Here goes.

"I wish you'd chosen differently. I get that you were scared, but I wish you'd have chosen us anyway. Toby and I didn't have you, and that hurts. But we're all doing the best we can. I've made mistakes, and I've been given second chances. I wanted to say, if it matters, I forgive you."

"It matters." Now her voice was tight as if she had a lump in her throat.

I steadied my voice. "I'm not going to be back in Tennessee soon, but maybe when I'm there next, maybe we could meet for coffee or something?"

"Absolutely. I would love the chance to get to know who you are."

"Happy Thanksgiving, Mom," I said. "I'll call again soon."

When I disconnected, I heard more sniffling from the direction of the couch. Jimmy and Eric were watching me, both with shiny eyes.

Jimmy blinked and fanned at his face with his hand. "So beautiful, Willa! I should cook more often, right? I didn't expect it to have such an enormous impact. At first, you ruined Thanksgiving. Like seriously shit all over it. But you've salvaged it."

"I'm going home to call my mum," Eric announced. "I'll be back in a bit to help with the dishes, Jimmy."

He waved him away. "It's handled. I've hired someone to come in and do it. I didn't want to put it on Willa, and I knew I'd be fucking exhausted. Come back to hang out later if you want." Then he looked at Oliver and me. "Oh, wait," he said. "Do you two want to be alone? Should I... go to Eric's or something? Third wheel in my own house," he muttered.

Oliver didn't take his gaze off me. "It's good, Jimmy. Maybe you want to come to my house later, Willa?"

"I do. Yes. I do."

"Maybe you'll even want to stay the night."

I grinned. "Yes, please."

Jimmy huffed out a breath. "Christ, this is weird."

Oliver patted the couch between them. "Willa, come sit with us for now."

"You want me to watch soccer with you guys?"

They corrected me in unison. "Football."

I snuggled in, my head on Oliver's chest. He put his arm around me and smiled at me. "It's like this now, yeah? We can cuddle like a normal couple."

"Just like a normal couple," I echoed, grinning like a fool.

Jimmy leaned against my other side, and I sighed happily. Eric rejoined us in a bit and helped himself to another slice of pie before he sat in front of the television.

I listened to the steady beat of Oliver's heart under my ear and let their sports talk swirl around me.

Soon, I'd be alone again with him.

Later, Toby would call to tell me he was home safely.

I'd meet with Hawk about a book tomorrow and probably spend the rest of the day with Jimmy, catching up on what needed to be done and making a plan to hire him a new assistant.

Benny was waiting with my dream job on the other side of the ocean, and, in the meantime, I had photographs coming out in new album liner notes and a spread in the next issue of *Offstage*.

It was a lot.

It was everything.

When the game paused for a commercial break, Oliver nudged me gently with his shoulder. "All right, Willa?"

"Mmhm. All right." I stretched to give him a light kiss on the mouth.

I was pretty sure I was going to love having it all.

Epilogue

As I was rushing around getting ready for my party, my phone kept buzzing with new messages. I ignored it. The whole thing was stressing me out. I hadn't even wanted to have a party. My loft in New York wasn't big enough for it to be practical, but I had been overruled.

"You absolutely fucking are having a party," Jimmy said. "You have a bestseller! Of pictures of me! Yes, fine, Eric, of *us*, I meant. It calls for a party, Willa. Shall we come to you, or do you want to come here?"

I was still on the fence, but then Benny's autobiography cracked the *New York Times* bestseller list. It was mostly his achievement, obviously. Still, the cover image and a section of photos in the middle were mine, and a party started to seem like a good idea. In celebration, he sent some new artwork for my apartment: an eight-by-ten-foot reproduction of the cover image, which, naturally, was his face.

I imagined how delighted Hope—and Oliver—would be and tried to come up with an unobtrusive spot to hang a massive canvas. Bathroom? No, that would be weird. There was nothing to do but let it take over the living room.

My plan to split my time fifty-fifty between London and New York paid off. I was the hottest new it-girl in the world of music photography. Being associated with Benny and Jimmy gave me a cool factor I would have probably never established without them. That, along with regular covers on *Offstage* and other magazines, album covers, and the program for Benny's play, added up to a robust body of work for an artist my age.

The last two years hadn't been easy. Spending half my time away from Oliver was roughly forty-eight percent more than either of us wanted, and to say he was jealous of the time I spent with Benny would be an understatement. To say he didn't take every occasion to rub it in his face would be a flat-out lie.

So it hadn't been easy, but it had been worth it. Still, the idea of mixing all the important people in my life and throwing them into one room was risky. The boys from Corporate were fully onboard because they loved coming to stay with me in New York. Benny thought it was the most brilliant idea anyone ever had. A chance to needle Oliver and flirt with Jimmy? No way he'd pass it up.

When Toby called and said he needed a reason to bring Chelsea to New York, I caved. Toby and I hadn't had as much time together as I'd like. I wanted to see Chelsea too. Odds were good she was going to be my sister-in-law, and I'd finally stopped pretending I didn't adore her. She was perfect for Toby, yes, but mostly I loved her because she was smart and funny and always up for a repeat viewing of *Jane Eyre*, minus the running commentary I'd get from the guys.

Now the big night was here, and the wheels were coming off. I couldn't get my dress zipped on my own, I'd broken the buckle on one of my lucky garters, my loft wasn't as party-ready as I'd have liked, and my damn phone would not stop buzzing. With a muttered curse, I gave in and picked it up. I had about a million missed messages.

Oliver: *IMPORTANT. Please do not speak to Jimmy until I'm there and you and I have talked. I'm serious.*

Jimmy: *I need to talk to you right away. Call me.*

Jimmy: *Srsly, darling. Call me stat. You're not answering your phone. Did you break it? Is it in another toilet?*

Jimmy: *I'm joking. I know it's not. The stalker app shows me you're right where you should be, snuggled in your loft in New York."*

Oliver: *Promise me. Do not speak to Jimmy.*

Jimmy: *Is your ringer broken? Call me.*

Toby: *Be there in an hour! Bringing Mom. Surpriiiiiiise! She wanted to see your place, and she's never been to NYC! Can you believe it? Tell Jimmy to be good. There will be grown-ups in the room.*

Hawk: *My invitation must have gotten lost in the mail, but I'm in town and got your address from the lads. See you tonight.*

Oliver: *We'll be there soon. Keep not answering your phone. I want to talk to you before Jimmy does. Please. It's important.*

Jimmy: *If you don't respond right now, I'm going to call the police. I can only assume the reason you're not answering is because you've fallen down those ridiculous stairs, which are not EVEN stairs, more like a ladder. I knew you wouldn't be safe. We must learn from the past or be doomed to repeat it, my sweet.*

Jimmy: *I'm referring to the other time you fell down the stairs, remember?*

Jimmy: *I HAVE TO TALK TO YOU BECAUSE I HAVE NEWS.*

Oliver wants to surprise you, but I know you hate surprises. Call me RIGHT NOW.

Hope: *Ken and I will be there soon. We're coming together, no big deal. Don't ask about it, just be cool.*

Ken: *Caught up with Hope in the airport. We're sharing a cab for no other reason, no big deal. I just didn't want you to get any ideas, ha ha. Be there soon.*

Benny: *Did you get my delivery? Make sure it's displayed prominently, Willa. Nothing puts me in the mood to celebrate like an enormous picture of my own face.*

Chelsea: *Willa, I'm nervous to meet Corporate. Toby and I are going to get there early so I can hide before Jimmy, Oliver, and Eric are there. I might puke.*

I let myself fall facedown into my bed. This. This right here was why I didn't want to have a party. Disaster already, and it wasn't even supposed to start for another hour.

What did Oliver have to tell me that was so important I'd need a heads up? Something good? Probably. It would be weird to bring me bad news the night of the party, but Jimmy's messages were freaking me out.

I picked my phone back up. He was right. I didn't like surprises. I'd call him and get the scoop so I didn't have it weighing on me when people got there.

As my thumb hovered over his name, someone knocked on my door.

Shit.

If it was a guest, they were early. I wasn't ready. "Hang on!" I called. "I'll be there in a minute!"

Oh well. Whoever it was could zip my dress.

~ * ~

The room was overcrowded and chaotic, and my neighbors were probably going to call the police if they hadn't already. The guests shouldn't have mixed well, but they did. My mom was uncomfortable at first, but Hawk went out of his way to put her at ease, employing a charm I'd always suspected he possessed underneath it all.

Uncle Ken and Hope made eyes at each other all night. Jimmy, Eric, and Oliver put on their full charm for Chelsea until Toby dragged her away. Even Benny was on his best behavior. He kissed me on the cheek when he got there, then kept his distance out of respect for Oliver.

The copious amounts of champagne probably helped. I somehow failed to remember I didn't have champagne flutes, so we drank from mismatched joke mugs. I was bombarded with hugs and kisses and champagne toasts. Everyone in the room loved me. Even

Hawk. And I loved all of them. A lot of them loved each other too, sometimes in a literal sense, as evidenced by Jimmy and Benny disappearing in my darkroom/closet for about half an hour.

In the chaos, Jimmy forgot what he was going to tell me. I forgot to ask Oliver about it until everyone had gone to sleep it off in their respective hotels, and he had unzipped the dress he'd zipped earlier. We spent some time reminding each other why this semi-long-distance relationship was more than worth it and then snuggled under my pink chenille bedspread.

"I love those garters." He sighed happily.

He was on his back, his hands clasped behind his head. I was resting on his chest, tracing the outline of a new tattoo on his chest . . . a lasso in the shape of a heart, with a cursive "Willa" in the middle.

"This is my favorite of your tattoos," I said, kissing it.

Then it came back to me. "Hey! What was it Jimmy wanted to tell me? He said you had a surprise for me."

Oliver smiled in a way that made me suspect he'd been waiting for me to bring it up. He slid out from under me and got up. I enjoyed one of my favorite hobbies, watching him be naked.

He picked up his pants and retrieved something from the front pocket, then crawled back under the covers with me.

He snuggled back in and rested his forehead against mine.

"I love you, Willoughby Reynolds," he said. "I want to be with you for the rest of our lives, however we can make it work. It won't be easy. I'll be on the road sometimes; you'll be on the road sometimes. Sometimes we can be on the road together even when we're not home. We'll have to be creative, and that's okay. We're up for it. I want this life with you, and I want it as your husband. Will you marry me?"

"Yes," I whispered, my eyes brimming over.

He slipped the ring on my finger. It was perfect. A plain, heavy gold band. "I'll get you diamonds if you want," he said. "This seemed more like you."

"I will be your wife, Oliver, because I love you with everything I am and ever will be. But listen to me."

"I'm listening, sweetheart."

I put my hands on either side of his face. "It's not fair that you asked for it with your voice."

"What other voice would I ask for it in?" His smile was so adorable that I wanted to lick his face.

"I don't know, but if you said, 'Willa, do you want to go swimming in a pool full of live sharks'—"

"Was that supposed to be my accent? Honey, no."

"—I'd probably say yes just from being bamboozled. But you don't have to bamboozle me because there is nothing I would rather do than be married to you." I held my hand out and admired the ring. "I love you, Oliver. I'm going to be the best wife in the world."

"You're pretty good at whatever you set your mind to. So that's probably true."

"I'm setting my mind to something right now, actually. How convenient you're in my bed, and we're both naked." I pushed him onto his back and then crawled on top of him.

My phone buzzed.

"Don't you dare answer," Oliver said, gripping my thighs. "He'll wait."

~ * ~

Later, I put on Oliver's discarded T-shirt and crept downstairs so I wouldn't wake him when I called Jimmy.

His voice was quiet when he answered. He sounded peaceful. "Are you happy, darling?"

I sniffed. "So happy."

"Don't do it," he warned. "I can't take it when you cry with your southern accent. Tell me you're as happy as you can stand. That's all I need to know."

I wiped at my eyes. "I'm as happy as I can stand."

He sighed happily. "Ahhh, it's so beautiful. My tied-for-best mate and my best girl, making it official. You're going to be good for each other. I'm glad I arranged this for you both."

I laughed. "Thank you. We're both blessed to have you choreographing our lives and making it all work. Listen, will you be my maid of honor? I mean my . . . whatever, my person of honor?"

There was a startled silence. "What?"

"I mean, I know Oliver will ask you, but I asked first. You're my best friend. Eric can stand up with Oliver. Okay?"

His voice was thick when he answered. "Fucking hell. You just wouldn't be happy until you made me cry. Well, congratulations."

I laughed. "Don't cry in an English accent. I won't be able to take it. Anyway, that means yes, so I'm hanging up now. Love you, Jimmy!"

"I love you too, Willa."

I went back upstairs and slid in next to Oliver. He was lying on his back, his face relaxed and peaceful as he slept.

I snuggled in against him and rested my head on his chest.

He was still the best pillow ever.

Acknowledgements

This book would never have left my head and lived on the page without the help of a community of people for whom I'm grateful.

Thank you to the whole Pitch Wars organization, and especially to my mentor and friend Michelle Hazen, who saw what I was trying to do with this book and helped me get there. Michelle, you taught me so much about how to write and how to find my own voice; my life is better because you're part of it.

Jana Hanson, who is clearly the best agent in the world. I appreciate your kindness, your directness, and your infinite patience. Thank you for believing in me and being part of this journey.

Cassie Knight and the whole team at Champagne Books, thank you for turning this story into a proper book and making a lifelong dream come true. Lindsay Flanagan, thank you for being such a patient, encouraging, wonderful editor. It was a pure joy to work with you.

My First Readers: Beka, Cookie, Sara, Stephanie. You put in the *work*, friends. Reading multiple drafts (so many drafts), brainstorming, solving problems, and fixing commas. For talking me up when I got discouraged, for caring so much about these figments of my imagination, for laughing with me, for encouraging me to keep going. This wouldn't be worth it if it wasn't fun, and it wouldn't be fun without you.

My brother, Jeff, who was appalled that I'd write a whole ass book and then *not* try to publish it. Thanks for the push, and thanks for believing in me.

The Slackers. Everyone always says "oh, it's the community you gain from Pitch Wars." Here to repeat it. It's the community you gain from Pitch Wars. I challenge anyone to find a group of funnier creative geniuses with bigger hearts and stronger feelings about mayonnaise. You all made me feel safe and surrounded during some really painful days, and I love you.

Gwynne, for being a friend, a tireless advocate for love stories, and for helping create and run such a supportive, inclusive group of writers. Cass, for reading and insisting there should be a sequel. Meryl, for encouragement, bonding, soap-making, and drinking coffee with me while a baby giraffe was born. Maria, for hours on the phone, and very specific and flattering feedback. Falon, for your thoughtful feedback that came right at the time I was ready to give up.

Jesse, Sam, and Gillian. Thank you for all the hours you helped me write, and the time we spent in the car brainstorming. Thank you for believing in me, grieving with me, and celebrating with me. You guys are my real world, and it's better than anything I could make up. I love you infinity (numbers don't stop).

About the Author

Eagan Daniels has a Master's degree in Literature, and a Bachelor's in Photography. If there were such a thing as an advanced degree in fangirling, she would certainly have earned that, as well.

Her interests include sports photography (but only of hockey), live music, literature, and male musicians who wear eyeliner. She lives in Michigan but spends about half her time in her head with imaginary friends.

Real life has gifted her with a wonderful husband, two amazing children, three naughty dogs, an arrogant cat, and a small tortoise who bullies them all.

Eagan loves to hear from her readers. You can find and connect with her at the links below.

Website/Blog: http://eagandaniels.com
Instagram: https://www.instagram.com/eagandanielsauthor
Pinterest: https://pinterest.com/eagandaniels/
Twitter: https://twitter.com/eagandaniels

Thank you for taking the time to read *Coming into Focus*. If you enjoyed the story, please tell your friends, and leave a review. Reviews support authors and ensure they continue to bring readers books to love and enjoy.

And now for a look inside *Some Assembly Required*, a fun and quirky story about a woman embarking on the new stage in her life after a divorce by Robin Winzenread.

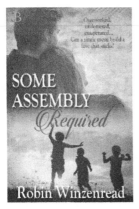

Can Ro Andrews, an overworked, undersexed, exasperated single mom, find love with Sam–a man allergic to chaos and crumbs—and make it stick, not sticky?

When new divorcee Ro Andrews moves her pack of semi-feral children to a run-down farmhouse, helping her brother restore the moldering homestead and living an authentic life—per the dictates of Instagram and lifestyle blogs everywhere—tops her to-do list. But romance? Hell, no. Between hiding from her children in baskets of dirty laundry, mentally eviscerating her cheating ex, and finding a job, Ro has a full plate.

Until she meets Sam Whittaker, a hunky Texas transplant with abs of steel and a nameplate that reads Boss. Clad in cowboy boots and surfer curls, this child-free stud has Ro on edge—and rethinking her defective Y chromosome ban. Somehow, this overworked, undersexed, exasperated single mom needs to find time to fall in love with a man allergic to chaos and crumbs and make it stick, not sticky.

Chapter One

As my young son's cries echo through this diner, I'm reminded again why some animals eat their young.

It's because they want to.

"Hey, Mom! Nick farted, and he didn't say excuse me!"

Normally when Aaron, my spunky six-year-old, announces something so crudely, we're at home, and his booming voice is muted by the artfully arranged basket of dirty laundry I've shoved my head into in hopes of hiding like an ostrich from a tiny, tenacious predator.

This time, however, Aaron yells it in the middle of a crowded diner in the small, stranger-adverse, southern Illinois town we're about to call home and, frankly, we don't need any more attention. Thanks to my semi-feral pack of three lippy offspring, we've already lit this place on fire, and not in a good way.

Despite our involuntary efforts to unhinge the locals with our strangers-in-a-strange-land antics, this dumpy, dingy diner, minus its frosty clientele, has a real comfortable feel, not unlike the ratty, stretched-out yoga pants I love but no longer wear because a) they don't fit any more and b) I burned them—along with a voodoo doll I crafted of my ex-husband (see my Pinterest board for patterns), after I forced it to have sex with my son's GI Joe action figure (see downward-facing dog for position).

Crap. I should have put the pictures on Instagram. Wait, I think they're still on my phone.

"Mom!" Aaron bellows again.

Right now, I'd kill for a pile of sweaty socks to dive into, but there's nary a basket of tighty-whities in sight, and that kid loves an audience, even a primarily rural, all-white-bread, mouth-gaping, wary one.

Frowning, I point at his chair. "Sit."

More than a bit self-conscious, I scan the room, hoping for signs of defrost from the gawking audience and pray my attempt to sound parental falls on nearby ears, earning me scant mom points. Of course, a giant burp which may have contained three of the six vowel sounds just erupted from my faux angelic four-year-old daughter, Madison, so I'll kiss that goodwill goodbye. I hand her a napkin and execute my go-to look, a serious I-mean-it-this-time scowl. "Maddy, say excuse me."

"Excuse me."

belch

Good lord, I'm doomed.

"Listen to me, Mom. Nick farted."

I fork my chef salad with ranch dressing on the side and raise an eyebrow at my youngest son. "Knock it off, kiddo."

"You said when we fart, we have to say excuse me, and he didn't." Finally, Aaron sits, unaware I've been stealing his fries, also on the side.

Kids, so clueless.

Nick, my angelic eight-year-old, is hot on his brother's heels and equally loud, "We don't have to say it when we're on the toilet. You can fart on the toilet and not say excuse me. It's allowed. Ask Mom."

Aaron picks up a water glass and holds it to his mouth. "It sounded like a raptor." He blows across the top, filling the air with a wet, revolting sound, once again alarming the nearby locals. "See?" He laughs. "Just like a raptor."

I point at his plate and scrutinize the last of his hamburger. "Thank you for that lovely demonstration, now finish your lunch."

Naturally, as we discuss fart etiquette, the locals are still gawking, and I can't blame them. We're strangers in a county where I'm betting everyone knows each other somehow and, here's the real shocker, we're not merely passing through. We're staying. On purpose.

We're not alone, either. My brother, Justin, his wife, Olivia, and their bubbly toddler twins kickstarted this adventure—moving to the sticks—so we're eight in total. Admittedly, this all sounded better a month ago when we adults hashed it out over too much wine and a little bit of vodka. Okay, maybe a lot of vodka. Back then, Justin had been headhunted for a construction manager job here in town, and I was in a post-divorce, downward-spiral bind, so they invited the kiddies and me to join them.

For me, I hope it's temporary until I can get settled somewhere, as in land a job, land a purpose, land a life. When they offered, I immediately saw the appeal—the more distance between me and the ex and his younger, sluttier girlfriend the better—and I decided to move south too.

Now I can't back out. I've already sold my house which buys me time, but I've got nowhere else to go. Where would I land? I've got three kids and limited skills. Plus, I don't even have a career to use as an excuse to change my mind or to even point me in another direction.

In other words, I'm stuck. Whether I want to or not, I'm relocating to a run-down farmhouse in the middle of nowhere Illinois to help Justin and Olivia with their grandiose plans of fixing it up and living "authentic" lives since, according to Instagram, Pinterest, and lifestyle blogs everywhere, manicured suburbs with cookie-cutter houses, working utilities and paved sidewalks don't count. Unless you're stinking rich, which, unfortunately, we, most definitely, are not.

Let's see, Justin has a new career opportunity, Olivia is going to restore, repaint, repurpose, and blog her way to a book deal, and me…and me…

Nope. I got nothing. No plans, no dreams, no job, nada. Here I am, the not-so-proud owner of a cheap polyester wardrobe with three kids rapidly outgrowing their own. I better come up with something, and quick.

Where's cheesecake when you need it? I stab a cherry tomato, pluck it from my fork, and chew. The world is full of people living their dreams, while mine consists of an unbroken night's sleep and a day without something gooey in my shoes. I take aim at a cucumber slice, pop it in my mouth, and pretend it's a donut. At least I don't have to wash these dishes.

Across from me, Olivia, my sometimes-vegan sister-in-law is unaware I'm questioning my life's purpose while she questions her lunch choice. Unsatisfied, she drops her mushroom melt onto her plate and frowns. I knew it wouldn't pass inspection. She may have lowered her standards to marry my brother, but she'd never do so for food. This is why she and I get along so well.

Olivia rocks back in her chair and smacks her lips, dissatisfied. "There's no way this was cooked on a meat-free grill. I swear I can taste bacon. Maybe sausage too." Her tongue swirls around in her mouth, searching for more hints of offending pork. "Definitely sausage."

Frankly, I enjoy finding pork in my mouth. Then again, I have food issues. Though, if I liked munching tube steak more often, perhaps my ex wouldn't have wandered. The bastard.

Justin watches his wife's tongue roll around, and I don't blame him. She's beautiful—dark, luminous eyes, full lips flushed a natural pink glow, cascading dark curls, radiant brown skin, a toned physique despite two-year-old twins. She's everything I am not.

She tells me I'm cute. Of course, the Pillsbury Dough Boy is cute too. Screw that. I want to be hot.

Regardless, I expect something crude to erupt from my brother's mouth as he stares at his lovely bride, so I'm pleasantly surprised when it doesn't. Instead, he shakes his head and works on his stack of onion rings. "What do you expect when you order off menu in a place like this, babe? Be glad they had portobellos."

Across from me, she frowns. Model tall and fashionably lean, she's casually elegant in a turquoise and brown print maxi dress, glittery dangle earrings, silky black curls, and daring red kitten heels that hug her slender feet. How does she do it? She exudes an easy glamour even as she peels a corner of toasted bun away from her sandwich, revealing a congealed mass of something.

"This isn't a portobello. It's a light dove gray, not a soft, deep, charcoal gray. I'm telling you this is a bad sandwich. I'm not eating it." She extracts her fingers from the offending fungus and crosses her bangle bracelet encased arms.

Foodies. Go figure. No Instagram picture for you, sandwich from hell.

Fortunately their twins, Jaylen and Jayden, adorable in matching Swedish-inspired sweater dress ensembles and print tights, are less picky. Clearly, it comes from my chunky side of the family. They may be dressed to impress, but the ketchup slathered over their precious toddler faces says, "We have Auntie Ro's DNA in us somewhere."

I love that.

Justin cuts up the last half of a cold chicken strip and shares it with his daughters, who are constrained by plastic highchairs—which I can't do with my kids any more, darn the luck—and, in addition to having no idea how to imitate raptors with half-empty water glasses like my boys or identify mushrooms by basis of color like their mother, they are still quite cute.

Love them as I do, my boys haven't been cute for a while. Such a long while. Maddy, well, she's cute on a day-to-day basis. Yet, they are my world. My phlegm covered, obnoxious, arguing world.

Justin wipes Jaylen's cheek and checks his phone. "We need to get the bill. It's getting late."

I survey the room, hunting for our waitress. Despite the near constant stranger stares, this place intrigues me. It feels a hundred years old in a good, cozy way. The diner's creaky, wood floor is well worn and the walls are exposed brick, which is quaint in restaurants even if it detracts from the value in Midwestern homes, including the giant moldering one Justin and Olivia bought northeast of town. Old tin advertising posters depict blue ribbon vegetables and old-time tractors in shades of red and green and yellow on the walls, and they may be the real antique deal.

They're really into primary colors, these farm folks. Perhaps the best way to spice up a quiet life is to sprinkle it with something bright and shiny. As for me, I've been living in dull shades of beige for at least half a marriage now, if not longer. Should I try bright and shiny? Couldn't hurt.

Red-pleather booths line the wall of windows to the left, and a row of tables divides the room, including the two tables we've shoved together which my children have destroyed with crumbs, blobs of ketchup, and snot. Of course, the twins helped too, but they're toddlers so you can't point a finger at them especially since all the customers are too busy pointing fingers at mine.

Bar stools belly up to a Formica counter to the right, and it's all very old school and quaint, although I would hate to have to clean the place, partly because Maddy sneezed, and her mouth was open and full of fries.

Kids. So gross.

Three portly gentlemen in caps, flannel, and overalls overflow from the booth closest to our table and, clearly, they're regulars. They're polishing off burgers and chips, though no one is sneezing with his mouth open, most likely because his teeth will fly out in the process. I imagine the pleather booths are permanently imprinted with the marks of old asses from a decade's worth of lunches. Sometimes it's good to make an impression. The one we're currently making, however? Probably not.

Nearly every table, booth, and stool are taken. Must be a popular place. Or it may be the only place in this itty, bitty town. It's the type of place where everyone knows your name, meaning they all stared the minute we walked in because they don't know ours, it's a brisk Tuesday in early November, and we sure aren't local.

Yet.

Several men of various ages in blue jeans and farm hats sit in a row upon the counter stools, munching their lunches. A smattering of conversations on hog feed, soybean yields, and tractor parts fills the air. They all talk at once, the way guys tend to do, with none of them listening except to the sound of his own voice, the way guys also tend to do, like stray dogs in a pound when strangers check them out and they're hoping to impress.

Except for one of them, the one I noticed the minute we walked in and have kept tabs on ever since. Unlike the others, this man is quiet and, better yet, he doesn't have the typical middle-aged, dad-bod build. While most of the other men are stocky and round, square and cubed, pear shaped and apple dumpling-esque, like bad geometry gone rogue, he isn't. He's tall with a rather broad triangular back and, given the way it's stretching the confines of his faded, dark red, button-down shirt, it's a well-muscled isosceles triangle at that. Brown cowboy boots with a Texas flag burned on the side of the wooden heel peek from beneath seasoned blue jeans, and those jeans cling to a pair of muscular thighs that could squeeze apples for juice.

God, I have a hankering for hot cider. With a great big, thick, rock-hard cinnamon stick swirling around too. Hmmm, spicy.

This Midwestern cowboy's dark-brown hair is thick with a slight wave that would go a tad bit wild if he let it, and he needs to let it. Who doesn't love surfer curls, and his are perfect. They're the kind I could run my fingers through forever or hang onto hard in the sack, if need be. Trust me, there's a need be.

His body is lean, yet strong, and beneath his rolled-up sleeves, there's a swell of ample biceps and the sinewy lines of strong, tan forearms. It's a tan I'm betting goes a lot further than his elbows. His face is sun-kissed too, and well-defined with high cheekbones and a sturdy chin. A hint of fine lines fan out from the corners of his chocolate-brown eyes and, while not many, there're enough to catch any drool should my lips happen to ravage his face.

Facial lines on guys are so damn sexy. They hint at wisdom, experience, strength. Lines on women should be sexy too, even the stretchy white, hip-dwelling ones from multiple, boob-sucking babies, but men don't think that way, which is why I only objectify them these days. Since getting literally screwed over by my ex, I'm the permanent mascot for Team Anti-Relationship. I blame those defective Y chromosomes myself. Stupid Y chromosomes.

Regardless, it's difficult not to watch as this well-built triangle of a man wipes his mouth with a napkin. I wouldn't mind being that white crumpled paper in that strong tan hand, even if I, too, end up spent on the counter afterward. At any rate, he stands, claps the guy to his left on the back, and I may have peed myself.

The sexy boot-clad stranger pulls cash from his wallet and sets it on the lucky napkin. "I've got to get back to the elevator, Phil. Busy day."

Sweet, a Texas accent. How very Matthew McConaughey. Mama like.

A pear-shaped man next to him raises his glass. "See ya, Sam. You headed to George's this afternoon?"

"I hope so. I need to get with Edmund first, plus we have a couple of trailers coming in, and I've got to do a moisture check on at least two of them." His voice is low, but soft, the way you hope a new vibrator will sound, but never does until the batteries die which defeats the purpose, proving once again irony can be cruel.

And what the hell is a moisture check?

I zero in on the open button of his shirt, drawn to his chest like flies to honey, because that's what I do now that I'm divorced and have no husband and no purpose—I ogle strange men for the raw meat they are. Nothing's going to happen anyway. Truth be told, I haven't dated in an eternity and have no real plans to start, partly because I've forgotten how; just another unfortunate aspect of my life on permanent hold. I've been invited to the singles' buffet, but I'm too afraid to grab a plate. At this point in my recently wrecked, random life, I would rather vomit. Hell, I barely smell the entrees. I'm only interested in licking a hunk of two-legged meatloaf for the sauce anyway. There's no harm in that, right?

Where was I? Right, his chest, and it's a good chest, with the "oood" dragged out like a child's Benadryl-laced nap on a hot afternoon. It's that goood.

Of course, as I mentally drag out the "oood," my lips involuntarily form the word in the air imitating a goldfish in a bowl. While I ogle this particular cut of prime rib, I realize he's noticed my stare not to mention my "oood" inspired fish lips, which is not an attractive look, despite what selfie-addicted college girls think. Our eyes lock. An avalanche of goosebumps crawls its way up my back and down my arms and, I swear, I vibrate. Not like one of those little lipstick vibrators that can go off in your purse at the airport, thank you very much, but something more substantial with a silly name like Rabbit or

Butterfly or Bone Master.

That, my friends, is the closest I've come to real sex in two and half years. Excuse me, but we need a moisture check at table two, please. Not to mention a mop. Okay...definitely a mop.

For a moment, we hold our stare—me with my fish lips frozen into place, vibrating silently in my long-sleeved, heather green T-shirt and jeans, surrounded by my small tribe of ketchup-covered children, and him all hot, tan, buff, and beefy, staring at us the way one gawks at a bloody, ten-car pile-up. All too soon, he blinks, the deer-in-the-headlights look fades, and he drops his gaze.

C'mon, stud, look again. I'm not wearing a push-up bra for nothing.

Big, dark, brown eyes pop up again and find mine. All too soon, they flit away to the floor.

Score.

Damn, he's fine. Someone smoke me a cigarette, I'm spent.

I scan the table, imagining my children are radiating cuteness. No dice. Aaron imitates walrus tusks with the last of his French-fries, Nick is trying to de-fang him with a straw full of root beer, and Maddy's two-knuckles deep into a nostril. And I'm sitting next to Justin.

Figures. My big, burly, ginger-headed, lug of a wedding-ring-wearing brother is beside me. Does this hunk of burning stud think he's my husband? Should I pick my own nose with my naked, ring-less finger? Invest in a face tattoo that reads "divorced and horny?" Why do I even care? He's only man meat. After all, was he really even looking at me? Or Olivia? Sexy, sultry, damn-sure-married-to-my-brother Olivia? I whip back to the stud prepared to blink "I'm easy" in Morse code.

blink *blink* *bliiiink*

With a spin on his star-studded boots, Hotty McHot heads toward the hallway at the back of the diner, oblivious that my gaze is rivetted to his ass and equally clueless to the fact that I have questions needing immediate answers, not to mention an overwhelming need to scream, "I'm single and put out, no strings attached" in his general direction.

Olivia pulls me back to reality with her own questions. "I mean, is it that difficult to scrape the grill before you cook someone's meal?"

She's still honked off about her sandwich, unaware I'm over here having mental sex with the hunky cowboy while sending my kids off to a good boarding school for the better part of the winter.

"I didn't have many options here," she rattles on, "even their salads have meat and egg in them. Instead of a writing a book, I should open a vegan restaurant. I was going to give them a good review for the ambiance, but not now. Wait until I post this on Yelp."

Eyeballing the room, Justin polishes off the last of his double-cheese burger. "Sweetie, we're moving to the land of pork and beef. Vegan won't fly here, and I doubt the help cares about Yelp. Did you notice our waitress? She's got a flip phone. Time to put away your inner princess and stick with the book idea."

Long fingers with bronze gel manicured nails rat-a-tat-tat on the tabletop. She locks onto him with dark, intelligent, laser-beam eyes. "Would it kill you to be supportive, honey bunch? You might as well say, uck-fay u-vay."

Apparently channeling some weird, inner death wish, Justin picks up an onion ring, takes a bite, then pulls a string of overcooked translucent slime free from its breaded coating. He snaps it free with his teeth, then offers it to her. "Your book is going to be great, babe, and it will appeal to a larger audience than here. Remember the goal, Liv. As for me, I'm trying to keep you humble. No one likes high maintenance."

The limp, greasy onion hangs in the air. She ignores it, but not him. "Okay, this time, sweetie, I'll say it. Uck-fay u-vay with an ig-bay ick-day."

Jaylen looks up from her highchair and munches a chicken strip. "Uck-fay?" she repeats through fried poultry. "Ick-day?"

Behind her an older woman, also fluent in pig Latin, does a coffee-laced spit-take in her window booth. I hope she's not a new neighbor.

Justin chuckles and polishes off the offending string of onion. Olivia stews. Time to implement an offense. Clearly, we need an exit strategy.

Where's our waitress? I spy her delivering plates of food three booths down and wave. She nods, so I use these few moments to ward off any drama. "Suggestion, you two. Let's not piss off the help. This may be the only place where we can hide from the kids and eat our feelings. Not to mention drink. Agreed?"

Justin snorts, but says nothing. Olivia rolls her eyes, but also says nothing. Success, although it's tentative. Time to leave.

Water pitcher in hand, our waitress returns to our table. She surveys the left-over lunch carnage, unaware my sister-in-law is both unimpressed and pissed off, and it's fairly obvious that, if we're all going to be regulars here, a sizeable tip, different children, or the offer of a kidney is in order. A middle-aged woman in jeans, T-shirt, and an apron with short, no-nonsense, dishwater hair, she refills our water glasses, possibly so I'll have something with which to wipe the seats or drown our young. Or both. I can't be sure. But I'm open to options.

She sets the water pitcher on the table and starts stacking dirty plates. "Ready for dessert?" She's a bit harried, and, with the possibility of an eruption from Olivia hanging over our heads, I pick up a napkin and start wiping. "We have cherry cobbler."

An indignant cry erupts from the booth behind us. One of the three portly gentlemen hollers—this is the kind of place where you holler— "Save me a piece of cobbler."

"Yeah, yeah, in a minute, Ernie." The waitress scowls. "What else can I get you? Pie? Cake? The coffee's fresh."

"Yeah, but it ain't good though," barks the man named Ernie. A fresh wave of snorts erupts from his companions.

I stifle a laugh, but it's a challenge, especially since Aaron's been flicking my salad croutons in their general direction throughout most of the meal and, despite my scolding, he's getting quite good with his trick shots.

"I bet you've done this before," I say to the woman whose name tag reads "Anna."

She glares at the booth. "Yep, they're regulars. Of course, I call 'em a pain in the butt, myself."

"Good to know, Anna."

"Name's Sarah. This is the only tag we had left."

Of course. Naturally, the crusty old guys are regulars in a diner where everyone knows your name, so you wear a tag that isn't your own, presumably for strangers who rarely show up on a Tuesday. I like this quirky town, even if it doesn't like me.

"Where are you all from? Chicago?" pries the waitress formerly known as Anna.

Olivia avoids eye contact and spit shines her twins. "Is it obvious?"

Curious, Sarah takes in the dress, the earrings, the bright red shoes. "Yep. What brings you through town?"

Backs stiffen throughout the room. Heads swivel in our direction. The general roar of conversation drops a decibel or two, all the better to eavesdrop, I assume.

I confiscate Maddy's spoon and add it to the pile of flatware on my salad plate, then plunge on before anyone at our table offers an unwelcomed critique of the menu. "We're moving here. They bought a place on Stockpile Road, Thornhill."

Eyes stare from all corners of the diner. Bodies sit taller. Ears bend toward us, and whispers swim across a sea of faces.

"Thornhill?" Sarah cocks her head. "You mean old lady

Yeager's place? I hope you're good with a hammer."

"It needs a bulldozer," shouts a voice from the back.

"Stick a sock in it, Ernie. Men," she mutters.

"I've got a toxic ex and a lot of frustration, so…" I imitate a manic hammering motion, but, getting no response from the masses, I load up Aaron's spoon with croutons and keep talking. "Justin's in construction—he's starting a new job here next week. He'll put us to work on the house. Should be fun."

Olivia stares at the hunk of sandwich left on her plate before looking pointedly at our waitress. "I plan to blog about the experience—articles on reclaiming the house, restoring the gardens, growing our own vegetables and herbs, recipes, homemade soaps. Think avant-garde Martha Stewart. It's what I do."

Sarah blinks rapidly as she digests Olivia's words. "Ah." She hesitates. "Want a doggie bag?"

Justin chokes on the last bite of his burger as he examines his phone. "Not necessary, but thanks. Can we get our bill though?"

A finger-painted, ketchup rendition of a farting raptor rambles across Aaron's plate. Sarah sets down her stack of dishes, rips our bill from the order pad in her apron pocket, and picks up my son's plate without so much as an appraisal. "So, you all are moving here. Good to know. I haven't been up there in years." She adds another plate to her stack, obliterating his finger art. "I hear it's a real project. Anyway, good luck, and welcome to town." She spins on her heels with arms full of dirty dishes. "You can pay at the register."

Justin tucks his phone in his pocket and wipes his mouth, pleased with his greasy, meaty lunch. "We need to get going. The movers will be here within the hour."

My heart does a double thump. Time to head to the new homestead. True, I'm a hanger-on in this adventure of theirs, just a barnacle on their barge, but I'm excited too even if I haven't been to the place yet. Desperate to reignite my life, the promise of a thousand potential projects, plans, and ideas leap to mind, calling out to me with hope. Maybe this is where I'll find myself. Or a purpose beyond wiping tiny hineys. Something. Anything, really.

Ready to settle the bill, I toss two twenties at Justin. "Here's my cash. Can you pay mine too? I'll run to the restroom, and then we'll get out of here. Sound good?

He grabs the cash. "Yep. Get going, sis. I got this."

My imagination whirls with anticipation as I rise. Roughly fifteen minutes from now, we should be there, home. Can a fresh start be far behind?

Oblivious to my growing excitement, Aaron considers me for a moment as I push back from the table, ready to roll. "Mom, if you fart in there, are you going to say excuse me?"

Nick polishes off his root beer and sets his glass on the table. "I bet she won't. I bet she'll sit there, fart, and say nothing."

Good gravy, will they get off this topic already? My stern gaze falls on blind eyes. Ignoring them, I make a hasty exit to the restroom, but Aaron once again sends shockwaves through the diner with his cry, "Will you tell us if you fart?"

sigh

Maybe I can outrun his voice. I rush away and turn the corner sharp, seeking sanctuary in the women's room. Instead, however, I spy something even better. Speeding toward me from an open door at the end of the hall is Hottie McHot-Stuff, the good-looking cowboy with moisture on his mind.

We both stop short. I sidestep right, as he sidesteps left into my path. We chuckle. Immediately we both dance the other way, blocking one another yet again.

I flash him a smile and grin. "Sorry about that. How about I stop, and you walk on by?"

Hints of vanilla, pine, and leather waft my way. He nods agreement, and our eyes connect. For a moment, we hold yet another stare.

Damn, he's even better looking up close and personal. I could get used to this. Heat rises in my face—where'd that come from? Moisture rises in my jeans—I know where that came from.

All too soon, he breaks our gaze and sidesteps around me. "Excuse me and thank you." Boots clack on the wooden floor, and he saunters away, dragging a steam cloud from my body in his wake. It's a wonder the candy-striped wallpaper in the hallway doesn't peel.

Happy to have a new hobby, I peek over my shoulder and gape at each swaying butt cheek. "You're welcome," I mumble as his blue-jean clad McNuggets disappear around the corner. "You are very welcome."

Into the diner restroom I go, daydreaming about hot cowboys and diner sex. A random inspection of my breasts, hoping they impressed, halts my midday revelry. Because, naturally, there's a hunk of crusted ketchup clinging to my left boob.

Perfect. At least there isn't a French fry in my cleavage. Or is there?

I scrape at the hardened blob with marginal success, preferring to study this fresh new stain on my old, dumpy T-shirt rather than the current flustered face in the mirror. I hate mirrors. The view always disappoints, even now after I've dropped a few dozen post-divorce, pissed-off pounds. But, as I de-crust and wash my hands, I finally look up.

Stain or no stain, I want to see what the cowboy saw.

A round, pixie face with a smattering of freckles that in twenty years when I'm pushing fifty everyone will assume are age spots. Bright green eyes with ex-husband anger issues and a twinkle of insanity. A hint of frown lines spreading across my pale, translucent forehead, explaining my new-found love of long, wispy bangs. Reddish blonde hair thanks to a box from the grocery store. A great big mouth built for yelling and eating. Yep. That about sums it up.

I pinch my cheeks for color because, nowadays, for sheer self-respect alone and in spite of my self-imposed dating ban, I'm making an effort. The truth is, in my full-time baby-making years, I'll admit I didn't most days. A relentless, nonstop tug of war between keeping it together or giving up and letting everything go to seed waged inside me as I confronted dirty diapers, dirty dishes, dirty underwear, and dirty socks. Clad in sensible shoes and something stretchy most days, I only wanted to be comfortable.

News flash. Husbands hate comfortable.

Which is why I am comfortable no more. Time to flush and flee. My old chubby life swirls down the crapper, and my new, uncomfortable, slightly less chubby, but even less focused one awaits. Halle-freaking-lujah, I'm a stalled work in progress.

Drowning in my personal funk, I toss a paper towel in the trash and bolt from the bathroom, far away from the mirror when—slam!

A tall, thin, elderly man sways, reduced to a sapling in a strong breeze, threatening to collapse to the floor under the weight of my rapidly advancing body. He's bundled up in a thick coat, and thank heavens, too, because his right lapel is the only thing that kept him upright.

I cling to it now, gripping with all my might as he steadies his skinny legs beneath himself. His dusty brown bowler hat tilts far forward on a patch of thin silver hair, and there's a spare quality about him.

A tired, watery stare falls upon me, and his initial alarm gives way to anger. "Young lady, watch yourself!"

Why couldn't I have slammed into the cowboy? I could have grabbed something more substantial than this old man's coat.

Letting go of the gentleman's lapels, I lurch backward. "Oh, my gosh, I'm sorry!"

He stands erect, but even with his dignity restored, his anger grows. "You, young people. You don't think, none of you. You have no concept of your own actions, no sense of responsibility!"

Holy crap. What do I say to that? I'm tongue-tied. After all, I did mow him down with my mom thighs. Plus, he thinks I'm "young people," and he sounds like he means it, possibly even enough to pinkie swear.

However, neither of us whips out a tiny digit. Instead, we stand there, locked in stony silence. "Sorry," I repeat for want of anything else to say.

Finally, he turns with a huff and disappears around the corner into the dining room.

Great. We've barely been in town an hour, and I am far from making friends.

Shaken, I hesitate. Please let this move be the right decision. Please?

It has to be because, right now, I'm a freaking mess. Somehow, I managed to abdicate control over my life to a man who eventually chafed under the responsibility. Now? Now, post-divorce, I'm a rudderless ship, a floating piece of flotsam bobbing downstream, willy nilly, with no real goals or plans other than to make this move, which may or may not be a smart move. What if this proves to be a dead end too? I can't have any more dead ends. Wasn't my marriage enough?

Everyone else has it together. Why the hell don't I?

Desperate for hope, I settle for a plea to the universe instead. Alone in the hall, eyes closed, back against the wall, I give it a go.

Hey, universe, will you please let this move be the right decision for me and my kiddies? Please? With sugar on top?

No one answers, God, Karma, the universe, or alien overlords for whom I am a rapidly failing SIMS avatar, nothing.

Was I expecting an answer?

sigh

No.

I'm alone in the hallway. No skinny old men or hot, buff cowboys walk my way. Regrets, fear, and second thoughts burn behind my eyelids, threatening tears. Steeling myself, I open my eyes, ready to swipe them away before any should fall when I notice it.

A bulletin board anchors the opposite wall, demanding my attention. It's plastered with everything from hay for sale (first cut too, which I assume is the deepest) to pictures of mixed-breed puppies alongside notices for church chili suppers. Bluegrass music drifts in from the dining area, and I drink it in, savoring the ambiance, searching for a sign.

Wait, what's this? An employment ad? For an actual job? Who

in the hell advertises on bulletin boards in this digital age? Better question, is it a sign from the universe? A random act of coincidence? A magical stroke of luck?

Who cares? It's an ad. I lean forward and read.

"Local businessman with multiple enterprises seeks organized, responsible individual to serve as part-time office manager with potential for full time available. Knowledge of basic accounting a plus. Requires good communication skills, customer service, and an ability to type. Pleasant office demeanor a necessity."

Oh my. It's a real job.

Snapping a picture with my cell phone, I give thanks to my short-lived pre-baby history of minimum-wage, part-time jobs at gas-stations and mini-marts. Customer service? No one rang up a carton of Marlboro Lights faster than me. Responsible? The Circle K condom dispenser in the men's restroom was never empty on my watch.

Is this my sign? It sounds like a stretch. Can I really do all that? I, mean, I wasn't exactly bred for this job, was I?

Bred for it? Ick, parent sex. There's an early Saturday-morning memory from age ten I don't need to recall right now.

Scratch that. It's time to be bold and bring on the next chapter of my life.

Lord knows, I need it.

Out Now!

What's next on your reading list?

Champagne Book Group promises to bring to readers fiction at its finest.

Discover your next
fine read!
http://www.champagnebooks.com/

We are delighted to invite you to receive exclusive rewards. Join our Facebook group for VIP savings, bonus content, early access to new ideas we've cooked up, learn about special events for our readers, and sneak peeks at our fabulous titles.

Join now.
https://www.facebook.com/groups/ChampagneBookClub/

19759886R00134